BARON OF BLACKWOOD

BARON OF BLACKWOOD

The Feud: Book Three

TAMARA LEIGH

Splitting Harriet 06/15 (ebook); 2007
(print): RandomHouse/Multnomah
Faking Grace 2015 (ebook); 2008 (print edition): RandomHouse/Multnomah

SOUTHERN DISCOMFORT: A Contemporary Romance Series
Leaving Carolina: **Book One** 11/15 (ebook);
2009 (print): RandomHouse
Nowhere, Carolina: **Book Two** 12/15
(ebook); 2010 (print): RandomHouse
Restless in Carolina: **Book Three** Mid-Winter
2016 (ebook); 2011 (print): RandomHouse

OUT-OF-PRINT GENERAL MARKET TITLES
Warrior Bride 1994: Bantam Books (*Lady
At Arms* clean read rewrite)
***Virgin Bride** 1994: Bantam Books (*Lady Of Eve* clean read rewrite)
Pagan Bride 1995: Bantam Books (*Lady Of Fire* clean read rewrite)
Saxon Bride 1995: Bantam Books (*Lady
Of Conquest* clean read rewrite)
Misbegotten 1996: HarperCollins (*Lady
Undaunted* clean read rewrite)
Unforgotten 1997: HarperCollins (*Lady
Ever After* clean read rewrite)
Blackheart 2001: Dorchester Leisure

***Virgin Bride** is the sequel to *Warrior Bride*
Pagan Pride and *Saxon Bride* are stand-alone novels

www.tamaraleigh.com

NOTE TO READER

—⊸⊱⊰⊶—

Dear Reader,

Welcome to the third book in *The Feud* series. As with all series shouldering an overarching plot, there will be some redundancy in storytelling. This is to orient the reader who read the first books months or years earlier and to ground the reader who enters the series out of sequence, allowing each story to stand alone. Of added benefit, pivotal events are experienced from a different—often more informed—point of view.

In *Baron Of Blackwood*, the love story begins the day Lady Quintin Boursier first encounters Baron Griffin de Arell when she rides on his castle to demand the release of her brother. This event falls four days after the abduction of Bayard Boursier in *Baron Of Godsmere*. Since my stories are—above all and wondrously so—romances, the first half of *Baron Of Blackwood* focuses on the developing relationship between Quintin and Griffin. Why did she draw a dagger on him? Why did he refuse to allow her to return to Godsmere with her brother? And what about Lady Thomasin's observation of how often they did not kiss when they clearly wished to? Now there's quite the tale...

Enjoy!

1

Barony of Blackwood, Northern England
Autumn's End, 1333

"Have a care, my lady. You are within range of their arrows."

So she was. But she did not fear them. Only a man not a man would order a bolt loosed upon a defenseless woman come unto his walls. True, the Baron of Blackwood was surely torn from the same foul cloth as his sire, but no word had she ever heard spoken against his behavior toward the fairer sex and few against his valor. Indeed, though it was much exaggeration, some said he was as formidable a warrior as her brother, The Boursier.

As for being a defenseless woman, that was also exaggeration. Quintin Boursier was no trembling flower. She was not trained in arms—her mother would not tolerate that—but she could wield a dagger beyond the capacity to reduce tough boar's meat to edible bites. After all, many were the idle hours in a lady's day.

"Pray, come away," entreated her brother's senior household knight where he sat his mount alongside hers. "Baron Boursier would not—"

"Nay, he would not, but he is not here, is he?" She narrowed her lids at the immense stone fortress whose walls evidenced they had been white-washed months earlier, and which were all the more stark against the bordering wood.

Sliding her gaze left and right, she searched for movement among the dense trees—a difficult undertaking. Even with all the leaves fallen, it was a dark wood, and when the weather warmed and a canopy once more spread over all, it would be a black wood, for which the barony was named.

Returning her gaze to Castle Mathe, she said, "Nay, my brother is not here—at least, not on this side of the wall."

"Tell me what you wish told, my lady, and I will ride forth and deliver your words."

Beneath her fur-lined mantle, she squeezed her arms against her sides lest the shiver inside ventured out, making her appear weak beside the knight seemingly unaffected by the late morning chill.

"I thank you, Sir Victor, but I shall deliver my demand to the Baron of Blackwood."

His cheeks puffed, and as he slowly blew out his breath, she guessed he was thinking of what her departed father had teasingly bemoaned—she would have fared better born a man.

Quintin did not concur. She liked being a woman, though there were times the limitations of wearing skirts rather than chausses chafed. This was one of those times.

She looked to Castle Mathe's gatehouse and the battlements on either side, the openings of which were filled with archers whose arrows were trained on the score of knights and thirty men-at-arms who had reluctantly accompanied their lord's sister to retrieve Bayard Boursier.

She was certain her brother was here—that the Baron of Blackwood had captured and imprisoned his daughter's betrothed to prevent the wedding two days hence. Thus, for defying the king's decree that the three neighboring families unite through marriage to end their twenty-five-year feud, the lands held by the Boursiers would be declared forfeit.

That Quintin would not allow. Somehow, she would bring her brother out of Castle Mathe.

She moved a hand from the pommel of her saddle to the one at her waist. No meat knife this. And no ordinary dagger. She gripped its pommel, knowing that were she to gaze upon her palm, the impression in it would be that of the cross of crucifixion, pressed there by the jewels forming it.

Though this dagger should not be on her person, before departing Castle Adderstone this morn she had gone looking for courage in the form of something better than a meat knife. At the bottom of her brother's weapons chest, wrapped in layers of linen, she had found that which had belonged to their father.

Having received his knighthood training from the Wulfriths at Wulfen Castle, a fortress centuries-renowned for training boys into men, Archard Boursier had been awarded a coveted Wulfrith dagger. And Quintin could not recall a day he had not worn on his belt what she now wore on her girdle.

Sacrilege? Likely. But were her father living, he would forgive her this as he had forgiven her much.

"Better born a man," she whispered and tapped her heels to her horse.

Sir Victor shouted over his shoulder, commanding the men of the barony of Godsmere to hold, then he followed.

Knowing she could not dissuade him from accompanying her, and not certain she wished to, Quintin moved her gaze embrasure to embrasure in search of the Baron of Blackwood. As told, he would be taller and broader than most men. As did not need to be told, he would not be one of those whose bow was fit with a flesh-piercing arrow. Griffin de Arell was a man of the sword.

Without warning shots or shouts, the castle garrison allowed Sir Victor and her to advance amid the sound of armored men shifting their weight, the breeze whispering of snowfall as it moved brittle grass at the base of the wall, the flapping of a flag that bore high the green and black colors of De Arell, and the shrill cry of a falcon overhead.

Not surprisingly, the drawbridge did not let out its chains.

If only Griffin de Arell were a fool, Quintin silently bemoaned. Of course, were he the one she was to wed to end the feud, that would not do. It would be disagreeable enough joined to an enemy without also suffering a dullard until death released her from one she could not respect.

Recalling the argument with her brother the day before his disappearance, she grimaced. She had tried to convince him it was better she wed Griffin de Arell since he already had an heir, but Bayard's choice of the man's daughter for a wife meant Quintin would be bound to a different enemy within the next few months—Magnus Verdun, the Baron of Emberly. Also not a fool, but likely in love with himself for as handsome as he was said to be.

Her long sigh misted the air. Her sharp breath cleared it when Sir Victor snatched her reins and jerked her mount to a halt.

"Near enough, my lady. Far too near."

He was right. They were less than twenty feet from where the drawbridge would settle to the ground were it lowered.

Fingers stiff from the cold despite thick gloves, she tugged to free her reins from the knight's grip.

He raised his eyebrows.

"Aye," she conceded, "near enough."

When he returned control of her mount to her, she raised her gaze to the roof of the gatehouse and looked from one archer-filled embrasure to the next. Just off center, she paused.

It was no highly-polished armor that revealed Griffin de Arell, and no bearing of self-importance where he leaned forward as if to look out upon a day that held no challenge though fifty of his enemy were outside his walls. Instinct told her here was the Baron of Blackwood. And his eyes that captured hers. And the smirk upon his mouth.

The hairs across her limbs prickled, but she did not avert her gaze, that being no way to preface demands.

Slowly filling her lungs in the hope he would not notice she sought to breathe in courage the Wulfrith dagger did not sufficiently impart, she drew a hand from beneath her mantle, freed the ties cinching the hood about her face, and pushed back the covering.

Something nearer a true smile, albeit crooked, moved Griffin de Arell's mouth as her jaw-skimming hair celebrated its liberation by dancing in the breeze before her face—the same breeze that moved the baron's dark blond hair back off his brow.

Momentarily wishing she did not eschew troublesomely long tresses that would have remained tucked beneath her mantle, she squelched the impulse to drag the hood back over her head and called, "I am Lady Quintin of Castle Adderstone, of the barony of Godsmere, sister of Baron Boursier."

"Of course you are," her family's enemy said across the chill air. "Though you are not the one I expected."

It was Bayard who should have ridden on Castle Mathe to collect his De Arell bride, but the young woman's father surely knew that was impossible. He but feigned ignorance. And not very well, for he had greeted Quintin's entourage with a raised drawbridge and archers ready to loose killing arrows. Hardly the way to welcome the man who was to be his son-in-law. Griffin de Arell was found out and prepared for Boursier wrath.

Returning his skewed smile, she said, "Come now, Baron. I may be the fairer sex, but I am no more fond of silly women's games than you, a warrior, should be."

She could not be certain, but she thought his smile wavered, then determined it must have. She *had* questioned his prowess before all.

"Ho!" he said as if with sudden understanding, though it was surely mockery. "Your brother has chosen to wed Elianor of Emberly rather than my daughter. And you are the bearer of tidings that could not please me more."

Quintin dug her nails into her palms. "That is not why I am here."

"Then since there must be a marriage between De Arell and Boursier, you deliver yourself." He flashed white teeth. "A most eager bride."

Amid the sniggering of De Arell's men, Sir Victor beseeched, "Lady Quintin!"

Warmed by anger, she held her gaze to the man she had told Bayard it was better she wed, and not only because the Baron of Blackwood already had an heir. Because she had wished to spare her brother marriage into the family of his greatest enemy, Bayard having been made a cuckold by Griffin's brother. Of course, Elianor of Emberly was nearly as unsavory, being the niece of Bayard's first wife whom he had found abed with Serle de Arell.

I assure you, Quintin's brother had said, *one Verdun wife was enough to last me unto death.*

Setting her chin higher, she called, "I would put myself through with a blade ere delivering myself unto one such as you, Baron de Arell."

He lost his smile, gained a frown. Yet she sensed he was more amused than dismayed. "Then as difficult as it is to believe of *The Boursier,* one must conclude he has decided 'tis better to forfeit his lands than wed a wee De Arell lass."

Now, before all, he not only scorned the name by which others esteemed her brother for his skill at arms, but questioned Bayard's prowess.

Quintin did not realize how quickly her breath came and went until Sir Victor leaned near. "Pray, my lady, let us withdraw that we may discuss the best course."

"This is the only course," she hissed and once more raised her voice up Castle Mathe's walls. "Release my brother, Baron de Arell, else not only will you forfeit your lands when the king learns of your treachery, but your life."

He gave a bark of laughter. "Then your brother *has* fled."

"He has not. As well you know, he was stolen from his bed. Now release him!"

To her amazement, he lifted what looked like an apple, paused, and called out, "Forgive me, but your arrival interrupted my dinner." He took a bite.

Realizing how far her jaw had descended, Quintin snapped it up.

Griffin de Arell chewed, nodded. "Were it true I held your brother, Lady Quintin, I might seriously consider releasing him—for you. But, alas, he is not inside my walls."

Ignoring what was made to sound like flattery, she said, "I would see for myself."

"My word I give."

Something in his tone tempted her to believe him, but that would require she accept what she could not—that Bayard could be dead, whether by De Arell's hand or another's.

"Your word I do not trust," she said and winced at the fear in her voice.

Though he had raised the apple for another bite, he lowered it. "Methinks this bears closer discussion, Lady Quintin. I shall come out to you."

Why? Because she had revealed vulnerability from which he hoped to benefit? Before she could think how to respond, he went from sight.

"I do not like this, my lady."

She looked around. "We are nearer to retrieving my brother, Sir Victor."

"I am not certain De Arell holds him."

"I believe he does. Thus, even if I have to be a woman to his man, I will make a way in." In spite of her short hair and, when riled, an inclination to speak as she wished to speak, she knew how to work her wiles. Providing she could hide from Griffin de Arell how much he repulsed her, she would tie him in a knot she would loosen only when he yielded what she required.

Or so I pray, she sent heavenward, and wished she had not said she would rather put herself through than deliver herself as his bride.

At the sound of her entourage advancing, doubtless signaled forward by Sir Victor, she said, "Send them back." Not only might De Arell decide against leaving the safety of his walls, but the men could prove too tempting a target for the archers.

"Nay," the knight said. "Ere long, I may once more answer to your brother, and that day I fear more than this."

"But—"

The drawbridge chains let out, and she caught her breath for fear the great planked beast would grind to a halt before returning to its upright position. It did not, though Godsmere's knights and men-at-arms reined in behind her.

The top of the portcullis came into view, and beyond its crossed iron bars she saw the buildings in the outer bailey, next the garrison. But it was the blond head and broad shoulders of the man striding—not riding—past the others that held her attention.

Surely he did not intend to leave his walls on foot? But as the drawbridge thumped to the ground, Griffin de Arell halted before the portcullis and it began to rise. When it was at waist level, he did not duck beneath so it might sooner lower and secure the castle entrance. And when his head easily cleared and he strode forward, the grating did not drop behind him. Of course, his archers did have Godsmere's men sighted down their arrows.

As the baron advanced, his eyes—were they the same intense blue as his brother's?—moved over Quintin's entourage, and she knew he measured Godsmere's men against the risk he took.

If he wore chain mail, she could not detect the metallic ring, nor the flash of silver links as she considered his black mantle that parted with each stride. All she glimpsed was a dark green tunic above black boots.

He was a bigger man than his brother, Serle, but not of fat—of large bones and thickly muscled like Bayard. And the nearer he came, the more she begrudged the appeal of him. His face too rough-hewn to be handsome, its weathered skin and several days' growth of beard making him appear older than the thirty and four years she knew him to be, he was still attractive, this man whose half-noble daughter was to have been Bayard's wife.

"Is to be," she whispered as her heart lurched over the slip of her thoughts. Bayard was at Castle Mathe and would wed before the deadline to preserve his family's lands.

The Baron of Blackwood halted before the drawbridge's threshold, less than twenty feet from his uninvited guests. Still he held the apple, and it looked more than half eaten, as if crossing from the gatehouse roof to the drawbridge had been but a leisurely stroll.

But if that was so, it was no more. He surveyed Sir Victor long and hard before shifting his regard to Quintin.

As she returned his scrutiny, the miserly sunlight reaching through the clouds revealed the hair at his crown was darker than that below. A sign he was often out of doors, just as the tanned skin of his face told.

"You may approach, Lady Quintin," he startled her.

Resenting the sudden heat in her chilled cheeks, hoping it was not as visible as it was felt, she urged her mount forward and Sir Victor followed.

One side of Griffin de Arell's mouth lifted, and he said dryly, "And you as well...Sir Victor, is it not?"

Quintin was momentarily taken aback, but it followed that just as Bayard knew the names of his enemy's most esteemed warriors, so would De Arell know those of Godsmere.

"It is," Sir Victor said and reined in five feet from the drawbridge.

Quintin did the same. Looking close upon her enemy, she was relieved that just as he did not mirror his brother's slighter figure, neither did his features—excepting the color of his eyes, a remarkable blue that dragged her back years to when she had hurtled herself between Serle de Arell and Bayard.

"So you believe I hold your brother, that I seek to deny him my daughter, thereby causing him to forfeit," Griffin de Arell returned her to the present where she found her fist pressed to her abdomen.

Tasting bile, she moved her hand to the Wulfrith dagger. "I do. Unfortunately, as evidenced by the history between our families, the word you give holds no meaning for the Boursiers."

"I grant that."

He did? She moistened her lips, and his gaze flicked to them—as expected. "Thus, I require proof you do not hold the Baron of Godsmere."

His lids narrowed, brow grooved.

"If what you tell is true, you can have no objection to me entering your walls, Baron de Arell."

"I can. And I do." He looked to Sir Victor. "However, to prove your lady's brother is not within and afterward invite her to my table, you would entrust her to me?"

"I would not!" It was said with more indignation than Quintin could remember hearing from the self-possessed knight. "Where she goes, I go, accompanied by a sufficient number of Godsmere men to defend her if needs be."

"Should I honor Lady Quintin's request and she observes the rules, I vow she will depart Castle Mathe the same as she enters."

While Quintin pondered what rules those might be, Sir Victor said, "As my lady has told, your word carries no weight with the Boursiers or those who serve them."

The baron exhaled a breath that drifted toward Quintin. "For your sake I tried, my lady, but it appears we are at a place from which neither party can be moved."

"We are not." She urged her mount forward, heard Sir Victor curse beneath his breath, and felt his arm brush hers. He caught her reins, but not before her horse's muzzle was a foot from Baron de Arell.

"A dozen escort." She asked for more than was needed. "Allow me a dozen, and we can move from this place."

He peered up at her, and she nearly winced at the perceived advantage she had that would not endear her to him. But then he stepped forward and, out of the corner of her eye, she saw Sir Victor close his hand around his sword hilt. And knew those behind did the same.

"Do not, Sir Knight!" Baron de Arell growled, once more causing the hairs across her limbs to stand, then he glanced behind at his archers. "At such close range, their arrows easily pierce armor."

She was to fault for that. When her brother's knight slid his gaze to her, she shook her head. He did not draw his sword, but neither did he remove his hand from it.

The Baron of Blackwood raised his own hands to show they were empty save for the half-eaten apple, then he parted his mantle, confirming he wore no chain mail over his tunic. There was, however, a great sword there. "Precaution only," he said. "No harm do I intend your lady." As the mantle resettled around him, he gripped the bridle of Quintin's mount. "A fine horse." Eyes that had been flint-hard once more gleamed with amusement. "Though methinks too tame for a Boursier."

She agreed, having pressed Bayard for a stallion, and for a moment felt kindly toward the baron.

Fool, she silently rebuked. Were she the one to wed into the De Arells, this man would not gift her a worthy mount. As his wife, a mare would remain her lot. He merely baited her.

After feeding the remains of his apple to her horse, he patted the animal's jaw and said, "Six men."

Though certain that would be enough, he must be made to feel she wanted more so his win would seem sweeter. "Ten, Baron de Arell."

"Six."

"Eight."

He released her mare's bridle and turned.

"Six!" she blurted.

"My lady!" Sir Victor exclaimed.

Griffin de Arell came back around, inclined his head. "Choose whomever you wish."

She looked to her brother's knight. "I leave it to you."

He muttered something, then summoned five of Godsmere's best men.

Wishing her personal guard were among them—Rollo, who had been called home to tend his ailing mother—she gripped the Wulfrith dagger beneath her mantle. If Sir Victor and the other knights could not keep her safe, she would see to it herself.

She guided her horse onto the drawbridge alongside Sir Victor, and when she drew even with the Baron of Blackwood, he turned and walked beside her.

"Methinks we are both pleased with our compromise," he said. When she shot her gaze to him, he added, "Though I would have allowed you a dozen men were it required to assuage your fear."

"Fear?" she scorned, and wished she had not. She ought to be charming him, not making her dislike better known.

As they neared the portcullis, she looked up at the archers. "For one who expected his future son-in-law, you make an unconvincing show of welcome."

"None was intended."

She frowned.

"I knew it was not Baron Boursier who rode on Castle Mathe, my lady."

"How did you come by that?"

He did not answer until they entered the outer bailey. "Just as I am easily picked from among my men, so is your brother by his size and the red in his hair. Too, though I would not be averse to Baron Boursier so fearing me that he deemed it necessary to bring a great number of armed men to his wedding, he does not."

Once Quintin and her escort were inside the outer bailey, the portcullis lowered, cutting them off from the greater body of Godsmere men.

"You will leave your mounts here," Griffin de Arell announced to her escort, then reached up and closed a hand over her reins and her gloved fingers that held them.

It was not flesh-to-flesh contact, but a peculiar sensation moved through her, so warm, languorous, and deep she did not attempt to correct his trespass—though she knew she should. And she met his gaze, though she knew she should not.

"I thought so," he said low. Eyes a darker blue than they had appeared outside the walls, he drew a thumb across her knuckles. "Yet another reason I would not have my daughter wed your brother."

Did he insinuate marriage between the houses of De Arell and Boursier be made through himself and her? Had her wiles worked that quickly? Or was she the one to fall victim to them?

That last freeing her from whatever hold he had on her, she snatched her fingers from his, twisted opposite, and dismounted from the wrong side. The mare did not like it, whinnying and sidestepping so sharply that had De Arell not brought the horse under control, she might have trod upon her mistress.

But Quintin would not thank the baron who was the cause of her unseemly dismount.

As she tugged her mantle into place, ignoring the curious looks angled at her by the men of Godsmere and Blackwood, De Arell came around the mare. "It seems I overestimated your ability to handle a horse," he said. "Indeed, this one may not be tame enough."

Closing her hands into fists, she said, "I await proof my brother is not at Castle Mathe."

He ran his gaze down her. "And so you shall have it, my lady. Let us begin here."

2

GRIFFIN KNEW HE should not have ignored his own counsel about Lady Quintin. But having too many days labored under the dark prospect of giving his daughter in marriage to one who, perhaps, had more cause to loathe the De Arells than the De Arells had cause to loathe him, the opportunity to nettle Boursier's sister was too tempting.

Unfortunately, she presented other temptations. Just as he should not have provoked her, he should not have said what he had when something between them had passed through him—and her—as he clasped her fingers. But like the squire of six and ten he had been when he had thought himself in love with a pretty chambermaid upon whom he had unknowingly fathered a child, the words had wanted speaking.

Not that he felt any depth of emotion for Lady Quintin. Attraction only, of which nothing could come since Bayard Boursier had chosen to wed Griffin's illegitimate daughter, Thomasin. The onset of that young woman's monthly having kept her abed this morn, he had expected her meeting with her betrothed would be postponed till the morrow. But if Bayard Boursier did not appear within the next two days, there would be no reason for them to ever meet.

Griffin narrowed his eyes at Lady Quintin where she stood in the center of the lord's solar he had opened to prove that just as her brother was not held in the outer or inner bailey, neither was he imprisoned in the great keep.

What had become of Baron Boursier? Though Griffin had suggested he had fled marriage, the baron was not such a man. Certes, he did not wish to wed a De Arell—would not even were the seventeen-year-old Thomasin fully noble—but more, he would not forego marriage at the cost of his lands. And as the king had known, neither would the Baron of Blackwood or the Baron of Emberly.

"Satisfied, Lady Quintin?"

She came about so quickly her mantle flared, and before its edges came back together, he saw an elaborate scabbard on her girdle of a length and breadth to encase not a meat knife but a deadly dagger.

Did she know how to wield it? Not that he feared he would find himself at her mercy, nor the mercy of Godsmere's men who had not been relieved of their weapons upon entering the walls. Curiosity only. And he liked curiosities, especially in women. Would Elianor of Emberly provide such when he wed her to end the feud between the De Arells and Verduns? All he knew of the woman was that she was beautiful and a widow to his widower.

"I am satisfied my brother is not in *this* chamber," Lady Quintin said, and once more he heard desperation in her voice that increased with each room that proved absent her brother.

She stepped forward. Framed by the solar behind with its fine chairs, tables, chests, and immense bed in which Griffin and, later, his own son had been born, he was struck by how well she fit this place that was long without a lady.

He ground his teeth. Had his dinner not been interrupted, he could have blamed such fanciful thought on having indulged in too much drink, but ale had barely wet his tongue before he was alerted to approaching riders.

Attraction only, he told himself. After all, the termagant gave him no cause to feel anything more, her efforts to encourage his attentions just that—the hope of gaining what he could not give.

He stepped aside and, as she passed him, pulled the door closed. The Godsmere men waited in the corridor, along with two Blackwood knights Griffin had chosen to accompany him—Sir Tilden and Sir Otto. The latter, ever attentive to his lord, had been less so these past hours. Though he surely tried to be discreet, his admiration of Lady Quintin was obvious. And bothersome.

"Do your duty, Sir Otto," Griffin said and strode past the knight and opened the door to his son's chamber.

The seven-year-old Rhys looked up from where he sprawled on his bed amid carved wooden soldiers. And flushed guiltily. As well he should, having been sent abovestairs to practice his sums following their interrupted meal.

"Father, I but—" The appearance of the lady at Griffin's side closed the lad's mouth.

"Lady Quintin of the Boursiers wishes to know if her brother hides beneath your bed, Rhys."

"The Boursier?" Rhys jerked upright as if he intended to drag the warrior out. But then he grinned and Griffin knew he was ready to play the game his father set before him.

"Alas, he has come and gone, my lady," he said, "and left not even an eyepatch to mark his stay."

Griffin nearly groaned. That was *not* the game, certainly not in the presence of one who had borne witness to the clash between the cuckolded Bayard Boursier that had ended in the loss of the baron's eye and Serle's sword arm. And then there was the injury Lady Quintin was said to have sustained—assuredly minor—when she had inserted herself between the warriors.

Hysterics, Griffin had named her foolishness, but now having met her, she whose breath had stopped so that anger might once more fill the space between them, he thought it more likely she had sought to aid her brother. Still foolish, but intriguingly so.

"You are satisfied?" Though it was the same he asked of each room she entered, this time he did so without teasing.

She turned and moved to the next door.

Rhys shrugged and lifted his palms.

The lad could not be faulted, for though Griffin knew Serle was more to blame for that day—for abandoning reason alongside faith—his brother had lost all to Bayard Boursier's sword. Thus, the ill will Griffin revealed in the presence of his impressionable young son, and that he did not better rein in his men who had also suffered at the hands of the Boursiers and Verduns, was responsible for words that should not have been spoken.

Determining he and his son would discuss it later, he jutted his chin at the wax tablet at the foot of the bed. "You are not to leave your chamber until your sums are completed."

Rhys grimaced. "Aye, Father."

Griffin closed the door. Though he had not expected he would ever apologize to a Boursier for anything, an apology was on his tongue as he drew alongside Lady Quintin.

But then she flicked her gold-ringed brown eyes at him and said, "Mayhap the De Arells are a lost cause after all. Poor King Edward. Such hopes he had for you." She sighed. "Me? Though I have not much expectation for any of these marriages, methinks it best I put all my hope in Magnus Verdun."

Whom she was to wed within months of her brother wedding Thomasin, leaving Griffin to complete the circle by wedding Elianor of Emberly.

Telling himself this was Lady Quintin's due, and there was no gain in responding in kind, Griffin knocked on the door. "My daughter's chamber. She was unwell this morn, so she may yet be abed."

When Thomasin did not call him inside, he opened the door. Her unmade bed was empty, as was the rest of her chamber.

Ulric, he thought. *She has gone abovestairs to visit him.* Which Griffin had refused to allow when, having learned of his daughter's existence three years past, he had brought her to live at Castle Mathe. But she did as she pleased, and he had accepted her visits to her grandfather once he determined the old man would do her no harm. Not that she knew Griffin was aware of her defiance.

He motioned Lady Quintin in ahead of him, but she said, "I am satisfied," and moved to the next chamber, which his senior household knight occupied when there were no guests of rank to accommodate. Neither did she enter that room, upon its threshold once more stating she was satisfied.

"You would also confirm your brother is not in the chapel?" Griffin jutted his chin at where it lay near the corridor's end.

"Of course." She crossed to it, opened the door, and peered into the dim. "Why are there no candles lit?"

He met her gaze across her shoulder. "As you know, the bishop of our diocese passed away a fortnight past. As you obviously do not know, Castle Mathe's priest succeeded him. Thus, we await his replacement." He removed the torch from the sconce alongside the door, and when she stepped aside, thrust it into the chapel to prove she would not find her brother there.

She swept her gaze around the confines, turned, and advanced on the narrow stairway that accessed the third floor.

Griffin caught her arm as she set foot on it. "You have seen all there is to see, Lady Quintin."

She pulled free. "I have not seen what is up there."

"Nor will you. The entire floor is my father's apartment, and he suffers no visitors." And in this moment, Ulric was surely aware of the potential for them. His little dog, efficient at alerting him to the approach of those who ventured abovestairs, was likely growling low as he did when his ears pricked at the sound of Griffin's voice. Once he sensed Lady Quintin's presence, that growl would become a fierce bark, alerting its master to the presence of a stranger.

"So these are the rules you spoke of," the lady said. "I may search out my brother only where you say I may." She started past him. "As I did not agree to such, I will see for myself—"

Once more he grasped her arm. And this time, Godsmere's men stirred in anticipation of the need to defend their lady. "As my father is not well, I will not have him disturbed. Thus, your search ends here."

She lowered her chin, stared at his hand on her, then raised her face. "It appears you have wasted my time and proved naught. My brother could as easily be at the top of these stairs as in any of the rooms you have allowed me to enter."

He released her, and though he expected her to distance herself, she did not.

"He is not abovestairs, Lady Quintin. You will have to accept my word on that."

Sir Victor strode forward. "My lady, we ought to depart."

As she held her gaze to Griffin, he saw plotting in her eyes. But rather than another attempt at bending him to her will with flirtation, she said, "You are not very hospitable, Baron."

As he was well aware. But of greater concern was how aware he was of her. And that could prove as dangerous to a warrior as leaving his helmet's visor raised amidst a hail of arrows.

"I have been more than accommodating, my lady. Thus, as Sir Victor tells, it is time you return to Godsmere where 'tis possible you shall find your brother."

"God willing I shall. But ere we part company, surely you can offer us food and drink to sustain us during our journey."

She sought to prolong her stay, doubtless in hopes of stealing up the stairs.

"Do you forget," she pressed, "you earlier invited me to your table."

He had not forgotten. "As the days of winter are short, the longer you delay, the more likely you will ride by moonlight."

She tilted her head. "Regardless, I am tired and hungry and would be grateful to sit awhile."

Imagining her at his side for an hour or more, wishing he were not attracted to one who should not appeal in the absence of long tresses through which a man could run his hands, he knew he ought to refuse. But he said, "Then you and your men shall join us at meal."

The turn of her lips seemed almost genuine. "You are all graciousness, Baron de Arell."

He motioned her to precede him, and she stepped past and was intercepted by Sir Victor.

Griffin could only hear the urgency in the knight's words, but he knew the man sought to convince her to depart immediately.

Surely wishing her response to be known to Griffin, she whispered loudly, "Aye, but the baron and I yet have games to play."

3

———

WHAT IF ILL befalls me whilst you are away, Daughter? What if I sicken and you are nowhere near to rouse me back to health?

Moving her gaze around the great hall in an attempt to put from mind the man seated beside her, Quintin winced over the memory of her mother's pleading.

Lady Maeve, once strong of mind and will, had become less so since the passing of her husband years ago. Now she seemed more like the daughter than the mother, and attending to her demands, worries, and fears was wearying—and sometimes alarming—but Quintin loved her dearly.

Though aided by Lady Maeve's long-time maid, she took upon herself much of the responsibility of ensuring her mother's comfort and peace of mind. And struggled against becoming foul-tempered when Lady Maeve perceived her daughter cared too much for others.

Quintin's brother was most often considered the interloper. Not that Lady Maeve disliked her stepson, whom she had raised from a boy, but she resented him for how much her daughter adored him.

You care more for your half-brother than you do for me, she had snapped when Quintin had taken to the saddle to go in search of him.

Quintin had assured her it was not so, but her mother had tearfully gripped her daughter's skirt and begged her not to leave.

'Tis not safe for you at Castle Mathe, she had cried. And when Quintin had gently loosened Lady Maeve's hold, her mother had warned that the devil walked Castle Mathe's corridors. Doubtless, she referred to the old baron who dwelled on the uppermost floor.

Quintin peered sidelong at Griffin de Arell. Over the past hour and a half, he had refused her attempts to draw him into further talk of Bayard's whereabouts and immersed himself in conversation with an older knight on his left. But now, as if feeling her gaze, he said, "Pardon, Sir Mathieu," and looked around.

She raised her goblet, put it to her lips, and sipped.

Motioning a servant to remove the remains of their meals, the baron angled his body toward her. "I am curious, my lady."

"Are you?"

He lowered his gaze to the bodice of her gown, lingered, and continued to her waist. "'Tis a fine dagger, one surely not meant to be worn by a lady."

"'Tis a——"

"Wulfrith dagger. I know of them, have seen them worn by men trained into knighthood at Wulfen Castle—as was your father, I understand."

Feeling as if she dishonored Archard Boursier and his accomplishment, she inwardly squirmed. "It belonged to him."

"He gave it to you?" It was said with disbelief, for such a treasure would be passed not to a daughter but a worthy son—in this instance, Bayard.

"That is not your concern, Baron de Arell."

He narrowed his eyes, inclined his head. "The day darkens, my lady."

She glanced at the windows. "I pray I will not have to further impose by requesting a night's lodging."

"Providing you depart within a half hour, you should make Castle Adderstone shortly after nightfall."

As she feigned consideration, she caught the scent of a dog, evidence a wolfhound was near again. The odor was not overly offensive, the dogs appearing well cared for, but she was not accustomed to being in close quarters with animals while at meal. Her mother did not allow it.

She lowered her goblet. "The sooner you honor my request to see what lies at the top of your stairs, the sooner you will rid yourself of me."

His mouth leaned into a smile that was becoming familiar—half hitched with humor at her expense. "My lady, do you not think that were your brother imprisoned in my father's apartment, I would have had him moved whilst we filled our bellies, and thereby see you satisfied and sooner on your way?"

She *had* thought that and, hoping there were no hidden passageways within Castle Mathe as there were at Castle Adderstone, had kept watch on the stairs lest a thing of good size was smuggled off them. But not even Lady Thomasin had appeared there, she who was as absent from the hall as she had been from her chamber.

Quintin frowned. Was it possible the young lady, who was said to be improper, was Bayard's jailer? Might that be the true cause of her absence?

Ignoring Griffin de Arell's question, she said, "If your daughter is well enough to leave her bed, why does she not join us at meal?"

He leaned nearer, and she caught the scent of ale on his breath. "You would know better than I, my lady, for I would not presume to fathom the life-giving secrets of a woman's body."

He spoke of menses, she realized and wished away the color in her cheeks and ache in her heart which, had she not removed her mantle before seating herself beside the lord of Castle Mathe, would have tempted a fist to her belly.

"Forgive me, Lady Quintin, I could think of no more delicate way to assure you my daughter would present herself were she able to."

Uncomfortable with how near he remained, wondering if others noticed, she swept her gaze around the hall. They were watched, not only by Sir Victor and the others of Godsmere seated at side tables, but openly by the handsome knight who had accompanied the Baron of Blackwood in escorting the Godsmere party around the castle. He offered a smile she did not return and set to whatever remained of his meal.

"I assure you," Griffin de Arell continued, "Thomasin would be eager to meet the one who is to be her sister-in-law."

"You speak as if my brother is not missing, that he will soon appear and fulfill the king's decree."

He drew back. "Since ill has not befallen him at my hands, there is little chance ill has befallen him at all."

She gasped. "That is rather arrogant."

"Nay, that is rather true."

"Even do I not see my brother again," she said between her teeth, "never will you convince me he abandoned his family to flee marriage."

"I would also be hard convinced of that."

Though his words seemed sincere, she pressed, "Where is he?" He knew. Had to. If he did not...

"My answer remains the same, my lady—I know not."

Again, spoken with sincerity. But it did not soothe. Far better Bayard imprisoned by his enemy than no longer subject to foul play.

"Whatever has become of my brother, it violates the decree. And that the king will not tolerate," she said, then blinked at the realization she had conceded Griffin de Arell might not be responsible for Bayard being stolen from his bed.

As if the baron also realized it, regret softened his expression. "Certes, Edward will not like that your brother has disappeared, but in the end he will have his alliances."

As much as it pained her to voice her next question, she said, "Without my brother, how will our three houses be joined?"

Regret more deeply grooved his face, and before he spoke she knew what he would tell. "The answer is in the king's decree. If your family is unable to meet the conditions, Godsmere shall be forfeited to the crown."

"But this is not our doing. King Edward will see that—will make allowances."

Dear Lord, she silently beseeched, *if the king stays true to his word that no excuse will he accept, not only will Mother and I lose Bayard, but our home will be dragged out from under us.*

"Of course…" Frowning, Griffin de Arell sat back.

"What?"

He moved his gaze over her. "'Tis possible the king could be convinced to amend the decree—for the sake of the Foucault name."

Her grandfather's name that was no more, the same as the barony of Kilbourne. Twenty-five years past, Baron Denis Foucault had united with his peers in protest against England's misrule, only to betray the baronage by turning spy for the inept King Edward II. His vassals—the Boursiers, De Arells, and Verduns—had then betrayed him to his peers. Upon Foucault's death in the ensuing confrontation, the empowered baronage had seen Kilbourne divided between the three vassals, and the embittered king had been forced to accept the barons of Godsmere, Emberly, and Blackwood. When Foucault's son, Simon, was killed in France shortly thereafter, the name had found its end.

Still, that blood flowed through Simon's sister, Lady Maeve, and half as strong through Quintin, whose sire had wed Denis Foucault's daughter. Though some spitefully said Archard Boursier had done it as penance for his betrayal, he had loved his wife.

Feeling the coursing of her Boursier-Foucault blood, Quintin narrowed her eyes at De Arell. "Amend the decree for the sake of the Foucault name? What mean you?"

He clasped his hands before him. "You have heard that when my father met with your father and Magnus Verdun's twenty-five years past to unite against Baron Foucault, they agreed that should they prevail and be granted the reward they sought, Castle Adderstone would be Ulric de Arell's."

Denis Foucault's own residence and the greater of his three castles. "This I know, as I know the reason it was awarded to my father. He proved the worthiest of those who revealed my grandfather's plotting."

She expected him to gainsay her, but he said, "A great loss for my sire."

"And for it, he loves to stoke the feud between our families."

Griffin de Arell further surprised by nodding. "I am thinking that if Godsmere is forfeited to the crown, eliminating the need for alliances with the Boursiers, I could suggest to the king that I be awarded the barony through marriage to you, Lady Quintin—for the sake of the Foucault name."

Her throat clamped so tight she did not know where she found breath to hiss, "For the sake of your coffers."

He smiled crookedly. "That, too."

This time she leaned near. "Had we not an audience, I would slap that limp smile from your face."

His eyebrows shot up. "Limp? Never have I heard it described so, though it does seem you and my sire are like-minded."

Not until she felt the jewels of crucifixion in her palm did she realize her hand was on the Wulfrith dagger. To be equated with Ulric de Arell—

"Neither does he like my smile. Though he thinks it arrogant, I think it amused."

"Amused!" Her voice rose, and she sensed more attention upon the high table.

The Baron of Blackwood glanced around. "'Tis mostly how I feel when my mouth hitches thus. But do I take you to wife, you will grow accustomed to it, likely find it appealing—as do most ladies—and long for me to press it to your own smile."

Quintin gaped. His father was right—arrogance was the better word for that smile. "You are a lout, a knave, an oaf, the lowliest of—"

He laughed. Loud.

"Lady Quintin!" Sir Victor called.

But she was on her feet. The Wulfrith dagger in her fist. The blade at the baron's throat. His laughter quieted. And the din of the hall put to bed.

4

⟨⟨⟨

Heart feeling as if the blood were being squeezed from it, Quintin held her gaze to the man whose head was back and eyes, like his mouth, no longer made sport of her. Indeed, the brilliant blue was barely visible, reduced to narrow bands encircling black pupils that put her in mind of what it must be like to stare down death.

Dear Lord, what have I done? And what am I to do now? she silently appealed, but if the Lord was speaking to her, His voice was too soft to be heard above the shocked and excited onlookers—and of more immediate threat, the growl of a wolfhound on the other side of the lord's high seat.

Certain her brother's men were too outnumbered to aid her, accepting it was too late to have anything to lose, she demanded, "Where is my brother?"

Griffin de Arell stared, and in that moment she realized anger, like fear, had a smell all its own—sharp and acrid, as she imagined fire would taste if one could touch tongue to it. And he had a right to be furious. Were it a man who had bested him in sight of his retainers, his pride would be injured. But that it was a woman and witnessed by his enemy's men...

"My lady!" Sir Victor again, his tone warning she had gone too far.

But it was too late to turn back. "Where is he, Baron de Arell?"

He drew a breath she hoped was meant to calm rather than ready him to move against her. "Had I to guess, I would say *The Boursier* has gone down a hole."

More derision as, before all, he marked her brother a coward.

"Where?" she snarled.

The wolfhound growled again, and when its great head and shoulders rose to the left of Griffin de Arell, she startled.

"Blessed be!" the baron rasped as a line of blood welled on his whiskered neck.

More growling, and now Quintin felt the wolfhound's hot breath ripple across her dagger-wielding hand and curl beneath her jaw.

"Down, Arturo!" Griffin de Arell bit as Quintin turned her face toward the beast whose teeth were bared and body bunched as if—

"Stand down, my lady!" Sir Victor shouted.

She would have if not for the iron band that turned around her wrist and wrenched her arm up and back. Then her feet came off the floor and she fell back. It was a short fall to the cloth-covered table, but she landed hard amid the sound of toppled goblets and voices that had been lost but now were found—shouts of surprise, outrage, her name.

She had her breath, and her head had not hit so hard she should lose consciousness, but all went black. However, when she tilted her head back, she saw it was only the darkly-clad Griffin de Arell pinning her to the table, jaw hard, eyes glittering.

Only Griffin de Arell. Was there a greater understatement?

She started to breathe deep, but when her chest rose toward his, made do with less air.

"Will you give over?" he asked in a voice so devoid of drollery she did not recognize it.

Surprised she still possessed the dagger, she said, "Will you get off me? 'Tis unseemly this."

"What is unseemly is a guest drawing a dagger on her host. And cutting him."

She opened her mouth to berate him for provoking her, but he was right. Fear over Bayard's fate and anger over the baron's suggestion he wed her so a De Arell might finally lay hands on Castle Adderstone had caused her to behave in a manner unbecoming a lady.

Grateful the other occupants of the hall now voiced their astonishment so loudly none could hear what passed between them, she choked down pride and said, "Forgive me. I did not intend that to happen."

"The dagger, Lady Quintin."

Knowing if she did not relinquish it, he would take it from her, she uncurled her fingers. "'Tis yours."

"So 'tis." He swept it from her palm.

She gasped. "I did not mean it is yours to keep!"

He pulled her off the table, and she so awkwardly stumbled against him she would have become a heap at his feet had he not gripped her arm.

Beset by the not entirely unpleasant scent of his man's body, she lurched back and searched out the Wulfrith dagger he held at his side. And just beyond it, the wolfhound stood, fiery eyes awaiting hers as if he wished her to challenge him.

She returned her gaze to the dagger. In Griffin de Arell's hand it looked less formidable, shorter and narrower than when she had held it. But that was fallacy. If he chose to wield it, a deadly thing it would be. And not merely because of a slip of the hand.

"The meal is at an end!" he announced, though most were already on their feet. "Be about your duties."

As the castle folk obeyed, Quintin winced over the cut on Griffin de Arell's neck, quivered over his flared nostrils, swallowed over the black of his blue eyes. "The dagger is not yours to keep, Baron."

He slid the blade beneath his belt.

She was tempted to reclaim it, as he must know—perhaps even wished her to challenge him, the same as his dog.

Proceed carefully, she silently warned as she should have earlier. "I spoke true when I told I regretted cutting you. Upon my word, it was not intentional."

He lifted a hand so suddenly she thought he meant to strike her. Instead, he swept fingers over the cut on his throat and glanced at the crimson streak. "That is the least of your offenses against my person, *Lady* Quintin."

True, for she had bled his pride.

"And the last offense." He pulled the meat knife from her girdle and tossed it on the table.

Chest constricting, she peered across her shoulder. Amid the disarray of those withdrawing from the hall, she found Sir Victor's gaze that had never before shone with such urgency. He and the other Godsmere knights were surrounded by Blackwood men, and they had been relieved of their weapons.

She moistened her lips. "It does, indeed, grow dark. 'Tis time my escort and I departed."

"Past time your *escort* departed."

Though prepared to be excluded, the fine hairs prickled across her limbs. "Baron, pray hear me. I—"

"Sir Mathieu! See Godsmere's men are removed from Castle Mathe as hospitably as possible."

Quintin longed to strain against his hold, but her struggle would cause the Godsmere knights to further risk their lives. Thus, she once more sought Sir Victor's gaze and inclined her head.

"Very good, Lady Quintin," Baron de Arell said. "Mayhap you are not a lost cause." His choice of words were a reminder of when his son had made sport of Bayard's eyepatch and she had bemoaned King Edward's hopes for the De Arells.

Lest her control slipped before her brother's men were clear of the hall, she seamed her lips.

"There is, indeed, hope for you," Griffin de Arell said as Godsmere's knights were marshaled outside.

When the doors closed, she looked up. "You have made your point, Baron. And I am repentant. Now, ere more damage is done—"

"I have not made my point, Lady Quintin, and you are not truly repentant. But I will, and you shall be, regardless of the damage."

"Baron——"

He pulled her after him along the back of the dais, and she did not resist, hopeful he but wished to put fear in her before tossing her out with Godsmere's men. And greater hope she had when he strode toward the doors leading to the inner bailey. But moments later, she was drawn up the stairs.

Did he mean to allow her what he had earlier refused? Though the possibility ought to gladden her, desperation wound through her. If he now permitted her inside his father's apartment, it was because Bayard was not there. And if he was not...

They reached the landing, and she followed him down the corridor toward the narrow stairway. But he stopped short of it and threw open the door to the chamber he had said belonged to his senior household knight, whom she now knew to be Sir Mathieu.

He pulled her inside. "Yours for the duration of your stay," he said and released her.

She whipped around. "What say you?"

The smile that lifted his mouth was far from limp. "As you boasted to Sir Victor, you and I yet have games to play."

So she had boasted, so sure of herself she had wished him to hear. Now she was not sure of anything save that she had made matters far worse.

"For the disgrace you made of my hospitality," he continued, "I will be compensated."

"Disgrace to which you added by landing me on the table," she snapped.

"Had it not been me, 'twould have been Arturo, against whom you would have fared most ill, for he is young and still much in need of correction—rather like you."

Anger jerked through her, but before she could respond, he jutted his chin at her waist. "Unfasten your girdle."

Ravishment was the compensation he sought? "I will not!"

She knew big men could move fast, her brother the perfect example, but she was unprepared for the speed with which De Arell did so. The Wulfrith dagger appearing in his hand as if it had leapt there, he lunged forward.

Quintin screeched and threw her arms up, but there was only air where he had been.

"Not your virtue, my lady." He held up her girdle from which the elaborate scabbard was suspended alongside the simple one that was as absent its meat knife as the other was absent its Wulfrith dagger.

He had cut it off!

"So worthy a blade requires a worthy sheath," he said and pivoted.

"Baron!"

He lifted a key from a hook beside the door, raised it. "To ensure untrustworthy guests do not take advantage of De Arell hospitality."

"You would lock me in?"

"Though I care not to be your jailer, especially as 'twould be a poor start to our marriage should our relations come to that—"

"'Twill not!"

"—I will not see my people further troubled or scandalized. Rest well, Quintin Boursier."

She launched herself at the door, but he was on the other side before she reached it. Then the key turned in the lock.

She landed a fist on the door. "You cannot do this!"

No response, only the firm tread of his retreat.

She struck again. "You cannot!"

Now the quick, vicious bark of what sounded like a small dog, then voices. Not caring to whom the latter belonged, she pounded on the door. Again. And again.

5

―⊸∞∞⊶―

"Is she as lovely as Rhys tells?"

Griffin turned to the young woman of ten and seven who had exited her chamber, then glanced at the boy at her side. Though the first was illegitimate, he did not think the two could be closer were their blood mixed from the same two pools.

Three years past, Griffin had received a missive from Thomasin beseeching his aid in escaping the lord to whom her mother gave her in service before abandoning her for a man. The proof provided that she was the daughter of Alice, whom Griffin had loved, had delivered him to the girl's side. That day, he brought her to Blackwood, not to live as a commoner, which was all she asked of him, but as a lady bearing his name.

Rhys had resented her—for all of six days. Though Griffin was uneasy with expressing affection, when Thomasin had come off the stairs with the motherless little boy on her hip, he had felt fatherly stirrings for the one whom obligation had caused him to claim. And more than stirrings all these years later. Thus, when she threw off her noble side in favor of the common, he corrected her only if improper behavior upset the household. Such had become rare, but he worried how Boursier would take to a wife whose untamed side would test his patience. For Thomasin, more than the possibility of his own gain, Griffin hoped the Baron of Godsmere forfeited all.

With his daughter and son staring at him out of eyes as blue as his own, his hard, angry reaches began to contract, though still Lady Quintin protested her confinement and Ulric's little dog protested her commotion.

Thomasin peered down the corridor at the door which lightly shuddered with each blow. "Rhys tells she is lovely," said she who was not as plain-faced as most believed, "that though her hair is rather short, 'tis black as a raven's wings."

Ash-black, Griffin silently corrected, as of a raven soaring above a consuming fire, its wings flecked with ash. "She is lovely," he conceded, keeping to himself the possibility her beauty was exclusive to outward appearance, "as you would have seen for yourself had you been in your chamber earlier."

Her smile wavered, but she offered no explanation, nor did he require one.

"Why is the lady in Sir Mathieu's chamber?" Rhys asked.

"And why have you locked her in?" Thomasin glanced at the key Griffin held, frowned over the cut on his throat.

"For her protection."

Rhys's eyebrows shot up. "From what?"

Grateful the boy had not completed his sums soon enough to join the meal belowstairs, for it would not do to see his father bested by a woman, Griffin said, "The lady trespassed on De Arell hospitality."

"You will punish her?"

"Forsooth, I have not decided what I shall do, but for now she remains at Castle Mathe."

"For how long? She makes much noise."

"Which the old baron will not like," Thomasin added.

"She will quiet ere long. As for you, Rhys, come to the solar ere supper this eve. I would speak with you."

The boy grimaced. "The eyepatch."

"Of that and other things." In spite of the humiliation Lady Quintin had dealt Griffin, his son must be prepared for talk of what had transpired in the hall and see clearly what his father might refuse to see if not that he aspired to provide a better example than Ulric had.

Rhys would know the true circumstances that had caused Lady Quintin to draw a blade on her host. More importantly, sense would be made of what had appeared to be a retaliatory attack. Had Griffin not landed her on the table, Arturo might have torn out her throat though he had been ordered down—evidence the dog required more training to overcome abuse suffered at the hands of a traveling merchant from whom Griffin had freed him. These things Rhys must know lest he believe it permissible to transgress against a woman.

"Continue with what you were at," Griffin said.

"Sums," the boy groaned. "Thomasin likes numbers. I do not."

"Still, you progress well," his sister said and urged him back inside her chamber.

Griffin continued to the solar and, as he entered, the lady's protests ceased. He paused in anticipation she but drew breath, but silence prevailed.

He grunted with satisfaction—and surprise. He had assured his son she would quiet before long but had not believed she would so soon prove him right. Quintin Boursier's claws were more easily blunted than expected.

Pacing. From one side of the chamber to the other. From one corner to the next. From the door to the bed. From the garderobe to the window. Mind mercilessly awhirl. Body miserably worn.

"Pathetic," Quintin muttered and halted before the window, opened the shutters as she had done often these past hours, and let the night air in.

Huddling into her mantle that had earlier been delivered with lit candles, coal for the brazier, and supper viands she had not touched, she stared at the glow beyond the castle's walls that evidenced Godsmere's men camped there. And regretted the discomfort for which she was responsible.

Fortunately, before departing Adderstone, Sir Victor had insisted on extra time to gather provisions should De Arell refuse them entrance, forcing them to camp outside his walls. It was terribly cold, but they had tents, blankets, fires, and food to allay the worst of it. But this was only the first night. If the Baron of Blackwood did not soon tire of the game she had challenged him to play, another night they would suffer.

And her mother...

Lady Maeve would become increasingly distraught. Though she only approached the edge of something dark on the anniversary of her beloved husband's death, what if worry over her daughter's prolonged absence drew her to that edge? There was only her devoted maid, Hulda, to gently call her back. And what if that was not enough?

Quintin's eyes teared. It might not be mere days ere she returned to Godsmere. It could be weeks.

Unless you become an exceedingly undesirable prisoner, suggested the Quintin who detested helplessness. *Unless you so disrupt Griffin de Arell's household he happily casts you out. And what better time than the still of middle night?*

She closed the shutters. Refusing to allow her gaze to fall on the bed her body longed for, she cleared a throat earlier roughened by shouts and examined the underside of her fists from which she had picked splinters gained from pounding on the door.

Catching her lower lip between her teeth, she considered the platter with its cold viands and the goblet she had emptied of wine to soothe her throat. Unfortunately, there were few other items about the chamber to add to her efforts. But she would make do.

She tilted the food off the platter onto the bedside table, snatched up the goblet, and crossed the chamber.

"Awaken, Baron!" She flung the goblet at the door, then the platter, and gave a satisfied smile as the dog above once more made himself her ally.

"Baron!" She slammed a fist on the door, and several times more before she conceded her hands could stand no further abuse and scooped up the goblet and platter and flung them again.

Without cease, she shouted and beat on the planks, causing such a din she would not likely hear the opening of doors, footsteps, or the key in the lock. But he would come.

When he thrust open the door, she jumped to the side and, before his robe-clad figure entirely filled the doorway, ducked beneath his arm.

She had not expected to make it into the torchlit corridor, but there she was, aided by the baron's underestimation of his captive. A glance to her right revealed a young woman, just past her Griffin de Arell's son, and coming up off the stairs were men-at-arms. Futility in that direction, gain in the other, she ran toward the old baron's apartment and felt the mantle tug at her neck. Blessedly, it slipped through her pursuer's fingers as she flew up the steps and onto a dimly-lit landing.

Griffin de Arell's cursing and pounding feet drawing near, she lunged for the door ahead and to the right, behind which barking and the scrabbling of claws sounded.

She gripped the handle, but just as she discovered the door was secured against her, she was wrenched back against what felt like a wall. "You are more in need of correction than thought," the baron rasped.

She strained opposite. "Loose me!"

"Griffin!" called one on the other side of the door. Despite the dog's vicious warning, there was no doubt it was an aged voice. But just because it did not belong to Bayard did not mean her brother was not there. And how unwell could Ulric de Arell be if he was not abed, as told by the strength of his voice and the shadow moving across the light slipping beneath the door?

His son turned Quintin from the door and thrust her at the man-at-arms who had followed his lord. "Return the *lady* to her chamber."

The man was not big, but he was strong. Despite Quintin's straining, he drew her toward the stairs as she tried to keep his lord in sight where he stood at the door speaking to the one on the other side.

Then the steps. Their negotiation was precarious owing to her resistance and the man-at-arms' attempt to keep them both upright. But moments later, Griffin de Arell appeared. His quick descent parting the edges of his robe to reveal bare calves, he relieved his man of her charge.

Quintin slapped a hand to the wall. Finding no purchase, she was pulled into the corridor where the baron's son and the young woman—doubtless, Lady Thomasin—remained outside their chambers, the latter's eyes wide with what seemed more excitement than outrage. In back of them stood a rumpled Sir Mathieu before a handful of men-at-arms.

To Quintin's surprise, her captor drew her past the chamber she had been given. Had she prevailed? Would he return her to her brother's men?

"Rhys, Thomasin," he said, "back to your beds."

The boy slipped into his chamber, but the young woman made no move to comply.

As her father neared, she captured Quintin's gaze. "You are as lovely as my father told, my lady."

"Now, Thomasin!"

She sighed and closed the door behind her.

Shortly, the promise of the stairs and the hall beyond was yanked out from under Quintin when the baron pushed her into his solar.

His disarrayed bed before her, she whipped around. "What is this?"

He slammed the door in her face.

"Baron!" She wrenched at the handle, but he held the door closed on the other side where she heard him speak low, then Sir Mathieu's equally unintelligible response.

Quintin slammed a fist on the door and recoiled over the pain. As she clasped her hand against her waist, the door opened, but this time De Arell left no space for her to slip past. He closed the door and gripped her arm.

She yanked and clawed as he drew her across the chamber, cried out when he thrust her onto his bed. She sprang to sitting, intending to launch herself off, but he barred her way.

"Again, I seek not your virtue, Lady Quintin. I but ensure you stay put."

As she stared up at him, she felt strangely assured he would not force himself on her. But then, for what had he brought her within? "A man's bed is an improper place for an unwed lady to *stay put*," she said.

"I agree. Unfortunately, the alternative is to bind you, and I am certain you would like that even less."

She caught her breath.

"Now stay, Lady Quintin." He strode to the foot of the bed.

She wanted to defy him, but the threat of being bound held her to the mattress.

He raised his eyebrows. "I think it best you look away."

Sinking her fingers into the fur coverlet that radiated the warmth of the one who had recently lain beneath it, she said, "Why?"

He loosened his robe's belt. "I assume—perhaps wrongly—your lady's sensibilities will be offended should I change clothes in your presence."

"For what do you do so?" she demanded.

"A robe hardly suffices against the chill outside."

Then he would release her?

He parted the robe to reveal a short undertunic.

"This is improper, Baron!"

"'Tis you who controls how improper it is."

She continued to glare at him, but when he began to shrug out of the robe, she jerked her chin opposite and was distracted by the bed's headboard. Elaborately carved into it was the mythical griffin, a creature composed of a lion, the king of beasts, and an eagle, the king of birds.

Such vanity! she silently denounced as her ears pricked to the rustle of clothes thrown off and pulled on, next the creak of leather.

She moved her gaze to the table on the far side of the bed, and there lay the Wulfrith dagger.

"'Tis increasingly obvious why you remain unwed," Griffin de Arell muttered.

Bitterness pouring through her, she kept her fist from her abdomen. "Obvious?"

"You are disagreeable, Lady."

Though tempted to inform him it was because of his brother she was not wed, she reached for the dagger instead.

"Leave it!" he snarled, and at her hesitation added, "I have no more patience."

Keeping her shoulder to him lest he was not yet fully clothed, she said, "My father gifted it to my brother. 'Twas not mine to yield."

"You did not yield it. I won it."

As she ground her teeth, she heard a sharp snap that told he shook out his mantle.

"Come, Lady Quintin."

She looked around. Relieved his eyes were once again more blue than black, she dropped her feet to the floor and said, "You have chosen the right course."

A corner of his mouth moved. "Have I?"

"I cannot say how much easier it will go for you, but certainly better than if you did not release me."

"You make it sound as if your brother is found."

Dear Lord, he will be, will he not? she silently appealed. *If not upon Blackwood, then...*

She raised her chin. "When he is found—"

"*If* he is found."

Knowing she would soon be outside Castle Mathe's walls, perhaps leaving Bayard inside with the deadline to wed quickly approaching, she pushed down pride and anger and placed herself in front of Griffin de Arell.

He narrowed his lids.

"Baron, I know our families have long been enemies, that you distrust my brother as much as he does you, but I vow, Bayard is a good man. Though he may never love your daughter, he will make a fine husband—will not mistreat her or cause her to feel unwanted. He will do his duty to our king, and he will do it well."

"Then I will rest easier should he appear in time to wed Thomasin."

Counseling herself to proceed with caution, she touched his arm. "He has to be here."

His gaze flicked to her hand, and she held her breath in anticipation of gaining what she sought.

But he reached past her, yanked the fur coverlet from the bed, and put it over his arm. "Follow."

"For what do you bring that?" she asked as she hastened after him.

"You will need it."

Something in how he said it nibbled at her. Considering what had transpired between them, it seemed too thoughtful a gesture to provide her such extravagant warmth once she was outside his walls. Was it, perhaps, a form of apology?

As she imagined crawling beneath the fur and yielding to fatigue, he led her belowstairs and through the hall. There was a restlessness about the great room, and she knew the commotion she had caused was responsible.

Passing the pallets of those seeking a comfortable position to resume their rest, she felt the glower of several and caught the words of one. "Deserves what's comin' to her."

Certes, she had made no friends at Castle Mathe. Fortunately, she needed none.

She gasped when she followed the baron out into a night so cold she was tempted to ask for the fur. And she might have before they reached the outer walls had that been their destination.

The portcullis that accessed the outer bailey remaining lowered, Griffin de Arell opened the gatehouse door and motioned her in ahead of him.

Sticking her feet to the ground, hugging her arms beneath her mantle, she said, "I thought you meant to deliver me to my brother's men."

"There is a chamber in the southern tower I did not show you earlier."

Certain all rooms were accounted for, since she had noted their windows before entering them to search out Bayard, she looked to the southern tower built into the inner wall. Only the first and second floor windows were visible from here, but she recalled the third floor room whose narrow window faced neither the keep nor the drawbridge in the outer bailey. Cut into the side, it allowed only a view of the inner wall to the right and the black wood flanking the castle.

"Do you not wish to see it?" the baron asked.

A hidden room, then? Where Bayard was held? She had considered there were such places within Mathe, and for it had paid close attention to the dimensions of the corridors and rooms she had been led through. But of course, of what use a secret room whose presence was obvious to one unschooled in building construction?

Ignoring the worry that continued to nibble at her, she stepped past him into the relative warmth of the gatehouse that warmed further when he closed the door.

The guard inside stood at attention, and though no word passed between the two men, he inclined his head as if in answer to an unspoken question.

"Stay near, my lady." Griffin de Arell stepped around her to lead the way.

To Bayard, and then home to mother, she assured herself as she followed him down a corridor whose closed doors he had earlier opened to reveal weapons, supplies, and stores of dried food.

The stairway at the end of the corridor accessed the tower, and upon reaching its third floor landing, he threw open a door. It was not locked, which should have made her pull back, but she was so hopeful her brother was inside that she entered first.

It *was* the chamber she had earlier been shown, though then the brazier had been unlit, the bed bare of covers, and no basin and pitcher present on the table. The only thing glaringly familiar was Bayard's absence.

6

QUINTIN SWUNG AROUND. "You have already shown me this room," she accused, certain that whatever he intended she had made easier for him.

He closed the door. "Aye, but now 'tis much improved—for you."

Recalling his exchange with Sir Mathieu when he had closed her in the solar, she knew he had sent his knight to ready the tower room for one he would not allow to disrupt his sleep again.

"You deceived me! You made me believe—"

"Only what you wished to believe, Lady Quintin. And all for the better, for I no more wished to put you over my shoulder than you wished to suffer the indignity."

Tears pricking, she stared at him. Regardless of whether she turned left or right, walked forward or backward, one wall after another rose up before her. And this was the highest.

Weighted by every minute of this day and night, feeling as if the bones were going out of her, she crossed to the chair beside the bed and sank onto it. And wanted nothing more than to be left alone so she could fold over herself and hold her throbbing head.

The baron strode farther into the room, dropped the fur on the bed, and gestured at the basket near the brazier. "You have a good supply of coal, but as it will be some time ere the floors and walls warm sufficiently to make the room comfortable, you may require the fur."

Quintin clasped her arms at her waist and allowed herself to lean forward just enough to more easily bear the burden clinging to her back.

"I trust now you will rest, as the castle folk and I shall, but should you decide otherwise, know that any effort to make a nuisance of yourself will mostly go unnoticed."

Hating the longing to rock herself, she tightened her muscles.

"There is only one window, and as it is small and faces not the keep but the black wood, this is where those who overly protest their *stay* are accommodated."

She closed her eyes and found such relief behind her lids she sank more into herself.

Impulsive, she silently berated. *Even when you think ere acting, you do not always think well. Mayhap you are not as distant from the young woman who believed she could turn aside the blade Serle de Arell sought to sink into your brother*—your warrior *brother, who needed not your aid...who believes he is to blame. But 'tis you who are to blame. And Serle. And Constance.*

She pressed a fist to her abdomen.

"My lady?"

Lifting her chin, she blinked at that man's brother as he lowered to his haunches before her.

Was it concern on his face? And how were his eyes so blue with but a single, unenthusiastic torch lighting the room?

"Oh, Griffin, once again I make a mess of all," she whispered, and distantly acknowledged she addressed him with too much familiarity—so much that even were he the one she would wed, she would not call him by his Christian name until they were husband and wife.

She moistened her lips. "You do not hold my brother, do you?"

His eyes widened slightly, and it was strange that it did not seem strange when he lifted a hand and cupped her jaw. "My word I gave, Quintin."

She wondered how a voice hardly more than a whisper could be so deep. And wondered again at the temptation to turn her mouth into his hand. To which she yielded. And he allowed—until she loosed her breath against his calloused palm.

"Nay, my lady." He drew back and stood, covering all of her in shadow. "This we will not do."

The woman who seemed to have stepped outside of her slipping back in, she said sharply, "What say you?"

Mouth so dour it was hard to believe it had ever known private amusement, he said, "Whilst you are another man's betrothed, this particular game I will not play."

"Game?" She struggled to traverse her thoughts, but they were sodden, as if she had consumed too much wine.

He bent, gripped the chair arms on either side of her, and put his face so near hers that her attempt to wring out her thoughts was doomed. "You told you would rather put yourself through with a blade. *That* I almost believe. *This* I do not."

She had said it—when he had mocked her ride on Castle Mathe and suggested she eagerly delivered herself as his bride. But what did he not believe?

Something shivered through her as she relived his hand upon her face, then her lips against his palm. Neither did she believe it, and yet she had done it, and with no thought for the game.

"As I intend you to learn, Lady Quintin, I am not my brother. Hence, no cause will I give you to put his sins on me."

For that he had said that while she was promised to another, he would not play *this* game with her, believing she had responded to him to gain concessions.

And perhaps I did, she considered, for it was the only way to make sense of the senseless. Without conscious thought—goaded by the need to not only return to her mother but to survive—she sought to work her wiles on him.

Relieved she was not so foolish to feel anything other than aversion for the Baron of Blackwood, she sighed back into the chair. "Alas, you have found me out. Doubtless, your betrothed, Lady Elianor, will appreciate your constancy. Though, of course, as she is a Verdun, you may find yourself cuckolded, the same as her aunt and your brother cuckolded my brother." She shrugged. "Unwitting justice, hmm?"

"Justice," he rasped. "You believe the Boursiers deserve more than already they have been dealt?"

"My brother lost an eye."

"My brother an arm."

"My brother lost his wife." She snorted. "Not that she was worthy to bear his name."

His eyebrows rose. "Serle lost his betrothed, which as you know, was the cause of the cuckolding."

She did, it being Bayard's greatest regret that he had been so entranced with Constance Verdun's beauty he had convinced her father it was better she wed a baron than a landless second son. And many times over he had paid for loving a woman who loved another man.

"Aye, the cause," she said, "but that does not make right that your brother and that…woman defiled the marriage bed."

He glanced down. His frown alerting her to the fist she once more pressed to her abdomen, she opened it and gripped that hand over the other in her lap.

"It does not make it right," he agreed, "but neither is it right that still my brother and Lady Constance pay the price."

Quintin knew that as well. For penance, Serle had been sent on a two-year pilgrimage from which he had yet to return—though surely it was by choice he stayed away—and in addition to Constance's annulment of marriage to Bayard, she had been sentenced to live out her days in a convent.

The baron leaned nearer. "Whereas, excepting the loss of an eye that hardly hinders your brother's ability to wield a sword, your family carries on as if that day never happened. No lasting justice for the wrongs done my family."

"None?" she nearly screeched. "I was there when——" She pressed her lips.

"Aye, I heard you were injured." He moved his gaze down her. "But as told, no lasting justice for my family."

Her hand sprang up, but he caught her wrist, denying her the satisfying sting of her palm against his cheek.

"So now we are alone, you would slap the *limp* smile from my face, hmm?"

Realizing she was trembling, and so strongly he had to feel it, she said, "Leave. Now."

His grip loosened, but before she could pull free, he turned her palm up. "You have hurt yourself."

She glanced at the abrasions on the lower edges of her hands. "I do not care to be locked in, as I am certain you would like even less."

"The other hand as well?"

"Aye."

He released her. "I will send salve and bandages."

And she would not thank him for it.

"Rest well, my lady."

When the door closed and the bolt slid into its hole, she allowed herself a small sob, then bent her head to her knees.

"Be here, Bayard," she whispered. "Even if it means Griffin is a deceiver, be here. If you are not…"

She clasped her hands between her chest and thighs. "Lord, You know where he is. Pray, loose whatever chains bind him and return him to his family. And me to my mother."

Griffin halted at the center of the bailey, dropped his head back, and stared at the light-pricked sky before allowing his breath to cloud it.

He liked women well, but not so much that his fondness for their company rendered him vulnerable. Ulric de Arell had refused to allow his heir to be overly distracted by the fairer sex, meting out punishment when the youth had shown too much interest in women to the detriment of his knight's training. And further Ulric had gone in denying Griffin knowledge of the first four and ten years of Thomasin's life.

Pushing down anger that had receded these past years, Griffin returned his thoughts to Lady Quintin and loosed a greater anger on himself.

Her defeat in the tower room should not bother him. Indeed, he should rejoice in it. But feeling her anguish and weariness as if his own, he had sought to reassure her though she had given him no cause. However, she had given him cause to be encouraged when she had spoken his Christian name, appealing to him in a voice he imagined she would use to call a man back to her bed.

So he had played her game.

Then she had conceded she might be wrong about him.

And more willingly he had played her game.

Discovering her face was silken beneath his touch, he had assured her the word he gave was true, and when he had spoken her name without title, she had moved her mouth to his hand in something nearly a kiss.

And forgetting it was a game, he had wanted more from her as she seemed to want from him.

But the man he had been before Quintin Boursier set herself at his walls had questioned how it was possible. And when her breath feathered his skin, he had realized it was only possible in a game—one seeking to prove he was no more honorable than Serle whose desire had moved him to claim what belonged to another.

Still, even when Griffin had said he would not play that game, he had wanted her to deny it was that. But without apology she had pled guilty and pointed out the sins of his brother with further talk of the cuckolding and the Boursiers' longing for more justice.

Griffin had not meant to defend Serle, from whom he had poorly parted once his brother's arm had healed sufficiently to allow him to embark on his pilgrimage. Nor had he intended to demand justice for his own family, but he had met fire with fire. And for it, the lady had nearly slapped him.

Remembering her trembling that had not seemed affected, he wondered what words she had bit back after telling she had witnessed Serle and Constance's sin. He had assumed she meant to point out the minor injury she had sustained, but was there more to it?

He shook his head. Whatever she had left unsaid had no bearing on his present or future—a future that would likely include Elianor of Emberly. Telling himself a better marriage he would make with the Verdun woman than Boursier's sister, he resumed his stride.

7

"HE INSISTS, MY lady."

Quintin considered the man in the hand's width she had opened the door—a different messenger from the one sent twice on the day past to invite her to meal.

Raising her eyebrows at the knight who had accompanied Baron de Arell in taking her around the castle and who had smiled at her during her ill-fated dinner, she said, "He insists? Then I must needs obey." As she began to close the door on him, she added, "Do not forget the bolt. Your lord would be displeased if—"

He thrust a foot into the room, clapped a hand to the door, and pushed.

Knowing it was futile to resist, she stepped back, and he opened the door wide but did not further trespass by crossing the threshold.

Quintin clasped her hands at her waist. "Your name again?" He had spoken it through the door after freeing the bolt and knocking, but it had not stayed with her.

"I am Sir Otto, and though I do not wish to force a lady to do what she would not, I must do as my lord bids." He smiled wryly. "Hence, I pray you will take pity on this poor soldier and come peaceably."

She nodded at the bowl of congealed apple pottage delivered this morn. "As you can see, I have no appetite." Even less than on the day past. Though her belly gnawed her backbone, foreboding clawed at her throat. If Bayard did not wed Thomasin de Arell this day, the barony of Godsmere would be forfeited.

"Regardless," the knight said, "you are to sit at table with the baron."

Then he would convey her to the great hall in whatever humiliating manner was required? She was tempted to test him but inclined her head. "Very well."

His gaze moved beyond her, and she followed it to the saddlebag Sir Victor had sent on the day past that contained the personal effects she had assembled ere departing Castle Adderstone—and which she did not doubt had been inspected before being delivered to her.

"I shall await you on the landing whilst you change, my lady."

She glanced down her rumpled gown. "I am suitably attired for the Baron of Blackwood." She crossed to the chair and lifted her mantle. "Where you lead, I will follow."

His brown eyes searched her face as she fastened the garment at her neck, then he stepped aside and motioned her to precede him.

She almost felt sorry for a warrior who feared giving a woman his back, but his concern was not unfounded. He had seen her put a blade to his lord's throat.

No further word did they exchange as she led the way from her prison out into a gray day stirred by the bitter wind that had rattled her window's shutters. Shortly, they entered a hall alive with the appetites of those gathered for the nooning meal.

Ignoring eyes that sped to her like arrows to prey—and those of Griffin de Arell who occupied the high seat—she halted to allow Sir Otto to draw alongside.

"Unless your lord requires you to lead me to table like a child, I prefer to make my own way."

He leaned toward her. "Methinks this suffices."

"I thank you." She walked farther into the room that was warmed by a fire blazing in the cavernous hearth.

Feeling as if on display, and she supposed she was since she was a prisoner and her family was as hated by De Arell's people as his family was hated by hers, she elevated her chin and met her captor's gaze. And refused to be grateful when amusement, not anger, moved his mouth.

She looked to his left. As during her first meal at Castle Mathe, Sir Mathieu occupied the seat on that side of him, and next to the knight were De Arell's son and daughter. Though the boy regarded her with distaste, Lady Thomasin did so with a smile of welcome. And it was almost enough to make Quintin take a liking to the young woman.

Griffin stood as she neared. "Though you missed the blessing of the meal, I am pleased you consented to join us, Lady Quintin."

"I am pleased to have been given a choice," she said and ascended the dais and traversed its backside.

The Baron of Blackwood pulled out the chair beside his, but when she stepped past him to gain the seat, he closed his hands over her shoulders and turned her to face him. "Allow me."

Knowing she would suffer further shame if she wrenched free, she stood stiffly as he unhurriedly worked the fastener at her neck.

"I have been told you are not eating well," he murmured, "and I can see neither are you sleeping well."

Realizing she had lowered her gaze to his thick neck, she looked up. "You did not order it. But as Sir Otto is eager to do your bidding, mayhap you ought to task him with ensuring I gain my rest this eve."

He raised an eyebrow. "As you will learn when you wed, my lady, a man and woman alone in the dark does not a restful night make."

Though she tried to turn away remembrance of being alone with him two nights past when his hand had touched her face and her lips had touched his hand, memories tumbled back as that same hand now brushed her collarbone.

Heat rising in her cheeks, she set her teeth as he parted her mantle and lifted it from her shoulders.

"Take your ease, my lady."

She lowered into the chair, and he draped her shed garment over its back. Then he seated himself beside her as he had done at this table over which they had first shared a meal—and upon which he had landed her. As if to recreate that event, a wolfhound slinked between their chairs.

Quintin averted her gaze lest it was the same one Griffin had said would have attacked her had he himself not taken her in hand. In this, she was certain the Baron of Blackwood spoke true.

"Go, Arturo!" Griffin commanded, and the wolfhound looked to its master who repeated the command.

With a low growl, the dog twisted around and padded across the dais.

"Your hands?" Griffin asked.

She splayed them atop her skirts. Having eschewed bandages, the abrasions were visible, but they were not as livid as before she had applied the salve Griffin had sent.

"They are fine," she said and nearly thanked him.

He motioned to a servant, and as the man poured wine into her goblet, asked, "Your accommodations?"

She looked around the hall to gauge the scrutiny to which she was subjected. It was much, as if the multitude awaited the moment the Boursier woman again sought to better their lord. But no further entertainment would she provide.

Angling her body toward Griffin, summoning a smile for the onlookers, she said, "Accommodations? A civil word for a less than civil place, my lord."

"Compared to the alternative—recall Castle Mathe's underground cells—'tis beyond civil, especially considering your trespass." He lifted his chin slightly, and she flicked her gaze over the healing cut on his neck. "And lest you forget, my lady, you were first given a comfortable chamber as befitting an honored guest."

"Which I am not."

"As you chose not to be."

Unable to argue that, she was grateful for the distraction offered by the squire who set before his lord a platter of sliced venison poured over with a dark red sauce. Then a separate platter with a smaller portion was placed in front of her.

The appetite she had thought long gone straining toward the scents of thyme, pepper, and wine, Quintin reached to her girdle. But just as there was no meat knife upon it, there was no girdle. Both were in the lord's solar, along with the Wulfrith dagger she must retrieve before departing Castle Mathe.

Griffin's hand appeared before her, his fingers around the hilt of a meat knife she recognized as her own. "Allow me to cut for you."

She turned her face to his. Only the ill, the aged, and young children suffered the indignity of having another cut their meat. Of course there were exceptions, as of lovers, wherein the man cut the most succulent piece of meat for his woman and offered it on the point of his blade.

As she and Griffin would never be lovers, she said, "I am capable of cutting my own meat, Baron."

He raised his eyebrows.

"My word I give that do you entrust my *meat* knife to me, I shall behave." She reached for it, but he did not relinquish it.

"The question is, my lady, can I trust your word more than you trust mine?"

She fastened a look of great thought on her face, held up a hand. "A moment. I am thinking how to answer truthfully, yet in such a way I gain what I seek."

He laughed, but before she could take offense as she had done the last time they had been here, he said, "Certes, you and my daughter would make good company between you."

Curious, having minutes earlier acknowledged an unfounded liking for the young lady, she said, "How come you by that?"

"Though a handful you will surely prove to your husbands, neither of you is dull. Thus, possibly worth the effort to keep you in hand."

"You assume we can be kept in hand."

He smiled, and this time it was no lopsided thing. Indeed, it was amiable.

How had a man publicly shamed so soon recovered that he was now more civil than before she had done him ill? Might he play his own game, hoping to catch her unawares to visit on her what she had visited on him?

"An assumption a wise man ought not make," he said and, increasing his smile, appeared years younger and much too charming. And dangerous—for she did not like him and did not wish to, and though two nights past she had done the inexplicable when he had touched her face, she was not attracted to him. Or was she?

Quintin did not realize the confused state of her face until his turned serious and he said low, "I am not wicked. I am not my father. I am not my brother. I am Griffin. And that man, Quintin, is who I would have you judge, if you must."

She tensed to hold in the shiver roused by him so intimately speaking her name. "Do you wish to be judged different, you will release my brother if you hold him."

"If," he murmured. "I am pleased we continue to make progress."

Suppressing the impulse to scoff, she continued, "And if 'tis true you do not hold him, release me so I may continue my search."

"Nay."

"Why?"

Lightly, he ran a thumb over the knife's edge. "Though there remains the matter of your trespass against me that could set a poor precedent were I perceived as too lenient, of equal import is that you are safer inside Castle Mathe than outside it."

"Safer? I am a prisoner, the men tasked with my protection set outside your walls."

"That is your doing, though I do concede it was ill mannered of me to provoke you. More, it was wrong to laugh at you before all. For that, I apologize."

He did? She blinked, pressed onward. "Tell me, how am I safer with you?"

"Better you suffer my company than resume a search that could see you set upon by men who would do far worse than lock you in a room."

"You speak as if I came alone and would go alone. Lest you forget, I departed Castle Adderstone with fifty knights and men-at-arms."

"The same who allowed *The Boursier's* beloved sister to lead them in a search for their lord, then permitted her to enter the lair of her family's enemy in the company of six." He widened his eyes. "Six."

Of which Bayard would be greatly displeased. But though she dreaded his wrath, especially that which would befall his men, she would welcome it before embracing its absence.

Be alive, Brother, she silently beseeched. *Come as angry as you will, but be alive.*

"Too, an early winter is upon us," Griffin continued, "one that promises to worsen long ere the sun once more warms the land."

"Our entourage is provisioned."

"Yet, I wager, they are miserable."

And he would not let them in, as neither would Bayard have allowed De Arell's men to enter Castle Adderstone.

"Nay, my lady, you are safer here. With me."

"When my brother—"

"Should he appear to fulfill the king's decree, relations shall be strained enough with my new son-in-law without adding to the strain by having been remiss in assuring your safety."

Quintin's imagination momentarily placed Bayard here alongside this man, and she would have laughed had she any light inside her. How strange that Griffin, but three years older than her brother, would become Bayard's father through marriage. *If* Bayard appeared.

"Now, my lady, let us to meal ere it grows colder."

She glanced at her venison, then his. No more heat wafted from the meat, much of the taste enjoyed by others in the hall lost to them. Though her appetite dipped, the hunger of her belly was painful, and so she reached for the knife.

Griffin sighed. "I am tempted to believe I can keep you in hand, but Arturo's instincts say otherwise." He nodded at the wolfhound who sat on the other side of the table, eyes fixed on the woman who had attacked its master. "Should a blade appear in your hand..." He shrugged.

"It is not within your power to send him from the hall?" she said tartly.

"Since he but does his duty to me, 'twould be a poor reward for his loyalty, do you not think?"

She smiled tightly. "Then it falls to you to cut my meat."

"My pleasure." He sliced off a piece, speared it on the knife's point, and carried it toward her mouth.

It would be more expedient to pick it off with her teeth, but she plucked it with her fingers and popped it in her mouth.

He smiled, cut another piece, and himself ate from the knife's point.

Quintin managed a half dozen bites swallowed down with wine, but once her hunger eased, she shook her head.

"That is all?" Griffin said.

"'Twill suffice." She looked sidelong at him. "I trust that if my brother does not arrive at Mathe this eve, you will allow me to return to Godsmere on the morrow so I might prepare my mother for the loss of our home."

He ate the venison she had refused, chewed it well. "Methinks the weather will prevent your departure, that there will be snow by nightfall."

A convenient excuse to hold her here. Where her hand rested on the table's edge, she gathered a fistful of the tablecloth. "'Twas not mere speculation that you wed me to gain Godsmere. For that, you would keep me prisoner—out of reach of Magnus Verdun so he cannot gain the barony through me." She curled her upper lip. "You condemn my brother for making another man's betrothed his wife, and yet you would steal my betrothal to gain Godsmere for yourself."

He set the knife on his platter. "Though wedding you was a consideration, on nearer thought, I find it is not viable on my front or the king's."

"Your front?"

"Should Godsmere be forfeited, still an alliance must be made between the De Arells and Verduns. Were I to take you to wife, it would fall to my daughter to make that alliance, and though I prefer she be joined with the Baron of Emberly rather than your brother, it would be better she wed neither. Thus, I shall make the alliance with Lady Elianor that is already in place."

Might he so deeply care for his daughter he would give up the possibility of doubling his demesne? In the next instant, she rejected the thought. He might wish to be judged as Griffin, but he was sprung from Ulric De Arell.

"I do not believe a daughter, even one of legitimate birth, would stand between a De Arell and that which they have ever coveted."

His pupils expanded, nostrils flared, and he curved a hand over hers gripping the tablecloth. "Again, you judge me wrong."

Striving to ignore the warmth and weight of his hand that caused something to ripple up her arm, she choked, "You want Godsmere!"

"Who would not? But that does not mean one should pay an unconscionable price—were it even for sale. And that brings us to the king. Young though he is, Edward is shrewd, and more so his advisers. The award of a forfeited Godsmere to the De Arells or Verduns could so rouse resentment in the one denied that, regardless of marriage-made alliance, the feud would continue. Thus, methinks the barony would go to another of the king's loyal subjects."

It made painful sense. If her prayers for Bayard went unanswered, she and her mother would be without a home. In which case, would it be better if Quintin's absence caused her mother to yield to that edge she teetered upon—to be unaware of losing what was nearly as beloved as her departed husband?

"Of course, 'tis possible the king will see you wed to whomever he awards Godsmere," Griffin said.

She blinked him back to focus and was surprised she did not want to spit at him for sensing her twisting and turning. What she wanted was to be alone.

"I..." Movement on the other side of him drew her regard, and she met Lady Thomasin's blue gaze before the young woman dropped it to her father's hand on Quintin's. A smile bowed her mouth.

Suppressing the impulse to yank free, Quintin said, "I would like to return to the tower."

Griffin had followed her gaze to his daughter, but neither was he quick to break the contact between Quintin and him. Eyes returning to hers, he said, "As you wish," and slid his hand off in what felt almost a caress.

Quintin rose.

He also stood and motioned one of his men forward.

It was only as Quintin crossed the inner bailey that she realized her escort was Sir Otto, and only because her gaze grazed his face as she glanced at the heavy clouds Griffin believed would soon turn the land white.

If prayers were answered and Bayard was this moment making his way to Castle Mathe, would he arrive ahead of the snow? Or would it thwart him—and cost him Godsmere?

8

A SLIDE OF the bolt. A rap of knuckles. A creak of the door.

"My lady—"

"Supper," she said, keeping her back to Sir Otto where she stood at the window staring into the white-flecked night. "He insists I join him?"

"Nay, my lady. 'Tis but an invitation."

That she did not expect, and it took her a moment to respond. "Then I decline, but thank him for me."

"'Tis chill in here, my lady. You ought to close the shutters."

Ought to. But she was listening, easier done before the open window.

Lowering her chin into the mantle shrugged up to her ears, she said, "I appreciate your concern, but the brazier serves me well." Not true with so much frozen air entering, but there was something strangely comforting about the discomfort of chilled limbs.

Hearing advancing footsteps, she looked over her shoulder.

"Forgive me if I overstep, my lady." Sir Otto pulled the fur coverlet from the bed, strode to her, and raised his eyebrows.

At her nod, he draped it over her shoulders. Then he crossed to the chair and moved it between her and the brazier.

"I thank you," she whispered.

He inclined his head. "Good eve, my lady."

As the bolt scraped into place, she stepped nearer the window to resume her vigil of listening for the thunder of hooves that would announce her brother's arrival.

It was dark, but not so dark he could not see the figure huddled in the chair angled between the weakly glowing brazier and the open window.

Fear lanced his breast. "Quintin?"

"Has my brother come?"

Silently thanking the Lord his fear was unfounded, he moved past her to the window. As he reached to secure the shutters against snow that had coated the ground outside to mark his passage from the keep, he looked out across the walls to the night-shrouded wood whose pine, oak, hazel, and birch trees ever sought to encroach on the castle—the blessing being they supplied abundant firewood to cast out winter's chill, the curse they provided too much cover for any who wished to steal upon Mathe. Due to that vulnerability, no town had been allowed to grow up outside the castle walls.

Griffin closed the shutters and turned.

The lady's legs were drawn up, knees clasped to her chest, and she'd had enough sense to wrap herself in the fur. The bit of light revealing she stared at the floor, she said again, "Has my brother come?"

In spite of the ill between their families and his opposition to his daughter wedding Boursier, Griffin almost wished the man had appeared. "He has not."

She nodded amid the fur framing her face and in a fainter voice said, "Is it past the middling of night?"

"It is."

Slowly, she raised her gaze to his. "You are here to taunt me."

Lord, he silently entreated, *not only the sins of the father and the brother, but my own.*

"I am not." Though Sir Otto had revealed he had found her before the open window, Griffin had not expected she would be there still, but as he had worked through correspondence in his solar, it had worried at him. And more so as night deepened.

"Then for what have you come?" she asked.

"With the weather turning more foul, I wished to ensure your comfort."

"Comfort…" She shuddered.

He took the short stride to the brazier and over his shoulder said, "Get yourself abed." He stirred the coals, added kindling, and as the slumbering flames awakened, placed more coal atop them.

When he turned back, she had not moved, and the brazier now lit the room well enough to reveal her starkly pale face. "You must rest, Lady Quintin."

Once again, her gaze climbed the length of him, and when her eyes met his, he saw the strain there. Had she not been crying, it was because she refused to allow the tears inside to squeeze out.

"Aye," she said and dropped her feet to the floor, leaned forward, and shuddered violently. "I cannot."

Griffin scooped her into his arms. Though he expected her to protest, she sank against his chest and slid a hand from beneath the fur and up around his neck.

It should not feel right, he told himself. *I should not concern myself with her.* And yet he longed to lower to the chair and hold her—to give his warmth to her until she was once more the fiery Quintin Boursier who would not allow him so near.

He carried her to the bed, but when he laid her on the mattress, she tightened her hold on him.

"You can loose me, my lady."

"Stay."

Was she delirious? "You would have me lie with you?" he said, certain that if he gave words to what she asked of him, she would come to her senses—and quite possibly strike him.

"I am so cold, Griffin."

Certes, she knew to whom she made the request. "'Twould be unseemly, my lady."

"Unseemly." She gave a bitter laugh. "What does it matter now?"

Now that only something approaching a miracle would prevent Godsmere from being lost to her family. "'Twill matter come the dawn."

Shuddering again, she said between her teeth, "Then I shall hate you come the dawn. Not now."

Leave, the rational Griffin warned.

Stay, urged the other who longed to hold her.

Silently vowing he would remain only until she was sufficiently recovered, he lowered onto his side facing her and drew the fur over himself as well to more easily pass his body heat to her.

"Nay, I will not hate you now," she murmured and scooted closer. "Mayhap not even come the morrow." She pressed her face to his chest and her lower legs to the tops of his thighs.

Unseemly, his rational side protested. *Improper. Foolish. Tempting.*

Still, he held her and focused on his breath to control the beat of his heart. Blessedly, it was not long before her own breathing told she slept. But her body was slow to warm—shivering one moment, easing the next—and so he curved an arm around her back and slid a hand beneath her waist.

As her quaking waned, he tried to turn aside thoughts that he would never again hold her thus, that it would be another who wrapped his body around hers and knew her more intimately.

Tried, but over the hours before the combined efforts of his body and the brazier warmed her, he thought them often enough that there was no danger of her awakening to find him asleep beside her.

Before dawn, he lifted his arm from around her and considered her shadowed face, from the fall of her lashes atop her cheeks to softly parted lips. Then he touched his mouth to her brow.

"Do not hate me, Quintin," he said low. And left her.

9

———◊◊◊———

"You are a Boursier. Be worthy." Over and over she repeated it where she sat in the center of the bed, the fur down around her hips, her head in her hands as she tried to keep the night past from drawing near. But each time she began to relax into her victory over memories on the far side of a doorway she did not want to go through, they appeared on the threshold, threatening to come to her if she did not come to them.

And that was when she glimpsed Griffin lifting her from the chair, her hand sliding around his neck, his face above hers as she beseeched him to stay, him lowering to the bed beside her, her curling into him as if vows spoken amid a world turning white had made them one.

She shook her head so hard it ached, but the discomfort was worth the relief of scattered memories. However, as they distanced themselves, she heard herself whisper, *Nay, I will not hate you now. Mayhap not even come the morrow.*

With a muffled cry, she pushed away the fur, swung her legs over the side of the bed, and stumbled upright.

"You are a Boursier," she said as she crossed to the window. "A Boursier!" She threw back the shutters and gasped as the frigid air Griffin had banished flung itself in her face.

Hugging her arms about her, she peered through the swirling snow at the stretch of inner wall adorned by men trudging the walks and moved her gaze to the wood beyond.

As expected, it was as white as the rest of her world. And it would be whiter ere the snow ceased its attempt to cleanse this corner of England—a futile purification greatly suffered by the men outside the walls. Men who, along with the barony of Godsmere, might no longer belong to her brother, regardless of whether or not he lived.

"Live, Bayard," she whispered and wished she had heeded Sir Victor and her mother and not left Castle Adderstone. The Godsmere knights and men-at-arms would be safe and warm within its walls and she would be there to comfort her mother.

She bowed her head as she had done on the night past when she had pleaded with the Lord to deliver her brother to Castle Mathe. "Let Bayard be healthy and whole," she tried again. "Let there be the peace of your presence upon my mother. Let there be safety and warmth and game aplenty to sustain my escort. And let there be a way for me to make right all I have made wrong. Amen."

She closed the shutters, crossed to the brazier, and opened her hands above coals that should not be so bright and warm. At this hour of the morn, they should be nearly exhausted.

"Oh," she breathed and dropped her hands to her sides. Griffin was not long gone. She had spent nearly all night in his arms, and after he had risen, he had fed the brazier to ensure the warmth he had given her was not lost.

Tears stung her eyes, and she did not understand the cause, for the only sense of them did not make sense. This day was but her fourth at Castle Mathe, far too little time to engage one's heart, especially a heart that knew not how to be engaged. And certainly not to the Baron of Blackwood who was too...

"Hated," she said, but it was a lie. She had not hated him last eve. And now it was the morrow, still she did not hate him. Because of his unexpected kindness? It must be. Too, the increasing likelihood Bayard was dead made her vulnerable—a sorry state for a Boursier. And she surely looked a sorry state, her gown more heavily rumpled than on the day past. Though she tried to push back imaginings of her skirts bunched between Griffin and her, they drew near the threshold alongside the memories.

"Enough!" Determined to make a straight line between her thoughts and actions, she once more reminded herself of who she was.

Regardless of the failure of the Boursiers to fulfill the king's decree, she would honor her father and brother's name. Never again would any man see her weak and needy as she had allowed Griffin to see her—Griffin whom, it was increasingly likely, she had wronged.

"Pride be trampled!" she rasped. A Boursier would apologize. Even had she not good cause beyond her own—the well-being of her brother's men—forgiveness must be sought.

She crossed to the saddlebag, shook out its contents, and began making herself presentable while she awaited the arrival of the one who each morning delivered a basin of fresh water and hand towels with her morning pottage. A meal whose every spoonful she would choke down, since it would be hours before Griffin once more invited her to his table.

If he invited her again.

This he had not anticipated, not after how he had found her on the night past and how he had left her ere dawn. Out of courtesy, he had once more invited her to join him for the midday meal, but the aged knight he had sent had not returned alone with palms raised apologetically.

Lady Quintin paused inside the doors to remove her snow-flecked mantle. Then, laced into the gold-trimmed dark orange gown Sir Victor had sent the second day of her stay, shoulder-length hair full and gleaming from a recent washing, she walked forward with chin high.

Were he a stranger here, he would think her the Lady of Blackwood—a lady the barony had not had since his wife's passing. Of course, even before Johanna was lost to him a year following Rhys's birth, such a lady Blackwood had not had.

Johanna had been too uncertain of her role, too eager to please those who ought to have sought to please her, too gentle a soul to have been wed to Griffin de Arell. Though they had been fond of each other, neither had loved. They had done their duty.

Only the woman who had borne Thomasin had Griffin loved, and then he had been a squire of ten and six and she a chambermaid. Impossible—and foolish, he had silently concurred with his sire when he learned Alice had deserted their daughter. Just as anything beyond what had happened between Quintin and him on the night past was impossible and foolish.

He stood. "Once more you grace us with your presence, my lady."

"I am pleased to have been given a choice." It was the same she had said on the day past, but this time lacking derision.

She crossed the back of the dais, draped her mantle over the chair beside his, and settled herself.

As he returned to his chair, the servants who had paused upon her entrance began placing bowls of steaming stew before those gathered. And the wine poured into goblets wafted as much heat, perfuming the air with the scents of cinnamon and cloves.

The lady raised her goblet and sipped. "A good drink for so cruel a day."

Doubtless, she spoke not only of the snow, but what appeared to be the loss of her brother and home.

"It warms the blood." Though not, he thought, as she had warmed his last eve.

When the lady's gaze remained unwavering, he wondered if she did not remember what had passed between them. Certes, she had been distraught, so much she had not seemed the one who had put a dagger to him, the same who, it appeared, sat beside him now—the confident, resolute Quintin Boursier he had wished back.

He took a long draw from his goblet, then settled it between his hands. "How were your dreams, my lady?"

A slight flicker in her gold-ringed brown eyes and a faint blush across her cheeks told she remembered. And now she would feign ignorance.

But a soft laugh parted her lips, and she blinked as if as surprised by it as he, then she further surprised by leaning near. "Unseemly they were, especially for a lady. And your dreams, my lord?"

Another game, but one he liked—at least at this place on the board. Wondering if meat had been served this day, rather than stew, she would have eaten from his knife, he said, "I dared not sleep lest I mistook reality for a dream and sinned in the belief I would be absolved upon awakening."

Her lips tilted further, and glimpsing white teeth, he realized that any bowing of the mouth she had heretofore bestowed had been but a semblance of a smile. "Then one should only sin inside a dream, Baron?"

"Whenever possible, my lady."

She straightened in her chair and took up her spoon.

Griffin did the same, and as he watched her display an appetite he had not believed her capable of, he pondered what had returned the backbone that had gone out of her last eve. But then Sir Mathieu returned him to the conversation her arrival had interrupted, and over the next hour he rarely looked her way, especially with Thomasin and Rhys so interested in what went between their father and his unwilling guest.

Feeling the languor about the hall, his retainers having settled into the warmth denied them outside, Griffin was reluctant to send them back out. But with ever more snow to be cleared to keep the baileys and walls passable, it was time.

He stood. "Return to your duties," he called and did not begrudge the men their mutterings as they pushed up off tables and scraped back benches.

A hand touched his arm, and he stiffened in remembrance of it sliding around his neck. Looking to Quintin where she had risen alongside him, he said, "My lady?"

She peered at him from beneath lashes that were thicker than they were long, making her eyes seem lined in black. "I have a boon to ask of you."

"For that you accepted my invitation?"

She inclined her head, and he was both disappointed and pleased she did not deny it. "For that and…" She swallowed. "If I have wronged you as I fear I have, I apologize."

Sincere? Or a concession to gain a greater concession? "What would you ask of me, my lady?"

Her hand on him tensed as if steeling her for rejection. "'Tis wicked cold outside, and you must agree my brother's men should not be made to pay any portion of my debt to you."

"I agree, but for the safety of my people, I cannot let inside my walls so great a number who wish me and mine ill. However, they are free to leave any time they wish."

"Without me."

"Without you."

"You know they will not."

"Thus, I sent food, blankets, and firewood last eve."

Her eyes widened, and she gripped his arm more tightly.

Thinking it strange he was more aware of his tilted smile in her presence than with his father, who had so disapproved of it during his son's younger years that punishment had been doled out, Griffin gave her one. "Perhaps further proof you have put others' sins upon me?"

She looked down, but not before tear-bright eyes provided another glimpse of the soft, vulnerable side her misery had revealed last night. "I thank you."

"Is that all?"

"All?"

Though certain his daughter watched, he laid a hand atop Quintin's. "Though I cannot permit you the full height and breadth of Castle Mathe, I would grant you more comfortable accommodations in the keep."

She shook her head. "'Tis best I remain in the tower."

That surprised, but he said, "As you will."

She drew her hand from beneath his. "And now I ought to return."

"Stay." He nodded at Thomasin. "On so dreary a day, my daughter would enjoy company at the hearth where she is to complete a piece of embroidery promised to me for near on a fortnight. Perhaps you might even aid her in mastering the stitches."

At Quintin's hesitation, he added, "I would be grateful were *you* to grant me this boon." What he did not voice was the hope it would distract her from whatever losses she had sustained that, were she alone, might return her to the state in which he had found her last eve.

"I shall grant it, Baron."

As he stared at her, he acknowledged what he should not. Beyond a good path for his children and peace for his people, he did not want much. But this he wanted. A woman quick of wit and tongue to walk and sit and lie beside him...to hold close and give his warmth to on long winter nights...to bear sons and daughters to raise into worthy men and women.

Impossible. Unless he—and she—defied a king and he cared not that his children were well provided for and his people found peace. Aye, impossible.

"Then 'tis time you knew my Thomasin," he said.

"Whom I shall not know as a sister-in-law," she murmured, then averted her eyes.

Having glimpsed what she held behind her resolve, he took her arm and led her forward.

An unladylike sigh, then, "I am hopeless."

Bending near the framed linen, picking out wayward stitches with more thought than was necessary to distract her from the fates of Bayard and her mother, Quintin said, "Not hopeless, Lady Thomasin. Inexperienced. It took years ere my own needlework was fine enough to be worn on the outside of garments."

The young woman seated beside her on the padded bench leaned forward and caught up her companion's skirt, revealing Quintin's ankles and calves to any who gave eye to the ladies before the hearth. "As my poor maid can attest, I will be an old woman who no longer has a care for pretty things ere I am able to stitch anything half as beautiful as this."

"Lady Thomasin!" Quintin dropped the embroidery in her lap, snatched the skirt whose lower portion she had months past adorned with vining leaves, and yanked it down her legs. And groaned when she saw Sir Otto, set to watch over her in his lord's absence, had naught better to do than give his full attention to her. He was not grinning, though only because he tightly pressed his lips.

"Forgive me," Lady Thomasin said. "I did not mean to embarrass you." Then she made a sound of disgust. "I do hope Sir Otto does not tell my father I forgot myself again."

Quintin once more took up the embroidery frame. "Would he be angry?" she asked, curious if the affectionate sire he seemed was only appearance.

"Not angry, but disappointed. Rightfully so, I suppose."

"He is a good father?"

"Indeed!" No hesitation. But then Lady Thomasin suppressed a grin as Sir Otto had done. "The woman he weds—and of late I wonder if 'twill be Elianor of Emberly after all—will have naught to fear when she places their babe in his arms."

Quintin knew what she implied, and to keep her fist from her belly and the ache in her breast, she resumed picking at the threads.

"I apologize," the lady said. "'Tis just that I have watched my father and you, and though I myself know nothing of great affection, I am encouraged by the way you look upon and touch each other."

Again, the embroidery landed in Quintin's lap. "I know not of what you speak, Lady Thomasin, only that 'tis improper."

The prettily plain wisp of a lady sighed. "So my father would say, but I like you, and if it passes you should become—"

"Why?"

Lady Thomasin blinked.

"Why do you like me? And how can you? Though you were not present when I put a dagger to your father, you must know of it."

"As do all. 'Tis true I was prepared to dislike you, but my father explained the circumstances to my brother and me, and once I had the opportunity to observe you, I did not see that you were of a bent to have followed through with your threat even had he not bested you." She leaned near and, lowering her voice further, said, "I do not think I could have followed through either, though a fist and well-placed knee have served in my defense against unwanted attentions."

Surely Griffin did not allow his daughter to be bothered by his men?

The lady gasped. "Not here. I speak of ere I came to live upon Blackwood—whilst I served as a maid at Waring Castle."

"Oh, I am sorry. For that your mother sent you to your father?"

Disbelief leapt off her face. "My mother?"

"Forgive me," Quintin said. "'Tis what I heard."

The young woman gave a bitter laugh. "My mother abandoned me. 'Twas I who alerted my father to my existence and appealed to him for aid."

And Griffin, who time and again proved he was not a villain, had done more than give aid. He had claimed his illegitimate daughter and made her a lady. "I am glad you are treated well here, Lady Thomasin."

She smiled. "Though I am misbegotten, none would risk my father's wrath. Or should I say blade? Too, I do not present as much temptation as I might were I the great beauty 'tis said Lady Elianor is—and you as well, my lady."

"I am no great beauty."

"Perhaps not great, but a beauty. Though you wear your hair short as if to deny a man's hands the glory of it, still men look upon you and long." She nodded at Sir Otto. "He and my father are not the only ones."

Quintin knew she drew the attention of men who looked first with the eye and, had they any substance about them, later the heart. As Lady Maeve was fond of reminding her daughter, Quintin was blessed with a pleasing face and figure. Were she still of a mind to wed as she had been before her brother's ill-fated marriage, she would set herself to maintaining long tresses, but since there was no longer any gain for her to willingly join with a man, she had better uses for her time.

Lady Thomasin lifted the embroidery from Quintin's lap and wrinkled her nose. "At least when your brother appears, he will not have to add to his loss of Godsmere a wife whose beautiful stitches he could proudly wear outside his garments."

When your brother appears...

It was said with certainty he would. Despite the fire at Quintin's back, a chill ran through her. Was it possible her apology to Griffin was unwarranted? That now the day required to wed was past, he would release her brother to suffer his losses? But then, what fool would he be to do that? He would have to know that an enemy all the greater for such treachery would exact terrible revenge. Even were Bayard imprisoned in such a way there was no evidence of who held him, he would look first to the De Arells as had Quintin.

Hating that the man who had held her last eve might be all she had first believed, hoping Lady Thomasin could believably explain herself, Quintin said, "What makes you think my brother will appear?"

"My grandfather—"The lady gaped. "Oh, have mercy!"

"What of him?" Receiving no response, Quintin laid a hand on the young woman's that gripped the bench's seat. "I fear for my brother. If you know anything of his disappearance, do what is good and right and speak."

Lady Thomasin glanced at Sir Otto who now conversed with another knight. "'Tis only speculation, of which I should have said naught."

"Why?"

"Though my father forbids me to visit my grandfather, I defy him. Pray, promise you will not speak of it."

"You have my word."

Thomasin studied Quintin's face. "My grandfather believes that if 'tis true The Boursier was stolen from his bed—"

"It is true."

"Then it is not intended he should die."

As was Quintin's belief. And hope. If Bayard's death was sought, why convey him elsewhere when it was easier and less dangerous to turn his bed red? Unless there was a purpose beyond the loss of Godsmere... unless a greater evil than supposed wished him to suffer long.

"He says that if your brother is as extraordinary a warrior as your father—well, he is not so civil as to use the word *extraordinary,* but 'tis what he meant—then The Boursier will free himself."

"Is it true your grandfather is unable to leave his apartment?"

The lady raised an eyebrow. "You think he may be responsible for your brother's disappearance."

Quintin shrugged. "As he has ever been our greatest enemy, he cannot wish to see a De Arell joined to a Boursier."

"He does hate your family, but I do not think he had a hand in this. Certes, not his own."

Though surprised the lady allowed he could be involved, and if so it would be necessary to enlist another's aid—surely his son's—Quintin forced her face to remain impassive. "Your grandfather is quite ill, then?"

Sorrow crimped her mouth. "Quite."

Quintin glanced at Sir Otto and his companion who stood between her and the stairs. Though tempted to try again to reach the apartment, were she able to, there would not be time enough to convince the old man to open the door. And if he did let her in, the wily Ulric de Arell would not reveal anything of consequence. As for Bayard being there, it would be too bold not to have moved him following Quintin's arrival at Castle Mathe.

The door to the great hall opened only enough to allow Rhys de Arell to enter on a gust of chill air. Mantle and chausses crusted with snow as if he had rolled around in the white mess, he narrowed his eyes at Quintin before giving his regard to his sister.

Recalling he had stomped off when his father had introduced the two ladies, and hoping to temper any concern over her interest in Ulric de Arell, Quintin said, "Your brother is not as willing to offer forgiveness."

The lady grinned. "Ah, but when he does, you will find him forever underfoot. Which is not all bad providing you watch where you step."

Quintin doubted she would be at Castle Mathe long enough to test that.

"I am to study my sums," the boy called as he strode toward the stairs. "Will you help me, Thomasin?"

Hoping she would defer, Quintin held her breath.

"Embroidery or numbers," the lady mused. "Numbers or embroidery." She smiled apologetically and stood. "It seems we shall have good cause to speak later, my lady."

Quintin also gained her feet. "I would like that."

Lady Thomasin hastened after her brother, and when she went from the hall, Quintin retrieved her mantle and crossed to Sir Otto. "I am ready to return to the tower."

Outside, the falling snow swirled in the biting breeze. If not for the efforts of the many who moved shovels and carts, she would have been up to her ankles in it.

As she and the knight neared the inner wall, he said, "It appeared Lady Thomasin and you had much to speak on."

Wondering if he might know something useful, Quintin said, "Methinks I would have liked her for a sister-in-law." What she did not say was that if the De Arells *were* responsible for Bayard's abduction, that would be impossible. Not only because they would never be forgiven, but the king had said—

Quintin halted. Regardless of who had taken Bayard from his bed, if he lived and escaped as Ulric de Arell believed him capable of, all might yet be restored. True, the king had said he would accept no excuse if the marriage did not take place by the appointed day, but surely an exception would be made for abduction. It would have to be proved, but if anyone could make good on that, it was Bayard.

"My lady?"

She smiled. "'Tis a better day than expected, Sir Knight."

His answering smile was uncertain, but it reached his eyes.

She blinked. "Why, Sir Otto, you have Foucault eyes!"

His smile jerked. "What say you?"

"A gold ring around the brown." She gestured at her own. "Of course, it sounds vain to claim an eye color for one's own. I am sure there are many who see out of such eyes."

"Indeed." He strode ahead and opened the door for her.

Quintin had not meant to offend, but it seemed she had. Might he be the son of a knight who had served her grandfather, Denis Foucault? One as disaffected as Boursier, De Arell, and Verdun had been?

She nearly asked but decided it was best to leave the matter be so they might sooner return to the easy company enjoyed before she had pointed out that Foucault blood ran as thick through her as Boursier blood. Too, more than any other at Castle Mathe, Sir Otto could prove an ally.

10

Two MORE DAYS, making this her sixth at Castle Mathe, and all that had changed was the snow had ceased to fall on the day past. Still no tolerable shelter for her escort. Still no relief for her mother who might have taken to bed. Still no further opportunities to speak privately with Lady Thomasin.

Hoping the dull ache in her head did not portend a miserable menses, Quintin looked across her shoulder at Griffin's daughter. The young woman sat on the stone hearth with her skirts tucked around her and leaned near her brother to explain a problem he worked.

Three days now, the boy had used the excuse of his studies to draw his sister away from Quintin, but this time Lady Thomasin had insisted they remain in the hall to provide a semblance of company to their father's *guest*.

Kind of her, but of no use. Only frustration—amid growing despair. As Bayard had yet to appear, there seemed little chance he would.

Breathing deep to hold in anguish lest it bounded out on a sob, Quintin considered the hall. The servants having finished setting it aright following the nooning meal, there were few about. But there were three wolfhounds. Two did not concern her, occupied as they were with snuffling among the rushes in search of morsels, but Arturo sat beneath the high table watching her.

As ever, Quintin looked away and stopped on the knight leaning in an alcove near the entrance to the hall. Not Sir Otto. Though the young knight was present for meals, he had not kept watch over her since the day she had offended him.

A groan. "Is this not what a steward is for? Why must I learn it?"

"As father told, Rhys, an ignorant lord is a bootless lord. If you would be baron and wish to remain baron, you must know what others do for you. Now try another."

Quintin did not wish to be alone, but fatigued from too little sleep and the struggle to keep a face on her inner writhing, she lifted her mantle from the bench and stood. Grateful brother and sister did not look around, she started across the hall.

The knight stepped from the alcove. "You are ready to return to the tower, my lady?"

"I am." She fastened her mantle about her shoulders, followed him outside, and wished she had departed sooner.

Griffin ascended the steps two at a time, his mantle flaring out behind him.

Though he halted a step down, still she had to look up to meet his gaze. "Mayhap I shall see you at supper, Baron."

"Mayhap?" There, that smile of his, and she could hardly bear it.

Affecting a lightness that had become increasingly necessary these past days, she said, "I am tired."

"And disheartened." He glanced at his knight, nodded the man away, and took her elbow.

She did not wish his accompaniment but was thankful his footing assured hers on steps that remained icy in places. She allowed him to retain his hold on her all the way to the tower room, but at the landing she pulled free and stepped past him.

"Why have we returned to where we were, Quintin?"

She slowly came around. "Returned?"

He closed the distance between them, and she had to put her head back to hold his gaze. "Two days past, you apologized lest you had wronged me. I thought trust might grow from there. But since, your accusations—albeit unspoken—are once more between us."

And she had thought she hid it well. "Trust, Baron? Pray, how is that to grow while still you keep me under guard and bolt my room?"

"'Tis not only a means of keeping you safe from yourself—"

"Myself!"

Annoyance flickered in his eyes. "Aye, Quintin Boursier, who left the safety of Adderstone's walls in foul weather and put a dagger to a warrior—in both instances risking her life alongside the lives of her brother's men."

She could not argue that.

"Too, methinks given the opportunity, you would again seek my father's apartment. That I will not risk."

"What have you to hide?"

"Not your brother."

She searched his face, wishing and not wishing to see a lie there. When only one wish was granted, she asked again, "What have you to hide?"

"My father loathes your family. Such a feeling I would not have loosed upon you. And his illness...especially not that."

"With what is he afflicted?"

"That which only allows him to watch from his windows as his grandson grows into a man. Leprosy."

She took a step back. "But your—" Nay, she had given his daughter her word she would not tell.

"Thomasin has told you then. So the question is why do I allow my daughter to visit him."

She caught her breath. "You know."

He inclined his head. "By the time I learned she defied me, she had been stealing abovestairs for a year. Since she had not been taken with the disease, and her grandfather's improved state of mind seemed a result of her visits, I agreed she could continue, providing my father kept a reasonable distance and allowed her to believe I remain unaware."

Quintin looked at the space between them. It was not much. "I see." But did she see right? And was it enough to absolve him of Bayard's abduction? Certes, it was not enough to absolve his father.

"I am sorry, Quintin."

She tilted her head back against the door. "For?"

"All your losses." He stepped nearer and laid a hand on her jaw. "Save one."

His touch felt so right she longed to lean into it. "One?"

"Verdun. I am fair certain you no longer belong to him."

Not if Godsmere was forfeited, rendering an alliance with her family unnecessary. Thus, if Griffin did to her what she believed he wished to do, no Serle would he be. If she allowed it. "That does not mean I belong to you, Baron."

"It means you belong to yourself and are free to do what you will. So what will you do, my lady?"

This, she longed to say. *What you wish to do.*

He lowered his mouth near hers. "What will you do?"

She was not breathing, though she did not miss that fullness in her breast whilst it held the fullness of him being so near and promising so much she had believed she would never want.

"As you told the night you asked me to stay," he said low, "what does it matter now?"

It did not. With a cry that could not be her own for how desperate it sounded, she pushed onto her toes and pressed her mouth to his.

This, she told herself as she wound her arms around his neck. *This,* as he drew her nearer. *This,* as she strained against his chest. *This* she wanted.

"Quintin."

And that. Her name breathed into her.

"Griffin."

He deepened the kiss, and his hand in the middle of her back moved to the small of it.

She shuddered. But a moment later, the door was holding her up more than Griffin. Wondering what had become of the press of his mouth and chest, she peered up into his face. Arm braced against the door above her head, his eyes were closed and nostrils flared.

"Griffin?"

His lids lifted. "Here we must stop, else we will not," he said raggedly. "And *this* does matter."

"This?"

He stepped back. "Lady Quintin," he titled her as if to remind her she was a lady, "I will not claim your virtue."

She drew a sharp breath. "What makes you think I offer it?"

"'Tis obvious you want this as much as I. Mayhap more."

It was not true. Was it? A kiss did not a harlot make. Did it? Regardless, he thought it—that had he not stopped, she would not have. But she would have, though when and where and how she did not know, having never before felt such turnings. She would *not* have lain with him!

Moved by anger she had last felt so strongly when she had stopped his laughter with the Wulfrith dagger, she pushed off the door. "I want it? Want you?" There again, the dull ache in her head. "What I want is my brother's release and to return home, and if I have to suffer your attentions to gain it, so be it."

He jerked, not as if slapped hard, but slapped nonetheless. "We are past this, Quintin."

"We are not!"

He expelled a half-growl, half-sigh. "Quintin—"

Footsteps sounded, and as he glanced over his shoulder, a voice called, "My lord?"

"What is it?"

"You are needed."

He opened his mouth, surely to inquire further. But as if realizing here was an opportunity to escape her, he gestured for her to enter the room.

She swung around, thrust the door open, and forcefully closed it behind her.

The slide of the bolt. Footsteps on the stairs and passageway. Silence.

Quintin crossed to the bed and dropped onto it. Staring at the ceiling, she touched fingers to her mouth. She was full-lipped, but never this full. Sensitive, but never this sensitive.

Though she told herself to think elsewhere, she closed her eyes and thought of where Griffin and she had been. So that was a kiss. That was what moved men and women to go beyond it. Would she have responded as ardently had it been one other than Griffin? The handsome Sir Otto?

She wanted to believe it but did not. She wanted to blame Griffin for all that had happened between them but could not. True, he had tempted her, but she had put her mouth to his and her arms around his neck. And not with the hope of gaining Bayard's release.

She snatched her fingers from her lips. Had it been a sacrifice she made for her brother, she could be forgiven. But Griffin was right. She had wanted to be that near him—and nearer yet. Thus, she had abandoned the possibility he was as much an enemy as ever.

Determinedly, she reminded herself of what had brought her to Castle Mathe. The De Arells had better reasons than any to abduct Bayard. Even more than keeping Thomasin from wedding their enemy, they would have the satisfaction of seeing Godsmere forfeited, and might even gain it for themselves. As for the old baron's leprosy…

It could be a lie, enabling Ulric de Arell to continue to work foul deeds that, for twenty-five years, had fed the feud between the three families.

Promising herself that what had happened between Griffin and her would not happen again, she muttered, "Cur. Knave. Miscreant." And found her fingers once more seeking her thoroughly kissed lips.

She groaned, flopped onto her stomach, and feeling the ache behind her eyes, dragged a pillow over her head. And prayed she would be spared the blessedly rare reminder of the day she had thought to keep Serle de Arell's blade from her brother.

The one known as The Boursier had come, as told more by his size and the red of his hair than the colors he flew—and the eyepatch that would ever bear witness to Serle's sin.

Sir Victor at his side, the knight having ridden across the melting meadow to receive his lord, the Baron of Godsmere guided his horse ahead of the men he had brought with him. Amid smoke from the encampment's fires, those who had accompanied his sister to Castle Mathe gathered to greet him. But his regard was mostly for his enemy's walls.

As well it should be, Griffin mused. He had ordered them more heavily manned than when Lady Quintin had come, the enemy having grown by dozens and now led not by an impetuous lady but a warrior worthy of respect—and all the greater for the anger he exuded. Unless by some miracle he still held Godsmere, he was no longer a baron, and now his sister was a prisoner.

"Archers, mount up!" Boursier shouted, and as a dozen retrieved bows and horses, he continued past the tents and across the land before the castle.

A hundred feet from the raised drawbridge, he halted his horse and called, "De Arell!"

Griffin pushed off the wall he had put a shoulder to and leaned into the embrasure atop the gatehouse. "Boursier!"

His enemy's singular gaze landed hard on him. "I have come for my sister!"

Griffin smiled, then a bit more knowing the turn of his lips would offend the brother as it had the sister. "For what do you think I would give over my prisoner—a woman who, in the presence of all, tried to murder me?"

Boursier reined his destrier around and walked it to a hooded figure mounted among knights. Setting a hand on the man's forearm, he leaned near. Words were exchanged that did not carry, then he reached up and swept back the hood.

Not a man. A woman.

"I have your daughter, De Arell," Boursier called. "Now deliver my sister to me!"

Ignoring the gasp of the one to his left, Griffin narrowed his gaze at the blond woman who was beautiful even at a distance and recalled the tidings received this morn. Could it be?

Wanting to laugh, he straightened and looked to Thomasin where she stood alongside the archer in the next embrasure. Wide-eyed, wearing a wondrous smile, she stared at her father.

He shook his head before she spilled words that were surely caught between tongue and palate. "Remain here and out of sight," he said low, then shouted, "Archers, make ready."

As they stepped deeper into the embrasures the better to be seen and mark their targets, Griffin descended to the outer bailey and called for his horse.

There he donned the chain mail hauberk he had sent his squire for after leaving Quintin in the tower and learning a scout had returned from patrol to report a great number of Godsmere men rode on Castle Mathe. Griffin had been fair certain one of those men would be Bayard Boursier.

Mounted, he ordered the lowering of the drawbridge and guided his destrier to the portcullis. Amid the clatter and grind of chains letting out, he stared through the iron bars as the descending drawbridge revealed first the sky, then the bordering wood, next the men outside his walls. Not surprisingly, Boursier's archers had also made ready—arrows nocked, bows raised, strings taut to loose missiles.

When the great wooden planks thumped hard to the ground, the portcullis began its ascent. While Griffin waited for it to complete its journey, he watched Sir Victor converse with his lord, who was clearly displeased with whatever was told him, and more so when the woman joined the conversation.

Once the portcullis cleared Griffin's head, he walked his horse onto the drawbridge.

In response, Boursier took control of the woman's reins, and the two left their escort to advance on the castle.

Halting his horse at the end of the drawbridge, Griffin settled his hands on the pommel of his saddle and his gaze on the imposter who might be near in height to Thomasin, but that was all. His daughter was lovely in her own way, but she was no beauty. How interesting—and amusing—that Boursier, who had surely been informed of what to expect of his betrothed, had been fooled. Twice in a sennight, Griffin was intrigued by a woman.

Baron Boursier—were he yet so titled—halted the two horses half a dozen paces from the drawbridge, and Griffin met the gaze of the man who had taken Serle's sword arm and seen him further punished with a pilgrimage from which he had not yet returned.

"Tell me, Boursier," Griffin said, "are your lands forfeit or nay?"

"Nay."

Griffin afforded the woman a glance. "Then you spoke vows with my daughter?"

A muscle convulsed in the other man's jaw. "As ordered by the king, the alliance was made."

"Bayard," the woman said, "he—"

"Now you will release my sister."

Continuing to deny the smile that sought to reveal all of itself, Griffin said, "I would, but should the king through some beneficence accept your marriage, it will fall to me to wed Lady Quintin."

Boursier leaned forward in the saddle. "It falls to you to wed Elianor of Emberly."

Griffin moved his gaze to the woman. "That is no longer possible, is it, my lady?" He lifted an eyebrow. "I am right about you, am I not?"

She inclined her head.

"I cannot say I am displeased." No *limp* smile, this. "Word came early this morn that you had gone missing from your guardian's demesne. Thus, he has ridden to Ellesmere Abbey to search you out." Griffin returned his regard to the man beside her. "Mistakenly, of course."

"What game do you play, De Arell?" Boursier demanded.

"Not I, though your *wife* makes my family part of hers by taking the name of one dear to me." Griffin looked over his shoulder. "Show yourself, Thomasin!"

11

———⤫⤫⤫———

THE ARCHER BETWEEN the battlements moved aside and Thomasin stepped forward.

"There is my daughter, Boursier. Younger than your *wife* by several years."

The formidable warrior stared, and Griffin almost pitied him for the dark emotions moving the muscles of his face, throat, and hands. Dangerous emotions that made Griffin calculate the time and space required to set his sword before him.

Boursier looked to the woman. Desperation also shone from her, though of a different sort from the man who, it seemed, had yet to name her.

The bitter, bloody rivalry passed to Griffin by his father and fed by Serle's losses surfacing, he said, "At last, the mighty Boursiers, ever taking what is not rightfully theirs, brought to heel. And by a woman, no less."

Boursier closed his hand around his hilt.

"Bayard!" The woman looked to the archers whose arrows were trained on him.

Not until Boursier loosed his hilt did Griffin address her again. "You took my daughter's name."

Her throat convulsed. "As 'twas assumed I was she, I did not dissuade Baron Boursier. I had to protect my family."

Griffin returned his gaze to the one she feared. "I knew something was afoul when you did not come for Thomasin—that never would you forfeit. Thus, it came as no surprise when your sister told that you had been taken. The only surprise is the one who took you." He offered the woman a smile of regret. "For all you tried to do, Lady—and I thank you—I doubt your uncle will be pleased."

Boursier's disbelief yielded to understanding that swept his heated anger across the chill air, and he narrowed his gaze on the lady Griffin was to have wed—Elianor of Emberly.

"I tried to tell you," she whispered.

"When you were without choice!"

Griffin shifted in the saddle. "What do you think the king will do with this?" Vows had been spoken between the two, but as Boursier's bride had done so in Thomasin's name—a story Griffin looked forward to hearing—the marriage was invalid. How would King Edward react when he learned of it? Would he grant Boursier grace for the deception worked upon him? Would that family once more enjoy greater favor than ever the De Arells and Verduns had received?

Feeling the resentment Ulric had sought to make run as thick through his son's veins as his own, Griffin said, "You know not how I yearned to shout from the battlements 'twas not my daughter you held. Though it would hardly please my brother that I did not, still I am satisfied."

Boursier drew his sword.

"Bayard!" Elianor of Emberly gripped his arm. Surprisingly, he stilled.

Eyes fast upon his enemy, Griffin left his own sword sheathed and gestured for his archers to hold. "Enough, then," he said. "I have my bit of flesh, and 'tis sufficient."

As told by Boursier's fiery gaze that burned through the chill air billowing white to reveal his breaths, he stood on an edge between reason and bloodlust.

Griffin believed he and his enemy were well matched, but he thought it possible that were they to come to blows, the other man would prevail.

Boursier looked to the hand on his arm. "Pray hard, Elianor of Emberly. For yourself and your accursed uncle."

Her beautiful green eyes widened. "Magnus had naught—"

"Another lie? Regardless, your family *will* suffer."

She pulled her hand from him, and he slowly lowered his blade. "I will take my sister now, De Arell."

"She is not yours to take." Griffin settled his restless destrier with a pat to the neck. "Your sister attempted to slay me, and for that none will deny my right to hold her. Thus, until such time as I determine what to do with Lady Quintin, she remains." He frowned. "Of course, she is not much of a lady, is she?"

Boursier's hand flexed on his hilt, but then he returned his sword to its scabbard. "A pity my sister did not kill you."

"I would not be surprised if that was her intent," Griffin once more goaded the man. "But worry not. As long as daggers are kept from her, she need not fear me."

"I would see her."

"I will allow it. Indeed, with day soon to fade, 'twould be ill-mannered of me not to offer you a night's lodging. Of course, the invitation is extended to your wife as well." Griffin once more gave teeth to his smile.

Boursier glanced at the lady who stared at the gatehouse roof and turned the lie she wore on her finger. The ring that proclaimed her Boursier's bride was too large for her fine-boned hand, but it would not long remain there.

"As it would be ill-mannered not to accept," Griffin's enemy said, "we shall avail ourselves of your hospitality."

"Then come." Griffin started to rein his horse around.

"Surely you do not think I would enter your lair without a watch upon my back?"

Griffin considered him, conceded, "I know I would not," and gestured at Godsmere's men. "Choose a half dozen if it pleases you."

"Three shall suffice," he said, then to Elianor of Emberly, "Remain here."

When it was only Griffin and the woman to whom he may or may not yet be betrothed, depending on what the king made of falsely spoken vows, she turned her face to him. In the absence of Boursier, she boldly studied the one who should have been her husband.

"So, you aspired to rid our families of the vile Boursier," Griffin said.

Anger flashed in her eyes. "Be assured, Baron de Arell, had it been possible to rid my family of yours as well, I would have."

He smiled, wondered if the bend of his lips offended her as much as it did Quintin. "Mayhap marriage to you would *not* be preferable to marriage to the Boursier woman."

"Assuredly not, for I would have cut your throat."

He snorted. "Your threat falls short of its mark, my lady. Were you capable of such, Boursier would not have gone missing from his bed. He would have been found dead in it."

Her lids narrowed.

"As already told, I thank you for sparing my daughter marriage to Boursier, for even your uncle is a better choice than what might have been."

"Better for your daughter, not Baron Verdun."

Griffin tensed. "If you believe Quintin Boursier a better match for your uncle, you cannot have met the termagant."

"'Tis not necessary to meet her to know—"

"You believe my daughter is unworthy of your uncle?"

As if realizing what she roused in him, her belligerent posture eased. "I did not say that, nor would I."

And no more would they speak on it, for Boursier neared, accompanied by three men—Sir Victor, a squire, and a priest.

A priest of note, Griffin mused, certain here was Father Crispin who had been a stable boy whilst he served Baron Denis Foucault. When something had roused Foucault's suspicions, he had set Crispin to follow De Arell, Boursier, and Verdun. But the vassals had rooted him out, and the boy had chosen to join them, reporting instead on Foucault's movements and betrayal of the baronage. Upon Archard Boursier's award of

Castle Adderstone, Crispin had received his priest's training. Since, he had served as God's legate upon Godsmere.

And now he served under Archard's son, Bayard, who captured Griffin's gaze and said, "Take me to my sister, De Arell."

As Griffin guided his destrier back across the drawbridge, he heard Lady Elianor say, "You wish to know why I did it?"

If Boursier answered, it was not with words.

When they entered the outer bailey, Griffin was pleased by his garrison's formidable presence on the wall walks above and the ground below. They were good men, as fiercely protective of their home as they were distrustful of the Boursiers.

Once more, he caught Lady Elianor's words. "I am sorry, Bayard."

"Not yet you are."

Boursier's anger was understandable. If he and his family lost all, it would be at her hands. Had she done the same to Griffin, in the dark of the moment he would make similar threats. Indeed, he had threatened Quintin with all manner of punishment her imagination could conjure, and he had lost but a few drops of blood—albeit amidst a spate of pride. But the only hand he had raised to her beyond retrieving the dagger was to comfort and caress.

As for Boursier, word was he had abused his first wife, but Griffin had not been as willing to believe it as Serle, who saw it as justification for making a cuckold of the man.

"You forget that I am acquainted with your revenge," Lady Elianor finally spoke. "You will not harm me."

She sounded confident, not challenging, but Boursier gainsaid her with, "All has changed."

When next she spoke, it was in a voice sorrowfully soft. "All has changed."

A flash of movement drew Griffin's gaze to the gatehouse steps. "Thomasin!" he called.

Mantle absent—surely left atop the roof—she lifted her heavy woolen skirts high, revealing hose-clad ankles and lower calves as she hastened forward.

Her lack of propriety making him grind his teeth, Griffin turned his mount sideways and, as she neared, extended a hand to bring her astride.

She ignored it and continued past him.

"Thomasin!"

"I would see who is me!"

"She is Lady Elianor of Emberly."

She halted alongside the lady. "Oh, Lady, that ye dared," she slipped into her commoner's speech as she sometimes did when excited or angry. "And against The Boursier! You must tell all!"

Griffin glanced at his enemy and once more felt the ire of the man who stared at Thomasin. Like many, she was in awe of The Boursier, but as a De Arell—more, the granddaughter of the man in whose company she spent too much time—she took exception to the wrongs inflicted on her family. Thus, he did not doubt she knew the effect of her words.

"Thomasin!" Griffin commanded.

Her shoulders slumped. "We shall speak later," she told Lady Elianor and turned.

Griffin lifted his daughter into the saddle. They continued across the second drawbridge into the inner bailey, and he did not need to look to the highest windows in the keep to know the curtains shifted as his father disapprovingly stared out at the world denied him.

Griffin halted his mount, lowered Thomasin to the ground beside him, and caught her back when she started toward Lady Elianor. "Make quick to the kitchen and tell Cook there shall be five more for supper."

She groaned but moved to do as bid. As she ascended the keep's steps, she passed Sir Otto whom Griffin had earlier posted before the doors to the great hall.

Griffin looked around and called to his squire, "Aid Lady Elianor in her dismount."

"Squire Lucas will tend her and keep watch over her in my absence," Boursier countered and swung out of the saddle.

"As you wish." While the man spoke low to his own squire, Griffin motioned Sir Otto forward and instructed him to escort Lady Elianor to Sir Mathieu's chamber.

"Where is she?" Boursier demanded.

Griffin glanced at the man advancing on him but did not answer until Sir Otto was fully versed in what was required of him. When his knight turned away, Griffin said, "Your sister is in yon tower," and moved past Lady Elianor as she was assisted out of the saddle by the Godsmere squire.

With long-reaching strides, senses trained on the man who followed, mind turning over King Edward's options, Griffin led the way to Quintin—she who, it was no longer impossible, might now belong to a De Arell.

12

⸻∞∞⸻

Not the Baron of Blackwood. But a man who rivaled him in size and presence.

"Bayard!" Quintin darted across the floor she had been pacing before boots on the stairs had caused her to don defiance to demand of Griffin what went within his walls, a view of which her flank-facing window denied her.

Her brother stepped past the door his thrust had caused to rebound off the wall. And when she landed against him, he wrapped his arms around her.

Feeling like a frightened little girl, she held tight and heaped silent thanks on God that Bayard lived. No matter what ill came of vows not spoken, he was not lost to her mother and her. No matter how much of the anger he exuded was her due, she would gladly do penance. All that mattered was that he lived.

She dropped her head back and looked into his face crossed by the eyepatch covering the ruin Griffin's brother had made of his left eye. "He has freed you?" she asked, and seeing the concern in the singular blue-green gaze searching her face, smiled reassuringly.

Some of his tension eased. "Never did De Arell hold me, Quintin."

She knew if she had to tell herself she was surprised, she was not. No matter how ill it made her look for all she had done and accused Griffin of, she was glad to be proved wrong.

And there he was past Bayard's shoulder. When he halted outside the room where he had not so long ago made something more of her graceless kiss, she searched for words to ask for forgiveness. But then he smiled so crookedly, arrogantly, and—to her shame—heart-stoppingly, it was far easier to be offended than allow him to further trample her pride as he had done in implying she wanted him enough to yield her virtue.

She swung her gaze back to Bayard. "I do not understand. If 'twas not that vile mis—"

"'Twas not this vile miscreant," Griffin drawled.

She leaned to the side the better to show her disdain and saw Sir Victor stood in back of him. "Aye, miscreant."

Bayard released her and turned. "I would speak with my sister alone."

Griffin settled a shoulder against the doorframe. "I await your apology, Lady Quintin."

"How gratifying to know you shall wait forever."

His smile tilted further. "That is not so long—at least, not for one who has the freedom to spend his days and nights as he pleases. You, however…" He considered her top to bottom, making no attempt to disguise his appreciation, while beside her, anger flew off her brother.

Griffin sighed, reached to the door handle. "A half hour, Boursier. That is all." He pulled the door closed.

Quintin turned so quickly the ache in her head that had eased enough to allow her to come out from beneath the pillow bloomed again. Wincing, she asked, "If not De Arell, who?"

"Elianor of Emberly."

She gasped. "Magnus Verdun's niece? She who makes of herself his leman?"

"The same you wished me to wed."

"But—"

"What harm has De Arell done you, Quintin?"

She harrumphed. "He is arrogant, ill-tempered—"

"He struck you?"

"He would not dare!"

Her brother breathed deep. "I would know all that befell you."

"The knave took my dagger!" Rather, the Wulfrith dagger. He would have to be told, but not now.

"After you cut him, I presume."

"Would that I had cut him deeper." She nearly groaned at her attempt to appear undaunted by what Sir Victor had surely told Bayard of that day. But better that than reveal how frightened she had been.

"What else did he do?"

She swept a hand around. "Know you how many days I have suffered this place?"

"Quintin!"

"What?"

"Has De Arell abused you in any way?"

Did the comfort of a night in his arms, reverent caresses, and a fervent kiss she had invited qualify? Feeling color run up her face, she snorted. "Did the baron beat me? Toss up my skirts and do unto me deeds most foul?"

"Quintin!"

She dropped to the bed's edge. "Griffin de Arell is a churl, a knave, a miscreant. But nay, those things he did not do."

She feigned interest in the lay of her skirts across her knees to keep her eyes from revealing what he *had* done—and with her consent.

"You should have sent for Rollo that he might accompany you."

She shrugged. "As I am sure you were told, his mother was ill. And 'tis not as if I did not have an impressive escort. Now tell, Brother, how did Lady Elianor do what she did? More, why?"

"The answer to the first is Agatha of Mawbry."

Quintin snapped up her chin. "Agatha." The devious, conniving servant whom Constance Verdun had brought with her to Castle Adderstone upon the lady's fateful marriage to Bayard. She who had done her utmost to divide husband and wife by drugging Bayard to keep him from Constance's bed. She who had been tossed out of Adderstone when her duplicity was discovered. And, it seemed, she who had made herself as useful to Elianor of Emberly as she had been to the wife whose marriage to Bayard had been annulled.

"As to why the lady did it," he continued, "'tis the same as our families have always done—to sabotage one another. In this instance, the hope that what appeared to be defiance of the king's decree would result in forfeiture of our lands."

Not the Boursiers' doing but the Verduns'. Quintin patted the mattress. "I wish to hear all of it."

Over the half hour Griffin granted, she learned that whilst she had grown increasingly frantic over Bayard's disappearance, he had been directly beneath her feet as she paced the hall above the castle's abandoned underground passages where he had been conveyed after his wine was drugged.

Finding himself chained to the wall of a pitch black cell and provided with enough provisions to last through the king's deadline, he had known forfeiture of Godsmere was the reason for his imprisonment and been certain Griffin was behind it. Thus, he had used his anger to free the old, rusted chains from the wall so that when his jailers returned, revenge would be his.

Bayard had only been mildly surprised upon discovering that the one he had overwhelmed upon her entrance into the cell was Agatha of Mawbry. But he had been well surprised by the woman who came after the witch—the one he had believed was Thomasin de Arell and who had not dissuaded him, the one Agatha had chastised for not allowing her to kill The Boursier.

In that dread place where Bayard had been held all those days, he had chained Agatha, then dragged the lady he believed to be Griffin's daughter into the hall. When he learned hours remained before the king's deadline was past, he had *persuaded* his captive to wed him. But as he had discovered in his attempt to use her to bargain for Quintin's release after days of snowfall delayed him from coming to Mathe, it was

Elianor of Emberly he had wed. A marriage made void by vows spoken in the name of Lady Thomasin.

When Bayard finished with yet more assurance her mother fared well despite worry over her daughter, Quintin asked the question whose answer could lay ruin to all. "Is Godsmere lost to you, Bayard?"

His dark silence was answer enough—a mix of anger and despair. But she sensed something more, something that pulled so hard at him it threatened the very weave of the warrior. What was it? And why did it bring Constance to mind?

"I will not easily yield it," he finally spoke, "but 'tis likely lost."

Suppressing a cry of anguish, she choked, "But when the king learns what Agatha and Lady Elianor did, surely he will grant you grace, heaping his wrath not upon the Boursiers but the Verduns—declaring *their* lands forfeited."

"'Tis possible, but as the king has said he will accept no excuse, it is just as possible our lands will also be lost."

She thrust off the bed and crossed the room. "Of the three families, Edward is best disposed toward ours." She returned to him. "You know he is!"

Bayard stood and laid a hand on her arm, but before he could gainsay her, she stepped quickly to the window. She opened a shutter, slammed it, and turned her back to it. "He granted you first choice of wife, and if not for that vile, wicked Elianor of Emberly—"

"Enough, Quintin!"

She blinked. Was his false bride the *something more* she had sensed beyond his anger and despair? Vows had been spoken, and it followed they would have been validated by consummation, but was it time enough for the woman to beguile him? She was said to be a beauty like her aunt, Constance, and as Bayard had proved with the latter, his fondness for a lovely face could be ruinous. He had pledged to never again fall victim to beauty—among his reasons for choosing to wed the plain Thomasin de Arell—but might he have betrayed himself?

She strode forward. "Tell me you do not concern yourself over the king's punishment of Lady Elianor."

His lid narrowed. "I do not."

She hoped he spoke true, feared he did not. But just as she was well enough acquainted with her brother to know the holes in his tale of Lady Elianor were dug there by him, she knew he would not be moved to fill them. "Good," she said. "I shall pray King Edward is just—that only the barony of Emberly is forfeited. So what will you do now?"

"Wait."

"And of Lady Thomasin—who I rather like, though methinks her youth will test your patience?"

"Wait," he repeated. "Since all may be lost to the Boursiers, De Arell is not so fool to allow me to wed his daughter ere the king makes his determination. Now you, Quintin. I would make sense of what has gone during your time at Castle Mathe." He glanced around the room. "Aside from De Arell landing you on the table to gain the dagger, this is all you suffered?"

As she had struggled to believe his enemy had not sought to injure the Boursiers by striking at her, so did he. Hoping to lessen his animosity toward Griffin, she revealed she had been given a chamber befitting a noble, and that only after causing a din and attempting to reach Ulric de Arell's apartment had she been imprisoned in the tower room.

Bayard showed his surprise that she had been treated well following her attack on the Baron of Blackwood, and again when she told him she had been allowed to join the baron at table and, under guard, linger in the hall. But just as he had left holes in his tale of the lady who had imprisoned him, she left them in hers. For naught would she undo the good she did in showing the sins of the father had not all been visited on Griffin. For naught would she see blood spilled over the impropriety of a night spent in the arms of their enemy, of caresses, and of a kiss that could have seen her undone if not for Griffin's honor—

Honor? She turned the word over as she embraced her brother at the door…as he vowed he would see her freed…as he once more assured her Lady Maeve was well…as he stepped to the landing…as the Blackwood knight slid the bolt into place.

She pressed her forehead to the door. The dishonorable Griffin de Arell was not as dishonorable as believed. But honorable?

She breathed out bitterness. What did it matter? She did not want him—did not want any man.

She touched her abdomen, traced the scar through the material of her gown.

And no man should want her.

Griffin could barely admit it to himself, but he knew there was a reason beyond Thomasin that caused him to examine the matter from every angle and search for a solution. Above all, he did not want his daughter to wed Boursier, but there was something else he wanted that he had thought he would never want again. And so great was the want, he could almost convince himself it was a need.

Had ever a warrior been so unmanned? Certes, were Ulric in his grave, he would find a way out to bedevil his son.

Staring at Boursier, who had not entered the hall wielding a sword and whose first words spoken were a demand for his sister's release, Griffin was confident the intimacies shared with Quintin had not been revealed.

Encouraged, even if she but sought to prevent bloodshed, he looked past Boursier at the two who had advanced only as far as the center of the hall. He dismissed Sir Victor, considered the priest whose services might soon be needed, and settled back in his chair. "Lady Quintin remains."

Boursier stepped nearer, set his hands on the table between them, and leaned in. "Your purpose, De Arell?"

Though there was now more to it than he had first declared when he had met Boursier outside Mathe's walls, he said, "*That* we have already discussed, Boursier. It has not changed, nor shall it, unless the king determines otherwise."

A muscle in his jaw convulsed. "Speak!"

Beneath the table, Arturo growled.

"Seat yourself." Griffin gestured at the chair Boursier stood alongside.

"I shall stand."

Griffin shrugged. "If Edward permits the delay in marrying my daughter, I shall return Lady Quintin to you—my new son-in-law." The least desirable course, and his enemy's singular gaze told he found it as distasteful. "However, if he orders a legitimate marriage between you and Lady Elianor..." He tilted a smile at Boursier. And wondered if he imagined a lessening of the man's distaste. Though it could not sit well with him to legitimately wed the lady who had made a fool of him, she was beautiful, and as told by Constance's betrothal stolen from Serle, he liked his women most fair of face.

"Thus, if Edward determines the house of Boursier should join with the house of Verdun through you and Lady Elianor, your sister and I shall wed shortly." It was the same as he had suggested outside the walls, but this time it was not meant to provoke. But it did.

"For what do you think my lands will not be declared forfeit?" Boursier bit.

The solution. And possibly viable. "Consummation, which was once said to make a marriage—providing both parties consented."

Did Boursier's gaze waver? If so, because what was proposed could save his lands? Or...

Griffin assured himself of the position of his feet should it be necessary to gain them, beneath the table moved his hand to his sword hilt, against his calf felt the wolfhound quiver in anticipation. "I wager you have had Elianor of Emberly to bed."

The muscles in Boursier's hands on the table strained as if to hold him where he stood.

When Griffin was fairly sure his enemy possessed enough control not to risk his life, he said, "You know Edward will conclude the same. And though 'tis true I would be satisfied to see you forfeit, I know you will not do so willingly—as I would not. Hence, Lady Elianor has handed me an opportunity I gladly accept. I shall suffer marriage to your sister providing my daughter does not suffer marriage to you."

Other emotions scrambled amid the anger mottling Boursier's face, but though too fleeting to name, Griffin was certain they reflected serious consideration of the proposal that might be his only chance to retain his title and lands.

Then Boursier's mouth curved. Not a smile, but satisfaction of a sort. He pushed off the table, reclaiming his impressive height. "If Edward does as you believe he shall, I wager you yourself will regret choosing my sister over forfeiture."

Griffin feigned puzzlement. He had knowledge aplenty of the difficulty of taking Quintin in hand, but the experience of having her in hand held promise that could outweigh the effort required to claim her.

"I shall take my men with me when I depart," Boursier said, "but I will depart only if Sir Victor remains behind to keep watch over my sister."

Griffin was not surprised, but neither did he like having Boursier's man underfoot. "No harm will she suffer."

"Let us be certain, hmm?"

Griffin inclined his head. "Very well, he may remain."

"One more thing. As you bore witness to Elianor of Emberly's deceit, I would have you add your words to those Father Crispin will compose to inform the king of what transpired that caused me to wed one other than your daughter."

"It would be my pleasure."

Boursier narrowed his one eye at Griffin. "Now, I must speak with my *wife*." He turned on his heel.

His wife, indeed. God—and King Edward—willing.

Boursier strode to his knight and his priest, conversed low, and peered across his shoulder. "Deliver my sister to the keep, De Arell. For so *joyous* an occasion, I would have her present."

Griffin smiled, and across the distance saw that just as Quintin found his expression offensive, so did her brother—a man who might soon call his enemy, the Baron of Blackwood, *brother.*

13

⎯⎯∞∞∞⎯⎯

ELIANOR OF EMBERLY was not beautiful. Perhaps to men who looked only with lustful eyes, but not to Quintin, who seethed as her brother once more sacrificed himself on the altar of Verdun treachery. His loss of an eye to Constance's cuckolding had been horrific, but it seemed a small thing compared to what he might lose now that he was wed in truth to the woman who had imprisoned him—a gamble that could further bruise his soul.

Hands cramping, the force of her fists causing her arms to quake, Quintin splayed her fingers and startled when those of her left hand brushed another's.

"For your brother's sake," whispered words swept her ear, "sheathe your claws."

Then there was Griffin, who stood at her side as if already they were bound to each other. And they would be, providing the king agreed that consummation sealed by this ceremony—as suggested by Griffin, to her surprise—fulfilled the decree.

With Godsmere's priest a blessing away from concluding the ceremony, his solemn voice appealing to God to safeguard the union, Quintin reflected that what she had urged Bayard the day of his abduction—that he wed Lady Elianor and she wed Griffin—had come to pass.

Holding in laughter that would be an ugly thing at this time and place, she looked up at the one who might now be her betrothed and thought his mouth much too firm. For some reason, she longed to see that arrogant smile he had not slanted at her since her escort to the keep.

Because I would rather foment over that smile than the hateful Lady Elianor, she told herself.

"Your claws, Quintin." He raised his eyebrows.

It was *her* mouth that moved with what felt like a sorrowful excuse for a smile.

His eyebrows jerked.

Her hand that once more splayed to brush the back of his.

His eyebrows lowered.

Her fingers that slid into the grooves of his and pressed their tips to his fingertips.

His eyebrows gathered.

Oh, how you lie, Quintin Boursier, she silently yielded. *As much as you hate Bayard wedding the Verdun woman, you are hardly tormented their union draws you nearer to joining with this man who, moment by moment, proves he is not his father.*

On the last of the breath she eased past her tight throat, she said, "Sheathed."

His mouth twitched, but still no smile.

He did not trust her intentions any more than she trusted them. The only things of which she was certain were how glad she was to have him at her side and that the ache in her head had receded.

When Bayard turned Lady Elianor to lead her from the chapel, Quintin snatched her hand back. Clasping it with the other, she tried not to miss the pads of Griffin's fingers as she watched the woman who was now Lady of Godsmere progress toward her.

Lady Elianor's eyes settled first on Thomasin, whose expression was more staid than heretofore seen.

And Quintin was ashamed she had not considered how affected the young woman might be to witness her betrothed's marriage to that thief. However, when Thomasin turned to watch husband and wife move past, Quintin glimpsed light in eyes as blue as her father's.

Was she merely behaving? Unconcerned that now she might wed the one who was to have been Quintin's husband? Magnus Verdun *was* said to be as handsome as his sister and niece were beautiful.

Quintin shifted her regard to Bayard's wife and glared when the woman's eyes met hers.

Without falter, the lady continued past. And so, to the wedding feast.

Quintin did not believe the meal could be more tense, nor Arturo more aware where he roamed beneath the high table, occasionally brushing her knees, at times growling. However, Lady Elianor caused relations to strain further when Griffin turned to where she sat on the other side of Bayard and said, "I have sent word of your marriage to your uncle, my lady." He raised his goblet toward his mouth. "Of course, such tidings will not likely give him ease."

"As it gives *you* ease to know you will soon wed a Boursier?" the lady retorted.

Knowing herself to be *that* Boursier, Quintin struggled to swallow words she wanted to spit. All were here now because of what this woman had dared. What *she* had done. If not for her, it would not fall to Griffin to—

Wed me, she silently acknowledged as she glanced from where he had stilled, to where Bayard had stiffened.

But Griffin is not completely averse to taking you to wife, she reminded herself. *Were he, never would he have shown you such regard, nor been so intimate.* And again she assured herself, *He already has his heir.*

But what if he wished more children? Many were the sons and daughters taken by illness and accident. He had only Rhys and Thomasin.

Griffin cleared his throat. "'Tis unfortunate for all, Lady Elianor, that we are forced into such marriages."

Unfortunate for all, Quintin reflected. But at least for Griffin and her, not as unfortunate as he made it sound. Or so she hoped.

The Verdun woman narrowed her lids. "Marriages that would have been unnecessary had you not laid ruin to six months of peace by raiding and burning the village of Tyne."

"Still, I maintain that was not the work of me or mine."

She drew breath to respond, but Bayard leaned near Griffin, blocking his wife's view of their host. "As you maintain you had naught to do with burning my crops last summer, De Arell?"

"I did that—after you slaughtered a score of my cattle."

A lie. Recalling the Baron of Blackwood's accusation against the Boursiers, Quintin's ire began to shift to Griffin.

However, with what was surely great effort, Bayard let it be. His wife did not—or would not have, had her husband allowed her further argument. Whatever words he spoke to her did not carry, nor her response, but it was obvious neither was pleased with the other.

When the meal ended, Lady Elianor held her head high as she followed Father Crispin across the hall to ascend the stairs to the chamber where she would be put to bed to await the groom.

Quintin was glad to see her go—and appalled to feel a tug of sympathy. Despite the lady's proud carriage, she exuded fear as of one being led to the noose. Were Bayard a different sort of man, she would have cause, but as she ought to know from having suffered no abuse following her imprisonment of the man who was now and evermore her husband, he would not raise a hand to her. Of course, her sins would be tenfold worse if the king determined his decree had not been fulfilled. That was certainly something to fear, though Quintin knew even then Bayard would not abuse his wife.

"I shall escort you to the tower, Lady Quintin."

She looked up at Griffin, then past him to her brother who watched them over his goblet. She started to summon a smile, but fearing its insincerity would concern him more than its absence, she nodded at Griffin.

He took her arm. As he assisted her out of the chair, she wondered if she imagined the possessiveness with which he did so—as if she already belonged to him.

Bayard did not like it, as evidenced by his grim mouth when he lowered the goblet. But perhaps that was Griffin's intent. Regardless, she allowed his gesture, knowing any objection would encourage her brother to intervene.

Griffin retrieved her mantle from the chair's back, draped it over her shoulders, and, to her surprise, guided her to Bayard.

Quintin kissed her brother's cheek. "All is well. And all will be well."

He nodded. "We depart on the morrow."

"I will be ready."

Something further disturbing his mouth, he laid a hand over hers and gently squeezed. "Good eve, Sister."

"I pray yours is as well." This time she did try to smile, and it felt passably true.

"So, 'tis done," she said as Griffin and she crossed the night-fallen bailey beneath the regard of patrolling men-at-arms.

"All that can be done by mere mortals. Now we wait to see if King Edward counts himself among us or ignores what has been set aright."

She peered up at him, thought how kind torchlight was to one whose face was more weathered than Bayard's. "Is it set aright? My brother has wed that…woman."

"Now your sister-in-law, regardless of what the king decides."

She stared at him, grateful his guiding hand assured her footing across the frozen ground. "It sounds as if you do not dislike her."

"I do not. Indeed, given time I might become fond of her."

After the words that had passed between the two at table? Quintin halted, and as he turned to her said, "You jest."

He arched an eyebrow. "I do not hide that I am fond of *you*."

It was too dim to read the blue of his eyes, but she felt the desire to be found there. "What has your fondness for me to do with Lady Elianor?"

"Methinks she may be your equal."

She would have taken a step back had he not held her. "What say you?"

"Like you, she is bold."

"Bold? She is criminal. With much forethought, she drugged and imprisoned my brother to steal his birthright!"

He gave a one-shoulder shrug she realized was nearly as common as his one-sided smile. "Very well, she is more bold than you."

She who had put a dagger to his throat without forethought. Did he truly admire Lady Elianor's conniving? "You find bold women appealing?" she demanded and, beyond him, saw two men-at-arms look around. She lowered her voice. "I thought most men preferred their women meek."

"I was wed to a meek woman—a good woman, who gave me a healthy son, but meek I would not wed again."

"Then you are to be pitied for having lost so bold a woman to my brother." As soon as the words were out, she knew they were bait.

And from the turn of his mouth, he knew it as well. "Methinks I would have been satisfied with Lady Elianor as a wife"—the hand he laid to her cheek was so warm she realized how cold her face had become— "providing you had not first set yourself at my walls."

He said what she wished to hear, and it made her heart hurt.

"Griffin," someone whispered, and she realized it was she when he looked to her mouth. She thought he might kiss her, but he lifted his gaze up the keep, then returned his hand to her arm.

"Come, 'tis cold."

Though tempted to look where he had looked, she faced forward as he led her to the gatehouse, and with every step imagined hostile eyes on her back. His father's? Did the leprous old man watch from a window?

Upon reaching the door to her room, Griffin said, "Let us return to the matter of Lady Elianor."

She did not try to hide her surprise, nor her aversion. "As it will not change that she is wed to my brother, I see no reason for further discussion."

"All the more reason, then." Before she could object, he said, "I have given more thought to her trespass against your brother and do not believe she did it only for her gain."

Quintin huffed.

"Had she, I would have been the one imprisoned so I could not take her to wife. Instead, she set herself at my daughter's betrothed. Why, do you think?"

"Should I care?"

"Quintin, this woman shall ever be part of your life. You do not have to like her, but 'twill ease your brother's burden if you can tolerate her."

She stared at him, wanting to argue but too speechless that he yet again tossed her hate back in her face. Griffin was not of a great age, and yet beyond his goading smiles and careless shrugs, wisdom dwelt.

"I am listening."

He glanced at the door as if he wished to be invited inside, but he put a shoulder to the wall. "Most know your brother's reputation as a man who beat his wife."

"He did not! 'Twas a lie Constance told to justify—"

He held up a hand. "I am inclined to believe you, but I do not think Lady Elianor does."

"Why?"

"You know that just as I am a widower, she is a widow?"

"I know."

"When the king issued his decree, I took it upon myself to discover more about the two women who might be my bride and, hence, mother to my young son."

Quintin supposed she should not be surprised, and was grateful so few knew of her secret pain.

"Unfortunately, it was difficult to learn much beyond the little I already knew about either of you. I was most curious about Lady Elianor's life after she wed Murdoch Farrow. What I did learn was that she bore her husband no babes and was reclusive, never leaving the castle and rarely the keep."

Griffin paused as if to allow her to catch up on the path down which he led her. "Does the one who drugged and imprisoned *The Boursier* seem one to huddle indoors like a frightened child?"

Grudgingly, she shook her head.

"The only one with whom she seems to have had any relation out-side of Farrow—a pig of a man, I am told—is Agatha of Mawbry."

Quintin caught her breath.

"What is it?"

"Pray, continue."

He stared at her, but finally said, "After your family ousted that woman from Godsmere, she returned to the Verduns. A year into Lady Elianor's marriage to Farrow, Magnus Verdun sent Agatha to serve her."

"So that is how it came to be."

"What?"

She hesitated lest she furthered the humiliation Bayard suffered, then determined the particulars of what it had taken to lay low the warrior would better serve him. "I am guessing my brother did not share with you that Lady Elianor was not alone in imprisoning him—that Agatha aided her."

His eyebrows rose. "He did not."

"They were only able to take him from his bed after drugging his wine, and then not far. He was imprisoned in Castle Adderstone's underground passages—was beneath my feet the entire time. And that is where Agatha is now, chained to the wall as they chained him."

After a long quiet, Griffin said, "It seems a good place for her, away from Lady Elianor who, likely, was too much in her company."

Quintin frowned. "You think Lady Elianor was influenced by that witch? So much she can be excused for what she did to my brother?"

"Very likely she was influenced, but perhaps more importantly, indebted."

"What do you mean?"

"Once her lovely hair was not so lovely. During her marriage to Farrow, it was shorn—severely, not merely shortened as you wear yours."

As punishment, he inferred. And if a man so publicly humiliated his wife, what might he do behind closed doors?

Quintin did not wish to understand where Griffin was dragging her, but she would have to do more than tightly close her eyes not to see what was well supported by the fear the lady had exuded as she was led abovestairs. "You believe Farrow abused his wife. That just as Agatha first drugged my brother to keep him from Constance's bed, she aided Lady Elianor."

He inclined his head. "And since it was Thomasin who was to suffer marriage to your brother, it is quite possible Lady Elianor moved against him to save my daughter from abuse."

If he was right, might the lady be forgiven for what she had wrought? Not that Quintin was ready to extend such, but for Bayard's sake, she prayed the woman to whom he was bound could be redeemed enough that the life he spent upon her would not be miserable.

"Pieces only," Griffin said, "but a good fit, do you not think?"

Quintin wondered how, in so short a time, they had moved from captor and captive to...

Was it possible they were compeers—equals? "What I think, Griffin, is that you think too much for a warrior."

He chuckled. "You forget who sired me."

"I do not. That is why you so surprise."

"Then, like many, you assume the acorn grew into the same oak."

"'Tis as I believed. Now...less and less."

"I am glad to hear it. And yet I do possess some of Ulric's undesirable qualities. Thus, I do think too much, but with good cause. My father does not well enough consider his words and actions, and so I learn from his mistakes that I might bequeath fewer to my son, often reminding myself to think much that I may regret little."

"Then you thought well on advising my brother to claim consummation fulfilled the king's decree?"

He hesitated. "Not as well as I should have. Recall what saw your blade at my throat that first day."

His suggestion that if Godsmere was forfeited to the crown, he could seek to claim the barony through marriage to her. For the sake of the Foucault name, had he not said? He had, but by aiding Bayard he had reduced the possibility the De Arells would gain what they coveted. Why?

"Aye," he said, and she realized he watched her closely. "If there is one thing upon which my father and I are of the same opinion, 'tis that Castle Adderstone upon the barony of Godsmere should have been our family's as 'twas agreed."

"Then?" she asked, though the real question was if he had aided Bayard for her.

"Thomasin," he said. "If she must wed, I would rather it be to Baron Verdun. Thus, lest the king allowed your brother's delay in wedding my daughter, I decided to remove all possibility of her being bound to him by seeing the Baron of Godsmere lawfully wed to Lady Elianor."

Though tempted to temper—to declare her brother would make a worthier husband than Magnus Verdun—Quintin reminded herself he had granted Bayard's request to add his testimony of Lady Elianor's duplicity to Father Crispin's, putting yet more distance between Godsmere and the De Arells. Had he done that for her?

"Too," he continued, "though I have good cause to dislike your brother, I do not doubt he was deceived when he spoke vows to fulfill the king's decree. And there is no honor in attacking a man from behind, even to gain a barony."

For Thomasin, then, and honor. And though he would not say it, she had to believe that, at least in some small portion, he had done it for her. "I am grateful for the aid you gave my brother."

"Are you?"

That smile of his! Deciding that instead of suppressing her longing to be nearer him, she would be bold as he claimed he preferred women, Quintin stepped forward. "You were right." She laid a hand on his jaw, thrilled at the rasp of his days' growth of beard against her palm, touched her thumb to the hitched corner of his mouth. "I have not only grown accustomed to this smile but find it holds much appeal. Indeed, I would have you press it to mine."

"Quintin." He closed a hand over hers. "Were I to kiss you, methinks you would be all the more angry after I tell you what your brother did not."

She frowned. "What?"

"You assume that on the morrow you will depart Mathe. You will not."

Were his hand not on hers, she would have dropped her arm. After the legitimization of Bayard's marriage which, with the king's acceptance, would see her wed to Griffin, she was to remain here? Yet more days parted from her mother? And her brother had known?

She resented that Bayard had not corrected her, but immediately forgave him. He had endured much this past sennight, and this night when he went to his wife, he would endure more. Quintin could not fault him for not giving his sister an opportunity to make what was difficult more difficult.

She pulled her hand from beneath Griffin's. "For what do you insist on keeping me here? After all that has passed, surely 'tis no longer retribution you seek for the dagger I put to you."

"That is a good excuse but now of little consequence."

"Then?"

"I believe 'tis best you remain at Mathe until we have word from the king. It will allow my people to begin viewing you not as the enemy who threatened their lord's life but as the future Lady of Blackwood."

"Should I become their lady, there will be time aplenty for that."

"Too," he said as if she had not spoken, "it will allow your brother and his wife to settle into their marriage."

Did he think she would hinder it? Had Griffin not fit for her the pieces of Lady Elianor, she supposed his concern would be founded, but surely he had seen she was receptive to the excuse he provided the lady?

She crossed her arms over her chest. "Of what benefit to you?"

When he did not immediately respond, she was certain she had asked a question deserving of an answer. "You and I have gained ground, Quintin. I would not lose it."

She opened her mouth to warn he would lose it if he did not allow her to leave, but he said, "More, I will not chance losing you."

Her heart stumbled, and it must have shown on her face, for he smiled—on both sides of his mouth. "The king is young, and the young can be fickle. Thus, when he accepts your brother's marriage, we shall wed without delay."

Aye, he had done it for her, as well as Thomasin and honor.

But what was this she felt for him? That which she had determined never to allow herself to feel? Or was it only desire? Did it matter? She was wanted by one she wanted, and that was not to have been. But would he want her when—

He has his heir, she reminded herself and winced at the realization she had done it so often it seemed almost a chant—as if its repetition would transform it into everlasting truth.

"My lady?"

As she returned Griffin to focus, he said in a voice whose rumble she felt all the way through, "I want you to want to stay."

"Even though you give me no choice?"

"Even though."

She looked down. "I would remain at Castle Mathe were it possible, but I have been gone too long from my mother."

"Lady Maeve is ill?" His concern sounded genuine.

"She is not." At least, in no way that was visible, she silently qualified. "Then?"

"She is surely sick with worry over me."

"Worry your brother can ease when he delivers tidings you are well."

"Aye, but...she needs me."

His brow furrowed. "Quintin, she is a grown woman and not of a great age."

"Still, she depends on me."

He thought on that. "She is the reason you are not yet wed, aye? For her, the king was able to make a puppet of you just as he did the rest of us."

"Nay, it was——" She stopped herself from revealing it was his brother and Constance who must answer for her lack of a husband.

"What?"

She shook her head.

He sighed. "Quintin, as your mother left her mother to be a wife, and surely when she had fewer years than you, is it not time you did the same? Though she will miss your companionship, she has your brother and, once she accepts his wife, Lady Elianor ought to make for good company. And outside of companionship, others can do for her."

He sounded like Bayard, who often warned that by bending her own needs and desires out of shape to fit her mother's, she made Lady Maeve's dependence worse. Were they right? Was she too protective, not only to her detriment, but her mother's? Would Lady Maeve accept and recover from her daughter's continued absence?

What if ill befalls me whilst you are away? her desperate beseeching returned to Quintin. *What if I sicken and you are nowhere near to rouse me back to health?*

Those words and others spoken over the years to keep the ties between mother and daughter tight had sometimes so suffocated that, even now, Quintin's throat constricted.

She has Hulda, she reminded herself of the maid who had been with her mother since she was a girl. And without giving it more thought, she said, "I want to stay."

He released a breath. "On the morrow, I will see you returned to Sir Mathieu's chamber."

Though she feared she would regret putting her wants ahead of her mother's, she nodded.

He pushed off the wall, lowered his head, and brushed his lips across hers. "Sleep well, my lady."

Wishing his mouth had lingered, she said, "Good eve, my lord," and entered the tower room, closed the door, and listened for what she hoped would be the absence of sound before that of boots on the stairs.

Silence did follow, then he slid the bolt into place—doubtless, lest she only said what he wanted to hear. And she could not fault him, for her mother's beseeching picked at her. Had Griffin provided an opportunity for her to return to Adderstone on the morrow, the temptation to grasp it might have proved too much. She was glad—selfishly so—he had not made it possible.

14

BAYARD WAS GONE. And with him his bride and Godsmere's men.

It had been a difficult farewell. On the night past, Griffin had not trusted her enough to leave her room unbolted, and this morn he had stayed by her side in the bailey lest she—or Bayard—determined she would, indeed, depart. Thus, few were the words spoken between brother and sister. But enough, she hoped, that Bayard was sufficiently at ease in leaving her. Not only was Sir Victor to remain, but she had revealed her acceptance of Griffin's offer to reside within the keep. And now...

She picked her gaze over the chamber that had briefly been hers—the same in which Bayard and Lady Elianor had spent their nuptial night.

"No more casting of platters and goblets, hmm?"

She had not heard Griffin move to her side but was not offended to find him so near. And she wondered at such easy acceptance of his presence. It was as if she were long accustomed to it, and yet it was hardly a sennight since they had met—and then as enemies.

"I shall do my utmost to refrain, as I am sure you will do your utmost to give me no cause to awaken the castle in the middling of night."

He grinned. "I shall behave. Now, is there anything you require?"

She looked around the chamber and was once more heartened to happen upon the tub that lacked only water to keep its promise of a bath long denied. Catching sight of Sir Victor where he stood in the corridor, she smiled. And felt the expression drop off her mouth when the wolf-hound Griffin had earlier commanded to his side put its head around the door.

She grimaced. "Bath water would be lovely."

"'Tis already being heated."

"I thank you. And what of Sir Victor's accommodations?"

"He is to have my son's chamber."

Then Rhys was reduced to a pallet on his sister's or father's floor. Because of her. Though the boy had to be displeased, Quintin was relieved her brother had not stipulated that Sir Victor sleep outside her door. She had half expected it since the alliance between Boursiers and De Arells was not yet made and she suspected Bayard was aware of the baron's attraction to his captive. And, possibly, that it was returned.

"Arturo," Griffin called.

The big dog did not bound inside but neither did it slink as it did when Quintin was in the hall. He came alongside his master and peered up at him with likely the same question that caused Quintin to raise her eyebrows.

Griffin touched her elbow, slid his hand down the inside of her arm, and caught up her fingers.

"Griffin?" She glanced at Sir Victor who had taken a step nearer the chamber's threshold.

The Baron of Blackwood raised her hand to his mouth, pressed his lips to the back of it, and drew it toward Arturo.

Quintin tried to pull free, but he held firm. "He will not harm you," he said and moved her hand to the dog's nose.

As Arturo sniffed where his master's mouth had been, Griffin said, "Protect, Arturo."

The dog made a sound between a growl and a whine, then dropped to his haunches.

"Protect?" Quintin said.

"As Sir Victor keeps watch over you for your brother, Arturo keeps watch over you for me."

She pulled free. "I am not to be allowed to move unhindered about Castle Mathe?"

"Within reason, my lady. I have business that needs tending and will not always be available to ensure your well-being."

She narrowed her lids. "Either that is an excuse to hide how little you trust the one who may become Lady of Blackwood, else I have something or someone to fear within your walls."

Or both, she recalled her mother's warning that the devil walked Castle Mathe's corridors. As Quintin had earlier concluded, it had to be the old baron she referred to. But though Griffin had revealed leprosy confined his father abovestairs, might Ulric de Arell venture out of his apartment? And if he did, would she be too much temptation for one who loathed the Boursiers?

"Father?" Now it was Rhys who put his head around the door.

"You have come to welcome Lady Quintin back amongst us?" Griffin asked, and Quintin saw his son was also a recipient of the uneven smile.

The boy dismissed her with a dart of the eyes. "I have completed my chores and would ride to the village of Lorria as you promised."

"That we shall." Griffin looked to Quintin. "Hence, Arturo, who does not like my father, nor his little dog."

Then perhaps more than keeping Ulric de Arell from her, he meant to keep her from the old baron lest she sought to steal abovestairs.

She shrugged. "Clearly, I no longer have cause to gain your father's apartment, but as you will."

He bent near. "Curiosity often suffices in the absence of cause, but know I but spare you exposure to his diseased body—and his cruel tongue." He drew a breath that broadened shoulders hardly in need of more width. "And so we go, Rhys." He strode toward his son, and when Arturo exited, left the key on its hook and closed the door.

"Come, Sir Victor," his voice carried, "your chamber has been made ready."

Quintin stared at the door, wondering how so much could change between them, then turned her mind to the arrival of steaming water.

"A bath," she said on a sigh and promised herself she would not move from it until it grew uncomfortably cool. She would sit and soak and pray Bayard's marriage to Lady Elianor satisfied the king.

But would that be enough? Was there not some way to strengthen her brother's position? To increase the chance Edward gainsaid himself, even at the risk of appearing weak? Certes, if the second alliance could be made soon—

She bit her lip. Aye, she would sit and soak and pray, and to those things add much thought as to the preservation of Lady Maeve's beloved home.

"Surely you can have no objections now," Griffin said, holding Quintin's gaze past his knife upon whose tip perched a cut of chicken. And caught a flicker of something in her gold-ringed eyes.

"As well you know, Baron, our union is not a given."

As he had done often since she had gained her seat beside him, he wondered what petals had been strewn upon her bath water and what soap she had worked through the ash-black hair falling in soft waves about her face and skimming her shoulders. "I believe 'tis a given," he murmured.

She moistened her lips. "You think the king holds my brother in such high regard he will alter his decree, though it may make Edward appear he only has teeth to bare, not bite?"

"Once the king learns the reason for the delay, he will have an excuse to merely bare, rather than bite. And since I added my testimony to Father Crispin's, methinks he will rule fairly."

She looked to the proffered chicken. "Then do I accept this intimacy, I am assured I do so from the hand of my betrothed?"

Griffin recalled the flicker in her eyes. She was clever, but not so much he did not know there was more to her words than the appropriateness of taking from the hand of a lover who did not yet have permission to approach her bed. She thought to fit a leash on him.

He lowered the knife to the platter they were to share during the nooning meal. "What are you about, Quintin?"

Another flicker in her eyes, then a glint, next a momentary lowering of lids as if accepting her leash might not have the reach required. "If you are certain I am to be your wife, I would ask that you do more than testify on my brother's behalf. I would have you wed me. Now."

His mind having begun to move in that direction as he pondered her words and behavior, he was not overly surprised. Neither was he overly willing. And he let it show.

She moved her gaze to the hall's occupants. "I have given it some thought and believe there is a greater chance King Edward will accept the delay in my brother's marriage if the second alliance—ours—quickly follows." She turned her face back to his. "Thus, you lend more credence to Bayard's marriage by showing you are as confident of his union with the house of Verdun as you are confident of your union with the house of Boursier."

He had said he liked his women bold, but if the king decided against her brother, this could prove too bold, his premature joining with the dispossessed man's sister of possible detriment to the De Arells—though not, he believed, to the extent he risked forfeiture of Blackwood. What he risked was Godsmere and Emberly.

Griffin was fairly certain the king would not divest Boursier or Verdun of their lands, but what he had not told Quintin on the night past, liking too well her gratitude for the aid given her brother, was what he would do if the baronies were forfeited.

Since one or both would be awarded to a vassal who held favor with the king, the De Arells being the one family that had not defied the decree stood a good chance of being granted their petition to lord those lands. As Griffin had suggested the day Quintin had drawn a dagger on him, marriage to her—for the sake of the Foucault name, which would likely appeal to Edward—could see the great barony of Kilbourne stitched back together under the De Arells.

Or not.

If he wed her without awaiting the determination about her brother's marriage, he could also be seen as defying the decree and, thus, the baronies would be awarded to another. However, if he did not wed her before the determination and still the king gifted the baronies elsewhere, so might Quintin be.

So wed her now to ensure he gained the woman he wanted? Or wait on the possibility of a barony three times the size of Blackwood, as it should have been when Archard Boursier and Rand Verdun pledged to support Ulric's bid to become the Baron of Kilbourne those many years ago?

Grunting low, Griffin retrieved the knife and considered the meat at its tip. Then he pulled it off and extended it.

Quintin blinked. "This is your answer?"

Regretting the strain in her voice that told she might draw back from the progress they had made toward each other, he said, "As you have given it some thought, so must I."

She opened her clenched hands in her lap, and he thought she would go from the hall, but she took the meat. "I thank you. If you would cut more, 'twill suffice to place it on the platter's edge."

She did draw back, but not as far as feared. Satisfied as much as was possible, he inclined his head.

However, when darkness fell over the barony of Blackwood and the castle folk once more gathered for a light supper, she sent a request for a tray to be delivered to her chamber. And Griffin allowed it.

Lights. So terribly beautiful they entranced, tempting her to reach... touch...run fingers through them. But she knew better. They were in her head.

"Dear Lord, let it go no further," she whispered. "This. Only this." Not the loss of sight, temporary though it was. Not the prickling along arms and legs that might turn numb. Not the faintness that could steal her consciousness whether she was on her feet or off them.

Still, to all these sufferings she would consent were she spared that which sometimes followed and could last hours, even days—an intense, persistent throb in her head, nausea, vomiting, and the cruelty of light that she imagined as viciously pierced her eyes as had the blade that pierced Bayard's eye.

Blessedly, the Lord most often answered as she pleaded, but once and sometimes twice a year, He did not.

The prickling began, moving up her fingers to her shoulders, then down her center to her toes. A whimper slipped from her, and she startled when it was answered by a whine from beyond the chamber—Arturo, that vile beast who had followed her abovestairs after the nooning meal.

She had feared he would try to enter her chamber, but when she had paused at the door, he had continued past her and stretched out at the base of the stairs to Ulric de Arell's apartment. By command of Griffin? Or merely a good vantage to watch her comings and goings without threat of being trod upon?

He whined more loudly, as if he put his mouth to the space between door and floor.

"Go away!" Quintin called and groaned over the slurred words and the sensation of the bed turning beneath her.

More whining, followed by scratching and growling.

"Accursed dog!" Lest his din attracted other unwelcome visitors, she clambered off the bed and bumped into the bedside table, causing the tray there to clatter. She tried to focus on the supper viands she had requested, since it was best to bide abovestairs as she did at Adderstone when the lights appeared, but the foodstuffs remained a blur.

It mattered not. She would not partake until fairly certain this thing did not progress to a painful head and nausea.

When a thud sounded against the door as if Arturo leapt at it, Quintin lurched across the chamber. There were fewer lights now, though only because blind spots vied for attention.

Her seeking hand found the door, and she opened it just enough to show she was not in need of protection. "I am well. Now go—"

The dog thrust inside, but she knew it only from the feel of him knocking against her legs. Holding tight to the door, she glimpsed him trotting around the bed, nose to the floor.

"Arturo, go!" She opened the door wider and stumbled as more blind spots usurped the lights. Fearing the loss of consciousness, she closed the door, held her hands out before her for guidance and balance, and gave thanks when her knees hit the bed.

She prostrated herself, but though she did not lose consciousness, she thought she hallucinated when a tongue ran up the hand of her arm hanging over the mattress.

"You are supposed to hate me," she mumbled and felt a wet nose bump the back of her hand. Then the ticklish hairs upon what might be the wolfhound's head brushed her fingertips. "Oh, let us hope that neither does the king bite with the teeth he bares."

She slept some, and upon awakening, tested the weight of her head and thanked the Lord she suffered no more than the ghost of an ache. When next she awakened, it was the same, and she allowed herself to believe this menses would prove but the usual inconvenience.

"You are awake?"

She flipped onto her back, and by the torchlight shining through the doorway saw Griffin leaned over her. She nearly demanded his purpose, but it was obvious, her chill limbs covered by the fur he had given her that first night. And strangely, his consideration made her long to cry.

He straightened. "When I saw Arturo was not outside your door, I hoped I would find him in your chamber." He laid a hand to the neck of the wolfhound at his side.

Quintin pulled the fur higher, tucked her chin into it. "Unfortunately, he insisted," she said, then asked, "Sir Victor?"

"Abed for the night." He nodded at the door he had left open. "But if he arises, he can be assured naught untoward goes here."

Still her brother's knight would not like finding the Baron of Blackwood at her bedside.

"I am sorry you are so distressed you could not bring yourself to join me at table this eve," Griffin said, "nor partake of the meal delivered you."

It had occurred to her he would believe her absence from the hall was due to his noncommittal response to her proposal, but though days past it would have been true—that she would have avoided being near him—she did not want the man who had covered her to believe that.

"I am distressed, but 'tis not what held me to my chamber and ruined my appetite."

As Arturo groaned and set his chin on the mattress alongside Quintin's thigh, Griffin prompted, "Then?"

Twinged by discomfort, she told herself it was silly for a woman to feel such, and more so for a man who had once been wed. Still, there was no cause to be blunt. She pushed up onto her elbows. "Methinks I shall soon require cloths."

"For?"

Perhaps somewhat blunt. "The curse of Eve."

Silence, then, "Ah. My departed wife called it the blessing of Eve."

"The *blessing?*"

"Her mother died birthing her sister. Being just as slight of figure, Johanna counted it a blessing each time her menses arrived. Two years into our marriage, it did not." His face was too shadowed for Quintin to glimpse emotions there, but she felt sorrow in the silence—and a tightness in her chest for what he had yet to tell.

"Rhys's birth was difficult, but Johanna survived. For a year."

As Quintin knew, tale having been carried to Castle Adderstone that his wife had rarely risen from bed following their son's birth. "I am sorry."

"As am I." He curved a hand around her jaw. "But I shall wed again and Rhys will have more siblings."

Her heart spasmed.

"I must needs think more on your proposal, Quintin, but know I do wish you to be my wife and bear my sons and daughters."

Emotions taking a messy turn, she nearly blurted that did they wed, she might herself count the arrival of her menses a blessing rather than a curse, but of greater fear than having to explain herself was the possibility he would reject her proposal outright if he knew the reason her fist once more pressed itself to her abdomen.

She lowered her head to the pillow. "Then I await your decision, my lord. Good eve."

After some moments, he said, "Good eve, my lady," and took Arturo with him and closed the door.

He has his heir, she told her conscience, *and if the king permits Bayard to remain Baron of Godsmere, Griffin will be bound to me no matter what I cannot give him.*

She drew the fist up her chest to where her heart beat, squeezed her lids closed. "The blessing of Eve," she whispered. Never would she count it that, for she did wish children at her breast.

And with God, it was possible, was it not?

15

⸻

"OH, HAVE MERCY!"

Quintin dragged her gaze from the skirmish that filled the air with grunts, shouts, and curses to the young woman who stood at her side near the stables in the outer bailey. "Mercy?"

Lady Thomasin tossed her eyebrows high. "They make a performance of this—for you."

Quintin looked back at the fenced training yard where knights and men-at-arms fought not with swords, pikes, and maces but with missiles formed from last eve's snowfall. The damp earth over which they moved was a muddy mess, most of its snow sacrificed to hands that shaped it into balls so hard and compact that, upon striking bare faces and hands, their glittering white explosions were sometimes flecked with blood.

"Men!" Lady Thomasin grumbled. "As soon as Sir Bertrand's snowball struck Sir Leeland between the eyes, he looked to you. Surely you know why."

Quintin did. Her attention was often sought at Adderstone, but here it was more amusing than annoying. Griffin's men remained openly distrustful of her though she had resided in the keep three days, and when her menses did not overly bother her, took meal in the hall and strove to give them no further cause to think ill of her.

Recalling their narrow-eyed stares, indignation pricked her, and she nearly laughed at herself. No matter how appealing they found her face and figure, they had good cause to be wary. Three days was naught compared to the twenty-five-year feud that had plagued not only the De Arells, Boursiers, and Verduns but their retainers. Too, though Griffin mostly showed her the regard due one thought to be the future Lady of Blackwood, still he did not allow her to cut her own meat—her public humiliation of him yet too fresh. But now that the worst of her menses was past, she would make a better effort to gain acceptance at Castle Mathe. Of course, she would have more cause to do so if Griffin agreed to her proposal.

"You know why, do you not?" Lady Thomasin prompted.

As Quintin tried to place herself back in their conversation, the young woman grunted. "Silly me. None need tell you the reason. 'Tis not as if only now, having caught my father's eye, you have transformed into what you were not before."

Quintin hurt for her. Though Thomasin's figure was pleasingly different from a man's—indeed, better proportioned than Quintin's—men who required gold, gemstones, and silk to be impressed would likely think themselves generous to name her pretty.

Quintin glanced at Sir Victor who stood behind and to the left, and seeing his attention was on those in the training yard, touched Thomasin's arm. "You are mistaken if you think I am the only lady who catches the regard of these men."

She scoffed. "They do not look at me as they do you. I am, if not overlooked, an annoyance."

Embellishment being in order, Quintin said, "I have seen many an admiring eye slant your way."

Hope flickered on her face, flickered out. "You are being kind."

"Am I?" She gasped. "Hold! Do not look at Sir Otto!"

Obediently, the young woman fixed her gaze on the battling men inside the training yard. "Aye?"

Quintin leaned near her, and the knight who had yet to participate in the hurling of snowballs frowned from her to Lady Thomasin. "As I have seen him do before, he looks kindly upon you."

"Kindly?"

Moving her gaze back to the young woman, Quintin paused on Arturo, who was ever near in Griffin's absence. When last she had looked, the wolf-hound had watched from a distance of twenty feet, but he had moved nearer now that villagers entered the castle through a door in the portcullis.

"Aye," Quintin said. "Certes, 'tis not with indifference Sir Otto steals glimpses of you." It was true, though very possible he was more curious as to what secrets passed between the ladies.

A blush further darkened Thomasin's chill-reddened cheeks. "Be he not most handsome?" she slipped into her commoner's tongue.

Tucking her chin into her mantle's fur-lined collar, Quintin said, "And kind. But, alas, if the king accepts my brother's marriage to Lady Elianor, Sir Otto will have to admire you from afar as the handsome Magnus Verdun claims your hand and your heart."

"I shall look now." A moment later, Thomasin muttered, "If he did admire me, he has determined you are more worthy."

"Men!" Quintin scorned as the younger woman had done. But in the next instant, one who was increasingly difficult to scorn drew alongside her, accompanied by his son.

She tensed. She knew Griffin's reputation as a man of war, and even Bayard, the worthiest of rivals, owned that the Baron of Blackwood was formidable. Thus, he would be displeased to find his men playing at the games of children.

But when she glanced at him, it seemed only with interest he surveyed the scene, then with teasing he said, "We men are much maligned, it sounds."

Thomasin laughed. "Not you, Father. Lady Quintin but remarks on Sir Otto's inconstancy."

"What has he to be inconstant about?"

"I complained that men do not look upon me with admiration as they do her, and considerate as she is, she made much ado that Sir Otto was admiring me. But when I peeked, his eyes were all for her." She sighed. "Inconstant."

Amid her inner groaning, Quintin followed Griffin's gaze to the knight. But where Sir Otto had been, he no longer stood.

Rhys stepped in front of his father. "Are we not going?" he asked with less petulance than when Griffin had invited Quintin to join their ride to the wood.

His father looked to the stables where ten horses were tethered, before them a horse-drawn wagon upon which perched four servants, who would make quick work of amassing the greenery needed to decorate the hall for the Christmas celebration four days hence.

"All looks to be in readiness," Griffin said. "Come."

As Rhys, Quintin, Thomasin, and Sir Victor followed, he ordered those yet engaged in throwing snowballs to return to their posts, called the names of the knights and men-at-arms who would accompany the party to the wood, and shouted for the portcullis to be raised.

When he took hold of his destrier's bridle and motioned Quintin forward, she faltered at the realization their armed escort numbered not five but six. With a glance at Thomasin and Rhys, who mounted their own horses, she said, "Just as I am not allowed to cut my own meat, neither may I guide my own mount?"

"'Tis but a courtesy," he said low and set his hands on her waist to lift her into the saddle.

She curled her fingers atop his, and too much liking how broad and powerful they felt beneath her smaller ones, was grateful her gloves were between them. "'Tis an intimacy I am loath to accept from one who has yet to confirm our union is a given." She raised her eyebrows. "Is it?"

He lowered his face so near hers, the cloud of his breath enveloped their faces. "I am near to deciding."

She struggled over the temptation to walk away, but beyond the deterrent of appearing childish, she was stayed by the longing to ride. Then there was her baser side that wanted his arms around her after what seemed weeks since last they had been so near. Hoping he also wished it, she eased her hands and lightly drew her fingers to his wrists. "Decide soon, Griffin."

His nostrils flared. "Mayhap we *should* ride separate."

"Mayhap you should decide."

With a chuckle, he lifted her onto his saddle. Then he swung up behind and slid an arm around her waist.

She reached back and pulled the edges of his mantle forward and over her shoulders. After all, what was one more intimacy?

"Do you work your wiles on me, my lady?"

His voice at her ear made her shiver. "I could say 'tis only a courtesy"—as he had with regard to sharing his saddle—"but aye, I work my wiles on you."

"Ah, Quintin," he murmured, "I do want you in my bed."

She sank back against him, laid an arm atop his around her waist, and slid her fingers into the grooves of his. "All the more reason to decide soon."

"Quintin Boursier," Otto murmured where he sat astride his mount, one of the handful set to watch over those collecting pine boughs, holly, mistletoe, and other branches and clippings with which to bring the sights and scents of the black wood inside.

Quintin Foucault Boursier, he silently added the surname that better defined her. Though she was lovely to gaze upon, it was Foucault blood, tainted though it was by Boursier blood, that gave her the greatest appeal. Or so he was made to believe.

He shifted his attention to Thomasin, where she applied a blade to a skein of ivy her brother tugged at. Her blood was tainted by a commoner's. More of a crime, he was also made to believe, and yet...

Feeling that which coursed his own veins, catching its thrum between his ears, he reminded himself that not only was Thomasin de Arell plain of face, but she was irksome. Lady Quintin was not. More, she was the prize. The only prize.

"Quintin Foucault," he tested the name on his lips.

As if she heard, though it was impossible at this distance, she turned where she stood alongside Baron de Arell, who had unloaded an armful of pine boughs into the wagon. Shading her eyes against sunlight that poked a hole in the gathering clouds and, somehow, found her amongst the dense trees, she smiled at Otto and turned back to the baron.

It bothered that he warranted little more than a glance and an obligatory smile, but it was hard to fault her. She could not know he would make a worthier husband than one whose father had greedily snatched away another man's property. But ere much longer, the truth would be revealed. God willing.

Or not, spoke the voice he was to pay no heed, the one that sought to unman him by provoking him to flee what had once been the barony of Kilbourne, the voice that made him fear for his soul.

Feeling the long years that had delivered him to this day, he dragged a hand down his face, slid it up the sleeve of the opposite hand, and fingered the scars climbing his arm. He remembered the getting of every one, as well as every promise he had made himself it would be the last. Was there any greater sin committed against one's self than that of lying?

Something smacked his shoulder, and he reached for his hilt a moment ahead of the realization it was a snowball.

Rhys stepped out from behind a tree. Mouth a great swag upon a face whose round, boyish curve was becoming lean, he proclaimed, "I stole upon you, Sir Otto!"

Lest it be known he had fallen prey to a child's stealth, Otto flicked snow from his mantle, laughed loud, and with great exaggeration called, "Why, I neither saw nor heard you draw near, young Rhys." He looked at Thomasin where she stood far to the right of her brother and winked.

Rhys's grin fell. "I did steal upon you!"

A year past, the boy would have accepted the condescension as truth and pridefully strutted away. A pity he now saw it for what it was, but for Otto's sake, he would have to suffer it to its end.

Finding Griffin de Arell's gaze on him where the baron and Lady Quintin stood beyond Thomasin, Otto made a show of suppressing a smile, gave a slight shrug, and returned his attention to Rhys. "Of course you did. You do your father proud."

Though the boy had only ever esteemed Otto, something different shone from his eyes, not unlike what often appeared when Rhys looked upon Lady Quintin. And Otto regretted it. But it would pass, he assured himself, and was relieved when the boy crossed to his sister.

Before they reached their father, Thomasin pried her brother out of his mood, as evidenced by his excited chatter. Then, blessedly, Griffin de Arell announced it was time to return to the castle.

But the blessing threatened to be short-lived. As they rode from the wood to the left of more villagers who braved the winter weather to conduct business at the castle, Otto picked out a hooded figure too familiar for his liking. Hoping he was wrong, that it was not that one, he steeled himself lest he was right.

There was something breath-stealing about going into the arms of a man whose touch she liked. Often she was assisted in dismounting, and there were times the one who lifted her down drew so near there was contact between their bodies as she slid to her feet, but never had she felt what she did with this man who kept space between them.

Too much space, Quintin silently lamented as Griffin released her.

"Once I have settled my horse, I will join you in hanging the greenery," he said.

Would he? On occasion, Bayard lent a hand, but it was mostly token since he preferred to spend his time practicing at arms or conducting demesne business. Of course, unlike Mathe, Adderstone was not without a lady to oversee such frivolity. Indeed, it had two—Quintin and her mother. Not that Lady Maeve was the force she had once been...

Once more pressed by worry, Quintin told herself, *Now she knows I am well, she is well. No matter how much she dislikes Lady Elianor, she has Bayard and Hulda. She is not alone.*

"You are bothered," Griffin said.

Embarrassed at staring at him as if he were empty space, she shook her head. "I am well."

His eyes told he did not believe her, but he said, "The servants have been informed they are to take direction from you."

As if I am their lady already, she thought and glanced at Thomasin, who reached to Sir Otto to lift her out of the saddle. "What of your daughter?" she asked, though she knew the answer.

"As I am sure you have witnessed, she is not comfortable ordering servants."

Too true. The young woman was quick to do for herself and others those things with which servants—especially her maid—were more often tasked. And this morn, a hushed argument between father and daughter had ensued when Griffin pulled Thomasin away from the ledgers to assist the cook in planning the Christmas Day menu. Quintin guessed her reluctance had much to do with the common life she had first led.

"Certes, she will thank you for it," he said. "Too, it will benefit her to see how the lady of a castle handles her responsibilities to her lord and people."

Quintin was tempted to point out she was not Lady of Castle Mathe, Griffin was not her lord, and his people were not hers, but it seemed petty. Too, he watched her so closely, it struck her this might be his way of revealing he would soon wed her.

Before she could ask again, he said, "I am near to deciding."

At least he moved in the right direction. "Then I am near to accepting."

He smiled, and when a shivering, snow-dampened Arturo appeared beside her, he reached to the wolfhound.

Alarmed to discover the dog had waited all this time for her return, Quintin watched as he swiped his tongue over Griffin's hand. Though she did not like the beast, she was touched by his steadfastness. It also helped that he no longer growled at her but suffered in silence.

"I will see you in the hall," she said to Griffin and, joined by his daughter, departed the stables with Sir Victor following. But hardly had they reached the inner bailey than Thomasin halted, pushed back her mantle, and searched a hand across her waist.

"What is it?"

"I tucked a sprig of mistletoe 'neath my belt." She peered over her shoulder. "Hopefully, 'twas lost in the outer bailey."

"There is plenty more." Quintin nodded at the wagon being unloaded at the keep.

"Ah, but this was a particularly pretty sprig. I will be but a moment." She hastened back beneath the inner portcullis.

Accompanied by Arturo—and more discreetly, Sir Victor—Quintin stepped nearer the gatehouse door that accessed the tower room she did not miss. As she watched Thomasin, a villager entering the door in the outer portcullis caught her eye. He was hooded, but something about the height, breadth, and slight hunch—even the stride—called to mind one who made her fist seek her abdomen.

But it could not be the woman who had aided Constance in drugging and cuckolding Bayard. As her brother had told, Agatha of Mawbry was imprisoned beneath Castle Adderstone. Surely she was still there.

"Aude!" Thomasin lifted her skirts and ran forward, then halted and slowly turned where she stood as if seeking the one she had called to. Shoulders dropping as if with a sigh, she began to search the ground for her mistletoe.

When she returned, it was with a muddied and crushed sprig between thumb and forefinger. "I ought to have put it in my pouch," she bemoaned.

"Aude?" Quintin asked as they continued to the keep.

"A friend. Though I have never known her to enter Mathe's walls, I am fair certain I saw her, but she so suddenly disappeared—" She gasped. "Do not look, but my grandfather is at his window. He has opened his shutters, and I saw the curtains move."

Was he watching now as Quintin was fairly certain he had watched that night his son had returned her to the tower room?

"He has asked after you," Thomasin said as they ascended the steps, "though not in words."

"What mean you?"

She laughed. "He is wily—knows well how to work a conversation around to where he wishes it."

"What have you told him?"

"That though 'tis true you put a blade to his son's throat, you would not have harmed him."

"He cannot be pleased."

She made a face. "He is vexed—indeed, nearly as much with my father."

"Why your father?" Because of what the old baron had looked upon the night Griffin and she had paused in the bailey and his son had laid a hand to her face and she had readied herself for his kiss?

"He has not visited the apartment since the night you attempted to breach my grandfather's sanctuary," Lady Thomasin said as they entered the hall where servants had gathered to transform the great room into a celebration of their savior's birth. "Thus, my grandfather feels more neglected than usual."

"Why does your father stay away?"

A great sigh. "Relations between Ulric and him have oft been strained—even ere my coming, I am told."

Given Ulric de Arell's unscrupulous reputation, Quintin was further encouraged by the young woman's account that there had long been discord between the two De Arells—more proof the man she had believed was as dishonorable as his sire was not.

Lady Thomasin leaned so near her shoulder bumped Quintin's upper arm. "'Twas my grandfather who concealed my existence," she said low. "Had my mother not done me one kindness ere she left me for her lover—providing me with my sire's name should I ever be in dire need—my father would never have known he had a daughter."

"Thus, he cannot forgive the old baron," Quintin said and was surprised by a twinge of sympathy for Ulric de Arell. The man whose jealousy had long lit the feud between the three families was not deserving of sympathy, and she would not judge Griffin ill for holding himself apart from one who had denied him the daughter for whom he clearly felt affection.

Quintin frowned. Why did he, unlike many men who cast their misbegotten children to the wind, care for Thomasin? So much he had not only come to her aid but claimed her alongside his legitimate son? Because the young man he had been had loved her mother deeply? Or did he but take responsibility for his wrongs? Regardless, it further evidenced how mistaken she had been about him.

Lady Thomasin halted before a table below the dais upon which the greenery was being laid out. "I believe my father has mostly forgiven the old baron"—she snapped a piece of mistletoe from a large bunch—"but still my grandfather can be most unpleasant."

"And you have forgiven him?"

She clicked her tongue. "I have, and I am fond of him—so much sometimes my heart hurts for how alone he is, that not even his beautiful cage gives him comfort of the sort he longs for." She looked to Quintin. "I cannot stand to be long indoors. Imagine a man who has ridden the breadth and depth of England reduced to walls whose only blessing— and greatest curse—are windows that allow him to look out upon a tiny piece of all that is now ever denied him."

Justice, perhaps? Quintin pondered. A righting of wrongs for all the misery visited on others? Not that she would suggest such to this one whom she wished in this moment were her sister-in-law, liking Thomasin as she doubted she would ever like Lady Elianor.

"Too morose!" The young woman waved the mistletoe. "I shall take this piece of the outdoors to my grandfather, allow him to satisfy his need to grumble at someone, and return to assist with the greenery." She turned but came quickly back around. "Forget not that my father is to know nothing of my visits to the old baron."

As she was not to know he was well aware of them. "I will say naught."

Thomasin grinned and departed the hall, leaving Quintin amid servants who grudgingly looked to her for direction. And so she instructed them where to hang and spread and wrap the greenery, faltering only when Griffin appeared, but quickly resuming her lady's duties beneath his gaze.

Hours later, finding herself alone with the Baron of Blackwood in an alcove whose opening they had draped with pine boughs, she stepped near to allow him to tuck a sprig of mistletoe in her hair. He tucked and stepped nearer yet.

And kissed her.

Oh, how he kissed her.

And how she wished he would decide soon.

16

~~~

"QUIETUS." ON MISTED breath that dipped and arched, Ulric de Arell sent that word's seven distinct sounds out of his body. And watched them dissolve across this day upon which others celebrated life.

Life, he bitterly mused. *Quietus* was the better of the two words. And how he esteemed it—that it was beautiful regardless if one shouted it loudly enough to bleed the ears or spoke it softly enough to soothe a wailing infant. More, he loved its meaning that was wondrously opposite that other word which promised much but disappointed more.

"Quietus," he said again and felt the tightness in his chest loosen as the exquisite word for death assured him of a release from pain, anger, and heartache. Of course, none would believe him capable of that last— except, perhaps, his son's great mistake.

Though he told himself he cared not whether his granddaughter came this day to tilt upon her stool and speak of what went in the castle, upon the barony, and in the world, he assured himself she would come.

On this Christmas Day, marked by sunshine that made a meal of the snow, she would slip abovestairs once she believed her absence would not be noted. And Ulric would suffer her impertinence and name her *Sin* and she would name him *Fiend*—which he rather liked, though he would not have her know it.

A boy's laugh, one especially treasured for how rarely it reached his ears, moved him to the side of the window to ensure he was not seen.

Gripping the curtain with a painfully bunched hand, he waited for his grandson to come into view. And as always, he ached over watching from a distance as Rhys grew into a man. How he longed to be nearer the one born of the loins of his loins. But it could never be.

Just as Griffin would not risk the boy inside the apartment, neither would the leprous Ulric. Rhys was the only De Arell heir, and even if the Boursier woman bore Griffin a dozen children, her foul blood would render all unworthy. Thus, there would only ever be Rhys to speak the De Arell name into the centuries.

When the boy appeared in the bailey below, Ulric bent his mouth into as near a smile as he was capable of. A finer lad there had never been—not even Griffin, of whom Ulric was more proud than he would admit. Though not as proud of recent.

It was one thing to be forced to wed the Boursier woman, another that force was not needed. Desire only, Ulric hoped. The longing to bed a woman could be satisfied with many a comely wench, whereas infatuation thinking itself love—that great crippler of men—could make ruin of all things, as when Griffin had become besotted with that lowly chambermaid.

If not for Thomasin's common mother, whom Ulric had refused to allow his son to wed, the divide between father and son would not have widened. If not for the revelation of Thomasin's existence, the foot-bridge the years had built across that divide would have strengthened sufficiently to bear more weight. But Thomasin had made herself known to Griffin who, too often taking responsibility for others' mistakes and misfortunes, had claimed that slip of a girl whom Ulric had once wished to see as diseased as he. Once...

Now Griffin came into view below—and the Boursier woman, who accepted the arm offered her by the one who would have fared better to remain her jailer.

Curse her! Ulric seethed. Then he cursed the body of Archard Boursier's wife that had pushed that one out into the world, thereby furthering the line that would otherwise have ended once Lady Maeve died—or should end. There were times Ulric sensed another Foucault hand was responsible for much of the feuding between the families. Impossible, but felt.

The hem of his long tunic shifted, evidence of the little dog who liked to travel alongside its master's feet. Then a wet nose bumped Ulric's ankle—one of many distinctive warnings issued by Diot when someone ventured to the third floor.

This time it was his granddaughter, as confirmed by another wet bump. Had it been Griffin, Diot would growl low, indicative of the strain between father and son. Were it a stranger, as on the night Quintin Boursier had sought to reach the apartment, a savage bark would sound.

Ever grateful for the warning his sanctuary was about to be trespassed upon, giving him time to set aright things for which he might suffer further humiliation, Ulric fumbled for one of many walking sticks Thomasin had fashioned for him. He detested the branches pared of their small limbs, their bulbous tops smoothed to aid the palm in bearing the weight of the body leaning into them. Detested, yet clung to one or another when he had only Diot in his great alone. It would not do for Thomasin to know how much he depended on her gifts, since it would make her happier than she had a right to be.

As Ulric concealed the walking stick behind the chest to the left of the window, Diot bumped his ankle again.

"Aye, she comes," he muttered and turned toward the door beyond one of several floor-to-ceiling hangings that shifted in the chill air wafting through the window.

There were her footsteps, the requisite rap, then silence as she counted to twenty to allow him to further prepare for her entrance.

Deciding against donning the carved mask that best hid his decaying face, he lifted the cowl pooled about his shoulders and drew it over his head and forward so its shadow concealed what none were permitted to look upon—none save the accursed physician whom Diot detested as much as he.

The door opened, and Thomasin called, "A blessed Christmas to you, Fiend."

Flexing the hand that longed for the support of a walking stick, he stepped out from behind the hanging and saw his granddaughter lingered in the doorway. "Get you in here," he snapped. "I would know what goes below."

"For that I have come." She entered and closed the door.

"Quintin Boursier," he said as she moved toward the stool from which she would deliver the outside world to him. "Is your fool of a father further besotted?"

She sat, drew her knees up and wrapped her arms around them, and leaned back. "Certes, where his lips cannot venture, his eyes go." She grinned. "As do Lady Quintin's—much to your displeasure, I am sure."

"Much," he rasped and hated there was no way to remove the temptation of the Boursier woman the same as he had done Thomasin's mother.

Curse King Edward! he seethed. *Curse Edward's throne! Curse Edward's kingdom! Curse this world that makes giants into bowing, scraping beings who only appear to be men!*

Drawing a great breath that caused his lungs to ache, he forced his weak legs forward until ten feet separated his diseased body from the one who bloomed with good health he wished he could begrudge her as once he had done.

When Diot had settled in, his small paws and nose jutting from beneath the tunic's hem, Ulric said, "Tell me more, Sin."

With a vaguely suppressed smile that bespoke satisfaction she possessed something he coveted, she began.

He was decided. Or nearly so.

Griffin grunted. After he and Quintin had hung greenery in the hall four days past and she had returned his kiss with a passion equal to his, the decision had mostly been made in favor of gaining the wife he wanted. Mostly.

The day's Christmas festivities soon to be put to bed alongside its celebrants, Griffin left Quintin in conversation with his daughter before the hearth and mounted the stairs. It was time to visit the one whose displeasure he had felt earlier in the day when Rhys, Quintin, and he had walked out of doors, allowing Thomasin an opportunity to steal abovestairs.

Griffin's tread moving from the corridor to the third floor stairs gave rise to low growls, the means by which the dog he had gifted to an unappreciative Ulric years past alerted the old baron to the new baron's approach. And the little beast, who had long forgotten its gratitude to the one who had rescued the pup following his mother's rejection, was far from welcoming when Griffin entered his father's apartment.

Growling more deeply, Diot nipped at the booted ankles of the intruder who swung the door closed.

"I wondered when the much too important Baron of Blackwood would next deign to visit his neglected, infirm sire," Ulric called in a grating voice from where he sat against the bed's cushioned headboard. Then he patted his thigh to return the dog to his side.

Diot scuttled away, sprang onto the mattress, and seated himself alongside his master's knee.

With further accusation, Ulric said, "Sir Mathieu visits me more often than you."

As Griffin permitted, Blackwood's senior household knight of nearly three score aged having served the old baron before he had served the new, and surely the nearest Ulric could come to calling another a friend. Not that he would.

Griffin halted at the foot of the bed and peered into the eye holes of the mask his father had surely fit upon being alerted to a visitor. The mask was another ill-received gift, but worn often enough to show it was appreciated—as were the walking sticks Thomasin smuggled abovestairs, though it was rare to catch sight of one.

"A good Christmas Day to you, Ulric." Griffin inclined his head.

"Good it has not been." The mask gave his father's voice a wooden cast.

"A feast of viands was delivered, you saw Rhys, Thomasin visited, and now I am here."

"Rhys," Ulric rasped. "Hardly did the boy fill my eyes ere that woman appeared and spoiled all."

"Her name is Quintin Boursier, and since you will be seeing her often, albeit from a distance, you must needs become accustomed to the sight of her."

"The only thing I must needs do is think on a way around the king's decree so you are not made to waste your life on a Boursier."

"There is no way around it." Certes, none he wished to find, Griffin mused. "Accept it and let it burden you no further."

"Accept! 'Twas ill enough when it was your misbegotten daughter who must wed one of them, but now it falls to you…" Ulric grunted, and Griffin inwardly grimaced that in this father and son sounded much alike. "Blessedly, much can happen ere you wed, especially now it is possible King Edward will reverse his decree."

Despite his diseased body, Ulric's mind remained shrewd. He knew Lady Elianor's impersonation of Thomasin, among the many things Griffin's daughter had surely shared with him, had caused Baron Boursier to miss the appointed day by which he must lawfully wed. What he did not know was that, regardless of the king's acceptance of Boursier's marriage, regardless of who would be awarded the baronies of Godsmere and Emberly should they be forfeited, the decree meant to bind the De Arells and Boursiers would likely be honored. And soon.

His father leaned forward. "You have something in mind."

Usually more heedful of his expressions in Ulric's presence, Griffin rebuked himself.

After a long, considering silence, his father said, "But methinks, not what I have in mind after what I witnessed between that Boursier woman and you."

Griffin raised his eyebrows.

"Spare me the arrogant smile, boy!"

Ulric's attempt to reduce his son from a man who had well-earned his spurs to a youth playing at swords did not anger as it once had, but it irked enough that though Griffin's smile had not been intentional, there was intent in allowing it to linger. "Alas, neither does Lady Quintin like my smile." *Rather, not in the beginning,* he silently amended. "She also thinks it arrogant."

Ulric jerked. "Unlike that termagant's brother, the son of Ulric de Arell has more right to be arrogant than most."

Griffin was not surprised his father took offense, and it tempted him to laughter. But he contained it, certain it would land them in no good place.

More silence, during which Griffin guessed that if not for the mask, he would glimpse on his father's face realization followed by dismay. Then Ulric cleared his throat. "Tell me what you are thinking so I might give counsel."

"I do not seek advice, Ulric. Though the king will be displeased Boursier was not wed by the appointed day, the circumstances of the delay give him good cause to be lenient—with the Boursiers if not the Verduns. Thus, I believe the decree will stand, I shall wed Lady Quintin, and she will be mother to Rhys and the sons and daughters made of our union."

His father's gloved, misshapen hands convulsed at his sides, causing Diot to move onto his master's lap. Cupping a hand around the dog's chest, Ulric slowly worked his fingers into its fur. "That is the only good of her—that she is no slight, frail thing like Johanna." He grunted. "A pity your wife proved such a poor breeder."

Griffin tensed.

Diot growled.

As if unaware of what he roused in his son, Ulric mused, "Or perhaps 'tis not such a good thing the Boursier woman is of good childbearing size."

Then he contemplated the same end for Quintin that had taken Johanna from her husband and their son. Meaning here they were again, Ulric never content to let be what Griffin also struggled to let be.

Though he often excused his father's words and behavior by telling himself they made the old baron feel alive amidst his slow death, Ulric went too far—just as he had done when he had sent Alice from Blackwood…when he had suggested his sixteen-year-old son's lover had run off with a man-at-arms…when he had not disclosed the chambermaid was with child…when he had denied Griffin knowledge of his daughter for fourteen years and Thomasin had suffered for it.

"Nay, not a good thing," Ulric said with finality. "De Arell blood is strong, but tainted by Boursier blood—"

"Enough!"

Ulric startled so hard his head struck the headboard. And Diot sped to the foot of the bed and loosed teeth-baring growls and sharp barks upon the one he believed was the aggressor.

The ache in Griffin's hands evidencing how much they longed to pound flesh and bone, he said, "We are done," and crossed the room.

"Griffin!" Ulric called as the door was flung open. "I should not have…"

Without looking around, Griffin said, "Nay, you should not have." And leaving his father to the regrets due him, he was all the more determined to gain the one whose loss would leave *him* with regrets.

On the morrow, then.

17

He had decided. She knew it the moment she lifted her lids on a morn that was so cloaked in dark it required every flicker of candlelight Griffin brought within to give shape to her chamber.

Filling her eyes with the man who halted near her bed, she whispered, "When?"

He smiled. "Now."

She pushed up on her elbows. "I am flattered you are so eager to deliver your tidings, but my patience could have stretched until the rising of the sun."

He stepped nearer, and as he set the candle on the bedside table, she noted he was fully clothed. "But my patience cannot await the rising of the sun, *my* lady," he said, and she noted the emphasis he placed on that one word. "As soon as you are dressed, we shall be on our way."

"Where?"

"As there is no priest at Mathe, we shall ride to the chapel outside the village of Cross. There a priest awaits us."

"But…" She shook her head. "Arrangements have been made?"

"Aye."

Quintin sat up, and as the coverlet pooled around her waist, saw his eyes move down her thinly-clad torso and was struck that if they did wed this day, this night she would be bared to him. And that thought so warmed her, she felt lightheaded. But the next thought so chilled her, she trembled. Were there enough light, he would see the scar. Were there not, he might feel it, though its ridge had smoothed over the years. Thus, Griffin would know their union could prove childless.

Tell him now, spoke the voice that knew truth was best served very warm.

It was, of course, too late for that, but were it not served until this eve, it would come to him deathly cold.

Tell him, else he might hate you for always.

Hate me for what his brother wrought? she bitterly countered.

Tell him.

She clenched handfuls of the coverlet. *What if he decides against wedding me? Of no use will I be in preventing Godsmere from being stolen from the Boursiers.*

"Is this not what you want, Quintin?"

She groped for words to explain her silence. Blessedly, an excuse was at hand. "I am but surprised that after keeping me waiting so long, of a sudden you deliver your answer. An answer you knew well enough in advance that a priest awaits us."

"There was much to consider—and yet to consider. But we will speak of it during the ride."

In the dark of pre-dawn, as if imperative they be away from Castle Mathe ere the sun shone.

Suspicious, she asked, "Sir Victor?"

"He shall not accompany us."

She looked to the door and saw Griffin had not left it open as in the past. And with good reason. "You think to wed me in secret."

He inclined his head. "As 'tis proper we not wed until word is received the king accepts your brother's delay in fulfilling the decree, it would not do to further stir Edward's displeasure. Do we, he might set himself against all three families."

Quintin tossed back the covers and dropped her feet to the floor. Assuring herself that receiving him in naught but her chemise was no less proper than all the improprieties thus far defining their relationship, she stood. "Lest you forget, the reason I proposed we wed sooner rather than later was to give further credence to my brother's marriage. If the king remains uninformed we have spoken vows, 'tis of no benefit to Bayard."

Once again, his eyes traveled down her, making her more aware of her thin chemise. "Very well," he said, "we will do this here." He retrieved the robe from the foot of the bed, handed it to her, and lowered into the nearby chair.

When the garment was snugged about her, Quintin perched on the edge of the bed. "Pray, explain."

"I believe the king will rule fairly, that consummation of your brother's marriage to Lady Elianor and testimony provided by Father Crispin and me are sufficient to ensure Godsmere and Emberly are not forfeited. And that it will then fall to the two of us to join our houses."

She frowned. "If you are so confident, why wed me now ere the king makes his determination?"

Candlelight flickering across his disturbed brow, he said, "You told I think too much and, certes, on this I have. Thus, I would be guilty of hubris did I not acknowledge the possibility I err—that the king shall decide against your brother."

"But if Bayard is dispossessed, a marriage between De Arell and Boursier will not be necessary."

Sitting forward, he clasped his hands between his knees. "Not necessary, but what I want. As much, methinks, as you want it."

She nearly denied it, but it would be a terrible lie.

His jaw shifted. "There is something else I would have."

Fully awake now, mind working backward and forward, she narrowed her eyes. "Godsmere and Emberly by way of marriage to one of Foucault blood."

"*If* they are forfeited."

She drew a sharp breath. "You would make me a piece on your game board."

Griffin pushed out of the chair, lowered to his haunches, and caught up her hands. "I would make you my wife, ensuring your place and your mother's."

Even if her womb remained empty as feared? "What if the king does not award you the baronies? If he gives them to another?"

"For that, we quietly wed this day—so he cannot also give *you* to another. Then I shall risk Edward's displeasure to make it known you are mine."

He seemed so sincere, and yet...

She dropped her chin as anger, fear, and longing wet her eyes and made her wonder at having never been as susceptible to tears as she had become since entering Castle Mathe.

Griffin lifted her face. "What does it tell you that it would be of less detriment to the De Arells were I to wait on wedding you?" At her silence, he answered, "That I want you enough to weather a king's wrath. Nay, I will not foolishly announce we speak vows this day, but if needs be to ensure I do not lose you, it will be revealed we are wed."

She pressed her lips inward. He wanted her, but he also wanted more children. Were Bayard denied and the baronies awarded to one other than Griffin, would her husband stay her side once his desire was slaked? The marriage being made in secret, he could disavow it altogether.

Nay. When first she came here, she would have believed that of him, but not this day. He might come to regret wedding her regardless of what the king decided about Godsmere and Emberly, but all the days of their lives they would pass as man and wife.

"Who will bear witness?" she asked.

"Sir Mathieu."

She liked the knight, though Griffin had revealed the man had served Ulric de Arell before him and remained in contact with the old baron. "You think he will hold close our marriage, even from your father?"

"Until told otherwise."

She forced a smile. "Then I ought to dress."

Relief smoothing the lines of his face, he drew her to her feet and lightly kissed her. "No regrets, Quintin."

"None," she agreed and sent to the heavens, *Lord, make it so.*

A simple ceremony, and yet Quintin thought it could not have been lovelier had it been properly public. As if the earth paused in its turning to bear witness to the man and woman standing outside the church doors, peace had girded all.

The only things to disturb that beautiful still as she had stood beside Griffin were low-spoken vows meant to entwine two lives into a single stronger strand, birdsong, the scuttling of small animals over frozen ground, the nickering of horses, and the sun sifting its dawning light through trees that were less dense near the village of Cross than those around Castle Mathe.

Despite disquiet over wedding in secret and the chill air that caused her to hold her fur-lined mantle close, Quintin had been warmed by the hand holding hers and the broad fingers sliding the ring into place. Then Griffin's lips lingering so long on hers that, forgetting to breathe, she gasped loudly when he lifted his head. As his mouth went aslant, she had pushed to her toes and kissed him again. He had chuckled, as had Sir Mathieu and the priest.

The nuptial mass that followed inside the chapel had been fittingly solemn, and then it was done.

Now as Quintin rode at a leisurely pace beside Griffin beneath a sun whose position told it was past the nooning hour, she looked at the ring on her gloved hand—somewhat ashamedly for how often it captured her regard. Not because it was beautiful, but because of what it symbolized. And her wonder that she should care.

She was the fourth De Arell bride to wear it—after Griffin's grandmother, his mother, and his departed wife, Johanna. The gold band was set with three stones, the amethyst signifying piety and martyrdom, the beryl purification, and the red jasper love. It was that last she looked longest upon and over which she chided herself for being fanciful. It was not at all like Quintin Boursier. Of course, now she was Quintin de Arell.

But love? That was hardly possible, though perhaps she would grow into it.

"You seem to like my ring on your hand as much as I," Griffin said.

She shrugged. However, the gesture was so lacking nonchalance she laughed. "I do like it."

"I am pleased," he said, and she sensed a lessening of his tension that was surely due to her unease over the circumstances under which they had wed. He jutted his chin in the direction of Castle Mathe that had come into view minutes earlier. "With regret, the ring must be removed."

Before they rode over the drawbridge with the felled deer that was to account for their early departure.

Quintin glanced at Sir Mathieu where he rode behind, leading the horse over which the two men had tied the deer they had hunted following the wedding ceremony. The fresh venison at table this eve would make their meal as near a wedding feast as was possible without any but the three of them knowing it was the Lady of Blackwood who presided over it alongside her husband—her left hand as bereft of a ring as it had been when first she had sat at table with the man who was no longer her enemy.

"Alas," she said and passed her reins to him. As he guided her horse with his, she unfastened her necklace from which a cross hung and threaded the ring onto it. Then she secured the gold chain about her neck and tucked cross and ring into her bodice.

"This eve, you shall wear it again when we are together as man and wife," Griffin said.

This eve. Once more, the prospect of being intimate with him thrilled and frightened her. She longed for the promise of what there was to learn beyond kisses and caresses, but how would he react when he saw the result of his brother's cuckolding? *If* he saw...

Not for the first time, she considered snuffing the candles and hoping his hands did not learn what his eyes could not. It would only delay the inevitable, but it *was* her wedding night.

Griffin reached her reins to her. "This eve, no mere imaginings of how you will fit against me," he said when their hands touched.

Warmth suffused her face, and feeling more a girl than a woman, she boldly said, "Methinks what remains of the day shall seem much too long."

He laughed. "'Tis good you have grown accustomed to my smile. Such talk inclines me to it—and makes me long to press it to yours."

She marveled at having previously deemed its half hitch arrogant and self satisfied—of course, it had been whilst they were enemies—but since Bayard's departure, she more often saw its wonder, amusement, and flirtation. Rather than offend, it made her smile in return, and so she did until they drew near Mathe's walls.

As expected, awaiting them in the outer bailey was not only Arturo, who had hours past accompanied them to the stables, but Sir Victor. A vexed Sir Victor, though few would know it to look upon him.

Quintin had known he would not like that she had departed without his escort, but Griffin had said Sir Mathieu's witness to their marriage would have to suffice since her brother's knight might insist it be delayed until the king made his determination.

"Baron de Arell," Sir Victor said as Griffin swung out of the saddle, "you ought to have informed me of your plan to take Lady Quintin hunting so I could accompany her as is the charge given me by my lord."

"I considered it." Griffin reached Quintin's side ahead of the other man and lifted her down.

Since she would not be so near him again until she joined him in the lord's solar this night, she was reluctant to lift her hands from his shoulders.

He must have seen it on her face, for he said low, "This eve," and turned to her brother's knight. "My apologies, Sir Victor, but 'tis a poor host who unnecessarily disturbs his guest's rest in the absence of need. And as you can see, naught befell your lady that might reflect ill on you. Her restlessness has been calmed by a day of riding and hunting, and she is all the better acquainted with the one she shall soon call husband."

Quintin stepped before Sir Victor. "I did not mean to cause you worry. Since the man I believed to have stolen my brother from his bed has proved himself an ally, I saw no harm in joining him."

"No harm? Regardless of whether or not you are to be his wife, Lady Quintin, 'tis unseemly you rode from Castle Mathe without me."

She smiled, and feeling one side of her mouth tug higher than the other, wondered what other mannerisms of Griffin's might find their fit on her face in the years to come. "No more unseemly than that I rode on Adderstone," she reminded him.

"You err, my lady, for then you had an escort."

She nodded at Sir Mathieu. "Baron de Arell and I were not alone."

Sir Victor's nostrils flared with a breath that returned composure to him. "I would have your word that whilst you remain under my watch, you will not venture forth again without me."

She glanced at Griffin.

"Your word," her brother's knight insisted, "else I shall eschew the chamber Baron de Arell gave me and sleep on the floor outside your door."

And no wedding night would she have. "Very well. Do I go venturing again beyond Castle Mathe's walls, I shall do so in your company."

He nodded curtly.

Griffin stepped forward. "As Sir Mathieu and I will be occupied in seeing fresh venison on the table this eve, and I am sure Lady Quintin would like to rest, I shall leave her in your care, Sir Victor."

"My lady." The knight motioned her to precede him.

Looking one last time at Griffin, Quintin slid a hand up beneath the cover of her mantle and touched the ring nestled between her breasts.

Upon reaching the great hall, she was relieved Lady Thomasin was not present, there being nothing Quintin wanted more than to enjoy a bath and a long rest in preparation for the night ahead.

Sir Victor saw her to her chamber, and at her bidding departed for the kitchen to arrange for bath water to be heated.

Feeling the fatigue of her early rising and all that had followed, Quintin crossed the room. As she sank onto the bed, she mused that she would not sleep there this eve. But then, neither might she sleep in Griffin's bed.

18

THE SLEEP OF the eternal, for which the one remaining Foucault might find it hard to forgive him.

Griffin stared at Thomasin who delivered grim tidings, she who was not to have known that when she ventured outside the walls, ever a knight followed at a distance to ensure her safety. But now she knew, Sir Otto having been forced to reveal himself when, during her return from a nearby village, Baron Boursier had overtaken Thomasin.

However, Otto's defense of his lord's daughter had been unnecessary. Boursier's ride across Blackwood had not been an act of aggression. He had come to deliver news to his sister of her mother's passing. And yet he had deferred that pressing duty when Thomasin inadvertently revealed the location of the hovel where a friend of hers dwelt—a woman she called Aude—whom Boursier had suggested might be Agatha of Mawbry. If so, had the one who aided Lady Elianor in imprisoning the Baron of Godsmere escaped her own imprisonment?

Griffin pressed his hands to the table in his solar where Thomasin had insisted she reveal that which made her nearly breathless. "Speak to me of this Aude."

"As I told The Boursier, she is a simple woman, a wanderer upon the three baronies who aids me in distributing food to the poor." She raised her eyebrows as if challenging him to rebuke her for taking food from Mathe.

But he knew about her ventures. And approved. "Continue."

"He wished to know when last I had seen her, and I told 'twas five days past here at Mathe." She frowned. "And peculiar that was since never have I known her to enter the walls, and as she did not seek me out after I lost sight of her, she seems not to have come for me."

Griffin looked to Sir Otto who stood alongside Sir Victor at the end of the table. As he was the knight most often tasked with following Thomasin, he asked, "You have seen this Aude?"

"I have, my lord. As Lady Thomasin tells, she appears harmless, so much methinks her simple minded."

It did not sound like the cunning Agatha whom Griffin knew only by word of mouth, but that did not mean it was not. He returned to Thomasin where she stood opposite him. "So now Baron Boursier rides for that woman's hovel you say is upon the lake where the three baronies converge."

"Aye, he seemed to think she is in danger."

In danger? Or *a* danger? Likely the latter, considering the import of informing his sister of her mother's death.

With whom had Thomasin been consorting?

She sighed. "He said he shall explain all later, and I should tell you and Sir Victor of Lady Maeve's death so you may be prepared to relinquish his sister for her return to Godsmere to bury and mourn her mother."

"He would himself reveal to Lady Quintin her loss?"

"Aye."

Griffin lowered his head between his outstretched arms. This day, the joy of a wedding was met with the sorrow of a death. While he had spoken vows with Quintin, had her mother, who would never know her Foucault blood would live on in the generations born of his union with her daughter, breathed her last? And how would Quintin receive the tidings?

He nearly groaned in remembrance of her concern over being long absent from her mother and insistence she depart Mathe with her brother. Though she had admitted she preferred to remain with Griffin, a daughter's loyalty would have returned her to Lady Maeve had he allowed it. But he had been determined to ensure the woman who entranced him was all the sooner his.

He looked up. "Did Baron Boursier reveal the cause of death?"

"He did not."

"When shall he arrive to escort her home?"

"He did not say, though surely by the morrow. What will you do, Father?"

He straightened. "Honor his wish that he be the one to tell Lady Quintin of her mother's passing."

And pray her loss does not come between us, he silently added.

The abundance of venison lent a festive air to the wedding feast though only three knew it for what it was. But most peculiar, that air did not extend to Griffin. The smiles he returned were forced and not one was uneven.

Under cover of the table, Quintin had placed a hand on her husband's thigh, and when he looked at her and she asked if all was well, his assurances had not been genuine. Something troubled him. As then, now her mind turned over the possibility he regretted taking her to wife. Still, when he came abovestairs, he would find her waiting.

Having remained in her chamber while others sought their night's rest—among them Thomasin and Rhys who shared a chamber and Sir Victor who had so often looked kindly upon her during supper he had surely forgiven her—she had slipped out after Griffin's squire finished readying his lord's chamber for the night. Though she had feared Arturo would follow her, he had merely raised his head and watched as she entered the solar.

Some of what the squire had done Quintin had undone. With the iron poker, she had rearranged the logs on the fire so they did not burn as bright. She had extinguished the candles except for the one on the table beside her. And sitting on the mattress against the headboard, she had drawn up to her waist the covers the young man had turned down.

And so she waited, often touching the stones in the ring she had returned to her finger and pressing her arms to her sides when shivers of anticipation ran through her.

At last, the sound of boots coming off the stairs. One set only. Had Griffin and she wed openly, he would have been accompanied by select guests who would put him to bed with his bride. She did not miss that ritual, though she prayed for Bayard's retention of his lands that would give Griffin and her occasion to wed before others. Her mother would not like losing her daughter, but she would wish to witness the ceremony.

The door opened, and she felt more than saw Griffin's gaze fall upon her as he entered the warmly glowing chamber.

He secured the door, crossed the solar, and halted at the foot of the bed.

Had there been only the hearth's fire at his back, she would not have seen the set of his face, but the candle beside her cast enough light to show it was solemn and his eyes did not speak to her as they had done this day upon their return to the castle.

"My bride is abed," he said, no eagerness in his words.

"You do not seem pleased, Husband. Though at meal you assured me all is well, something troubles you."

"I received ill tidings late this afternoon."

"Of?"

"Naught you need worry over, though I think it best we delay our nuptial night."

Disappointment gripped her. "'Tis quite serious, then."

"It is."

"I am sorry to hear it but relieved 'tis not me who causes you to be distant. I feared you might regret your haste in wedding me."

"Nay, Quintin, I am pleased you are my wife."

In this he seemed sincere—and determined to hold her gaze lest what lay beneath her chemise proved too much temptation.

"Then come to bed." She turned back the covers on his side. "Even if only to hold me again as you did that night I feared all was lost."

And might yet be if the king denies Bayard, the thought slipped in. But she would not think there.

Griffin nearly smiled. "Certes, this time I would not be satisfied with only holding you."

"Then do not. Whatever has happened cannot be undone, aye?"

His jaw shifted. "It cannot."

"Then its worries can save until the morrow." Or could it? Might the tidings be something over which she ought to be concerned?

"I do wish to lie with you," he said, "but—"

She drew a sharp breath. "Have you received word from the king? Has he decided against Bayard?"

"Nay, no word yet."

"Then?"

"I cannot say, Quintin."

Her anger stirred, but a quarrel was not how this eve was meant to begin and end, not after the vows exchanged this morn and the words passed between them on their return to Mathe. She wanted what they had promised each other, no matter what might be learned of her.

She pushed aside the covers, revealing bare calves and ankles beneath the hem of her chemise, dropped her feet to the floor, and stepped forward.

Griffin opened his mouth as if to protest, but his eyes had strayed where he clearly did not wish them to.

She halted before him. "No matter what the day has wrought, Husband, first it beautifully wrought you and me." She slid her hands from his chest to his shoulders. "As you advised my brother, consummation is as much a measure of marriage as the speaking of vows. So on our wedding night, let us be one." She leaned up and offered her mouth.

"Quintin," Griffin groaned and took her face in his hands. It was no gentle kiss, nor was her answer to it. It was long and of such hunger that, were it of the belly, she thought she might not cease filling it even at the risk of death.

Then it ended, though only long enough for him to swing her into his arms. Reclaiming her mouth, he carried her to the mattress, followed her down onto it, and began drawing up her chemise.

As air whispered up her knees and thighs, followed by his hand, she remembered. And reached to pinch the candle's wick, leaving them in naught but the fire's glow.

Eyes glittering above hers, Griffin asked, "Is this modesty, Wife?"

That, too. More, it was the scar and his brother, neither of which had any right to her wedding night.

She laid a hand on his jaw. "Did you not once say a man and woman alone in the dark does not a restful night make?"

His laughter fanned her face. "I did, though methinks not so dark a husband's eyes are denied being as intimate with his bride's lovely form as his hands."

"Might your eyes be jealous?" she quipped, though her stomach cramped with fear he would relight the candle.

"Indeed," he murmured, "but there will be other nights. So this one...You would not have it be restful?"

She moved a hand to the belt about his tunic. "For this, I slept hours ere supper."

"You, Quintin de Arell"—he lowered his head—"are a most eager bride."

"Meaning you, Husband, ought to take advantage."

He did, and when night began to move toward day, his contented wife tucked her head beneath his chin and whispered, "I am yours."

"Of course you are," he said, and she smiled in remembrance of those being the first words he had spoken to her the day she had come before his walls and announced she was Lady Quintin of Castle Adderstone, of the barony of Godsmere, sister of Baron Boursier. Now she was of Castle Mathe, of the barony of Blackwood, wife of Baron de Arell.

And as she drifted toward sleep, it struck her that the only thing that would make her happier was tidings that Godsmere remained Boursier.

19

ꞏꞏꞏꞏꞏ

WERE IT POSSIBLE, Griffin would have his only regret of the night past be that he had not been careful to ensure his bride did not conceive whilst their marriage remained unknown, but there would be other regrets.

He should not have succumbed to Quintin's sweet seduction. Once she was told of her mother's passing, *she* would regret they had known happiness during a time better given to grieving. Though Griffin had honored the behest that Bayard Boursier be the one to inform his sister of her loss, her guilt would manifest itself in anger.

Almost wishing that when she had pressed about the ill tidings, he had delivered them, he set another log on the fire, causing the flames he had coaxed from the embers to begin an exploration of the new addition that would ensure the chamber was comfortably warm when his wife arose. It was a task usually left to his squire, who had tried the door a quarter hour past and, finding it locked, departed.

As for the maid who straightened the chamber each morn, Griffin would tell her to leave it be, allowing Quintin to sleep as long as her body asked it of her. Hopefully, a long rest would allow her to better endure her loss.

He straightened and looked around. While he had tended the fire, Quintin had turned from her side to her back. Black hair beautifully stark against the white pillow, displaced covers revealing the tops of her breasts bared by the absence of the chemise he must have rid her of during their lovemaking, she tempted him to return to her. It was good she yet slept.

He meant only to rearrange the tangled covers over her, but when he drew alongside the bed, his jealous eyes bade him look upon that which his hands had known.

He drew back the covers, and as firelight flicked at the shadows and danced across her skin, his eyes agreed with the rest of him that Quintin de Arell was beautifully formed. If not for a long, thin shadow across her belly that did not join in the dance, he might have lain down with her again.

Remembrance in his fingertips, he rubbed a thumb across them. He had felt that shadow that was not a shadow during their lovemaking, but had spent mind and body on desperate murmurings, kisses, and caresses rather than questions that could wait. Or so he had believed...

It was not necessary to touch the scar to know it was not recent, but that was all he was certain of—until he gave himself over to thought.

He had heard tale of only one injury done Quintin, and though he had thought it could not be dire, this one had been life threatening. Was it the same she had sustained in setting herself between her brother and Serle?

Lowering to his haunches, he moved his gaze to her profile. How many times whilst they were at odds, especially at mention of his brother, had he seen her press a fist to her abdomen—to that scar whose length and placement told all, the result of which could prove satisfactory to Ulric?

Or perhaps 'tis not such a good thing the Boursier woman is of good child-bearing size, his father's cruel words returned to him.

Anger having no place here and now, Griffin determinedly put Ulric from his mind, dragged a hand down his face, and returned his attention to the scar.

So *this* was what had been done to Quintin. Because of *this*—rather than her being disagreeable as he had once suggested—her betrothal was broken after Bayard Boursier's cuckolding. For *this* Griffin had sensed her unease when he spoke of children. And on the night past, *this* had made her snuff the candle, as if the scar would provide an excuse for him to seek release from their marriage.

Certes, his talk of wanting more children had given her cause to think such. And since she did not yet know him well, he could hardly begrudge her silence and…Was it deception?

Considering his family and the Verduns were largely responsible for what could prove an inability to birth children, if it was deception, neither could he begrudge her that.

What he wished to know was if she viewed the likelihood she would give him no more heirs as his family's due for what had been taken from her—vengeance of a sort, for unless she was a rare woman, she also wanted children.

Nay, unless he knew her not at all, it was not in the company of vengeance they had consummated their marriage. It had been one woman wanting the one man who would have remained unknown to her had her brother wed a De Arell.

He frowned. Was this the reason the Baron of Godsmere had chosen to wed Thomasin—so his sister would not herself suffer marriage to a De Arell? Likely, for better she wed the brother of the woman who had cuckolded, than the brother of the man who had not only cuckolded but whose bloody clash with Bayard Boursier had caused her injury.

Am I thinking too much? he wondered. *In the wrong direction?*

Too much, he decided. For now.

He stood, and as he set aright the covers as much as possible without disturbing Quintin, he discovered her chemise. His hands renewing their acquaintance with its delicate material and finding it intact, he tried to recall divesting her of the garment. He could not, but he did remember the wonder of discovering the skin beneath his hands was more silken than that woven on a loom.

Griffin folded the garment, placed it on the bedside table, then opened the drawer hidden in the table's underside and removed the

Wulfrith dagger he had taken from Quintin that first day. He laid it atop the chemise, along with her meat knife he had worn on his belt alongside his own.

Trust. As was befitting one's wife.

He turned back to her, bent, and touched his lips to her brow. "You could have told me what was done to you," he whispered.

Her lids fluttered and she murmured, "But I do not yet love you." She sighed. "I think."

Griffin straightened. In her half-dream state, was love what she believed he wished she had spoken of? And why, amid the disquiet of learning she was scarred—in the midst of foreboding over the tidings to be delivered—this twinge of pleasure she would even consider loving him?

Because if there was love, their one night together would not be the best he ever had of her. With such depth of emotion, she would get past the anger and mourning to come. The woman he had possessed, as she had possessed him, would return to him. And their dark beginning would yield to the light of an agreeable marriage.

Prayer, he determined. First prayer in the silent chapel, then he would begin his day as if it were the same as any other.

I am wed.

It was the first thought that moved through Quintin's awakening mind, and the next was that she would have liked to find her husband abed. But as revealed by the light slipping past the closed shutters, it was well into morn—might even be approaching noon. Too, with the folk of Blackwood ignorant that the solar was now a nuptial chamber, it would have seemed peculiar had Griffin not arisen in the absence of illness.

She sat up. And caught her breath when the covers fell down around her waist. She did not recall the removal of her chemise. What she did recall were the thousand and one sensations roused by her husband making all of her known to him.

"All," she breathed and pushed aside the covers and peered at the scar. It was years beyond the raw, livid thing it had been, but had Griffin's hands found it in the dark?

She touched the place where the edge of her brother's sword had begun its journey across her abdomen, closed her eyes, and traced the line all the way to its end.

Had Griffin felt it? Nay, he would have questioned it if he had. Thus, he would be told of it at a time of her choosing. But it would have to be soon, for she wished to feel again what he had made her feel.

She slid her gaze to the covers. Some were spread around her, others hung over the side and dusted the floor. Near the foot of the bed, portions of the sheet were twisted around the blanket and the blanket around the coverlet, all three connected as if they had made love as enthusiastically as...

Heat rose in her cheeks, and she snorted at being embarrassed with only her thoughts to attest to the loss of her virtue. There would be occasions aplenty to blush when she went belowstairs and faced Griffin— which she must do soon to dispel curiosity over her late rising.

She looked around and, discovering her chemise on the bedside table, gasped when she saw what lay atop it. And sweetly ached for what the Wulfrith dagger and meat knife told of how far Griffin and she had come.

With a smile so true she thought it might never leave her lips, Quintin donned her chemise. But as she belted the robe over it, out of the corner of her eye she saw red. The bottom sheet also attested to her loss of virtue. And when the solar was set aright, it would tell a tale that could not yet be told.

She stripped off the sheet and considered putting it on the fire. However, since it might later be required to prove consummation and that she had come to her husband a maiden, she folded it and placed it at the bottom of Griffin's clothes chest.

After making the bed, she cautiously exited the solar and gave thanks when she reached her chamber with only Arturo to witness her stealth.

And a good thing his vigil was, causing any who might have sought her out to believe she was inside.

The sun's position revealing she had two hours before the midday meal, she did not hurry her ablutions, using the time to compose herself lest something in her manner, eyes, or voice alerted others she was as changed as she felt. Though she had long been a woman, this day she felt older—as if, in truth, she had been but a girl.

Why? she wondered as she brushed her hair. Because in the most binding, intimate way possible, she was now a wife?

She considered her face in the hand mirror. She looked the same, though her eyes appeared softer and her mouth much liked its smile—a smile that would surely falter when Griffin learned of her injury.

"Pray, prove the man I have come to believe you are," she whispered. As she lowered the mirror, she noticed the ring. It was snug, as if it did not wish to be parted from her finger, but she wiggled it off.

When she stepped from the stairs a short while later, the ring once more hung alongside her cross beneath her bodice.

She was not surprised Griffin was absent from the hall while preparations were made to bring the nooning meal to table, but she had expected Sir Victor would be there to ensure she did not depart Mathe without him. How curious he was not—and nearly as curious that Lady Thomasin was not at the hearth since Quintin had not heard her voice, nor her brother's, in passing their shared chamber.

Only Rhys was here. Looking small where he alone occupied the high table, he was on his knees in a chair beside the lord's seat, elbows on the table, face clasped between his hands as he frowned over his wax tablet.

Quintin touched the shoulder of a servant who cast dried herbs across the rushes. "Have you seen Sir Victor?"

"Aye, milady. A messenger arrived from Godsmere a short while ago and my lord and Sir Victor withdrew to the steward's chamber to receive the tidings."

Quintin's heart sped. Had the king made his determination about Godsmere? "I thank you," she said and hastened toward the short corridor to the left of the high table.

"Lady Quintin?"

She looked to the boy who had addressed her directly—something he did only as was required of him in his father's presence, and on occasion with Thomasin, who prodded him to be civil.

Though anxious to know the tidings, Quintin longed for the boy's acceptance, and more so now she was his mother.

She altered her course and ascended the dais. "Rhys?"

He heaved a sigh. "These sums are difficult. I cannot hold the numbers long enough in my head to find the right answer. Will you..." He scratched the back of his neck. "...help me?"

Staring into eyes so like his father's, Quintin smiled. Granted, he asked for aid the sooner to be done with a task that required him to exercise his mind before he could exercise his body, but it was a beginning.

"Of course I shall." She sat beside him and, for a quarter hour, helped him work the numbers. When his answers were pressed into the wax, he pushed the tablet away and grinned—though only for a moment, as if he realized he was not ready to be so friendly. Stiffly, he thanked her and was across the hall and out the doors before Quintin reached the short corridor.

The door to the steward's quarters was closed, but as she set a hand to it, the voice of her brother's knight defied the door's attempt to render his words incomprehensible.

"Thus," Sir Jerrard said, "Baron Boursier was forced to alter his plan to retrieve his sister this day."

Bayard had been coming for her?

"Still he would be the one to tell Lady Quintin of her mother's passing?"

She stopped breathing. Those words...those ugly words spoken by Griffin found no fit in the woman who had awakened in his bed. They could not be meant how they sounded.

"Aye, whether you deliver the lady home this day or my lord comes for her on the morrow, he would be the one to speak it."

Quintin gave her head a shake. Though more and more Lady Maeve was of a weak disposition, she was not dead. At worst, she was abed and but needed her daughter to aid her in rising from it.

"I shall myself escort Lady Quintin to Godsmere so she may bury and mourn her mother, Sir Jerrard."

Bury. Mourn.

Quintin's hand on the door shook so violently the handle rattled.

"My lady?"

She snapped her head around and met Thomasin's wide-eyed gaze where the young woman stood at the mouth of the corridor.

Then the door was wrenched open. "Quintin!"

She knew her mouth was open, but when she looked to Griffin, she could not close it. Nor work her tongue around words that waited on the breath trapped beneath her throat.

He wavered before her, as did Sir Victor and Sir Jerrard beyond him.

Her husband settled a hand on her arm. "I am sorry," he said, his face so distorted it seemed she was beneath water looking up at him.

Tears, she realized as she felt warmth spill onto her cheeks. Wasted tears. There was naught over which to cry. Misunderstandings did not warrant such.

Griffin's arm was around her now, and she knew what he invited though it would be unseemly to turn into him. Perhaps had she suffered a great loss, but not over a misunderstanding.

She looked up. And how she feared the regret in his eyes! "'Tis not so." She shook her head. "Pray, explain it, for I know I heard wrong."

"I wish you had." He began to draw her near. "But—"

"Nay!" She stepped back. "You do not know what I ask. I thought I heard…But I cannot have. My mother…"

"Quintin, Lady Maeve—"

"Is well. Aye, she refuses to stir from her bed—makes much of a small ache of the head—but when I return to her, she will be on her feet again."

Griffin cupped her face between his hands, reminding her of last eve when he had done the same, but then it had been to kiss her. "Hear me, Quintin. This is not how you were meant to learn of your loss, and I am aggrieved you did, but what you heard is true. Lady Maeve——"

"Cease!" She raised her palms between them. "I do not like this."

"As I do not, but 'tis the truth."

"What my father tells is so," Lady Thomasin said. "Your brother revealed it to me and Sir Otto on the day past."

Quintin nearly rejected her words as well, but when Thomasin stepped alongside Griffin, such pity swam amid her own tears that what needed to be a misunderstanding paled. Then Sir Victor appeared over the shoulders of father and daughter.

"Your mother has passed, my lady. You have my sympathy."

She looked back at Griffin, heard again Thomasin's words. "The day past? You knew ere this day? Ere last eve?"

"I did."

Her knees softened, and he gripped her forearms to support her.

"This is the ill tidings you received last afternoon."

"'Tis."

The reason he had wanted to delay their wedding night. Honorable, and yet he had allowed his ignorant wife to convince him to consummate their marriage. And Quintin, having had few thoughts of how Lady Maeve fared since telling Griffin she wished to stay at Mathe, had not been with her mother in her time of need. What had it been? Her head? Her heart?

"Your brother insisted he be the one to tell you," Sir Victor spoke, as if in Griffin's defense.

"Why is he——?" Her voice broke, and she swallowed hard. "Why is he not here?"

"My lady," Sir Jerrard said, "the baron shall explain all upon your return to Adderstone."

If only she had returned sooner, had found a way past Griffin's determination that she remain here. Even had she failed, the effort would be of some comfort. Or would it?

What if ill befalls me whilst you are away, Daughter? her mother had pleaded. *What if I sicken and you are nowhere near to rouse me back to health?*

Something was thrusting against Quintin's insides, seeking a way out. All it needed was one crack, and when Griffin spoke her name again, that terrible thing burst past too many cracks to count.

Denying herself the comfort of her husband's arms—the longing to cling to him no matter what might be revealed about their relationship—she shoved her hands against his chest. Freed of him, she jumped back and came up against the wall.

"You said naught!"

He raised a hand. "We must needs speak. Let us go abovestairs and—"

"Oh, you would like that! To seduce me into forgetting 'twas you who denied my mother's need for me to return to her. To deny me the right to give succor and receive her farewell and give my own."

"Quintin!"

"There is naught you can say that will make right what you made wrong."

Staring at his wife, Griffin was tempted to sweep her into his arms and, no matter how she railed, carry her abovestairs.

She took a step forward. Eyes chill, she said, "Had I been a daughter rather than a prisoner, I might even have prevented her death."

"I shall take you—" He had nearly said *home,* but regardless of her anger, Mathe was now and would ever be her home. "This day, I shall return you to Adderstone for your period of mourning."

And only that, he did not say.

"I do not require your escort." She looked past him. "I shall be ready to depart within a half hour, Sir Victor." She started down the corridor.

"Forget not," Griffin's daughter called, "this all began with you, Lady Quintin."

"That is enough, Thomasin."

Ignoring her father, the young woman hastened to where Quintin halted. "It began with you," she repeated and stepped in front of her.

"You who falsely accused my father of imprisoning your brother. You who drew a dagger on him. You who but suffered comfortable confinement for an offense so dire none would have disputed a dungeon cell was more fitting."

As Griffin reached his daughter's side, Quintin lowered her chin and said, "Then the sooner Mathe is shed of me, the better for all." She stepped around them and went from sight.

"Oh, have mercy!" Thomasin raised moist eyes to her father. "I am sorry, but I love you too well and like her too much not to speak in truth."

Griffin had meant to rebuke her for not heeding his warning to leave Quintin be, but he drew his daughter against his side and kissed her head. And felt all of her ease. He did not understand why it was so hard to say he loved his first born, but he did feel that for her though he had known her only half as long as he had known his son. He ought to tell her. And he would when the time was better and it would not seem like a mere aside.

"Worry not, Daughter. All will come right." He released her. "And now I must prepare to ride to Adderstone."

"But she does not wish your escort."

"Still, 'tis my duty." *Foremost as Quintin's husband,* he silently added and strode away.

20

GUILT-SPAWNED ANGER, Quintin acknowledged what his daughter, for all of her youth, had known. It had made her turn on the man who might bear some of the blame, but not as much as she. Blessedly, there was some comfort in knowing that, regardless of what illness had stolen her mother, it would likely have done its thieving even had Quintin been present.

Draped in her fur-lined mantle, riding behind Griffin who had added a dozen knights to her escort, Quintin longed to apologize to her husband. And yet she was still angry with him though it was more her fault. He had wanted to postpone consummation, and what further excuse could he have given, having honored Bayard's wishes that he be the one to reveal her mother's death?

Dear Lord, she silently prayed and looked to the sky that would be black by the time they reached Adderstone. *Ease this anger and longing to cast upon Griffin guilt not due him. Humble this pride so I might make my regret known. Let him forgive me so I am not alone with my grieving.*

That last was selfish, but he had vowed, just as she had, to be with her for better and worse. Thus, she wanted his arms around her when she lay down in her chamber beside her mother's barren chamber.

She lowered her gaze to Griffin's back that was so tall and broad it looked capable of bearing burdens that would bend and break the backs of other men.

Here, Lady, is your husband, the priest had said. *Here, Lord, is your wife. Love each other as our Heavenly Father loves you.*

Quintin tapped her horse's sides, urging the animal to greater speed.

As if Griffin sensed her advance, he looked around and, meeting her gaze, slowed his destrier and raised an arm to command the others to ease back.

"My lady?" he said when she drew alongside.

"My lord."

He raised an eyebrow.

She moistened her lips. "'Twas ill of me to say what I did. Lady Thomasin is right. I am more responsible for not being at my mother's side."

It would hardly be appropriate for Griffin to give her a half-hitched smile, but she would not have been offended had he, she so longed to see it. But he stared at her.

"Pray, forgive me," she beseeched.

He glanced at the others, who had fallen back to allow them privacy. "I fear you will regret seeking my forgiveness, Quintin."

"I do not see how."

He grunted. "Unfortunately, there is more to the tale besides your mother's passing."

She sat straighter. "What?"

"Again, the Baron of Godsmere binds my tongue, but we are not long from Adderstone. You will know soon enough."

"You frighten me."

"I do not mean to. I but prepare my wife as best I can."

She hesitated, then reached to him, uncaring what any thought of the intimacy she sought that was hardly intimacy compared to the wondrous things learned in the nuptial bed.

Griffin closed his fingers around her gloved hand. "You wear it, do you not, Quintin?"

Then he believed it possible she had cast off his ring. "It lies above my heart."

A corner of his mouth convulsed, but still no smile. "Promise that no matter how this day ends, until my ring can be displayed on your finger, you will keep it on your person."

"You have my word. And my thanks."

"For?"

"The return of my dagger and knife."

He inclined his head. "I hoped that would please you."

"It does, though…"

"Aye?"

"I have become fond of you cutting my meat."

There, a smile, albeit slight. "Have you, indeed?"

"I have."

"I would be honored." He glanced behind. "And now, with regret, we must resume our pace to reach our destination ere night grows long. Will you ride at my side?"

"I shall."

"Then to Adderstone."

And what he told—and she tried not to think upon—was more to the tale.

Grim. There was no kinder word to describe their reception. As was fitting, Castle Adderstone was in mourning, the sorrow and pity coming off the castle folk who stood on the walls and walked the baileys nearly suffocating.

Grim even better described the Baron of Godsmere's expression as Sir Victor, having dismounted ahead of the others to draw his lord aside, revealed Quintin's knowledge of the reason her mother was not on the keep's steps.

Thus, Lady Elianor was the first to greet Quintin. "'Tis good you are home, Lady Quintin," she said with a smile so small the torchlit bailey nearly rendered it flat.

"'Tis unfortunate it is under such circumstances I return."

As the lady's eyes widened, doubtless in alarm that Lady Maeve's passing was known, Quintin's anger stirred. More than Griffin, this woman was responsible for her absence from Adderstone. Had Lady Elianor not abducted Bayard, there would have been no ride on Castle Mathe and no reason to leave Lady Maeve behind.

The gentle squeeze of Griffin's hand on Quintin's arm reminded her of his intercession when Bayard and Lady Elianor were properly wed. Griffin had urged her to sheathe her claws for her brother's sake. So she must again—for Bayard's sake and, perhaps, his wife's considering what Griffin believed had caused her to work ill on the Baron of Godsmere.

Quintin drew a deep breath. "Still, 'tis good to be at Adderstone."

The lady inclined her head. "I am sorry for your loss."

Quintin could only nod.

"And you, Baron de Arell, are welcome at Adderstone."

"I thank you, my lady."

Lady Elianor's eyes lowered to Griffin's hand on Quintin's arm, and her mouth curved a bit more. Though her note of his close attendance was disconcerting, it was not enough to cause Quintin to pull away.

Bayard strode forward. He could appear barbarous owing to the eyepatch and his size, but in the midst of night and wearing a grim expression, he seemed more so.

"I am sorry, Quintin," he said and took her into his arms. "Dear Lord, so sorry."

She clung to him, and he let her be the one to draw back. When she did, he said, "You are tired and hungry. Let us see to your needs."

She thought it would be on his arm she once more entered the great hall, but as was his duty to his wife, he turned to Lady Elianor and led her up to the keep.

But Quintin had Griffin, who also knew his duty and aided her ascent of the steps.

"First, food and drink," Bayard said as Lady Elianor and he entered the hall ahead of them.

Then the chapel, Quintin thought and was grateful Griffin's grip allowed her to arrest the impulse to fly to that place where her mother awaited their reunion. Considering what lay ahead, it would behoove Quintin to first wet her dry mouth and put something in her belly.

Upon the dais, Griffin assisted Quintin with the removal of her mantle. As he handed her into the chair beside the lord's high seat, she saw her brother similarly attended Lady Elianor—and was surprised to see what was beneath the lady's mantle. Her arm was in a sling, and when Quintin looked upon the lady's face that was better lit inside the hall, she saw fatigue amid scratches. And was that a bruise on her cheek?

Bayard put his mouth to his wife's ear, said something that made her smile softly, then settled between his wife and sister.

"As told, there is more to the tale," Griffin murmured, and she was comforted that he had taken the chair on her opposite side.

She looked back at her brother and, finding his singular gaze awaited hers, leaned near. "Though I know Lady Elianor's injuries were not dealt by you," she whispered, "are they a result of further plotting against you?"

"Nay, all is well with my wife and me."

So it appeared, but it was so unexpected considering the circumstances of their marriage that Quintin said, "I find that hard to believe."

His mouth curved. "As do I, but 'tis so."

Though she could not yet think kindly of Lady Elianor, after what Griffin had surmised of the woman's first marriage, it was impossible to dislike her as much as before. And she did hope all was well between Bayard and his wife. He deserved happiness and, perhaps, Lady Elianor was also due it.

Wine was poured ahead of the arrival of platters of bread and cheeses, but Quintin had taken only two swallows of drink and a bite of bread before a woman rushed off the stairs and cried, "My poor lamb!"

Barely recognizable with her hair a mess, eyes swollen and face flushed, it was her voice that revealed it was Lady Maeve's maid.

Bayard surged to his feet. "Return abovestairs, Hulda."

The woman's step faltered, but she continued toward Quintin. "'Twas murder that took your lady mother!"

Murder. As that word seeped into Quintin's emotions, the cracks of which were too recently repaired by her apology to Griffin, Bayard sprang over the table. One of his size should not be able to do so with grace, but he made it appear effortless and intercepted Hulda before she reached the dais.

"You vowed you would not leave your mistress's side," he gently rebuked as he turned her toward the man coming off the stairs—Father Crispin, who had wed Bayard and Lady Elianor at Castle Mathe. A gray cast to the priest's face evidencing he was ill of health as he was often of late, he put an arm around Hulda.

"But my lord," she bemoaned as she was urged opposite, "my poor lamb is home." She peered over her shoulder at Quintin. "You should not have left your mother. How she ached for you. And now…"

When she disappeared, Quintin stood. "Say 'twas not murder, Bayard. Tell me Hulda is but mad with grief."

He did not—instead ordered all but her, Griffin, and Lady Elianor to ease their hunger and thirst in the kitchen. "Sit, Quintin," he said upon his return to the dais.

Ignoring him, she moved her gaze to her husband and hated that his face was as grim as Bayard's. "*This* is more to the tale?" she demanded.

His nod was weary.

Though tempted to voice her anger, she had prayed she would not further punish Griffin for things not of his doing. And so she said, "Surely you could have better prepared your…" She had nearly named herself his wife, and though she was now tempted to name herself his prisoner, she said, "You could have better prepared your betrothed."

Bayard touched her shoulder. "I would have had this wait until you were rested, but since my wishes are once more ground underfoot, I bid you sit so I may explain."

She lowered into the chair.

"Over a sennight past," he said as he regained his seat, "Agatha escaped the underground. Upon encountering my wife, she threw her down the steps and left her for dead. Blessedly, the worst Lady Elianor suffered was a broken arm."

Quintin glanced at the lady. "Why would Agatha harm the one she aided in imprisoning you?"

"She was not the ally Lady Elianor believed, but we will speak more on that momentarily."

"Then tell me who released Agatha."

He drew a deep breath that made her hold hers. "Lady Maeve."

Quintin was on her feet again. "Your wife released that vile being! She but puts the blame on my mother. And you…" She pointed at her brother. "Once more you are under a woman's spell, just as whilst you were wed to the faithless Constance Verdun. Thus, you prefer to believe the one who betrayed is the woman who raised you as if you were her own."

"Nay, Quintin, when I confronted Lady Maeve, she admitted to releasing Agatha."

Quintin blinked. "It cannot be. My mother hated that witch for the aid she gave Constance in making a cuckold of you."

"Aye, she loathed Agatha, and all the more because the witch controlled her."

"How? And why?"

"Your mother believed their alliance was the only way to keep you safe."

"What say you?"

"Whilst Agatha served as Constance's maid at Adderstone—ere I ousted her for drugging my wine—she killed our father."

Quintin's legs weakening, she yielded to Griffin's hands on her shoulders easing her down. As he resumed his own seat, she reached to him and he enfolded her hand in his.

Looking back at Bayard, she saw he noted the intimacy between Griffin and her, just as Lady Elianor had earlier. "Continue," she said.

"Your mother suspected Agatha was responsible for Archard's death and confronted her. The witch admitted she had hastened his passing and threatened that unless Lady Maeve did her bidding, she would end your life as well. Thus, though I cannot know what your mother did for Agatha all these years, she served her."

A pounding behind her eyes, Quintin narrowed her lids. "For what does Agatha hate us so?"

"Lady Maeve said Agatha did ill in the name of the Foucaults—aiding in cuckolding me, imprisoning me, and setting our families against one another."

Movement beside Quintin drew her gaze to Griffin, and she saw from the lean of his body and intensity of his gaze he turned all this over.

"She seeks revenge, Bayard?" she asked.

"Aye. More, your mother believed she and others sought to restore the barony of Kilbourne by tearing our families asunder."

"What others?"

"Lady Maeve believed there is at least one Foucault supporter at Castle Mathe."

Feeling Griffin's hand tense, Quintin recalled the day she had prepared to go in search of her missing brother and her mother had begged her not to leave. Lady Maeve had said her daughter was not safe at Castle Mathe, and when she had warned the devil walked its corridors, Quintin had thought she referred to Ulric de Arell. But surely he was not a Foucault supporter.

"Agatha is a Foucault?" Quintin's voice trembled.

"Your mother would tell no more. She said your safety depended on her silence. However, she said that if I brought you home, she would reveal all she knew of Agatha and the others. Thus, I agreed to ride for you the next morn."

"But then found her dead."

He nodded. "The night before, she was so anxious I sent the physician to her. He assured me that though her heart troubled her as oft it did when she was overwrought, she but required a draught to help her sleep. The next morn, ere I departed for Mathe, Hulda discovered your mother had passed."

"And says she was murdered."

"There being no sign of struggle, it was thought her heart failed, but I did have doubts. Alive, she would have been of detriment to those whose tale she meant to reveal. Dead, she would take her secrets to the grave. Keeping my word to her, I left Adderstone to bring you home, but as I neared Mathe, I met Lady Thomasin in the wood and our talk moved to a friend of hers named Aude."

Quintin gasped. She had first heard that name the day greenery had been gathered to decorate the hall for Christmas and Thomasin had been certain she had seen her friend inside the castle walls.

"What is it, Quintin?"

She shook her head. "Continue."

"I suspected Lady Thomasin's Aude was our Agatha, and when Baron de Arell's daughter yielded up the location of the woman's hovel on the lake where our three baronies converge, I turned back in hopes of capturing her."

"Is she the same?"

"She was."

Quintin frowned over her brother speaking of the woman as if she were of the past. "You found her?"

"Aye, and she had my wife with her."

Quintin snapped her gaze to Lady Elianor, who inclined her head.

"After I departed for Castle Mathe, the entire household was drugged and my wife taken to the lake so Agatha could question her about what your mother revealed ere her death."

Quintin shivered. "Then 'tis true my mother was murdered. By Agatha."

"Murdered, aye, but Agatha told my wife it was another who took Lady Maeve's life. And Elianor thinks the man she heard conversing with Agatha outside the hovel may be the one who did the deed."

The deed. As if the taking of life was an achievement.

"Agatha said it amused her to work ill on our families, ensuring discord between those who had betrayed Denis Foucault. When she tried to end my wife's life, Elianor set the hovel aflame and escaped into the night as my men and I rode on it. By the fire's glow I saw her run from Agatha onto the frozen lake. Agatha tried to break the ice to send Elianor into a watery grave, and failing that, followed. It was her weight that broke the ice, she who went down into the freezing water. The experience was hellish. Thus, I had to deliver Elianor home ere coming for you."

Quintin lowered her chin. Though it was unlikely she could have saved her mother had an ill heart stolen her away, had she done her daughter's duty, she might have prevented Lady Maeve's murder.

Do not think there, she told herself as tears fell, *for there is Griffin where you would not have him be.*

Because I am selfish, she countered. *Just as I preferred to remain at Castle Mathe with him rather than be burdened by my mother's needs, I would absolve both of us of wrongdoing.*

She felt a squeeze on her fingers and knew her husband sought to comfort her. She who had no right to be comforted, and certainly not by one who—

Once more, she turned from casting blame on him.

"Quintin." He lifted her chin.

Longing to go into the arms she had allowed to replace her mother's, she said, "Selfish. Little thought I gave her these past days, thinking only of what I wanted. Not what she wanted—and needed."

"Quintin—"

"I cannot make it right." She pressed a hand to her chest, groped upward, and gripped the chain about her neck. "Cannot undo what might not have been done had I—"

He laid a hand over hers on the necklace, leaned near. "You gave your word," he said low. "It remains."

She squeezed her eyes closed. She had made a promise she should not have because she had also wanted what he asked of her. Her wants. Her needs. Her happiness of greater import than her mother's life. Happiness she did not deserve with this man who...

She opened her eyes, and as she stared into brilliant blue, tried to quell the self-scourging anger lest it turned outward. And perhaps she would have succeeded had he not spoken what next he did.

"You are not to blame for this. Each of us here played a role, as did others who are not present, even——"

It seemed the warrior who thought too much did not think well enough in this moment, certain as Quintin was of the name he pulled back from his lips.

"Even my mother?" she said sharply.

He inclined his head. "Your mother as well."

Releasing the chain, she snatched her hand from beneath his. "Leave me! It hurts too much to be near you—to look upon you."

A hard light entered his eyes but quickly dimmed. "I shall leave you, but only for now. We are far from done, you and I."

When he moved to rise, she lunged to her feet. "You are my brother's guest, so stay, eat, drink, seek your entertainment and rest—whatever you wish. I am the one who should leave. I am the one with grieving to do."

The muscles in his jaw jerked, but he did not try to detain her as she stepped between their chairs.

She passed behind him and crossed the hall amid the silence of the dead—her mother's silence that was also present in the candlelit chapel. But it lasted only until Hulda heard footsteps. Slumped on a bench beside the table Lady Maeve lay upon, Father Crispin standing behind her, she lifted her head.

"Ah, lamb," she choked and slowly rose.

Not yet ready to look near upon her mother, Quintin crossed to Hulda and saw tears brimmed in the old maid's eyes.

"Pray, forgive me, my lady," Hulda croaked. "I should not have spoken to you as I did."

"As I deserve."

"Nay, you do not deserve such." The maid put her arms around her lady's daughter. "Oh, how I hurt, lamb!"

As Quintin returned her embrace, she looked to Father Crispin. He smiled sorrowfully and turned away.

The two women held each other, tears falling, sobs sounding, and when Hulda sagged, Quintin helped her onto the bench. For minutes, she hovered over the maid, holding her back to the fateful reunion. Then she turned.

Lady Maeve in eternal repose was heart wrenching. And nearly breathtaking, owing to Hulda having lovingly prepared her mistress for all who wished a last glimpse.

As revealed by candles, Adderstone's lady was dressed in a gown she had not worn since before her husband's death—

Rather, his murder, Quintin corrected.

The gown had been Lady Maeve's favorite, fashioned of wine-colored samite and edged with ermine. On her small feet were black velvet slippers, across the toes of which marched pearls. But of greater note when Quintin stepped to the head of the table was that every hair was perfectly arranged on her brow and around her cheeks and jaws, softening the lines age had pressed into a face that had become sorrowful since widowhood. Indeed, Lady Maeve had not appeared so lovely and at peace for years.

"She look pretty, don' she?" a slow voice moved out of a shadowed alcove.

Quintin nearly jumped at the sound and sight of the big man stepping into candlelight—her personal guard, who had been unable to accompany her to Castle Mathe.

Resentment flared that he had not earlier shown himself, but it was momentary. Not only was she fond of Rollo, but he had a right to be here. Quintin's father had been convinced that though Baron Denis Foucault had not acknowledged his illegitimate son, Rollo was a Foucault. Thus, upon Archard Boursier's award of Castle Adderstone, the new Baron of Godsmere had made certain the boy was given every opportunity to grow into a man whose skills provided him a good living. Rather than a life spent beneath a plow's yoke, Rollo's days and nights were marked by an extraordinary facility with weapons that had elevated him to the rank of a man-at-arms.

Later, following Quintin's injury, Bayard had assigned him to be her guard. She had chafed at being unable to leave the castle without his escort, but her mother had liked it even less, though for a different reason. But regardless that neither had Lady Maeve acknowledged Rollo as a Foucault, the man was her brother. And Quintin's uncle.

"Aye, she looks pretty, Rollo."

He halted on the opposite side of the table and nudged his sister's shoulder as if to test for wakefulness. "She be at peace," he said, and Quintin's tears flowed again at hearing her own comforting thoughts come off his lips. But then he added, "At last."

Another sob fled her.

Rollo came around the table and patted her back. "There now, my lady, I not say it a God thing."

Sorrowful laughter opened her mouth. In this instance, he did not speak of the divine but substituted the name *God* for the word *good* as he often did.

"Nay," he said, "but it be a blessing her pain is done and sleep long. She was tired and lonely without her Archard."

Quintin turned into him and held to him as she had held to Hulda. It was a comfort. And yet the arms she longed for were those of the man she had spurned.

Griffin was right. They were not done with each other. Should be, but were not, especially if...

She pressed a palm to her abdomen. Might she carry his child? And if that was possible, would they be done with each other if their babe did not make it out of her afflicted womb? Certes, if mother's and child's lives were both forfeited. But, perhaps, they would not be. Nine months from now, her heart's cry might be answered beautifully when her husband bent over her to peer at his new son or daughter.

Rollo drew back and frowned. "Your belly aches, Lady Quintin?"

She looked into his moist eyes. "I but fear 'tis empty, my friend."

She expected him to think narrowly, in terms of a belly hurting for lack of food, but his brow became weighted and the words he spoke proved he was not as simple as others believed.

"'Tis for the Lord to decide, my lady." He released her and lowered to the bench beside Hulda where the two kept the night-long vigil with her.

Griffin had remained well into the new day to attend the burial and find an opportunity to be alone with his wife. But Quintin remained at her brother's side, and each time her eyes moved in Griffin's direction, she averted them as if she truly could not bear to look upon him.

Though tempted to swing her into his arms, carry her to the chamber he had been given on the night past, and lock them in until she responded to him, he controlled himself. Thus, he and his men departed Castle Adderstone before the nooning meal.

While he waited on the king's determination about Boursier's marriage, he had lands to administer, measures to take to protect his people if the Foucault threat had not died with Agatha, and a Foucault supporter to root out if one did reside within his walls.

I shall find you and make misery of your life as you have made of ours, he silently vowed as he urged his horse over Adderstone's drawbridge. *Your revenge shall become my own.*

Revenge. Such thoughts he was usually wise enough to reject once he had the satisfaction of entertaining them, but he did not know he could do so in this instance. Certes, not now with murder so fresh and of such pain to the woman he...

What? he asked himself.

The woman I desire, he answered, then spurred forward and did not look back lest he suffer disappointment Quintin was on no wall nor in any window watching him go from her.

21

Barony of Godsmere
Early Spring, 1334

I am with child. Pray, come soon that I may wear your ring for all to know I am yours ~ Quintin

Twice more she read the words she had put to parchment a day past. Words that were to have been received by Griffin when next Bayard sent a missive to the Baron of Blackwood. Words that now would never know the caress of those very blue eyes.

The child was lost to them, the cramping and bleeding having awakened her before dawn. All evidence of her failed pregnancy, save her pallor, shivering limbs, and heartache, had been removed by Hulda, the sole person with whom Quintin had shared her secret—and only because the woman had guessed her lady's state two months past just as Quintin herself accepted her menses were not merely late.

A joyous day that had been, tentatively so over the knowledge a child grew in her, unquestionably so owing to Bayard's receipt of the king's acceptance that the Baron of Godsmere had fulfilled the decree. Though that same missive had granted Quintin a stay of marriage for grieving, she had longed to send word of her pregnancy to Griffin, and Hulda had encouraged it once she was entrusted with the secret her lady was wed. However, Griffin would have come for her immediately, and she had not been ready to receive him. More, even at the risk of appearing to have conceived out of wedlock, she had wished her pregnancy further along the better to be certain it held.

It had not. Though she knew she ought to be grateful the longing to be with Griffin that had caused her to write the missive a month sooner than intended had been curbed by her body, it was impossible.

"You ought to sleep, lamb," Hulda said. "I shall tell Lady Elianor your menses keep you abed."

Elianor, whom Quintin did not wish to have a care for but did, especially for how much the lady seemed to love Bayard and he loved her. As ever, Quintin was struck by how strange it was they felt such for each other. But more unbelievable it would be if Griffin and she...

She shifted her gaze from the parchment to the woman who sat in a chair near the bed. "My menses," she murmured. "The truest lie possible."

Hulda wrung out the cloth she had dipped in water, but when she reached to once more cool her lady's brow, Quintin shook her head. "You have helped all you can. Now I will rest."

"Then I shall sit here and—"

"I thank you, but I would be alone."

After a long consideration, Hulda stood.

Quintin handed her the missive. "Pray, burn this."

"I shall, my lady."

Quintin turned away, drew her knees toward her chest, and tugged the coverlet over her head to give herself to the dark. And why not? The light growing in her had gone out.

As another lump moved up her throat, she told herself what she knew to be true no matter how it made her ache—better her loss now than later when it would hurt more...when she would miss the flutters and turns and kicks of the child Griffin and she had made...when she could no longer draw her husband's hand to her beautiful burgeoning.

"Cease," she hissed. But when the door closed, her mind returned to her losses.

My father. My mother. The babe Griffin and I made. And likely my marriage.

She bit her lip. She was wed and would remain wed—indeed, would properly wed Griffin in accordance with Edward's decree—but she could not give him all he wished of a wife.

Serle's fault. Constance's fault. Agatha's fault. And mine.

She shuddered over that last that had been her first thought the morn she had regained consciousness following the clash between Serle de Arell and Bayard and the physician had revealed the extent of her injury. Foolishly, the girl she had been had thought she could stop two warriors from coming to blows that could see her brother lost to her. Impulsively, she had set herself between arcing blades without a care for whose blood they sprayed. Tragically, it was Bayard's sword that opened her, and for it he had claimed responsibility which she had rejected, hating herself alongside Serle, Constance, and Agatha those first years.

And tempted to once more hate herself for the little life lost.

"Serle, Constance, Agatha," she spoke the names aloud. But though Griffin was sensible enough to recognize her injury was more the doing of others, he would also know that had he been made aware of it, King Edward might have agreed to alter his decree so a baron with but a single heir did not risk the possibility of none should ill befall the one.

Remembering how her mother had bemoaned her inability to bear her husband another son, Quintin ached that it was her own fate—that desire alone did not an acceptable marriage make.

"Ah, Griffin," she whispered, "I should have told you."

It was little better than a lie not to have done so. But what she feared as much as his reaction to the revelation was how she would respond—that she would aggressively defend her right to hold close her injury by casting blame on him for being Serle's brother. Afterward, she would regret doing so as she had long regretted rejecting Griffin the night he had returned her to Adderstone.

And she had good cause to worry, this new loss threatening to muddy the waters of grief which, when she had composed her missive to Griffin, had settled enough they had begun to clear. Would the king grant her a second stay of marriage—a few more months so she would not be so raw when reunited with Griffin?

Her palm convulsed on her abdomen where it had strayed as had become habit since she had first pressed it there in wonder. Now it was only remembrance that made it seek that place. And how she longed to make a fist of it!

She slid her hand across the mattress and over the side. And, strangely, wished Arturo were beside the bed, his mangy fur beneath her fingers.

Chest tightening, she drew her hand to it. Through the material of her chemise, she gripped Griffin's ring until sleep offered the only comfort to be had. As she was drawn down through its warm, soft layers, she prayed the king would give her more time so she might salvage something of her relationship with the man whose arms she longed for.

22

Barony of Emberly
Mid-Spring, 1334

Aɴᴏᴛʜᴇʀ sᴛᴀʏ ᴏꜰ marriage. Unlike the first, the second had surprised—
and angered. He had accepted Quintin needed time to grieve, but it was
over four months since Lady Maeve's passing.

Unfortunately, the king had once more been lenient, ordering
that the De Arell and Verdun alliance be made before the De Arell and
Boursier alliance. Thus, this day Griffin gave his daughter into the keeping of the Baron of Emberly. More unfortunately, he did so in the absence
of the Boursiers, who were unable to attend the wedding due to a sickness of early pregnancy. Lady Elianor was with child.

Griffin had been disappointed the Boursiers had not come, having
wished to inquire into Quintin's well-being. The only thing of which he
was certain about her beyond her extended grieving was that, unlike the
Lady of Godsmere, she was not with child. After he had discovered the
extent of her injury, he had thought it unlikely she would conceive. Still,
it had been a question, and its answer was given by her silence.

Had their one night miraculously produced a child, Quintin would
have alerted him the sooner to see them properly wed to lessen talk
their babe was illegitimate. In which case, he would not have had to give
Thomasin in marriage this day, the timing of which could not be worse,

as evidenced by the bride who stood between her father and new husband outside the chapel.

While they waited for the king's wedding gift to be delivered to the bailey, as ordered by Edward's man who had attended the ceremony, Griffin considered his daughter.

She was lovely in her wedding finery, but the bruises and scratches on her face, that no amount of powder could hide, continuously drew his regard. And made him long to see those responsible suffer.

Nearly a sennight past, during a visit to one of the villages, she had slipped away from the knight set to watch over her and been attacked by brigands who sought to ravish and, likely, kill her to prevent her marriage—possibly the same Foucault brigands who had recently attacked Blackwood villagers in their fields, killing four and injuring three.

Most strange, it was Magnus Verdun who had happened on the three men as they sought to undo Thomasin. He had injured two, but all had escaped, and he had left an unconscious Thomasin with a villager to tend her injuries. Thus, not until the night past had the Baron of Emberly learned the identity of the woman he had believed was merely a commoner. And how Verdun had learned…

Griffin sighed. One thing was certain. Thomasin would make the rigid man an interesting wife.

She peered over her shoulder at those who had exited the chapel behind them, on one side Emberly's men, on the other Blackwood's. And among the latter was Sir Otto who, unbeknownst to Verdun, would remain at Castle Kelling to ensure Thomasin's safety until her husband proved capable of doing so himself. Certes, that news would not be well received, but such was the baron's lot.

Thomasin looked forward again, and Griffin followed her gaze to the men who led two horses beneath the raised portcullis, one a palfrey of deepest black, the other a destrier of silver-gray. And face-down over each were bloodied corpses.

"What is this, Cartier?" Verdun demanded.

Muscles seizing, Griffin shot his gaze to the king's man who stood on the other side of the Baron of Emberly. Sir Francis Cartier was a mercenary whose reputation preceded him, though not only because his sword and the men who followed him were useful to King Edward. Of equal note was his fire-ravaged countenance that fit well the man who had earlier taken perverse pleasure in naming Griffin's daughter an *all too common nobleman's indiscretion*.

Had Thomasin not been quick to point out that just as Cartier could not control the effects of the fire that had sought to consume him, neither could she control the circumstances of her birth, Griffin might not have been able to keep his hand from his hilt—and it became more difficult when the mercenary had said she could not be pleased with the marriage required of her and mockingly sympathized over the price of dirt.

Now, hand once more tempted to the hilt, Griffin growled, "I would also know, *king's man*."

The mercenary's eyebrows rose above brown eyes that gave Griffin pause. "As told, wedding gifts, the destrier and palfrey given by King Edward, the brigands given by me."

"Brigands," Thomasin breathed, the dread in her voice pulling Griffin back from the edge of something toward which his thoughts had moved.

"They attacked as we crossed from the barony of Godsmere into Emberly," the mercenary continued, "and paid with as much pain as could be carved from their flesh ere they forswore this world." He chuckled. "A worthy excuse for being late to your wedding. Eh, Verdun?"

"Where were you attacked?" Thomasin's husband asked.

"Near a small, heavily wooded lake."

"The lake that lies at the center of the three baronies?" Verdun said, also turning over the possibility it was where Thomasin's friend, Aude, had tried to murder Lady Elianor.

"I think that is the one." Cartier shrugged and stepped toward the horses that had halted twenty feet distant. "Come see."

Verdun looked to his wide-eyed bride. "Remain with your father."

As Griffin drew her near his side, she asked, "Do you think they are the brigands who...?"

Her attackers. He narrowed his gaze on the horses who stood restless beneath their gruesome burden. "I almost wish it were not those knaves, for I would myself bring them to ground." *As for Cartier,* Griffin silently added, *were I my father, I would kill the miscreant for bloodying my daughter's wedding day.* In the next instant, he said sharply, "Do not look!"

But she held her gaze to the spectacle, watching the king's man lift the heads of each of the brigands to show their faces to Verdun.

"They are known to you?" Cartier asked.

"I recently encountered them working ill upon Emberly and sent them running," Verdun said.

Two of Thomasin's three attackers, then.

"How disappointing they eluded you." Cartier clicked his tongue. "But that makes my wedding gift all the sweeter—at least, for me."

"My thanks to you and the king." Verdun's voice was tight with control.

Wearing a hideous smile courtesy of the puckered skin of his burned lower face, Cartier moved it from the Baron of Emberly to Thomasin. "I speak for King Edward in saying we are pleased to have made this day more memorable for you and your bride."

Verdun nodded stiffly.

"The Verduns, ever in control," Griffin rasped, then corrected, "rather, the men." None could gainsay Constance Verdun had lost control in cuckolding Bayard Boursier with her lover, Serle.

Griffin's thoughts having stumbled over his brother, he pulled them back. A fortnight past, one of his patrolling men had sighted a traveler who resembled the younger De Arell. But before he could verify that one's identity, the patrol had spotted riders in the distance and set off after them—surely brigands, though that also went unverified, the riders evading their pursuers.

So had Serle returned to Blackwood? If so, why did he not show himself at Mathe?

"You have searched these men to determine whence they came?" Verdun's voice returned Griffin to the present.

"Thoroughly and gave them chances aplenty to spill their secrets ere we spilled their innards," Cartier said. "But they proved uncooperative."

"Thus, you have naught to give me but silent bodies."

"Far more than you had ere I gifted them."

"Indeed." Thomasin's husband waved two of his men forward and gave the horses into their care. "Sir Francis," he said as the animals were led away, "if not that you are too occupied with the king's business to tarry, I would invite you and your men to partake of the wedding feast. But I am certain King Edward would rather you further his interests than mine. Thus, I bid you Godspeed."

Cartier laughed. "Surely you can be less obvious with your dislike of the king's man, Verdun."

"Surely I cannot."

The mercenary clapped Verdun on the back, causing the baron to exude something that told he was nearing the end of his control.

"We are much the same," Cartier said. "Thus, for the sake of our kinship, I leave you and your wife to celebrate the alliance of your families." Then he called to Thomasin, "Dear lady, mount that mare with caution. A palfrey she may be, but she is spirited."

His words taunted, and in them Griffin perceived a threat. "The tales told of Sir Francis Cartier are not exaggerated," he said as the king's man strode from the bailey. "Indeed, they may be too kind. There is something black in that mercenary's breast."

Eyes on her husband's advance, Thomasin did not comment.

Verdun's gaze momentarily fell to his wife's father, and there Griffin saw the roiling within and, at a corner of his mouth, a spasming that revealed its depth. Fortunately for the baron, Griffin's instincts told him Thomasin's husband was honorable enough he would not visit his anger and frustration on one who was not responsible for them. Still, Griffin was glad Sir Otto would remain at Castle Kelling to keep watch over her, just as Ulric had suggested.

Now to see if Magnus Verdun could maintain control when he learned he would have to prove he could be entirely entrusted with the daughter of Griffin de Arell.

The next morn, as those of the barony of Blackwood rode beneath a gray sky threatening to make their return to Castle Mathe a wet one, Griffin tried to be comforted that he did not leave his daughter without recourse should his instincts about her husband prove wrong.

As predicted, Magnus Verdun had not liked that Sir Otto would remain at Castle Kelling. Indeed, so greatly had he been offended that Griffin and he might have come to swords had Thomasin not stepped between them.

Displaying a calm and depth of maturity that had surprised Griffin as much as on the day past when Cartier had taunted her, she had entreated the two warriors to accept each other's respective role—Griffin as her father, Magnus as her husband.

Thus, Verdun had grudgingly consented to allow Sir Otto to remain. For a time.

Tasked with keeping watch over her—of greatest concern once she began to steal away from Kelling to acquaint herself with Emberly's common folk and provide for those in need—Sir Otto would ensure no ill befell her as Griffin was fairly sure the knight would have done had he been the one to watch over her the day of her attack in the wood.

Aye, if anyone could keep her safe from the Foucault supporters, it was Sir Otto.

23

Barony of Blackwood
Spring's End, 1334

THE FIRST TO fall was unintentional, the tidings delivered to the old baron causing him to snatch hold of the hanging to keep his frail legs beneath him. But the second and third hangings partitioning his apartment were willfully wrenched from their ceiling hooks as he lurched from one to the next.

"A Foucault!" he raised his voice as near a shout as his ravaged throat allowed. "An accursed, puking, half-faced, God-forsaken Foucault!"

As Griffin looked upon his father's leprous face, revealed when the shawl draping his head slid to the floor, he acknowledged Magnus Verdun was not the only one to exercise great control over his emotions.

Ulric's reaction over the news from Castle Kelling could not be half as great as that which prowled beneath Griffin's skin, panting and growling as it searched for a way out. But he would not become his father, even under circumstances that gave him good cause to turn his thoughts to the merciless taking of life—circumstances that proved if Ulric de Arell was not capable of love as Griffin had long believed, something had shifted in him that allowed him to become so attached to another he would likely kill were he able to crawl out of his incapacitated body.

The old baron stumbled to the next hanging, but as he clawed at it, a whine sounded from the bed beneath which Diot had scrambled when his master's raging threatened to trample him.

Ulric dropped to his knees, fell to his hands, and called, "Diot, I did not mean to frighten you." He patted the floor. "Come. Come."

The dog crawled forward, revealing its front legs and nose, and that was all.

Griffin retrieved the shawl and returned to his father.

Ulric jerked his face aside. "The mask," he croaked. "Beside the bed. And a stick. In the wardrobe."

Griffin secured the first but was slower to gain the second from the immense upright chest whose contents were heretofore unknown to him, though he had suspected it was where his father hid the walking sticks Thomasin fashioned for him.

Thomasin…He closed his eyes and gave thanks the tidings delivered this day told she lived, as did her husband. That was not to have been. Had the one who was to have kept the Lady of Emberly safe succeeded in a quest far different from that with which he had been tasked, all that remained of Magnus and Thomasin Verdun would be burned corpses.

Verily, I could kill too, Griffin silently admitted. Beyond the necessity of defending family, people, and land, and with only sufficient thought to determine where best to sink his blade, in this moment he could deal a mortal wound to the one who claimed he was Foucault on one side and Agatha of Mawbry on the other.

"For what do you tarry?" Ulric demanded.

Retrieving a branch pared of its small limbs and rubbed smooth, one of many that stood like sentinel trees in barren winter, Griffin caught sight of his hand reflected in the mirror hidden behind the walking sticks. And pitied his sire for the ghastly wound leprosy had also dealt his vanity.

He returned to his father, who fit the mask before climbing his hands up the stick to regain his feet.

"Diot," he called once he was stable.

The dog crept out, rumbled at Griffin, and darted beneath his master's long tunic.

Ulric turned his wooden face to his son. "Otto must die. You will see to it?"

Certes, Griffin had desire aplenty, made all the greater by the knowledge he had long harbored the murderous traitor at Castle Mathe—more, that he had entrusted Thomasin to him, never suspecting him capable of such duplicity. Of murder!

Self-loathing skinning another piece off his warrior's pride, Griffin said, "'Tis not for me to do. Otto is the Verduns' prisoner." Blessedly, rather than their executioner, the knight having planned to set their bedchamber afire to eliminate the Verduns and their claim upon Emberly. But he had failed, just as the attempt to murder Lady Elianor at Christmas had failed.

"It is not for you to do?" Ulric snapped. "He tried to kill your daughter! Had he succeeded, his attempt to take back the baronies and make them one again could have seen Rhys dead."

Griffin knew that. Enough was revealed in the missive to acknowledge a war was not newly arrived at their gates. For years, it had lived and breathed amongst them. It might even extend as far back to when the three families were each awarded a piece of Kilbourne and jealousy—regrettably, Ulric de Arell being the greatest offender—birthed the feud.

"And it still might see your son murdered!" Leaning heavily on the stick, the old baron crossed to the bed and lowered to the mattress edge. "I care not that Otto—that misbegotten, pus-filled scab—confirmed his father's death. Methinks it quite possible Simon Foucault lives."

As Griffin had concluded. Though it was long known Baron Denis Foucault's heir had died in France shortly after his father's lands were forfeited, and while Otto had lingered over killing the Verduns he had confirmed the death of the one who had sown him on Agatha, Simon's misbegotten son had claimed he took orders from another. And who might that be but his sire?

Hopefully, Otto's imprisonment at Castle Kelling would yield answers that would allow the three families to escape the web spun around them—a web that, it was told, included Thomasin's mother.

Griffin lowered his lids. Such a struggle it had been to forgive Alice for deserting their daughter, and he had not entirely, though he had known his father—and he—bore much of the responsibility for making her life so hard she had made that choice. But now to learn the man for whom Alice had left Thomasin had aided Sir Otto…

"Did you hear me, Griffin?"

"Be assured, just as I am aware Simon Foucault may live, I know Rhys is in as much danger as Thomasin was as a child."

Through the mask's eye holes, Griffin saw his father blink. "You have not told all!"

Deciding not to waste breath on reminding Ulric his outburst had interrupted full disclosure of the missive's contents, Griffin said. "I speak of Alice, the woman I loved, whom you sent from Blackwood with Thomasin in her belly."

His father snorted. "She was a girl. You were a boy. And you but thought yourself in love. 'Twas best for all I sent her away."

"And yet, as learned this day, she returned."

Ulric jerked. "What say you?"

"Alice returned, but not to Blackwood—to Emberly."

"For what?"

"She took a lover, unaware he was a Foucault supporter sent to murder her and Thomasin. Apparently, he was so besotted with her, he instead convinced her to abandon her daughter and follow him to Castle Kelling where he took work as a man-at-arms to keep watch over the Verduns."

"Then Thomasin has been reunited with that—" Ulric caught back the foul thing he wished to name Alice. "Your daughter has been reunited with the woman who abandoned her?"

"She has not. A year after Alice arrived at Emberly, she died."

"Ha! Forgive me if I do not mourn her."

The concealed Diot growled, evidencing he felt the surge of Griffin's anger.

"What of the man-at-arms?" Ulric asked.

Griffin did not answer until he was sufficiently calmed to pry his fingers out of his palms. "It was with his aid Sir Otto nearly fulfilled the task given him."

"I would see him dead as well."

"Then you will be pleased to know it was with his final breaths he revealed to Thomasin what became of her mother."

"Beyond pleased. So what now, Griffin?"

"I fulfill the king's decree."

"And wed the Boursier woman."

A second time, Griffin reflected. "Best I claim the prize ere another tries to steal her away."

"Prize?"

"Something else I have yet to share."

"Then share!"

"Sir Otto boasted Lady Quintin is the prize in all this and that he, her cousin, was to wed her." As Griffin had done several times since reading those lines, he sifted through instances of the knight in Quintin's presence. He had seen the way Otto looked at her and had not liked it, but he had understood—at least, until Boursier's marriage to Lady Elianor had advanced the likelihood Quintin would become a De Arell. But even then, the knight's lingering gaze had been no more offensive than the regard of Griffin's other men.

"Foucault blood strengthened by Foucault blood," Ulric said.

"Aye. Thus, it occurs that the leader of the Foucault uprising is one who holds great favor with the king such that, with the elimination of our families, 'tis possible he will gain the baronies as a whole, putting Kilbourne back together through marriage to Lady Quintin." Ironically, it was the same strategy Griffin had entertained—that had the king decided against Boursier and Verdun, the De Arells might be awarded the forfeited lands, their claim strengthened by Griffin taking to wife one thought to be the only hope for the survival of the Foucault line.

"You do not believe Sir Otto is the leader." Ulric said with the same certainty Griffin felt.

"He is too young to have set this in motion, and he admitted to taking orders from another. But though he was convinced he would be the one to gain the prize, I think him but a pawn. Were he legitimate-born, it would not occur, but he was birthed by Agatha of Mawbry."

Ulric grunted. "Then Denis Foucault's whelp does live—that arrogant, bootless maggot is the one plaguing our families."

Many times with the unwitting aid of Ulric de Arell, Griffin once more kept thought from his tongue. "Aye, I believe Simon lives."

"And you think he is the one who seeks the prize."

"I am fair certain. However, he does not do it in the name of Simon Foucault. He has become another. Someone who would be permitted to wed his niece with none aware he violates the laws of consanguinity in the most perverse way."

"You know who it might be?"

"There is one I suspect." Griffin stepped nearer his father. "Tell me, would you recognize Denis Foucault's son?"

"When last I saw him, he was aged a score of years and some. But though he would be fifty or more now, I believe I would know him. Even if age has much lined and sagged his face, it was distinctive, and more so his eyes—Foucault brown, we called them. His father and sister, Lady Maeve, had them. And I would guess his niece as well."

"Brown, ringed by gold," Griffin said, memory setting Quintin's lovely face before him.

"Aye, most unusual. This one you suspect has such eyes?"

Letting Quintin's face drift away, replacing it with one who would approve of his daughter dying by fire, he said, "Certes, they are brown. Unfortunately, I did not draw near enough to determine if gold is at their outer reaches. And brown is a common color."

"What of Sir Otto's eyes?"

"Brown. But again, I have not looked near enough to say they are touched by gold."

"Otto is a Foucault," Ulric said firmly. "Now if he can be made to talk."

Griffin nodded. "Regardless, if the Foucault threat is to end, we must set a trap."

"We?" There was something childishly hopeful in that single utterance.

"Aye, Father. We."

Barony of Godsmere

The prize.

It made her quake with anger and shiver with fear.

The prize.

It tossed the contents of her stomach and tightened her throat in anticipation of bile.

"The prize," she said low to determine if it was as offensive to the tongue as its written form was to the eyes.

Far more offensive, further reducing her to chattel—in this case, that of Sir Otto. Her cousin!

"Quintin."

Gripping the parchment so hard it would forever be creased, she turned to her brother who stood alongside his wife in the solar. A quarter hour earlier, Lady Elianor had glowed. Now she was pale. But as disturbed as she was by the tidings from Emberly, hope was beneath the hand she pressed to the slight bulge below her waist.

Quintin's remembrance of the comfort of her own hand knowing what the eyes of others were incapable of confirming caused the missive to further protest its abuse.

"Beyond the horror of what Baron Verdun and his wife endured and nearly suffered," Bayard said, striding forward, "you understand what this could mean, do you not?"

When he halted, she said, "It means I am the perverse hope of the Foucaults. Ah, but if only they knew how false that hope!" As soon as she spoke, a thought struck her, and she caught her breath. "Mother did not reveal to Agatha what her scheming with Constance and Serle de Arell wrought. Had that witch known I am not likely to revive the Foucault line, I would have been of no use, as easily disposed of as were my father and mother."

"Once again, your mother was protecting you," Bayard said and took the missive from her. "There is good in this, Quintin. It further evidences the feud was instigated by Foucault supporters. And though two marriages have already been made, the third need not be."

A laugh parted her lips, and she nearly confessed that what need not be done *was* done—even before Baron Verdun and Thomasin wed.

"Satisfactory marriages," she said and looked to his wife. Despite the lady having imprisoned Bayard, regardless of what Quintin had lost that the other woman had gained, Elianor was agreeable.

Though in Quintin's darkest moments she sometimes wrestled with envy, once she emerged from that darkness, there was happiness in seeing the two together. So quietly—and intensely—in love.

Quintin looked back at her brother. "Very satisfactory marriages," she reiterated, referring also to what she had witnessed of Magnus Verdun and Lady Thomasin's marriage when they had traveled to Castle Adderstone a fortnight past.

Naturally, her thoughts returned to Sir Otto, who had been part of the Baron of Emberly's entourage when, attacked en route to Adderstone, it had prevailed over the brigands. Quintin had exchanged few words with the knight while he was at Adderstone, but she had been glad to see him—dangerously unaware that, as the devil her mother had said walked the corridors of Castle Mathe, he had stood to benefit from that first of two attempts to leave the barony of Emberly bereft of lord and lady.

For what seemed the hundredth time, she regretted the bitterness that had caused her to be curt with Thomasin during that visit. But Griffin's daughter had been intent on speaking of her father and Quintin had hurt to discuss the man with whom she was incompatible.

"I can petition the king to release you from marriage to Baron de Arell," Bayard pulled her back to the moment.

Of comfort to him. He loved her too much to see her risk trying to birth babes out of a craven womb. And, unbeknownst to him, there was now more evidence he had good cause to worry—were she capable of conceiving again.

"That is what you want, is it not?" he pressed.

It was not. But she had not dissuaded him from believing her emotions remained tattered over her mother's death and her belief Griffin bore much of the blame. She missed her mother, but her womb's rejection of the child made with Griffin was responsible for her continued grieving.

She sighed. "I want what you have, Brother—and, certes, the Baron of Blackwood wishes it as well—but I fear 'tis not possible for me. Indeed, a better use for your sister might be to give the Foucault supporters their *prize* and bring their line to an end."

"Do not speak such!"

She winced at her indulgence in self pity. "Forgive me. It but feels dirty that I am a Foucault."

Bayard grasped her shoulders. "That blood gives you life the same as Boursier blood. And that is all. It does not mean you are responsible for the ill done by those who share it. Indeed, you are more a victim than the rest of us."

She stepped from beneath his hands. "I am sick unto death of being a victim. And a pawn. Even more distasteful is being made a man's prize." Unless, she silently added, that man was one who wanted her as much as she wanted him.

She shook her head. "Woe to any who tries to make me such, for they will not find anything lovely to unwrap, and I might well enjoy proving I am every bit a dirty Foucault." She skirted her brother and exited the solar.

As she traversed the corridor toward her chamber, the chapel drew her regard. Though tempted to seek Father Crispin's counsel, it was of an hour he would be abed, allowing one of the two draughts she daily prepared for him to provide relief for the cancer he had finally revealed was the cause of his poor health.

Two months past, the physician had said the priest would not live a month. A month past, he had said Father Crispin would not live a fortnight. A fortnight past, he had asked the man of God to reveal the makings of the draughts.

Though still frail, Father Crispin had himself written down how to prepare the duckweed and honeywine extract prescribed for cancer by Hildegard of Bingen, a long-departed Benedictine abbess, as well as the peppermint and dandelion draught that eased his aching belly. The final ingredient of both he listed as prayer—to which Quintin knew she ought to apply herself now.

She closed herself in her chamber, but her mind, knees, and hands would not settle heavenward. And so she paced the room until she caught her reflection in the corner mirror.

She returned to it. "The prize," she hissed, resenting that she looked like one. She was not as beautiful as Lady Elianor, but Lady Maeve had passed her comeliness to her daughter, and Archard Boursier had improved upon it by providing Quintin with a strong chin unlike her mother's slightly recessed one.

Quintin stepped closer to the mirror and considered her eyes— Foucault brown, the same as Sir Otto's, as she had noted at Castle Mathe. His reaction to her observation had caused her to believe he had taken offense, but fear of exposure had made him walk away.

"My cousin!" she spat, then squeezed her eyes closed and counted her breaths until the flames within sank to their haunches amid the embers.

She opened her eyes, raised them to her dark hair that had grown too long, shifted them to the pale green gown that flattered her figure unlike the black, shapeless garments she had worn her first months following her return to Adderstone. Though this morn she had promised herself she would soon wear the beautiful gown Lady Elianor and Hulda had sewn for her months past—of a shimmering dark blue fabric that called to mind Griffin's eyes—perhaps she ought to make black her habit again. As for her hair...

She crossed to the bedside table, opened its drawer, and hesitated over the Wulfrith dagger. Months past, she had returned it to Bayard, and he had not rebuked her for taking it. After she confirmed it was the one she had put to Griffin's throat, he had surprised her by giving it into her care, saying Archard Boursier's daughter, who had courageously led men against their enemy to rescue her brother, had as much right to it as his son.

Realizing she was smiling, she lifted the dagger out and removed it from its scabbard. Scissors would serve better, providing more control over the cut, but this blade was sharper and would make quick work of the task.

Before the mirror again, she pushed fingers into her hair and drew them out to its ends. But as she moved the blade near, she remembered.

Griffin's face above hers. Warm breath on her brow. Fingers pressed to her scalp. His attempt to wrap shorn tresses around his hands. Her longing for him to do so.

She lowered the dagger, then her head. "Oh, Griffin, I shall have to tell you. And you will have to accept that a bedmate and companion is all I will ever be."

Though, perhaps, acceptance of her failings would not last overly long. If Bayard's fear for her was realized, Griffin would find himself twice a widower. That or suffer the loss of babe after babe unable to thrive in its mother's womb.

Were he not already bound to her with vows and consummation, Bayard's proposal to seek her release from the king's decree would be best for Griffin so he could make more heirs with another lady. But he was her husband, and the king would wish proof of the final alliance—a public wedding that it was possible the Foucault brigands would try to prevent.

The miscreants would fail, she told herself, just as they had failed to stop the other two alliances. But of course, that would make them all the more desperate to succeed this time.

She dropped to her knees, clasped her hands beneath her chin, and closed her eyes. "Forgive me, Lord, for the wrongs I think…speak…do. Give me strength to accept blame that is my due and right its wrongs." The words tumbled forth, and she did not heed her aching knees until she was empty but for one final beseeching. "Pray, Lord, do not let my marriage be soaked in blood."

24

Barony of Blackwood
Summer, 1334

HIS PATIENCE WAS at an end. He wanted his wife, even if she did not want him.

Quelling the impulse to call for his men to ride, Griffin braced his palms on the table, dropped his head between his shoulders, and breathed long…breathed deep…breathed in Griffin de Arell who was not his father.

"Now think," he commanded that which always served him well. "Think much. Regret little."

Which would not be necessary had Boursier and Verdun done the same. Instead, at Boursier's prompting, Verdun had sent word of Otto's treachery to King Edward. And this morn, the detestable Sir Francis Cartier had arrived at Castle Kelling to deliver the knight to Edward's prison for questioning.

Thus, the trap Griffin had been laying was rendered worthless by the loss of its bait. He would have set it sooner if not that Rhys, a quarter of his garrison, and a goodly number of servants had been laid abed by a coughing sickness that had taken the lives of a man of such great age he was no longer capable of walking and a little girl just beginning to walk.

But the ruined trap was not the only reason Griffin urged himself to think before acting. He must consider Boursier's motive for alerting the king to Otto's crimes. Based on further evidence the feud between the families was mostly instigated by Foucault brigands, Quintin's brother wished her released from the decree. Which meant the lady yet held close her secret that the king's solution to the feud was fully realized.

Griffin pushed off the table and dragged a hand down his face.

As proved by his wife's silence and the second stay of marriage, she continued to grieve the loss of her mother and blamed the one who had refused to allow her to return to Adderstone. But though she was obviously not eager to claim the role of Lady of Blackwood, neither did he believe she meant to disavow the marriage that made her a De Arell in the eyes of God and Church. Thus, he was fairly certain she was not behind the request to release her from the decree. She might even be unaware of it.

The anger that had been moving toward Quintin pulled back, as it did from her brother. Ignorant of his sister's marriage, Boursier but tried to do right by her, likely believing her continued grieving and anger toward Griffin warranted intercession. But soon enough, the Baron of Godsmere would relinquish his sister to her husband. As for Sir Otto and the trap from which Cartier had sprung him...

Upon this, Griffin had not thought enough. Hence, he regretted much, the anger flaring anew directed at himself.

Sensing it, Arturo growled as if in sympathetic agreement and slunk out from beneath the table.

Griffin met the dog's doleful gaze and wondered if the great wolf-hound continued to feel Quintin's absence. That first month following her departure, he had been more temperamental than usual and given to pacing the second floor corridor—ironic considering he would have torn out Quintin's throat that first day and, when made to watch over the one who had attacked his master, had exuded resentment. But then, the same could be said of Rhys who had grown fond enough of Quintin that several times he had asked with exaggerated indifference when she would return.

"Soon," Griffin muttered and shifted his thoughts to the trap. Since it would have required the cooperation of the Baron of Emberly to make it work, he had intended to reveal to Verdun his plan to flush out Simon Foucault. However, he had erred in not sooner enlisting his son-in-law's aid, nor Boursier's. Had he, Otto would not have been collected by the king's man and quite possibly freed—or quite possibly killed, depending on whether or not Cartier could wring some use from the knave.

"Live and answer for what you did to my daughter," he rasped. "Live that you suffer alongside Simon Foucault."

And that required the construction of a new trap—beginning with arrangements for the ride to Godsmere, a missive sent to the Baron of Emberly, and instructions to Sir Mathieu who would serve as lord in Griffin's absence. Then a climb up the stairs to give Ulric this day's tidings.

He is here, was all Quintin could think as she stood before the hearth from which she had turned when the arrival of the Baron of Blackwood and a sizable escort was announced.

Barely breathing, she touched the braid her lengthening hair had allowed her to fashion for the first time in years.

"Lady Quintin?"

She looked to Elianor who had gained her feet, leaving on the bench the bit of gown she embroidered for her unborn babe.

Fearing what brought Griffin to Adderstone without warning and so far into the eve, wondering if it had to do with this day's tidings that the king's man had collected Sir Otto, Quintin said, "I shall go as well," and started across the hall as Bayard strode from it into the torchlit inner bailey.

Though she lifted her skirts and ran, she did not catch up with her brother until she ascended the outer wall's steps.

"Bayard!" she called as he moved toward the embrasure nearest the gatehouse, beyond which could be heard the restlessness of a great number of armed and mounted men who faced a greater number of Godsmere men gathered on the walls.

Bayard looked over his shoulder, but before he could rebuke her, she said, "You may order me to return to the keep, but I shall remain and know the reason my betrothed is here."

His singular gaze catching light, he said, "I know why he comes."

She halted before him. "You speak of the tidings from Emberly?"

"I do not. I speak of the reason—"

"Boursier!" Griffin's voice sprang over the wall as if he and his men were much nearer than the edge of the great void presented by the raised drawbridge.

Dear Lord, Quintin silently beseeched, *I did not realize how much I longed to hear his voice.*

She laid a hand on Bayard's arm. "Of what reason do you speak?"

"That for which Sir Otto came to the king's attention such that the knave has been taken from Castle Kelling."

She frowned. There had been no mistaking Bayard's disquiet over the news from the Baron of Emberly, but there was more to it than believed. "Tell me."

"I convinced Verdun to send word of Sir Otto's treachery to King Edward as further proof the feud he tries to remedy is not of our making."

"And?"

"I asked that you be released from your betrothal to Baron de Arell."

As he had suggested weeks past and she had believed was forgotten.

"Doubtless, Baron de Arell is now aware of my request. That is why he has come."

For me, she thought. *At last.*

Bayard's hand closed around her arm. "I would not see you sacrificed, especially now there is no gain from a Boursier and De Arell alliance.

Is there not? her selfish side argued.

Certes, there is little for Griffin, countered the other side that liked to remind her of what she could not give her husband.

"I wait Boursier!" The anger in Griffin's voice had sharpened.

Bayard drew Quintin to the wall alongside the embrasure and, denying her a view of Griffin, leaned forward. "Baron de Arell, what do you
riding upon my walls in the dark of night?"

"I am here to collect my bride."

Back pressed to the wall, Quintin quelled the temptation to push
a place beside Bayard, who called back, "Your bride? That is premature
whilst we await word from the king who may yet decide you are free to
wed whomever you please, as is my sister."

A long silence, then, "If you do not yield what belongs to me,
Boursier, another feud there shall be, and this one born not of Foucault
treachery."

"You have no claim on Lady Quintin."

"Do I not?"

She caught her breath. Did he mean to reveal their marriage?

"What say you, De Arell?" Bayard demanded.

"As the king has decreed our families ally, your sister is promised to
me. Hence, my claim upon her."

"You err. Until she speaks vows, she belongs to no man."

"Lady Quintin!" Griffin called.

He but guessed she was near. Her exchange with Bayard had been
low and, since her brother had shown himself, he had not glanced at
her. Now, out of sight of those beneath his walls, he raised a hand to her,
directing her to remain unseen.

She stepped alongside him.

"Quintin!" he snarled.

But her attention was on the man illuminated by the torches his
arrival had caused to be lit upon the walls—as his attention was on her.

Then Griffin smiled that crooked smile, and her heart jolted so hard
she felt as if punched in the chest. "It seems our roles are reversed, my
lady. This time, 'tis I who demands entrance to your walls. You who shall
grant my desire."

Desire. Did he intentionally choose a word that made her shudder
in remembrance of their one night together?

As if he saw the emotions on her face, his own face—rough with several days' growth of beard—softened.

They stared at each other, then he called, "Tell your brother to whom you belong—whose wife you would be, *my* lady."

Bayard laid a hand over her two clasped atop the embrasure. "The morn will be soon enough to discuss his ride on Adderstone."

She shook her head. "Let him in. He is our ally."

"Not yet."

"As you yourself allow, Bayard, no matter the past, in this present Baron Verdun and you retain your lands in large part due to Baron de Arell's words on your behalf."

His jaw shifted. "You are at stake, Quintin, not Godsmere."

"Pray, let him in."

"You no longer hold him responsible for your mother's death?"

"I have not for months."

His lid narrowed. "*Do* you wish to be his wife?"

"I do, though he may not when he learns…" She looked down her front. "But I would belong to him."

"Then I should not have asked the king to release you from the decree?"

"Only for Griffin's sake."

He looked nearer upon her. "Do you love him?"

"I…" She moistened her lips. "…do not know."

He returned his gaze to Adderstone's visitor, murmured, "Mayhap you are not the only one who does not know if they love."

A laugh escaped her. "Certes, Griffin desires me."

"Mayhap as I desired Elianor as I grew toward her in love, hmm?" He raised his eyebrows, then stepped away and signaled a man-at-arms to order the lowering of the drawbridge.

"Quintin!" Griffin called.

She leaned farther into the embrasure. Surprised by how light she felt in that moment, though aware later moments would reveal that which could turn him from her, she said, "You are an eager groom, Baron. I suppose we shall have to let you in."

The smile that had dropped from his mouth whilst she conversed with Bayard returned, and she knew he remembered her appearance outside his own walls when he had suggested she was an eager bride and she had retorted she would rather put herself through with a blade. How her feelings had changed!

"I am pleased this bears closer discussion," he furthered the game, reminding her of when he had said the same to her from atop his wall, denying himself another bite of the apple he had chewed while they conversed.

"Alas, had I only an apple, Baron de Arell."

His laughter warmed her, then it was muted by the drawbridge's chains.

Avoiding her brother's gaze, Quintin descended the wall on his arm and remained at his side while he ordered a squire to alert Lady Elianor that refreshments would be required. Then the portcullis rose and Griffin and his men guided their mounts over the drawbridge.

Other things besides her feelings for Griffin had much changed, she reflected as one and a half score of Blackwood men entered Adderstone's walls. When she had entered Castle Mathe, she had been allowed only six and Bayard fewer. And her brother was just as cautious as Griffin, meaning he believed an alliance between the Boursiers and De Arells had been forged even in the perceived absence of marital vows. But lest he erred, his knights and men-at-arms on the ramparts and around the bailey were prepared to loose arrows and swing swords.

As Griffin advanced, the lightness that had supplanted Quintin's worries over their reunion returned to the shadows. There were too many months between this night and the night he had returned her to Adderstone. And so much to be told and, God willing, forgiven and accepted.

She shivered, and Bayard leaned near. "Should I not have let him in?"

"You should have, and I thank you."

"I have waited for you to speak of what goes between you two. Will you now?"

She swallowed. "Soon."

He straightened and widened his stance to receive the man who drew near. "You are welcome at Adderstone, Baron de Arell," he said when Griffin reined in.

Though Quintin's husband gave the greater part of his regard to Bayard, he looked to her, and how she wished this were the day she had donned the dark blue gown. But though the one she wore was simple, it fit well. Best of all, it was not black.

As she smoothed its cream-colored skirt, Griffin said, "I am pleased, Baron Boursier, especially since the tidings received this day from the Baron of Emberly indicated you and I are no longer at peace."

Bayard released Quintin's arm and took a stride forward, becoming a barrier between her husband and her. "My sister assures me we are at peace. Hence, I invite you and your men to refresh yourselves and gain a night's rest in my hall."

"We accept." Griffin gestured for his men to dismount, swung out of the saddle, and crossed to Bayard. "We have much to discuss, Baron Boursier."

"So it seems."

Griffin looked to Quintin. "My bride awaits her groom. May I pass?"

After a hesitation, during which her brother's gaze surely shone with warning, Bayard stepped aside.

Mouth and throat so dry her tongue cleaved to her palate, Quintin could only stare when her husband halted before her.

He reached to her slowly, as if sudden movement might set her to flight, and closed a hand around hers that gripped her skirt. Then he eased her fingers open and carried her hand to his mouth.

"It has been long, my lady." He kissed her knuckles, turned her hand, and put his lips to her wrist. "Much too long." As sensations tripped over themselves in their eagerness to be better known to her, he added, "I pray you feel the same," and lowered her hand.

Though Quintin's tongue had loosened, her voice barely made it past her throat. "I am glad you have finally come."

He raised an eyebrow. "You make it sound as if I am responsible for delaying our marriage before all—indeed, for seeking to absolve us of marriage altogether."

She momentarily closed her eyes. "Forgive me. The delays are of my doing, but I would have you know that until your arrival this day, I was not aware my brother sought my release from the decree."

"As thought, and upon which the baron and I must needs talk."

His hold on her eased, but she gripped his fingers. "Pray, let there be no ill between Bayard and you. He only did what he thought best for me."

"'Tis not best for you—for us. But fear not, providing he makes no further attempt to deny me my *prize,* we shall remain allies."

There was anger and bitterness in the word to which Sir Otto had referred to her, and she did not doubt much was directed at himself for entrusting his daughter to that knight. Otto was fortunate he was destined for the king's prison rather than Castle Mathe.

Moving his hand to Quintin's elbow, Griffin turned to Bayard. "We shall follow, Baron Boursier."

It was staggering what had been accomplished in the short time given Lady Elianor to prepare her hall. A half dozen tables had been placed before the dais and set with goblets to which servants applied pitchers as the first platters of viands arrived.

"Baron de Arell," the Lady of Godsmere called as she crossed the hall, and beyond her shoulder Quintin saw Rollo, the big man-at-arms who was as protective of his lord's wife as he was of his lord's sister, slip into an alcove. Such was his habit, deferring to Bayard to protect the ladies of Adderstone when the baron was present.

"Lady Elianor." Griffin released Quintin, accepted the hand extended him, and kissed it. "I thank you for your hospitality, but if it is not too much trouble, would you have food and drink delivered to the solar where your husband and I can converse in private?"

Uncertainty flashed across her face, but after a glance at Bayard, she said, "Of course."

As she moved away, Griffin turned his attention to Quintin's brother. "Be assured, 'tis best we speak behind closed doors."

Obviously on the matter of Bayard's attempt to release Quintin from marriage. But did he intend to reveal that was impossible regardless of the king's determination?

Griffin returned to Quintin and bent near. "It remains between us. For now."

She turned her face up. "I must needs speak with you."

"If not this eve, on the morrow."

This eve, she hoped, the morrow too distant now he was so near.

He pivoted. "I shall follow, Baron Boursier."

As his men settled in to satisfy their appetite, Quintin watched her husband and brother ascend the stairs. Though she also wished to depart the hall—to make herself ready should Griffin come to her, she set herself to aiding Godsmere's lady with their guests.

An hour later, as Bayard's men bedded down in the hall among the castle folk, Griffin and Bayard had not reappeared.

"Join me at the hearth?" Lady Elianor said, moving toward it.

"I thank you, but I shall gain my bed."

The lady retraced her steps, smiled softly. "I do not know if you are ready for me to call you Sister, but you are that to me, and I hope if I am not that to you, I shall be."

Quintin did not know how to respond, and when she remained mute, Elianor said, "I pray you will find with Baron de Arell what I have with Bayard." She stepped close and kissed Quintin's cheek. "Sleep well, Sister."

Quintin moved toward the stairs, halted, and looked around. Her sister-in-law's hand on her abdomen nearly checked Quintin's words, but she chastised herself for not first feeling joy for the blessing that awaited Elianor and Bayard.

And I shall be the little one's aunt, she reminded herself.

"You *are* that to me, Elianor," she said and ascended the stairs. As she neared the solar, she heard the muffled voices of the two within but continued to her chamber, hoping she would be awake when Griffin retired to the chamber down from hers.

To her surprise, Hulda awaited her. To her further surprise, the maid held out the parchment she had been instructed to burn. "You will tell him, my lady?"

Quintin curled her fingers around the missive. "I shall."

"Then all will come right, lamb." Hulda moved past and exited the chamber.

A quarter hour later, Quintin sat robed on her bed. This night, she determined, once she was certain Bayard and Elianor were abed, she would go to her husband. And reveal all.

25

THEY WERE IN accord, and Boursier's encounters with the miscreant, who Griffin believed to be Simon Foucault, made it certain that the one who had fathered Otto, likely murdered Lady Maeve, abducted Lady Elianor, ordered the assault on Thomasin, slain Thomasin's attackers to present as wedding gifts, and led the raid on the Verdun party en route to Adderstone was the same who had this morn taken Otto from Castle Kelling.

Simon Foucault was not dead. He had become Sir Francis Cartier. And for his aid in securing the young king's crown, the mercenary had the trust and favor of England's ruler.

The Baron of Godsmere had expressed regret that his attempt to prevent what he thought an unwanted marriage had ruined Griffin's plan of openly transferring Otto to Castle Mathe to draw Cartier there. Ulric being the only one of an age to recall the visage of the Baron of Kilbourne's son, he was to have confirmed that what remained of the man's face belonged to Simon Foucault.

Then Boursier had pointed out that had Griffin included Verdun and him in setting the trap, he might now have his prey in hand. Having concluded the same, Griffin had tried not to take offense.

Well before the end of his meeting with Boursier, it was agreed the three families would unite to expose Cartier. Meaning that just as their fathers had done more than twenty-five years past, the sons would gather to plot against a Foucault—this time to hold on to their lands.

Near the middling of night, Griffin thanked Lady Elianor for delivering him to the chamber he had been given near the chapel.

She nipped her lower lip and said in a rush, "I am glad you came, Baron de Arell."

"As am I."

"I was frightened and angry when I was a guest at your table on my wedding night. I pray you will forgive me."

"Of course. The circumstances were…difficult, and I was a poor host in the absence of a wife to temper my mood. But soon the king's decree will be fulfilled on all three sides, giving Blackwood the lady it deserves and securing all our lands."

"Know that I am grateful for your aid," she said, "not only with regard to your suggestion that consummation validated our first marriage, but that you sent to King Edward your witness of the events, without which Bayard and my uncle might have forfeited."

"'Twas the right thing to do."

The lady's smile increased. "Despite the ills our families have suffered at one another's hands and the hands of Foucault supporters, does it not strike you how delighted the Lord must be to bring us out of that darkness and not merely into the dim?"

Griffin did not mask his surprise that she shared that observation.

"What I mean," she said, "is that 'tis surely by His hand enemies have become lovers in heart as well as body."

"In heart?"

"I love my husband, and he loves me, though never would you have believed it possible the day you revealed to Bayard the fool I made him, aye?"

"There was much strain between you. Hence, 'tis a blessing your husband and you have proved well matched."

"As has your daughter and my uncle. When they visited six weeks past, there was love there as well."

It was as Thomasin had expressed in a missive sent to Castle Kelling shortly after Otto had nearly murdered her and her husband. Griffin could not have been more pleased—unless, of course, he was certain Verdun felt the same.

As if Lady Elianor knew his thoughts, she said, "'Twas mutual, methinks, though Magnus Verdun holds close what goes behind his eyes."

"I thank you for that, my lady."

"Now all that remains to be seen is how you and my sister-in-law fit together. What think you?"

Did she hope for a declaration of love? "I threatened a feud of my own making if your husband refused me my bride. Thus, I am assuredly of the belief marriage to Lady Quintin will be satisfactory."

For the second time since she had escorted him to his chamber, he noted her hand on her abdomen and wondered if she was aware of the injury Quintin had sustained that would likely deny Griffin and his wife the blessing the Boursiers were expecting.

"A winter babe?" he asked.

Her hand fled her belly. But then she gave a joyous laugh. "December, a year after the beginning of Bayard and me."

"My congratulations."

She opened her mouth, but closed it as if the words she had nearly spoken were best left unsaid. Had she thought better of returning the kindness of wishing Quintin and him the same blessing?

"Alas," she said on a sigh, "'tis late, and I should be abed. Good eve, Baron."

When she was gone, Griffin considered his packs that had been delivered to the chamber—and listened for the closing of the solar's door.

It *was* late, but when he had followed Lady Elianor down the corridor, he had seen candlelight beneath the door of the chamber he knew was Quintin's from the night he had spent here after returning her to Adderstone.

Still, he should wait 'til the morrow to speak with her. *Should*, he told himself again as he unhurriedly completed his ablutions, giving Quintin time to come to him.

A quarter hour later, he went to her.

She did not hear his footsteps. Nor had she expected she would. He did not knock. Neither had she expected he would.

As he eased the door closed, she saw that though his tunic was belted, no sword hung from it—only a dagger—and he was without boots. The absence of both made him look more the lover than the warrior.

"I meant to come to you," she said as he turned to where she sat on the end of the bed.

Dear Lord, he fills my eyes, she silently exclaimed, then prayed her thoughts and convictions would not further stray from the path she had set them upon. But stray they did, the sight of him making her long to be nearer this man who was tall and broad, blond and blue-eyed, and not handsome enough to appeal as much as he did.

She swallowed. "I meant to but could not."

"Thus, I am here." He did not move from the door.

She glanced down her robe-clad figure. "Unseemly either way."

"Only to those who do not know 'tis as husband and wife we are reunited."

"That is everyone," she said, then remembered Hulda. But it would not do to speak of the maid, for Hulda knew her lady was wed only because she also knew what Quintin had lost.

Quintin shivered. Having promised herself that at the first opportunity to be alone with her husband she would reveal all, it was time.

"I would rather you be cold than frightened of me," Griffin said, "but methinks you suffer from the latter."

She rose from the bed and clasped her hands at her waist. "I have wronged you, and my apology is months past due."

"Lady Maeve."

"Aye, I should not have spoken as I did. I have no excuse other than my own weakness that the blame for not being at my mother's side was too heavy to bear alone."

She sniffed and wished that after all these months she did not continue to succumb to tears. Through them, she saw Griffin tense and sensed he held himself from crossing the divide between them—a divide he would learn was wider than believed.

She breathed deep. "I pray you will forgive me this one thing. And more."

He strode forward. "Already I know," he said, and before she could make sense of that, her face was between his hands, his mouth on hers. He kissed her hungrily, and she returned his kisses. Then his hands were in her hair, gently pulling apart her braid. "You have let your hair grow," he said against her lips.

"For you."

"God's breath," he groaned, "I have been too long without you."

She also felt the months beyond the months of that first stay of marriage, but his words reminded her that before their long parting could be remedied, he needed to know the reason for the second stay of marriage.

She slid her palms up his chest and leaned back. "There is more to be told."

Candlelight flickering across his face, he repeated, "Already I know." Did he? Had he seen...? Nay, he spoke of something else. She stepped back and, when he let her go, loosened the robe's belt.

But as she parted it to reveal her bare body, his hand closed over hers. "Quintin, I know. Whilst you slept the morn after we made love, I saw the scar. And I understand what it may mean."

She gasped. "Still you want me."

"You are my wife."

Her chest convulsed. "I should have told you ere we wed. Perhaps the king would have altered the decree and allowed you to marry another."

"Regardless, I would have taken you to wife."

He could not possibly understand. She opened the robe and touched the scar's upper curve. "How near did you look upon this?"

His eyes moved down her, pausing on the ring strung on the necklace, then continuing to her belly. "As told, I know what it may mean."

"But you do not know what it *does* mean. You believe it possible I can still bear children, as I also hoped, but now..."

"Now?"

She shuddered. "The second stay of marriage was also for grieving, but not for the loss of my mother—for the child we made."

Griffin's blue eyes darkened beneath lowering eyebrows, nostrils flared, hand dropped from her. "You carried my child and did not send word."

Defensiveness soared through her, carrying with it Serle's name and tempting her to shout that it was all the fault of the De Arells. But nay, not the De Arells. Not Griffin.

"I am sorry," she choked. "When I realized I was pregnant, I yet mourned my mother and was still wrongly angry with you. But more, I feared my womb would fail. And it did."

From atop the mattress, she retrieved the missive Hulda had returned to her. "The eve ere my body gave up our babe, I wrote this, but come the morn there was no longer a reason to send it—naught I could do to change what happened, naught you could do."

As Griffin stared at the woman who had denied him knowledge of his child, an ire similar to the one he had directed at Ulric for hiding Thomasin from him gained strength. Without consideration of the consequences its release might cause, it wanted out.

"Griffin," she said softly.

He took the missive from her. *I am with child,* he read. *Pray, come soon that I might wear your ring for all to know I am yours ~ Quintin*

She is mine, he told himself. *Unless I lose her in this moment.*

He touched the ring between her breasts and urged himself to think much so he would regret little. Finally, he said, "'Tis late, and I am tired." He turned away. "We shall talk more on the morrow."

He heard her indrawn breath, felt her hurt, and continued to the door.

"I am sorry, Griffin. There seems no end to the wrong I do you."

Struck by the difference between the Quintin of Christmas past and the one of summer come, he stilled. Were that fiery, resentful young woman present, it was anger she would sling at him, not apology. She would defend her actions by placing the blame on Serle—indeed, all the De Arells, including her husband—and it would be understandable, for much of the blame was theirs. But though grateful she did not speak against the family that was now hers, he missed her fire.

"Pray, Griffin, know that if 'tis possible to gain an annulment, I will not oppose you."

Think much. Regret little, he silently commanded. And yet something warned he would regret much if he left her alone with her grieving and unanswered request for forgiveness.

He pivoted and returned to his wife whose brown, gold-ringed eyes were large in her pale face. "There will be no annulment. Before God I vowed to be your husband and protector to my end days. That does not change because you cannot bear children. That is not the man I am, nor the man I would become. Aye, I wished more sons and daughters, but it was not a requirement. Indeed, had the king not decreed I wed again, I likely would not have. Thus, the only thing I ask of you is that you be wife to me and mother to our son, Rhys."

That last made her startle.

"Aye," he said, "*our* son, he who may not admit it but would have the Lady of Blackwood return."

Griffin lifted the necklace off over her head and, as he removed the ring from the chain, said, "Our lives are entwined. Children or nay, I wish you for my wife." He tossed the necklace on the mattress, lifted her hand, and slid the ring on her finger. "You are claimed, Quintin de Arell, as am I. And as I will not relinquish my claim, I would not have you relinquish yours."

Tears spilled. "I am forgiven?"

"I would that you had sent word you carried our child so I also would have known the joy, brief though it was—more, that you would not have been alone in grieving our loss—but that ache and disappointment will heal. So if forgiveness is needed, 'tis given."

She dropped her chin and began to cry—softly at first, causing him to pull her into his arms, then more loudly, prompting him to carry her to bed. He lowered the missive to the table, next his dagger-hung belt, then stretched out beside her and tucked her into his chest to muffle her misery so it would not rouse her brother who would be far from genial to find the Baron of Blackwood in his sister's bed.

Quintin continued to weep and hold to him until two of the three candles guttered out, then she slept. But when he pulled away, she awakened.

"Stay."

"'Tis dangerous."

"But a while longer."

He eased down, promising himself that as soon as she slept again he would depart.

But she began to talk. "At Castle Mathe, you believed I was not sooner wed because I was so disagreeable, but it was because of my injury—and at my request—my first betrothal was broken."

"'Tis as I thought when first I saw your scar." He frowned. "The headache you suffered ere your menses is because of the injury?"

"I believe so. Never did I endure such before then."

"A painful reminder."

"You understand, do you not, my injury is the reason Bayard wished to keep me from fulfilling the decree?"

"I do."

"'Tis not just that I am unlikely to bring a live babe into the world. The physician warned that if a child remained in my womb nine months, the birthing could kill us both."

The possibility of which Griffin had considered while holding her and reflecting that once more he was wed to a woman with good cause to fear childbirth. But having lost Johanna to lingering complications a year after Rhys's birth, Griffin would not lose Quintin to the same.

"Mayhap the physician is wrong," she whispered. "'Tis possible a child of ours would survive."

Also possible it would be left motherless the same as Rhys. "Nay, Quintin, I will not put another child in your belly."

She gasped. "But I would be your wife in bed as well as in name."

"You shall be, as I shall fully be your husband."

"How?"

He pushed up on an elbow, turned her onto her back, and brushed tear-dampened hair off her cheeks. "Wife of mine, there are ways to intimately love and be loved without conceiving, and those ways we shall teach each other."

"But the Church deems conception the sole purpose of husband knowing wife."

And considered intentionally childless marriages little better than prostitution, he knew. "So it does, and yet it embraces the saying *Si non caste, tamen caute.*"

"Meaning?"

"If not chastely, at least cautiously."

"Oh," she breathed.

"Too, the Lord made such relations pleasurable—pleasure that does not end when a woman is past child-bearing age. Self-serving it may sound, but surely lovemaking is also meant to bond a couple so ever they long for the arms of the one to whom they pledged their lives." He drew a thumb across her lower lip. "As ever I shall long for you, Quintin de Arell."

She caught her breath. "And I for you."

He lay down. "We will be one again, but this night I grieve with you the loss of our child."

She did not respond. But after a time she relaxed and, as her breath deepened, murmured, "Methinks it possible I love you."

He tensed, disturbed and yet tempted to try the words on his own tongue. Did he love her? Certes, the last time he had so wanted a woman was when he had known Thomasin's mother. But that was not this.

This was no young man's exaggeration that his life would upend were he denied the woman he longed for. This was Quintin, and what he felt for her was not all desire. It was more simply being near her... speaking with her...breathing her...holding her.

He kissed her brow. "Then this—what you think love—is where we begin anew."

26

―∞―

Soon every morn I shall awaken thus, Quintin silently clasped the promise to her as she peered into Griffin's restful face.

The chamber was dim, dawn having begun to relieve night of its duty. But by the purple-gray light passing through the window, she saw the line of her husband's jaw and its dark whiskers, the curve of his lips and straight descent of his nose, his lowered lids whose lashes deepened the shadows atop his cheeks.

Seeing these things, she was reminded of that first night they had spent together in the tower when, muddled in misery over the belief all was lost and Bayard possibly dead, she had beseeched Griffin to stay. Just as on the night past, that night he had only held her as she had needed him to do. However, this morn he was yet with her, which he had not been even on the morn following their nuptial night. And she could think of nothing she liked better than greeting a new day whilst in the arms of this man.

She leaned up and touched her mouth to his. "You stayed with me."

"Hmm. Dangerous." He narrowly opened his eyes. "But I do like awakening to my bride."

She smiled. "I was thinking the same of my groom."

"Then we must give the king his wedding."

"When?"

"Soon. Doubtless, Simon Foucault will be far less inclined to fail at preventing our union than he was with the others."

She frowned. "Simon Foucault?"

"Aye, Sir Otto's father and your uncle. Your brother and I have concluded he lives and for years has been known as Sir Francis Cartier."

Of a sudden, breath eluded her.

"You have seen him?" Griffin asked.

"Nay, I have only heard of the king's man—of his visage ruined by fire. Has he Foucault eyes?"

"At Thomasin's wedding, there was no occasion for me to draw near enough to determine if the brown is ringed by gold, but your brother says 'tis so."

She nodded. "Bayard met him at King Edward's court, and I understand he was here on Christmas Day ere my mother—" She recoiled. "'Twas he who killed her? Her own brother?"

"That is what we believe—lest she revealed the puppet he made of her. I am sorry."

She trembled. "Dear Lord, he has been among us all these years—plotting, raiding, burning, killing."

Griffin drew his fingers down the curve of her face. "The revenge wreaked on us shall end. Your brother, Verdun, and I will see to it."

"How?"

"That must be determined, but if the Baron of Emberly is as eager to end the Foucault threat as your brother and I, he will soon appear at Godsmere in response to the missive I sent ere departing Mathe. And we will lay our plans." He rose above her. "Regrettably, I must return to my chamber."

She laid a hand on his arm. "I am glad you came for me and truly sorry I left much unsaid for so long."

After some moments, he said, "'Tis of no benefit to be anxious over things that cannot be changed, whether because God Himself has taken them in hand or..." He slid his hand inside her robe and spanned her belly.

"Griffin?"

"Regret is a bane to the soul, but know that ever I shall rue Serle and Constance allowing Agatha to tempt them to a place that caused my brother to take something so precious from you."

Though she did not wish to speak of that day, there was something he needed to know. "Though I have long held Serle as responsible for my injury as he is for Bayard's, his blade did not cut me."

Griffin drew back a space. "What speak you?"

She gripped his hand, moved it to where the sword's point had begun its destruction, and drew it to its end. "This was done by my brother's blade. Foolish me. And foolish Bayard. When Constance tried to get between him and her lover, my brother left himself open to save her, and Serle's blade took his eye. Fearing I would lose Bayard, I did what Constance failed to do. I set myself between two raging warriors and Bayard...Blindly, he retaliated for the injury done him, unaware I would be the one to suffer his wrath. And then he took your brother's sword arm."

Griffin sank into silence, but finally said, "Many assumptions I have made, my brother having revealed little of that day. But this I know—though it was Bayard's blade, that does not absolve Serle of responsibility. No matter that he loved another man's wife, regardless Agatha of Mawbry incited him to make a cuckold of your brother, he must answer for it."

"I thank you," she said low. "Now you better understand why my brother is so protective? That he ever tries to right what he believes was his wrong—bearing guilt of which he is undeserving?"

"I understand. Indeed, 'tis possible I may come to like *The Boursier*." This time when he titled Bayard such, the derision was half-hearted.

Quintin drew a breath of relief. "I pray you shall."

He brushed his lips across hers. "From this day forward, let us aspire to suffer as few regrets as possible."

"Aye, lord husband."

He stood, retrieved his belt, and buckled on the dagger-hung leather. Then he reached for the missive in which she had revealed what was to have been tidings of joy. And looked to her. "I would have come immediately, Quintin."

"This I know."

He nodded stiffly and tucked the missive beneath his belt. "I will see you in the hall for the morning repast, and you will sit at my side."

"I shall."

Thanking the Lord all was coming right, praying Simon Foucault's terror would soon end, Quintin watched her husband stride opposite. But as he cleared the end of the bed, a knock sounded. He halted and reached for the sword he had not brought within her chamber.

Yanking her robe closed, fumbling to secure its belt, Quintin sprang off the bed. "Quick, Griffin—"

The door opened, carrying Hulda inside. But the woman halted so abruptly she had to stumble two steps forward to keep her feet beneath her. "Baron de Arell! What do you—?"

"Quiet, Hulda!" Quintin rushed forward, but someone had heard, as revealed by booted feet moving at a run down the corridor.

"Stay behind me!" Griffin threw out an arm to hold her back.

"But I can explain—"

His head snapped around and, blue eyes gone black, he snarled, "Did you learn naught from the last time you placed yourself between a De Arell and a Boursier?"

Her hand made a fist, and as she struggled to keep it from her abdomen, Bayard lunged through the doorway. He paused just inside the chamber and, singular gaze fierce, moved it down Griffin to his bootless feet, then to Quintin where she stood just over her husband's shoulder. Unlike Griffin, his seeking hand had attained his sword, its blade halfway out of its scabbard.

"Do not!" she cried and would have proved foolish again had Griffin not gripped her arm to hold her back.

"Baron Boursier," he said, "think much on this ere the past revisits us."

But Bayard did not break stride until his blade's tip was at Griffin's throat. "Unhand my sister!"

"Hear me, Bayard," Quintin beseeched.

"Unhand her!"

"And risk her trying to save her brother again?" Griffin's voice was dangerously calm. "Nay, she stays behind me, and you shall lower your sword."

Bayard pushed its point nearer Griffin's throat. "*If* I deign to lower it, 'twill not be whilst you hold my sister."

"As already told, she is mine to hold."

"I said release her——"

"Bayard!" Lady Elianor's arrival caused all within the chamber to startle, and Griffin's growl made Quintin fear her brother's sword had cut him.

"Take yourself and our babe from here, Elianor," Bayard ordered. "Now!"

She halted, protectively crossed an arm over her abdomen, and looked from Quintin to Griffin to Hulda. "Surely there is an explanation, Bayard."

"There is, Lady," Griffin said.

"Leave, Elianor!"

She took a step forward, and her voice met Quintin's as they both entreated, "Bayard!"

"Blessed rood!" he bellowed. "Can not a husband protect his wife and sister without argument?"

"It seems not," Griffin muttered, then put across his shoulder. "Shall I explain or will you, Quintin?"

"Pray, tell him, my lady!" Hulda cried.

"You know what goes here, Hulda?" Bayard demanded.

Her eyes widened. "I…" She glanced at Quintin, whose quick shake of the head beseeched her to remain silent over her lady's loss. "I do know, my lord. As Lady Quintin has ever been my lamb, not much escapes these old eyes and this old heart."

Bayard looked back at Quintin. "Speak!"

She raised her left hand, revealing the ring her husband had moved from the necklace to her finger on the night past. "I do belong to Griffin, just as he belongs to me."

His brow, crossed by the eyepatch, creased heavily. "How?"

"Your sister and I have been wed these six months," Griffin answered. "She is my wife as much as Lady Elianor is yours."

Bayard returned his regard to the man whose throat remained intimate with his blade. "By way of vows spoken before a priest or"—he glanced at the bed—"consummation only?"

"First the former, then the latter. Regardless that Sir Otto sought to revive the Foucault line by taking his cousin to wife, regardless of the king's answer to your missive, in the eyes of God and Church, your sister and I are wed."

Bayard held his offensive stance so long Quintin was thankful her husband was not one to behave rashly. At last, her brother lowered his blade. "Wed in secret. For what?"

Quintin started forward, but Griffin tightened his grip.

And when Lady Elianor moved as if to gain her husband's side, Bayard rumbled, "Stay where you are, Wife," then repeated, "For what, Baron?"

"Your sister tried to save you again by proposing I wed her ere a determination was made about your marriage—a show of support she believed would more likely move the king to decide in your favor. However, as I did not believe it would be of any more aid than that which I had already given, I saw no reason to tempt Edward's wrath."

"But still you wed her."

"For other reasons, the first being I wished her for my wife and feared that if the king declared your lands forfeit, eliminating the need for an alliance between our families, he would wed your sister elsewhere. In that event, I would have revealed a much too eager groom and bride had chosen to wed rather than sin."

Griffin's choice of words eased Quintin's fear, but only for a moment. Bayard's sword remained unsheathed.

"What other reason?" her brother demanded.

Griffin put his head to the side, reminding her of that first day when, looking down upon her from atop his wall, he had assessed the threat her entourage presented.

With what sounded like a smile in his voice, he said, "You will not like this, Boursier."

"Thus, my blade keeps close company with my sword arm."

"In addition to wanting Lady Quintin as my wife, it occurred that were Godsmere and Emberly forfeited, the king could be moved to award the lands to the family originally promised the whole of Kilbourne. And were that not enough, my claim on them would be strengthened by marriage to one believed to be the last hope for the Foucault line."

Bayard considered that, then said, "You cannot have been pleased the king accepted my marriage to Lady Elianor."

Griffin grunted. "*Think,* Boursier! Were I set on gaining your lands, why would I provide you the solution of consummation? Why would I bear witness it was Lady Elianor's deception that caused you to miss the appointed day by which you were to wed?"

Bayard stared.

"Forsooth, I was not averse to enlarging my holdings. What man would be? But who better to gain them than one willing to give your sister and her mother a home?" He raised his eyebrows. "Or would you have preferred that, in addition to the king awarding Godsmere and Emberly to a favorite—mayhap his man, Sir Francis—he awarded your sister?"

"What he speaks is true," Quintin said.

Bayard looked to her. "And yet only now you wish to take your place as Lady of Blackwood?"

"I..." She pressed her lips for fear revelation would pour past them. She could not tell him the reason for her prolonged grieving. Far better he believe her incapable of conceiving than know that what his blade had wrought had caused her to lose a child. Too much guilt. Too much pain.

"I have been stubborn and grudging, as you know I can be," she finally said, "but now I would wed before all and accompany my husband home to Castle Mathe." It was with intention she claimed Griffin's home as her own, and she was pleased to see a softening about Bayard's face.

"As soon as Father Crispin is well enough to perform the ceremony," she continued, "I would have it done." After she spoke it, it struck her

that the beloved priest would then have presided over all three marriages. There was something very right about that.

Her brother nodded and slid his sword into its scabbard. "'Twill be
done. But until then, De Arell, you will not enter my sister's chamber
lest one outside the five of us bears witness and sets tongues to wagging."

Griffin inclined his head. "Then all the sooner we must see your
priest risen from his bed."

"Indeed."

Griffin released Quintin. When he turned, she saw Bayard's sword
had drawn blood from her husband's throat. But it was not as deep as the
cut she had made there last Christmas, presenting as a thin crimson line.

"You will have to remove the ring," Griffin said.

She glanced at it and, assuring herself it would not be long ere it was
forever on her hand, nodded.

"I shall meet you belowstairs, my lady," he said.

She inclined her head, and as he turned away, she noted the missive
beneath his belt, the contents of which she prayed her brother would
never know.

Her husband strode across the chamber, and Bayard stepped aside
to allow him to pass.

Upon hearing Griffin's chamber door close, Quintin said, "Now you
know what goes between us, Bayard."

"You should have told me sooner." He momentarily closed his eyes.
"Had De Arell a sword upon him, I do not know I would have hesitated
to engage him and…Almighty! You would have set yourself between us."

"I did not think—"

"As you did not five years ago!" He splayed his hands as if the fists
made of them ached, shook his head. "Forgive me. I am to fault for that."

"You are not."

His gaze lowered, and realizing she had once more put a fist to her
abdomen, she dropped it to her side.

"Does he know?" Bayard asked.

Tears sprang to her eyes. "He knows."

"And?"

"Still he came for me. Still he would pass his life with me." She gave a short laugh that did not taste or sound as bitter as once it had. "He has his heir, Bayard. 'Tis a wife he wants. Me."

"He knows 'twas my blade?"

"Aye, and as I do not hold you responsible, neither does he."

With a glance at Lady Elianor and Hulda, Quintin crossed the room and put her arms around him. "My husband is a good man."

"I pray 'tis so, otherwise I will do worse than score his throat."

She leaned back. "'Tis so."

His jaw shifted. "If he...If you..."

She knew his worry—that which had made him seek to release her from marriage. "He says he will not risk getting me with child, that there are ways to..." Her face flushed.

As did Bayard's. "I am pleased you are happy with him," he muttered.

"Quite. And I am sorry I did not sooner reveal all. These months have been difficult."

He kissed her forehead. "I know."

But he did not know all. And that was as she would have it.

He drew back. "I shall let you make ready for the day." He turned to his wife. "Elianor?"

"I will aid Hulda with your sister, then join you at meal."

He nodded and closed the door behind him.

There was something Elianor wished to say, Quintin sensed, and it was more than the words she spoke minutes later as she tightened the laces on one side of her sister-in-law's gown while Hulda tugged on the right.

"It seems," she murmured, "that if you do not already have with Baron de Arell what I have with your brother, you will be blessed with a good semblance of it."

And it made the lady happy, Quintin knew. "I did not expect to feel this way about any man, especially Griffin de Arell."

Elianor laughed. "Oh, what surprises God had for the three ladies of the baronies—and their lords. Love."

"I did not say I love Baron de Arell," Quintin said sharply.

The lady came around. "Only you can know how much you feel for your husband, but I wager you now walk a path that runs in the same direction as the one I traversed when your brother set aside my trespasses to soothe away my past."

Recalling what Griffin had believed of the lady, Quintin said, "Your first marriage was horrid, aye?"

Her lashes fluttered, mouth trembled. "Such that I often cease whatever I am occupied with that I might look near upon my surroundings to be certain they do not waver as they would in a dream from which I might awaken to find myself returned to the nightmare."

Quintin glanced at Hulda who, having secured the other laces, had taken a step back and now looked between the ladies.

Satisfied Elianor was comfortable conversing in the maid's presence, Quintin said, "I am sorry for what you suffered, Elianor."

"I would not wish it again, but where I am now with Bayard is surely because of where I was without him, and so I try not to begrudge my past and instead look upon it as the terribly steep mountain I had to climb ere I could begin to make my way into the beautiful valley on the other side." Eyes tearing, she turned aside. "Come sit. Hulda and I will plait your hair."

Quintin lowered onto the bench before her dressing table, and once more the women each took a side of her. "I thank you for making my brother happy," she said as she stared into the mirror on the table. "Certes, he was not ere you came."

"And I thank you." Lady Elianor paused halfway down the braid that would just barely drape Quintin's shoulder. "For not telling Bayard."

"For not—?" Quintin snapped her gaze to Hulda, whose face reflected surprise.

"As much as I do not wish to be right in this," Bayard's wife said softly, "it would explain much. Am I right?"

Quintin swallowed. "You are."

"Oh," the lady breathed, "I am sorry."

Her sympathy stirring up more tears, Quintin said, "When did you know?"

Elianor took up the braid again. "It first occurred you were with child when I noticed how often your hand was on your belly—the most natural response when a woman knows she carries life. However, I reasoned away my suspicion, reminding myself Baron de Arell and you were but betrothed and telling myself your hand there was because of the injury done you—that something made you think on it. It occurred to me again when, your grieving for your mother having eased, of a sudden it returned, and I noted you no longer pressed a hand to your belly. 'Twas a fist instead."

"Then you knew I had lost our babe?"

"Nay, once more I believed I guessed wrong. Thus, I did not know until this morn when I learned you are wed, your marriage consummated, and I saw your reaction when it was revealed Hulda knew of your marriage." She sighed. "I ache for your loss. And as told, I am grateful that with the scent of blood on the air, this day you did not reveal it to your brother."

"I would not have you tell him."

"Of course not. 'Tis for you or your husband to reveal."

"Never," Quintin said firmly, then peered into the mirror and wished for the customary veil upon her hair that signified she was no longer available to wed.

Soon.

27

Two days passed before the Baron of Emberly and his bride rode upon Castle Adderstone. Their escort, numbering two score strong, evidenced that just as Griffin and Bayard did not believe Sir Otto's departure for the king's prison ended the Foucault threat, neither did Verdun. And as would soon be learned, the Baron of Emberly had more cause to suspect the danger was far from past.

Though Griffin insisted his wife stand at his side to receive the Verduns, when he strode forward to greet his daughter, whom he had not seen since giving her in marriage at Castle Kelling, Quintin remained at the steps and clasped her hands hard in remembrance of how aloof she had been when last Thomasin was at Adderstone. Quintin had hurt one who had not known of the loss that made it difficult to be reminded of Griffin.

"My lady."

She looked to her husband, who had halted halfway between his daughter and her to reach a hand behind, then glanced to where Verdun had lifted his petite bride from her horse and had yet to release her. Returning her gaze to Griffin, Quintin reluctantly stepped forward and slid her hand into his.

He leaned near. "She is also your daughter," he said, and for a moment she was angered that he pressed on her something she was not ready for. But he meant well, and when Thomasin hastened forward and threw her arms around him, Quintin realized how alone she would have felt had he let her be.

Their embrace was long, Thomasin laughing and chattering and pecking kisses on his cheek, Griffin chuckling and twice lifting her off her feet. Then, with a contented sigh, Thomasin moved out of her father's arms and stepped before Quintin.

"Another wedding we shall have, aye?" She radiated such hope—and forgiveness—all Quintin could do was nod.

"Soon we shall be kin!" Thomasin took a chance only she would take, putting her arms around Quintin and, when the gesture was not spurned, hugging the breath from her. "Methinks 'tis more than wishes to kiss the Baron of Blackwood that finds you at his side," she said low.

Quintin nearly laughed. "Far more," she allowed and looked forward to sharing with the young woman that already they were kin.

Thomasin drew back. "Though the black yet hangs over us, I am so happy I can barely behave the lady."

Quintin raised her eyebrows. "Thomasin de Arell Verdun, you have only to be yourself to be adored."

The young woman beamed, then shifted her gaze to the two who approached. "Oh, have mercy! 'Tis she who made The Boursier believe plain could be so beautiful."

Lady Elianor and Thomasin embraced and laughed over little words exchanged, then arm in arm ascended the steps whilst the three barons, all in one place for the first time, greeted one another with less enthusiasm. But they were men, and they seemed genuine enough that Quintin started after her sister-in-law and stepdaughter.

"I thank you for receiving us so well, Baron Boursier," Verdun said low. "Unfortunately, I bear ill tidings."

Though foreboding pierced Quintin, her feet did not falter. She knew the Foucault threat was not past, but perhaps it was nearer than believed. Did Thomasin know the tidings her husband would share with Griffin and Bayard? If so, Quintin would soon know them as well.

It was told he was dead, that he had met his end during the journey to the king's prison when his escort was attacked.

Though the brigands had succeeded in freeing Otto, Sir Francis had given chase, and one of his men had overtaken the knight and engaged him at swords. Surrounded by brigands, the mercenary's man had sustained a fatal blow—but not before spilling his prey's innards. Thus, the end of Sir Otto.

Rather, the *presumed* end, the knight's mount having fled with its dying rider fallen over its neck.

"Convenient," Griffin said when Verdun finished delivering the tidings received prior to his departure from Castle Kelling.

"Indeed." Verdun nodded. "If Sir Francis is Simon Foucault as your missive told, he has eliminated the possibility of exposure."

"You do not believe the two are the same?"

"On the contrary. Though we gained little from Otto during his imprisonment at Kelling, the man-at-arms who aided him in seeking to murder Thomasin and me revealed ere his own death that the Foucault uprising was led by Aude and her man. He said we would not know that man's face, but we would know his name. And so we do, and now Simon Foucault's son runs with the brigands."

"That," said Boursier where he stood before the open window, his back to his allies, "else dead by means other than those recounted for the king. Otto failed his father, and as a much-informed witness who could be broken by Edward's interrogator, he may have been deemed throwaway. Regardless, 'tis further proof Simon disguises himself as Sir Francis Cartier."

Pleased the Baron of Godsmere thought much, Griffin looked to his son-in-law. Did the youngest of them think well behind his inscrutable face? A face that, despite the circumstances uniting the three the same as their fathers had united a quarter of a century ago, was nearly absent the facial tics for which he was known?

Thomasin, Griffin concluded. His impetuous, perilously improper daughter was good for Magnus Verdun. Though the baron might not hold his wife in great affection, he liked her well. That Griffin had concluded when Verdun had lifted her from the saddle before Adderstone's keep and lingered over her, returned her whispers, and smiled wide enough to show teeth when she bounced to her toes and touched her mouth to his.

"Better Otto dead," Verdun said, "but until I see his corpse, I will not render my wife or people vulnerable by believing it." He pushed off the table he had leaned against since entering the solar. Throughout, he had stood an arm's reach from Griffin, allowing only a glimpse of amusement when told of the secret marriage. But his feelings had become more readable with the delivery of his own revelation about Otto's supposed death, so deeply grooving his face he appeared older.

"So it comes to a head," he said. "For Cartier, a desperate head. God willing, his successes in furthering the feud all these years will make his recent failures cause him to act rashly."

More and more liking his son-in-law, Griffin reached to the platter at the center of the table and retrieved an apple. He took a bite, and the crunch turned Boursier from the window and caused Verdun to peer over his shoulder.

Griffin swallowed. "The hours between dinner and supper are long." He nodded at the platter Lady Elianor had ordered delivered to the solar. "Join me."

Shortly, all three were seated and devastation of the viands began in earnest.

It was Verdun who returned them to Sir Francis. "We require bait." He flicked crumbs from his fingers. "I have a proposal. However, 'tis one I do not believe either of you will like."

There being only one whom Boursier and Griffin had in common that neither would risk, Griffin growled, "Think again. And not any-where near my wife."

"Stay away from my sister, Verdun," Boursier snarled.

The Baron of Emberly looked between them. "I would feel the same about my wife and niece, but neither qualifies now both are wed and, thus, so far out of Cartier's reach their only value lies in death. And as told by Otto, Lady Quintin is the prize—whether his or his father's, meaning she is in less danger—"

"Enough!" Griffin and Bayard said in unison, and if not that Quintin was under discussion, Griffin would have been impressed by how unconcerned Verdun seemed though he roused two warriors whom he might triumph over individually, but not collectively.

"Hear me," he continued. "It has only to appear as if he might gain his prize. And more desirable that prize will be if it is believed the marriage between De Arell and Boursier has yet to take place."

"Lady Quintin and I are to wed publicly as soon as Father Crispin is well enough to perform the ceremony," Griffin said. Which could be within the next few days, the priest having made it to the hall for supper last eve. Though he had partaken of little, there had been color in his face, and he had conversed with those on either side of him during the half hour before Rollo assisted him abovestairs.

"I say you wait," Verdun said. "If we are to end the Foucault threat, we must set the trap with the *appearance* of that which will cause Simon Foucault to risk the snap of iron teeth."

Though Griffin longed to end the conversation, Boursier's brooding curbed his tongue and fists. Quintin would not be the bait, but perhaps this was the starting point of the plan to bring Simon Foucault to justice.

"I am listening, Verdun, but only that." He looked to the Baron of Godsmere. "Boursier?"

"Speak, Verdun."

"First, what do we know of Simon Foucault?"

Boursier settled back in his chair. "He was born to Baron Denis Foucault around 1280, meaning he is now over fifty years aged, the same as Sir Francis. He received his knight's training in France and, upon earning his spurs, was called home to administer Kilbourne in preparation for the day he would gain his father's title."The Baron of Godsmere raised his eyebrows. "But he refused, citing my father was capable of administering the barony as he had done for Denis Foucault, and would continue to do once Simon gained his inheritance."

Griffin nodded. "After his father died while taking up arms against the earl from whom he held Kilbourne, still Simon did not come. What is not known is the reason. Believing all was lost, his inheritance divided between our families, did he decide to remain in service to his French lord? Or did the skirmish he is said to have died in occur ere he could cross the channel and attempt to take back the barony?"

"The latter," Verdun said. "And I wager, 'twas in that skirmish he was burned." He looked to Griffin. "Recall Thomasin's exchange with Sir Francis after our wedding when she said she could not imagine how one survived the agony that had befallen him. For that, methinks Otto was ordered to murder my wife and me by way of fire."

As when Griffin had received tidings of what had happened in the lord's solar at Castle Kelling, he felt a burn in his belly of the sort that only vengeance might cool—and which threatened to make him regret much in thinking little.

"Simon Foucault's ruined face allowed him to return to England bearing another man's name," Boursier said. "Now let us speak of what we know of Sir Francis Cartier. When he arrived in England, he brought his lover with him—Aude, whom most know as Agatha—and either in France or here, she birthed Otto."

"Who was raised to believe he was the hope of the Foucaults," Verdun said, "and trained up under the eye of King Edward II, who likely knew who fathered Otto."

Griffin's anger stirred more violently. He had trusted the knight the old king had sent to serve upon the barony of Blackwood years past. He should have been wary, but a score of years had passed since the De Arells, Boursiers, and Verduns had made an enemy of that king by revealing to the barons united against him that Baron Denis Foucault served as Edward II's spy. Aye, the king had to have known the baseborn Otto was a Foucault.

"But when Edward II's queen forced him off his throne," Verdun continued, "seating their son on it with the aid of her lover, Mortimer, and making Edward III their puppet, Sir Francis would have had to look elsewhere for favor. Thus, he aided the young king in wresting power from his mother and slaying Mortimer."

"And he has made good use of Edward III's favor in plotting to bring about our ends," Griffin said and looked to Boursier. "You know Edward III better than we. Do you think he is aware of Cartier's true identity?"

The Baron of Godsmere rose and returned to the window. "I do not believe our present king knows his esteemed mercenary is Simon Foucault. Not only would Sir Francis have no cause to confide in him, but because of who Edward III has become since he cast off his mother's fetters. He wants what is best for England, even if he must threaten his nobles into submission, as he did in forcing our families to unite. He is hardly perfect, but he is determined he will not make the mistakes that cost his father the throne. And Sir Francis is such a mistake, one that could threaten Edward's rule."

"So how do we turn that to our advantage?" Verdun asked.

"Bait," Griffin said, "but not my wife."

Boursier narrowed his gaze. "De Arell?"

Griffin knew his smile was crooked, and he let it be. "'Tis something my father suggested, which I shall enlarge upon now we better know Simon Foucault."

Quintin caught her breath—just as Thomasin had done when Quintin had revealed to her she had long been wed to her father, just as Quintin and Elianor had done when Thomasin had revealed the tidings of Sir Otto's supposed death.

A hand to her mouth lest a sound of distress slipped past the door that granted access to the solar on the other side of Adderstone's hidden passages, she stared into the darkness.

She knew she should not listen in on the barons' conversation, and for that she had not revealed to Thomasin and Elianor what she intended. Though the former might have joined her, the latter would have protested. Not only was Elianor with child, but it was within the inner walls that Agatha had nearly ended the life of Bayard's wife. Too, Quintin did not trust Elianor to withhold from her husband his sister's trespass.

"Dear Lord," she breathed, "whatever comes of this baiting, let us not lose the men we love."

She closed her eyes. "I do love Griffin," she whispered. And there was no pain in acknowledging it, for she was not alone in this. In many ways—determination and perseverance, kindness and consideration, patience and understanding, gentle embraces and sweet caresses—Griffin had first revealed he loved her.

Though she would cherish those words if ever he spoke them, she did not require them. But she would tell them to him, lest being a man he did not understand or acknowledge such wondrously reckless feelings.

She opened her eyes and told herself to listen, that there was more she needed to know so whatever part she played in outing Simon Foucault, she would be prepared. God willing, she would not have to place herself between two warriors, but *the prize* would do it if it kept Griffin alive for his son and daughter, Bayard for his wife and unborn child, and Magnus for his Thomasin.

Once more, she pressed her ear to the door, but all she heard was the silence of what might have become an empty chamber. Had those within departed?

There. The scrape of chairs and boots across the floor, the sounds of which she used to cover her softer retreat.

28

THE PUBLIC WEDDING was to be delayed a fortnight, as told in a missive sent to King Edward, in which Bayard had retracted his request to release his sister from marriage, citing she had agreed to do her duty now her grieving was past.

A fortnight. Time enough, Griffin said, to allow Father Crispin to recover more of his health. As Quintin knew, unlike Elianor and Thomasin, though the priest yet suffered, he was not so ill he could not preside over a marriage ceremony.

Unfortunately, whatever plans the barons had settled on, she was uninformed, further discussion of Simon Foucault surely having been conducted the past three days whilst the men were outside the keep. All Griffin, Bayard, and Magnus confided to their wives was that plans were being laid to bring the mercenary and his brigands to ground so their children would grow up free of the feuding that had defined their fathers' rules.

Now as Quintin rode beside her husband upon their return to Castle Mathe, where she would begin settling into her role in advance of speaking vows that would officially acknowledge her as Lady of Blackwood, she sensed they were watched.

Glancing at the black wood that, unlike when first she had ridden on Mathe, was so heavily roofed in leaves it looked as if night were upon it, she reached inside her mantle and touched the Wulfrith dagger Bayard had given into her keeping.

When the castle's towers were in sight and Griffin had slowed his men, she nudged her horse nearer his. "Methinks we are watched."

Keeping his gaze forward, he said, "We are. Regardless, our escort is too sizable to draw out those who prefer to lurk in shadows until they can take their prey in the back."

"You will not tell me your plans?"

He looked to her. "You will know all you need to know when you need to know."

"But——"

"Quintin, allow me to protect you as is my honor and responsibility."

Resentment ran through her, but she did not wish to have harsh words with this man she loved—though he did not yet know that was what she felt. If he had come to her chamber since her brother had found them together, she would have declared herself, but he had stayed away as Bayard required. However, once they were inside Castle Mathe...

She frowned. Much depended on Rollo, who accompanied her, resuming the guard he had been tasked with for years—but now only until the Foucault threat was slain. Afterward, he would return to Adderstone, wed Elianor's maid, and become personal guard to the Lady of Godsmere and her babes as they came into the world.

Babes. Quintin hurt some, but it was not hurt fed by jealousy. Though she would ever wish children born of her own body, there would be nieces and nephews and grandchildren. Her arms would never be truly empty.

I thank You, Lord, she silently praised. *You have delivered me from that day.*

She looked to the fortress ahead and thought how different it appeared since that winter day she had ridden on it. Then, its white-washed walls had offered little contrast against the ghostly pales of the season. Now Mathe stood beautifully stark amidst the greens and yellows of high summer.

"You are going home," Griffin said.

She smiled. "When I had to beg and bargain to enter your walls, never would I have believed I would one day call it that."

"As I would not have, though perhaps I wished it."

"Verily?"

The turn of his mouth wonderfully crooked, he said, "Hence, my jest that you eagerly delivered yourself to be my bride."

She *tsked*. "A lady of shorn hair who brought forces against you, who accused you of things you were innocent of, who said she would rather stick herself with a blade ere offer herself to you."

"Irksome," he drawled, "and exciting. For that, I did not turn my back on The Boursier's impudent sister but came out to look nearer upon such a woman. For that, in the hope she would find me as intriguing—*and* for the blade at my throat—I made her my prisoner. And now…" He was silent so long she nearly demanded he continue. "Now what I did not know was missing from me I would never cease to long for were it lost. Thus, I will do whatever is required to keep you safe."

Quintin did not realize how still she had gone until he said low, "Breathe, Wife."

She did so, and on the exhale said, "You make it sound as if you love me."

His canted smile spread to the other side. "So I do. But I know no better way to say it."

Her heart leapt. She had thought to speak love ahead of him, thinking him incapable of expressing such feelings, but he had told it first—just as he had shown it first.

"Certes, no better way," she agreed, "For you, who think too much."

He raised an eyebrow. "You would rather I speak three small words? Nay, they do not suffice."

Strange they should now seem inadequate.

"In the press of time, they serve well," he said, "but when time slows, there are better ways to say and show it."

Her wish to declare her own feelings using those small words dwindling, she determined she would also find better words. Until then… "You do know I feel the same?"

He chuckled. "I suspected, but sometimes false hope disguises itself as truth." He laid a hand over hers that gripped the saddle's pommel.

"Much is owed the meddling King Edward. Indeed, methinks I could forgive him almost anything—even his ignorance of Sir Francis."

Further hating that fiend for being here in this moment, Quintin asked, "Are you confident your plan will free us of him?"

"As with all things, there is room for error in judgment and calculation, but I believe we will see the last of him, and our lands and people will prosper as has been denied them all these years. And ever you shall be at my side and I at yours."

"We will grow old together."

"Very old, my lady." He jutted his chin at Castle Mathe. "Within those walls, we shall see Rhys become a man worthy of spurs, of lording Blackwood, of a fine woman, and of fathering children. Then we shall be blessed to start again with his children."

"I thank you."

"For?"

She turned her hand up into his. "This day. It could not be better."

Serle.

It was too many years since Griffin had seen his brother, but in the moment it became obvious Quintin recognized him—the younger De Arell's blue eyes staring out of a darkly tanned and bearded face—it seemed too few years.

Quintin cried out, and as her palfrey sidestepped, thrust a hand inside her mantle to gain the weapon there.

As Griffin's right hand was filled with his sword, he shifted control of his destrier to his thighs and snatched hold of his wife's reins with his other hand. "Fear not, Quintin!"

"Fear not?" Her eyes darted to the man who regarded them from atop his own horse. "That is—"

"I know."

"He is the reason Bayard…" She swallowed loudly. "And I…"

Having brought his horse tight alongside hers, Rollo having done the same on her other side, Griffin released her reins and set a hand on her arm. "I am with you."

She stilled, but her eyes remained fiercely wide as she looked between the brothers. And Griffin was grateful his resemblance to Serle was mostly of the eyes, his brother being of slighter build and finer features that, in his youth, had made him appear almost pretty. Now he was gaunt.

Griffin had known something was amiss when the drawbridge was not lowered as he and his entourage neared, and he had soon seen the lone rider before his walls. Lest the man was of Foucault, Griffin and his men had drawn weapons as they spurred forward, and Rollo had come alongside Quintin opposite her husband to shield her.

It did not seem necessary, but her fear was real. And understandable. Here was the man she had last seen when his trespass against Bayard Boursier had left brother and sister bleeding, one losing an eye, the other her woman's gift. And for it, Serle had given his sword arm, as evidenced by his black tunic's empty right sleeve.

The brothers had not parted on good terms when Serle had recovered sufficiently to set out on the pilgrimage imposed as punishment for his adultery. And from the chill in those blue eyes, Griffin suspected the man Serle had become during his exile was no more amiable than the angry one who had demanded his brother and father find a way to release Constance and him from the consequences of their sins.

Thus, Griffin was not surprised by the bite of his brother's voice when he said, "'Twould seem I am no longer welcome in my own home." He jerked his head to indicate the raised drawbridge. "Hours I have sat here, refused entry not only by Sir Mathieu but our father, who sent word he shall await his *heir's* determination as to whether or not I may enter."

Griffin glanced to the gatehouse roof where Sir Mathieu looked down on them.

"And now," Serle said, "such a cool—rather, absent—greeting from my brother and his..." He shifted his gaze to Quintin. "...betrothed."

Then he knew of the king's decree. What else did he know?

"Not that I expect kindness from the lady. After all, did she not bleed as much as I?"

Beneath Griffin's hand, he felt Quintin tremble, likely more from anger than fear.

Serle shrugged, worked his right shoulder forward and backward. "After all these years, I ought to be accustomed to how light this side of me feels." He gripped that shoulder with his left hand, slid his palm down the upper arm, cupped the stump of an elbow. "But alas, I am not. And for that, my lady, apology escapes me. But tell, how does your brother— the mighty, one-eyed Boursier—fare?"

As a strangled scream escaped her, Griffin snarled, "That is enough!"

"Is it?" Serle said, then laughed when Quintin thrust a blade past the part in her mantle.

Pointing it at Serle, she said between her teeth, "You vile, cuckolding, worthless—"

It was Rollo who quieted her, gripping her wrist and stilling the Wulfrith dagger twitching in her hand. "'Tis not a God thing, my lady." His coarse voice was strangely soothing as he gently pried the hilt from her fingers. "Do cuttin' be needed, I do it for ye." He nudged her mantle open, returned the dagger to its scabbard, and looked to Serle. "Meanin' ye best shut yer mouth, knave."

Serle leaned forward. "Rollo, is it not? Baron Denis Foucault's misbegotten lump of a son?"

As the rage below came above, Griffin glanced at Quintin. She was pale, a sharp contrast to eyes whose pupils were so large the gold was barely visible. Feeling near murderous that this day, which she had minutes earlier declared could not be better, had become a nightmare, he demanded, "What do you upon Blackwood, Serle?"

"My pilgrimage is done, and so I come home. To this." He threw his arms wide, the palm of one heavenward, the stump of the other no higher than the horizon, then he settled his eyes on his brother's sword.

Though now the reported sighting of Serle was verified, proving he was not recently returned to Blackwood, Griffin decided to hold close the knowledge that carried the scent of Foucault. "'Twas not a five-year pilgrimage to which you were sentenced," he probed. "Tell, what took you so long to show yourself at Mathe?"

Serle shrugged again. "I liked France and Spain. And I had not anything to return to, had I?"

"And yet now you do. What has changed?"

"The king's decree. I heard our feuding families were to make peace through marriage. Hence, opportunity."

"For?"

"Constance." Her name was said with such reverence Griffin pitied him for loving so long the one denied him. Remembering that lady, who had been granted temporary leave of the convent to attend her brother's marriage to Thomasin, and the discovery she was not much more agreeable than in years past, Griffin said, "Are you aware Bayard Boursier and Lady Constance have made peace, that the Baron of Godsmere has appealed to Church and king to see her released from the convent?"

Serle's eyes widened and face slackened, making him appear almost a youth. "And?"

"Thus far, the Church is unmoved and the king unwilling to prod them."

The hard edges returned to his face. "Then 'tis good I returned."

"You think to bring Constance out?"

"Not I," Serle pitched his voice low to prevent those on the walls and those beyond Griffin from hearing, "but there is one—or another—who can do it for me."

Griffin felt his stomach turn as if on a spit above a well-fed fire. He did not want to believe what his brother alluded to, but there it was. And he allowed understanding to show on his face.

Serle nudged his horse forward.

The ring of chain mail announcing Blackwood's knights and men-at-arms prepared to defend their lord, Griffin commanded, "Halt, Serle!"

His brother reined in and moved his gaze to the sword on his belt. "Do I not come with empty hands—er, *hand?*"

"And, 'twould seem, as a traitor to your family," Griffin growled.

Serle glanced at the men who formed a wall twenty feet behind their lord. Keeping his voice low, he said, "As you have learned, 'tis difficult to find the Judas lurking amidst the loyal."

He referred to Sir Otto.

"Thus, 'tis better we speak in private, meaning it is time you welcome the prodigal with..." Serle raised his eyebrows. "...if not open arms, an open gate."

"Do not let him in!" Quintin hissed.

Serle flicked his eyes toward the wood. "The longer you delay, the greater their suspicion. Thus, if you wish them to believe I play the game by their rules, you must let me in, Brother."

Griffin looked to Rollo. "Remain with your lady," he said and raised a hand to command the men at his back and upon the wall to hold.

"Nay, Griffin!"

Ignoring Quintin's plea, he returned his sword to its scabbard, walked his destrier forward, and drew rein when the muzzle of his horse was a hand's width from that of his brother's mount.

Loud enough for Quintin and Rollo to hear, but not others, he said, "You think I would knowingly allow a betrayer within my walls?"

Hurt moved Serle's face, but a tight-lipped smile pushed that emotion aside. "You know me as such only because I allow it."

In that he was wrong, but better he believe it.

"And there is more you must know, *if* you wish my aid."

Though the plan was mostly laid to put down the brigands, there was room for error, as Griffin had warned Quintin. What aid might his brother give to lessen the possibility of failure? And what price paid for it? "How came you to make a pact with the devil, Serle?"

"'Twas out of necessity. But no more will I speak of it until you give the appearance of welcoming me home."

Griffin stared at him.

"*Their* rules, Brother."

Griffin inclined his head. "Providing you understand that once you are inside Mathe, you will be no better than a prisoner."

Above the sound of Quintin's gasp, Serle said, "So be it."

Griffin did not wish to believe his brother capable of murdering one of his own, but with the younger De Arell too bitter and too near the brigands to trust, he took stock of Serle's weapons. Upon his belt were two daggers and, despite the loss of the arm trained to wield it, a sword. Finding no evidence of concealment beneath thin tunic and hose, Griffin urged his horse alongside the other, put an arm around Serle, and drew him near in what would appear a brotherly embrace.

"As soon as you are inside my walls, prodigal," he rasped, "you will tell me of the *necessity* of playing by the devil's rules."

"As soon as I am inside."

Griffin pulled back, shouted to Sir Mathieu to lower the drawbridge, and motioned those behind forward.

Feeling Quintin's ire, he was prepared when she reached his side opposite that which his brother sat to await entrance to Mathe. He leaned near. "I am aware you do not like it. Neither do I. But you must trust me."

Her chin snapped around, and there was fire in eyes made brighter by tears.

"I would not let him in did I not believe there is gain in doing so." He lowered his voice further. "Remember the reason I shall do whatever is necessary to keep you safe. Pray, trust me."

As Quintin stared at the man who had said he would never cease to miss her were she lost to him, the drawbridge began to lower. Amid the clatter, her fear, resentment, and hatred began to fray. But only that, her fist against her abdomen reminding her of Serle de Arell's sin.

Trust Griffin, she told herself, and when the planked beast thumped to the ground, sending dirt billowing up around them, she said, "After what he did—and what he spoke to me this day—you ask much."

"This I know. And I regret so beautiful a day has turned ugly."

She jerked her chin. "I hate this, but I shall trust you."

No more was spoken as they crossed the drawbridge into the outer bailey where Griffin dismounted and was received by Sir Mathieu, who eyed his lord's brother as the younger man climbed down from his horse.

"My lord," the knight said, "I have sent word to the keep to have your son await you in his chamber."

"As I would have it."

Then Sir Mathieu had known Griffin would not wish to expose Rhys to the uncle he likely did not remember. Finding some comfort in further proof her husband did not trust his brother, Quintin went easily into his arms when he lifted her down, only to stiffen when Serle stepped near. Blessedly, Rollo inserted himself between his lady and the traitorous De Arell with a heave of his shoulder.

Serle stumbled back and looked to Griffin. "How long am I to be accorded the appearance of being welcome?" he asked.

"As long as you give no cause to accord you the reality of being a prisoner. Hence, when we enter the keep, you shall relinquish your weapons."

Serle gave a curt nod.

Lightly grasping Quintin's arm, Griffin led her from the outer bailey into the inner, accompanied by his brother on his left and Rollo on her right.

"Our father," Serle said as they ascended the keep's steps. "I would see him."

"Not whilst you straddle the bloody line between De Arell and Foucault." Griffin jutted his chin at the shifting curtains high above. "He knows you are returned."

And I, Quintin thought, ever discomfited by the old baron's eyes on her.

29

—⧉—

UPON THEIR ENTRANCE into the great hall, Griffin directed the porter to take his guest's weapons. As they continued forward, servants paused, acknowledging their lord's return with nods, smiles, and murmured words of welcome. Some extended the same to Quintin, surely aware her return evidenced they would soon answer to her as their lady.

What surprised was that, other than curious glances, Serle went unacknowledged. But she guessed his unkempt beard and thin frame that had once been muscular rendered him unrecognizable. But soon they would know the prodigal had returned.

As they neared the stairs, a wolfhound slunk off the steps.

Though Quintin recognized the big dog, she did not expect him to approach her. "Arturo," she said with more warmth than she ought to feel.

He gave a low groan and bumped his nose against the back of her hand.

"He has missed you," Griffin said.

"Me?"

"Aye, surprising considering how you first became acquainted, but he has been annoyingly restless since your departure."

Were Serle de Arell not present, she might have smiled. Setting her hand on the dog's head, she said, "I may have missed him as well."

"Then I hope you will not object to him once more watching over you."

She glanced at Rollo. "What is one more?"

Griffin dropped his hand from her. "I will leave you to gain your chamber and await the arrival of your packs."

"Nay, I would hear what your brother has to tell."

His brow lowered. "Quintin——"

"In this, you must trust *me*."

"Forgive me, my lady," Serle said, "but you presume much for one who is not yet a De Arell."

"Do I?" she snapped.

"Aye, Quintin *Boursier*."

She swung her gaze to Griffin. "Is that all I am to you—Quintin *Boursier?*"

His darkening eyes told he understood what she left unspoken, the evidence of which nestled between her breasts. "As the lady is soon to take my name," he begrudged, "she may join us."

Serle made a sound of disgust. "She has twisted you around yourself, dare I say the same as that chambermaid you got with child?"

Feeling his hands begin to fist, Griffin opened them. "You dare not," he said and strode forward, leaving the others to follow.

His steward, who had risen from a chair at the far end of the high table, nodded at him. "My lord."

"We shall require the use of your quarters," Griffin said and continued down the corridor.

He threw open the door and strode into the room that, despite being of good size, was cramped with the tools of the steward's trade—a table set around with four chairs and upon which ledgers were stacked, a cushioned stool drawn up to a tall writing desk whose top was scattered with quills and ink pots, and two walls of shelves weighted by books and parchment.

Quintin followed him inside, Arturo on her heels.

"The misbegotten one as well?" Serle jerked his head at Rollo who entered behind him.

Almighty, Griffin silently appealed, *keep my fists from him.* "If 'tis as my betrothed wishes," he said when Quintin stepped alongside him at the center of the room.

She raised her eyebrows. "I do wish it."

As Rollo closed the door and crossed to stand on the other side of his lady, Serle eyed his brother. "Obviously, 'tis not mere talk that desire for your betrothed makes you vulnerable."

Griffin resented that, though he knew it was true. But there was also strength in what he felt for one who gave him more cause to defend well what was his. "I am guessing you learned that from the traitorous knight who tried to kill my daughter."

"Your daughter." Serle twitched a smile. "When I heard you had claimed her, it occurred to me my brother might have become impulsive as ever he accused me of."

Griffin stared.

Serle sighed. "Aye, I heard it from Sir Otto, whom you now know to be a Foucault."

To be. Either Griffin's brother was uninformed about the knight's death, or he knew it for a lie.

"Not that he told it to me directly," Serle said. "I overheard him discussing it with another." Before Griffin could ask who that other was—likely Sir Francis—his brother continued, "But now I see Lady Quintin and you together, I am thinking 'tis more than desire you feel for her. Most peculiar, since I was also privy to a conversation in which it was told she put a dagger to your throat."

"I did," Quintin said, "and when I put one to yours, you will not fare as well."

He narrowed his lids. "I marvel, Lady."

"At?"

"Those who would see Kilbourne restored to generations of Foucaults believe 'tis best done through marriage to you. They think you are the prize at the end of this feud."

"And I think you a swine."

"Were I, my lady, I would have enlightened the brigands as to what your naked form shall reveal, which would render you no safer than the rest of us."

She sucked a breath.

Serle smiled at Griffin. "As I see no confusion on your brow, I wager you have sampled your betrothed and know of what I speak."

In the next instant, he gave a choked cry as Griffin closed the distance between them. Jumping back, he narrowly avoided the hand that sought the neck of his tunic and came up against the door where he splayed his arms and the palm of his one hand. "Calm thyself, Brother. I do not mean to offend."

Longing to strike that gaunt face, Griffin held his feet firm to the floor. "Aye, you mean to!"

Serle turned down his mouth. "Being so long without civilized company, I forget how to conduct myself in the presence of those easily offended."

"There are lessons for that," Griffin said, then pivoted and strode back to Quintin.

"Worry not, milady," Rollo said, "I kill 'em brigands do they try to harm ye." He jabbed a finger toward Serle. "That 'un, too."

Griffin saw the struggle on his brother's face—that he knew he should let the big man's threat pass—but Serle thrust off the door. "Do you remember the water, Rollo?"

The expanse of flesh between the man-at-arms' eyebrows pinched. "Water?"

"Aye, yet more overheard—a question as to whether or not you are capable of recalling how cold and deep runs the river near the cottage where you were born. Alas, 'twas concluded your brain is too addled."

Rollo's frown grew larger.

"What about the boot upon your back?" Serle tilted his head to the side. "And—I am only guessing—mud in your mouth?"

The big man's eyes bulged. "Tried to kill me."

Serle nodded. "How ever did he fail?"

Feeling Quintin's rage, Griffin struggled to keep control of his own. "Who was it, Rollo?" he asked, though he would be surprised were it one other than Simon Foucault, whose attempt to end his illegitimate brother's life was likely responsible for Rollo's simple-mindedness.

The man-at-arms grimaced. "Don' know who held me under. I was a wee lad." He rubbed a hand across his mouth. "Near choked on mud."

"Still you taste it?" Serle said.

"Miscreant!" Quintin cried, and Griffin once more lunged forward.

This time, he thrust his brother up against the door. "I have no more patience for your cruelties and petty games. You entered these walls with a plan. Now reveal them else return to your brigands and tell them you failed."

The fear on Serle's face was genuine, and had good cause to be. Griffin was on an edge with a sheer drop, the only other time he had come this close to thrashing Serle being when he had discovered his brother had not accepted Constance Verdun was another man's wife. Had Griffin bruised and bloodied him with fists rather than words, preventing him from rising from his bed for days, Serle would not have been able to keep his fateful rendezvous with Constance Boursier. And Quintin—

He snatched his thoughts away from what could not be undone and, seeing Serle gasp for breath, released him and stepped back only enough to allow his brother to stand away from the door. But Serle remained pressed to it, breathing deep as he held his gaze to Griffin as if to look away would provoke another attack.

"Tell me," Griffin said, "beginning with when you first became acquainted with the Foucault brigands."

Serle swallowed loudly. "Upon my return to Blackwood two months past, they captured me two leagues from Mathe. Though I gave the name of another, they knew me and determined to kill me—slowly, painfully, and with much humiliation." He ground his teeth. "They would have ended me, but I played my part well—and easily since I hardly played."

"Your part?"

"The same as the brigands play. I felt and still feel the anger that bade me curse my brother and father for refusing Constance and me aid in fleeing the Church's punishment. And so the brigands think to use the divide between my family and me. Though I am not wholly trusted, if I gain them what I have promised, they will give me what they have promised."

"What have you promised?"

"To be their eyes and ears within Mathe the same as Sir Otto was and…" He drew a deep breath. "…when instructed, let them in."

Griffin clamped his hands closed. *Better fists,* he thought, *than a hilt.* "You would betray your nephew…brother…father?"

"Father," Serle drew out the word. "At first I thought it strange his death was sought ahead of yours, but vengeance goes deep—all the way back to the roots of our families' betrayal of their liege."

And for it, the brigands would risk entering Mathe's walls, Griffin reflected. But that must be avoided to keep safe those harbored during the wedding celebration to come. "Our father," he said, "the last living betrayer of Denis Foucault."

Serle shook his head. "There is also Father Crispin."

It was true, though when De Arell, Boursier, and Verdun had united against Foucault, the priest had been but a stable boy. "You would betray," Griffin said, "fully aware that betrayal would mean the death of your family *and* a holy man?"

"Loyalty does not flow only one direction, Brother. You must give to get."

"Thus, the question of what you would have *me* give."

Serle looked to the chair before the brazier. "May I? The day has been long."

Griffin inclined his head.

Once Serle was settled, he said, "The brigands have promised to deliver Constance to me and allow us to go free."

"Which you wish above all, so why reveal the bargain made with the devil?"

"If I fail them, and I know it possible in setting myself against you, Constance dies next."

A powerful reason. "So I am to believe you would risk the woman you love to side with me?"

"As told, I played my part well. Thus, the brigands believe my ill feelings toward father and you are cause enough for me to betray my own. But I have learned the way the world turns, and I do not doubt that, regardless of how well I serve those who avenge the Foucaults, Constance and I will remain as vulnerable to their revenge as the rest of you."

Griffin saw truth in his brother's words, that his only hope was to band with the three families to defeat the brigands, even if he did not truly believe it himself and played both sides to the best end possible.

"I know what you want, Serle. Now speak."

His brother sat forward. "I would make the same bargain with you— Constance freed of the convent and both of us bound for the continent with enough coin to keep us well for a year. Promise me that, and I shall mislead the brigands however you wish."

There was merit in what he proposed, but only a fool would readily agree. Griffin looked at Quintin and Rollo. His wife was stiff with disapproval, the man-at-arms lax with uncertainty as if he could make little sense of what was spoken around him.

"What say you?" Serle pressed.

"Where do the brigands encamp?"

"They do not stay in one place long—constantly moving across the three baronies and even upon those that border, including Orlinde. Twice we were there."

"Once inside Mathe, how were you to communicate with the brigands?"

"By way of the farmer from Cross who daily supplies the kitchen with vegetables."

"He supports their cause?"

"Not knowingly, methinks. Whilst he is inside with the cook, I am to check for missives attached to his cart's underside and affix my own in answer to theirs, as well as reveal anything of import."

It did not sound as if the farmer was an accomplice, but he would be watched. "Tell me about Sir Otto."

Serle smiled small. "You wish me to verify or disavow his death."

"I do."

"You will give me what I ask?"

"I have not decided."

"Then why should I tell you?"

"To prove your worth. A bargain is no bargain unless the buyer knows he shall gain something of value."

Serle went silent so long that Griffin said, "We are done."

"Nay!" The younger De Arell thrust out of the chair. "Sir Otto lives."

As thought. "How does he live?"

"What mean you?"

"I understood he was severely injured during his escape from the king's men."

Serle shook his head. "Certes, he is hurting, but 'tis from punishment for failing to kill your daughter and her husband."

Recalling what Verdun had told—that Otto had revealed to Thomasin numerous scars upon his arm that represented his failures, Griffin asked, "Who dealt the punishment?"

"The one who leads the brigands."

"Who?"

"I know not. I have spoken with him, but never has he shown his face. What I do know is that he is cruel. He enjoys inflicting pain—methinks nearly as much on Sir Otto as he did on me."

"What did he do to you?"

His brother unfastened his belt and lifted his tunic.

"Dear Lord," Quintin gasped.

Serle gave a sharp laugh. "And you thought your scar terrible, my lady. Granted, mine are only skin deep, but..." He tucked the hem of his tunic between chin and chest to free his one hand, which he then drew up over numerous welts covering his abdomen and chest. All were livid, especially those more recently carved into his flesh. "Sixty-six cuts, one for every day of captivity, including this day." He tapped a cut near his collarbone. It yet bled, though the dark of his tunic had hidden the seepage.

Griffin's stomach was not easily turned, but it rolled. Though there was much about Serle to dislike, he did not deserve what had been done him. However, there was a perverse good in it. It allowed Griffin to better understand and tolerate his brother's behavior.

"And here"—Serle turned his back to them—"is where it began. Sixteen cuts that, I am told, form the word *traitor*."

It did.

Serle released the tunic and came back around. "Unsightly, aye? But as he said, such is the price of dirt."

Griffin felt his blood course faster. He knew the one who had done this to his brother was Simon Foucault who now called himself Sir Francis Cartier, but those words—the same spoken to Thomasin at her wedding when the mercenary had mocked that marriage to her enemy was the price of dirt—enraged him.

"So now a question for you," Serle said. "Do *you* know who leads the brigands?"

Griffin wished he trusted him enough to reveal what was no longer suspicion so if it was true Serle was unaware of the identity of his tormentor, he might find some comfort in knowing how near the man was to justice.

"Since we know Simon Foucault and his lover, Agatha of Mawbry, are dead," Griffin said, watching his brother closely, "the leader is likely an obscure relation."

"You are certain Simon Foucault is dead?"

The question gave credence to his brother's ignorance of the identity of the brigands' leader, but not enough that Griffin would take him into his confidence. "His death was reported twenty-five years past, and Sir Otto confirmed it when he was captured at Castle Kelling."

"That does not mean 'tis true."

Griffin inclined his head. "It does not, but methinks 'tis another we search for." And in a manner it was, he mused—Simon Foucault in the guise of Sir Francis.

"Now that my worth is proved," Serle said, "you will have Constance delivered inside the safety of Mathe's walls?"

That last so surprised that Griffin nearly did not think before speaking. "Do I bargain with you, Serle, 'twill not include bringing your lover here. For the sake of my betrothed"—he glanced at Quintin—"but also lest the brigands learn of Constance's removal from the convent and their suspicions render useless your ability to mislead them."

"But they could take her from there."

"'Tis possible, but methinks unlikely. Thus, on this I will not be moved."

Serle's single hand opened and closed, then he said, "Very well. But once the brigands are defeated, aye?"

"I will think on it."

"Think on it?" Serle spat.

"Aye, little brother, something I oft advised you to do. And in the absence of thought, you lost an arm."

Serle's jaw trembled. "When will you give answer?"

Griffin glanced at Quintin. Though the anger she had exuded before the baring of his brother's scars had returned, it was not as evident. "This eve you will know my decision."

"Until then?"

"Until then and thereafter, you will be under watch."

"Until I gain your trust."

Griffin did not answer.

"Ah," Serle snarled, "you do not think I will."

Griffin looked to the big man-at-arms. "I would have you remain here with my brother whilst I escort Lady Quintin to her chamber."

Rollo looked to his lady.

"As my brother told," she said, "I am safe in Baron de Arell's company."

"Then I will keep watch, my lord."

Griffin held out a hand, and Quintin took it. Followed by Arturo, neither spoke until they entered the hall.

"Methinks you will accept his terms," she said with distaste.

"I shall."

"And risk incurring the wrath of king and Church by stealing Lady Constance from the convent."

"If it must be done, I will find a way to do it that will make it difficult—even impossible—to see my hand in it." He moved his grip to her elbow as they ascended the stairs. "Of more immediate concern is the possibility my brother plays both sides. Thus, those set to follow him will do so discreetly lest Sir Otto is not the only one the brigands have inside Castle Mathe."

He led her down the corridor and, halting before the door to the chamber that had been his daughter's, noted Arturo continued to the stairs that led to Ulric's apartment where he would watch over Quintin. "I think you will find Thomasin's chamber better suited to a lady than Sir Mathieu's," he said.

"I thank you." She started to turn away.

"I apologize for what my brother said, Quintin. Though I care for him, he is much changed from the one alongside whom I grew into a man."

Her jaw shifted. "I would not wish to love as he has loved. Indeed, what he and Constance share make love seem more a disease than a blessing."

Griffin pulled her close. "What we share will be a blessing."

He felt her soften a moment before she once more stiffened. "I pray so." She stepped out of his arms and reached for the door.

"Father!"

Griffin was not surprised by Rhys's appearance, having caught the whisper of hinges. Hoping his son would behave appropriately, having informed Rhys that when he returned to Mathe it would be with the woman who was to be his mother, he looked across his shoulder.

Rhys's wide smile eased as he moved his gaze from his father to Quintin, but it remained genuine enough. He halted alongside his father. "I am pleased you have returned, Lady Quintin. Now you are to wed my father?"

Her face gentled. "I am."

"You would have me call you Mother?"

"Only if you wish it."

"I will think on it."

Griffin nearly laughed to hear his son speak the same words recently spoken to Serle.

"You will let me know what you decide?" Quintin asked.

"I will, my lady."

She glanced at Griffin. "I will leave you to the things of men."

Telling himself they would speak more later, whether she came to him in the night or he to her, he inclined his head.

When her chamber door closed, Rhys said, "'Twas acceptable, was it not—telling her I would think on what I shall call her?"

"Aye, you were honest but kind." Though it seemed natural to swing his son into his arms and embrace him—even after so short a parting— he resisted. Now eight years aged, Rhys was increasingly resistant to such displays of affection, but that was expected of a boy aspiring to manhood.

Setting a hand on his shoulder, Griffin said, "I have missed you."

"As I have missed you!" He smiled broadly. "You must come to the training yard and watch me tilt at the quintain."

"Must I?" Griffin teased.

"Aye, on the day past, I made a dozen passes ere it knocked me out of the saddle."

"A dozen? You do not exaggerate?"

Rhys's nose twitched. "Ten. I vow!"

"Most accomplished. I have business to attend to, then you will show me—"

Rhys groaned.

Griffin chuckled. "You are right. My son first, then business. Don your gear and meet me in the hall."

The boy hastened back inside his chamber, and Griffin descended to the hall to make quick work of setting a guard on Serle and discovering if the woman who was to be his wife's maid had arrived at Mathe.

30

She had thought herself stronger than this.

Quelling the impulse to rock herself where she sat on the edge of the bed with an arm squeezed around her middle, Quintin wondered that after all these years she could be so affected. Since the night she had revealed to Griffin what Bayard's blade had done, she had not felt as broken as she had before telling him. But seeing Serle again, and then his taunting...

God forgive her, she had hated the knave. And yet, much of the black had drained out of that emotion when he had revealed his scars. She did not like him, but she felt for him.

She pulled up her skirts and stared at her own scar. "I do not wish to feel for him," she whispered. "He deserves every scar. He——"

She thrust her skirt down. "I know he does not deserve them, Lord. I know." Serle had sinned, but he had not meant for his sin to harm her, certainly could not have known she would provide an easy meal for keen blades. And she must not forget Agatha's influence—that Serle and Constance were also victims of those who sought revenge against the families.

Though it would be nearly as impossible to forgive them as it would be to forgive Sir Otto, perhaps eventually that which scraped at her soul would retract its claws. But not now with the recent loss of her child.

A knock sounded, and she stood. "Enter!"

The door opened, and a lovely woman stood on the threshold. "My lady." She dipped her head. "I am Nanne, sent by your husband to be yer—"

"Mother," a voice inserted itself, though the one it belonged to remained out of sight.

The woman looked across her shoulder. "Hold, son."

"How long?"

Nanne returned her gaze to Quintin. "Forgive me, my lady. My son is not accustomed to being among nobility. But he will learn."

"His name?"

"Eamon, my lady. A good boy."

"Eamon," Quintin called, "let me see you."

His head came around the door—a large head that looked all the larger for the slight body that followed. Halting alongside his mother, he peered at Quintin from beneath long lashes.

"Welcome, Eamon," she said. "How many years are you?"

"Seven, m'lady."

A year younger than Rhys. Quintin returned her regard to Nanne. "You said my husband sent you?"

"Aye, I am to be yer maid—unless you do not approve."

Quintin blinked. "Why would I not?"

The woman's compressed lips eased. "I thank ye, my lady." She laid a hand on her son's shoulder. "As Eamon is still young, and I am not ready to give him in service that would take him long from my side, Baron de Arell assured me he may also serve ye."

Quintin had no idea how she would make use of the boy. Indeed, so accustomed was she to tending her own needs, she was not sure how she would occupy his mother's time. "Of course I will not separate you, though I fear you will become bored, Eamon."

He shrugged.

"The baron's son is not much older. Mayhap you could pass time with him."

"Ah nay, my lady," Nanne said. "My son must learn his place."

Though Quintin was well aware of the distinction between noble and commoner, she did not like it. But for now she would leave it be. "You come from a nearby village? Cross?"

"We are from the barony of Orlinde, my lady."

Quintin frowned. "That is a long way to come—beyond Emberly, aye?"

"'Tis," Eamon said. "Baron Verdun sent us here."

"He did?" Surprise raised Quintin's pitch.

"Aye, he is my friend."

She looked closer at the boy. If he was the result of an indiscretion of Thomasin's husband, it was not apparent in his features.

"I am a widow, my lady," Nanne said. "My boy's father has passed."

Embarrassed to be easily read, Quintin said, "I am sorry for your loss." Though she sensed there was something more to it, she had no right to Nanne's secrets. "I am mostly accustomed to doing for myself, but as the wife of the Baron of Blackwood—once I am that—I shall surely require more aid."

"For that, the baron believes we are a good fit. I have never served as a lady's maid and will require patience."

"Then we shall learn together." Quintin raised her eyebrows at the boy. "And when you are not doing for me, Eamon, perhaps we can attend to your education."

He groaned.

Nanne smiled. "Baron Verdun would like that. He takes an interest in my son."

"I care not for learning," Eamon muttered.

"Eamon!" Nanne chided.

"Well, I do not. I would rather my fingers blackened by the oil and ash of a bladesmith than the ink of one who is always at letters and numbers."

"Forgive him, my lady."

Quintin raised a hand. "Better honest than falsely proper. And all the more reason your son could prove a good companion to Rhys de Arell. Neither does he care for letters and numbers."

"That could invite trouble, my lady."

She was probably right. But Quintin understood enough about boys to know they needed other boys to grow into worthy men. And during her winter stay at Mathe, she had noted that, outside of training at arms, Rhys spent much of his time in his sister's company. Now that Thomasin was gone, he must be lonely.

"It could invite trouble, Nanne, but that does not mean 'twill be of detriment."

Irritation flickered across the woman's face, then uncertainty.

"'Tis only a thought," Quintin said.

"I thank ye, my lady." The woman smoothed her skirt. "Now how may I serve?"

"It was a long ride to Mathe. Would you arrange for a bath?"

"Of course. And I shall scrub your back and wash your hair. 'Tis as a lady's maid would do, aye?"

"'Tis."

Nanne ushered Eamon out of the chamber, and as she closed the door behind her, the boy's voice slipped through. "I like her. Do you?"

"I hope I shall."

Hope, Quintin mused as the door fit in its frame. So much possibility in that word. Unfortunately, also disappointment.

Keeping her arm and fist from her middle that offered little hope a child would flourish there, she ignored the appeal of the bed and crossed to the window to stare out across her new home.

And pray that the plans of Griffin, Bayard, and Magnus would set all aright.

"You think him false?" the ravaged voice asked.

Griffin turned from the window to consider his father whose hood allowed the mix of moonlight and candlelight to reveal glittering eyes. "Not entirely false, but enough that he cannot be trusted in the keep at night, even with a watch over him."

"If there are other Foucault supporters inside our walls, 'twill appear suspicious that the prodigal is welcome only enough to warrant a chamber outside the keep."

Not the same tower room in which Griffin had held Quintin. He had not liked the thought of his brother in that chamber where first Griffin had begun to feel for his Boursier bride something beyond desire. Thus, another room had sufficed.

"For that," he said, "Serle was instructed to insist, in the hearing of many, that rather than displace Sir Mathieu, he wished a tower room." Which had been expressed after Griffin called an end to the supper that had bristled with whispered talk of the second son's return, and through which Quintin had sat mostly silent on one side of Griffin.

"He cannot have liked that," Ulric said.

"He did as told."

Griffin's father grunted. "How will you make use of your brother in ridding us of Simon Foucault?"

"The misinformation he tells he is willing to pass to the brigands fits our plan well."

Ulric sighed, then moved out of sight, his labored footfalls nearly obscuring the patter of Diot's paws.

Griffin stepped around the hanging that fluttered in the night breeze and followed his father to the bed. As Ulric lowered to it, Diot shot out from beneath his master's tunic and launched himself onto the mattress.

As the little dog settled on the pillow beside the one Ulric would lay his head on, Griffin said, "Serle wishes to see you."

Amid the silence, Griffin once more sensed his father's roiling and guessed he was thinking of the torture that would forever brand his youngest son a traitor. Such foul words Ulric had spewed, the violent swing of his walking stick sending precious objects flying. But now he issued another sigh. "Nay. If 'tis to be believed death is near, he must not know the true strength of my illness." With a creaking of joints, he eased onto his pillow. "Were he to rouse me to anger…"

Pleased—though not surprised—he and his father were in accord, Griffin nodded. Should Serle stand more the side of Foucault, the plan laid down by the three barons could be compromised, its success and the safety of their loved ones dependent on the final confrontation occurring outside these walls. Thus, by way of Serle, the brigands would learn of Ulric's impending death which, hopefully, would give them less reason to try to enter Mathe.

"I shall keep Serle away," he said.

"If he proves loyal to his family, there will be time aplenty."

The words were so low and lacking force Griffin wondered if *he* knew the true strength of his father's illness. "Sleep well," he said and started for the door.

"Griffin."

"Father?" he once more accorded him the title.

"Would you betray your family for a woman?"

Certain Serle's dangerous obsession with Constance Verdun was behind Ulric's question, Griffin said, "Though I pray you know the answer to that, I will speak it. I would not betray Rhys or Thomasin for a woman." Never would he endanger the lives of those he had loved longer and more fully so he might have Quintin—though as told, ever he would long for her were she missing from him. "Nor would I betray you," he added.

"I do know it," Ulric said wearily, "but I also know there is more to your answer."

There was, and Griffin wished his father did not see him so well. "I would not betray my family, but methinks I would betray myself."

"For Quintin Boursier."

"I would risk much of myself for the chance to finish life with her at my side."

"You love," Ulric growled. "Again." It was said with accusation, but less disgust than expected. "Do you remember my response when you declared you loved Thomasin's mother and would wed her even if I disowned you?"

"I remember." Ulric de Arell had told his son of ten and six that he mistook love of the loins for love of the heart. And since Griffin had little evidence his father knew anything of the latter, he had rejected his counsel, determined to have Alice even at the cost of his inheritance. Thus, Ulric had made Thomasin's mother disappear.

"I do not know if 'twill console you any, or even if I wish it to," Griffin said, "but I now know the difference between those two loves and, as I have found with Lady Quintin, though that of the heart carries greater weight, the two are best served together."

After a time, Ulric said, "I suppose I shall have to be content with that—providing she is good to Rhys and accepts him as your heir no matter how many sons she bears you."

Panged by the reminder of the loss of their child, he said, "Then I am certain you will not be disappointed. Good eve." He turned and closed the door harder than intended.

As he came off the stairs, he had to step over Arturo the same as when he had ascended them, the wolfhound having settled in for the night.

Griffin halted before Quintin's chamber. He was certain she did not sleep and, thus, was grateful Rollo had honored her request to make his bed in the hall. The man-at-arms had objected, but the assurance Serle was outside the keep and Arturo on one side of his lady abovestairs, Griffin on the other, made him acquiesce.

Lest a knock was heard by those sleeping nearby, Griffin did not announce his entrance.

Illuminated by a single candle, Quintin was wrapped in a robe where she sat against the headboard, loose hair draping her shoulders.

He closed the door quietly. "Methinks you expected me."

"I hoped." Her smile was not as certain as he wished it, but it called him to her. He halted alongside the bed, and she dropped her head back to hold his gaze. "Not here," she said. "Our nuptial chamber."

He frowned. "'Twould be more discreet for us to remain in this one."

"Our nuptial chamber."

"As you will, my lady." He scooped her up, and it was she who reached to quietly open and close the door, then the solar's.

He lowered her to their bed and drew back to look upon her face and the black hair falling back from it. "You are lovely, Wife."

"And you make me wish to forget there are things left unsaid."

He grimaced. "Serle."

"I did not expect there to be so much distance between your brother and you—and of such depth he should hate you."

"I had hoped that need not be told."

"But now he has come, and so bitter is he you cannot trust him to be true to his family."

Griffin straightened. "I would like to believe he will not betray us, but 'tis possible he will do as Simon Foucault bids—that to gain Constance he would turn his back on me even were it in his power to cut a noose from 'round my neck."

Quintin touched the place beside her. "Come to bed."

"Do I, I am not certain things left unsaid will take precedence over things left unfelt."

She scooted to the center of the mattress and turned onto her side toward him. "I will do my best not to tempt you."

"I cannot promise the same," he said, then removed his belt and grinned when she quickly shifted her attention to the headboard into which the mythical griffin was carved.

Once he had shed all but his undertunic, he stretched out beside her.

"Tell me about this," she said, tracing the griffin's rear body and feathered breast, the former of a lion, the latter of an eagle.

"What would you have me tell?"

She pulled her hand back. "My first night at Mathe, when you tossed me on this bed, I believed the carving evidence of your vanity and arrogance. But now I know better."

"Thus, you do not think so ill of me."

Her pretty teeth showed. "Oh, you are still arrogant, but not so much it offends as once it did."

He felt his own smile pull to one side. "Because I have good cause to be arrogant?"

"Because I do not believe 'tis show—that you are truly confident of who you are and what you do because 'tis so."

"Wife," he said low, "you told you would not tempt me."

She laughed. "I did not know a man's desire could be stirred merely by complimenting his person and behavior."

He captured her hand and kissed her fingers. "To be thought of so well by the woman he wishes not only to dream with but to pass his waking hours with? Aye, Quintin, such rouses a man—and more so when that woman is in his bed with naught but the parting of her robe between them."

"Then I must needs save my compliments until you have told me about Serle. But first…" She nodded at the headboard.

He glanced at the great, winged beast. "The griffin denotes strength, courage, and leadership, a symbol my father esteems. For it, he gave his firstborn son the name, and when he became baron of these lands, he had this headboard made."

"I should have guessed it was him, since this was his solar ere it was yours."

"Then you think me even less arrogant?" At her grin, he continued, "As the griffin is also known for guarding priceless possessions, when I was young, I liked to think the headboard reflected my father's feelings for my mother. But I never saw evidence he felt affection for her, and when she passed shortly after he gained Blackwood, his behavior seemed more a show of respect for the dead—and irritation that the household did not run smoothly without her."

"I know what it is to have one's parents love and respect each other and think it must be difficult when they but share a chamber and meals. I am sorry your father could not love his wife."

"Or perhaps she could not love him."

Quintin grimaced. "He is a…"

"…tyrant. Aye, this I know, just as I know that were it possible to strip away all the atrocities done us by those who avenge the Foucaults, still my father would have stirred up enough dissent that peace between our families would yet be difficult."

"Does he know 'tis not merely obligation that made you take me to wife?"

Griffin chuckled. "I was with him ere I came to you. If he did not know before this eve, he knows now."

"And disapproves. Not only did my father gain the castle and land he wished, but I am as much a Foucault as a Boursier."

"Though I would have him think well of you, Quintin, what he feels does not affect who you are to me and who you will become to Rhys."

She drew her lower lip between her teeth. "I hope Rhys will accept me as his mother."

"I believe he will, that he is only as resistant as he deems necessary to ensure you are aware 'tis a place you must merit."

She smiled. "'Twould seem he thinks much—like his father."

"I pray he does and, God willing, will regret little in this life."

After some moments, she said, "Methinks he must be lonely now Thomasin is gone, that he ought to be more in the company of boys his age."

"Since my daughter's departure, I have seen to that as much as possible, but you have more to say on it?"

"I am thinking of the son of the maid given to me—and for which I have not thanked you."

"You are pleased?"

"I am unaccustomed to close attendance, but she seems agreeable, as well as her boy."

"She told you she is from the barony of Orlinde?"

"Aye, that Magnus Verdun sent them here. Is he…?"

"The boy is not Verdun's. I know not the details, but the Baron of Emberly feels responsible for him and his mother, and his involvement with them has led the Foucault brigands to believe Eamon is his son. Thus, as that endangers them, Thomasin asked that I make a place for them here."

"That is kind of you."

"And self serving. If there is more to Verdun's relationship with Nanne than is told, the farther from my daughter's husband she is, the better. But of Eamon…You are suggesting he become a companion to Rhys?"

"I have little with which to occupy the boy, and as the two are of a similar age, it occurs. Too, Rhys may be more receptive to his lessons if he has someone to learn alongside."

Griffin nodded. "I will think on it."

"Of course you will," Quintin murmured.

"My wife learns me well." He slid an arm beneath her and drew her to his side. As she settled her head on his shoulder, he said, "Now, ere there is not enough remaining of the night to attest to this being our nuptial chamber, I will tell you of the breach between my brother and me."

Her silken hair against his skin and the fit of her curves with his firm planes too sensual for his thoughts to remain on a straight path, he wished he had not pulled her so near. But he supposed he would have to suffer—and all the sooner be done with the tale.

"As you know, Serle was betrothed to Constance Verdun at a young age. Though relations were often strained between the De Arells and Verduns, albeit not nearly as strained as with your family, Serle and Constance saw each other fairly often and fell in love. Thus, when her father broke their betrothal to make a more advantageous marriage of his daughter to your brother—a baron, rather than a second son who had only knighthood to his name, 'twas a blow."

"If only she had refused."

"Aye, but she did her duty to her family. Serle was angered, as was my father, who believed the Boursier-Verdun alliance threatened to turn the feud to our great disadvantage. Having recently assumed our father's title, I forbade Serle the revenge he vowed and tried to keep Ulric and him separate, knowing no good would come of their combined hatred."

Griffin drew his hand up Quintin's back and slid his fingers into the hair at her nape. "As the months passed and Serle's mood lightened, I believed he was accepting his loss and eased my watch over him. A year after Constance wed your brother, Serle asked for a considerable sum of money so he might cross to France and make his fortune in tournaments. I refused."

"You did not believe him."

"Nay, so great a sum was not necessary. Too, though he was proficient at arms, his successes in tournaments were few. I told him that if he wanted the money, he would have to convince me of his need, beginning with the truth. And he told it. He planned to take Constance with him to France, and the money would provide them a living until he could pledge his sword to a lord."

"Did you give him the money?" There was wariness in Quintin's tone that made Griffin more grateful he had again refused Serle. "I did not, though he reminded me that once I had loved as deeply, so much I had been willing to cede my inheritance to take Alice to wife. Our argument was loud enough to bring Ulric out of his apartment, and I steeled myself for his support of Serle in stealing another man's wife. But he surprised us both by instructing Serle to forget Constance."

"What did your brother do?"

"He attacked me, and I struck him down. I have often thought I should not have stopped there, that I should have done worse to ensure he remained at Castle Mathe. Had I, he could not have gone to Godsmere to steal Constance—at least, not for a time. Perhaps the delay would have been enough to get his thinking right."

"You could not have known."

"Truly, I did not believe he would go to her penniless. But then, I did not know Agatha of Mawbry goaded him."

Quintin saw the lines of regret in her husband's face as candlelight moved its glow over it.

"He left Mathe, and I was certain he would return within a sennight, hopefully resigned to life without Constance. But the following day, your brother's men left him outside our walls—strapped to his saddle, clutching the cauterized stump of an arm." Griffin turned his face to her. "Though there was some satisfaction in knowing The Boursier had lost an eye, I longed for vengeance until I reasoned myself down from it. Serle spoke little of what happened, but I knew he was more at fault—was fairly certain The Boursier had witnessed being made a cuckold." His hand moved again, down her side and in to her abdomen. "I did not know what was done to you, but I vow there was no satisfaction in learning you had been injured."

"This I know." She laid a hand on his stubbled jaw. "Serle blamed you for his failure to take Constance from Adderstone?"

"That was the foundation on which he built his hatred when our father and I refused to bribe the Church to set aside his and Constance's punishment. He believed enough coin would allow them to be together, and when I refused, he left on pilgrimage cursing me."

"I am sorry."

Griffin sighed. "Serle did not think, though more than before, I begin to understand why he did not."

"What do you understand?"

He turned her onto her back and leaned over her. "Are you being coy, Wife?"

"Only a little. As told, I would not wish to so cleave to another it would cause others harm."

"That is why I feel you down through me, Quintin."

He was speaking love to her again, she mused, and as his head lowered, she wished she had found words of her own to express her feelings. When he was not distracting her—warming her lips beneath his, enticing her to open her mouth to him—she would tell of her feelings beyond those three words that, as small as they were, held much.

Winding her arms around his neck, she urged his chest down to hers.

His kiss deepened before moving to her ear, jaw, and neck, then he parted her robe and, barely touching her skin as if for fear his calloused fingers would mar her, moved from her collarbone to the base of her throat. And stilled.

Quintin opened her eyes. "Pray, do not stop."

"What would you have me do?" he rumbled like a great storm in the distance warning that soon it would arrive to bend trees, scatter leaves, and make rivers run swift.

"Show me what you promised," she whispered of his assurance they could be intimate without making a child. "Show me the ways to love and be loved that I may know the joy without later the pain."

"Love but for love's sake," he murmured. "Aye, Wife, I will show you."

31

━━◦◦◦━━

CASTLE MATHE BRIMMED, the impossible of a year past made possible now the king's decree was honored in its entirety. And four days hence, it would become official when the Baron of Blackwood publicly wed the sister of the Baron of Godsmere following six days of celebration.

God willing, on that day there would be more to celebrate than a marriage—namely, a funeral, the feud that had plagued the three families for a quarter of a century buried so deep it would be as unknown to future generations of De Arells, Boursiers, and Verduns as it was now known to their forebears.

But much depended on the hunt. That of the day past had borne no fruit other than a bounty of venison from the deer brought to ground by those who had made themselves bait.

Bait, Griffin reflected as he stared at the one who impaled him on the hook of information and misinformation fed to Simon Foucault the past ten days by way of the farmer's cart. And on that hook with him was Boursier and Verdun.

Serle had mostly stayed out of sight since the arrival of the barons of Godsmere and Emberly two days past. And he was wise to do so. Though Griffin's brother-in-law was reasonable enough to acknowledge the prodigal's aid could be of benefit in ending the Foucault revenge, the scent of blood was on the air when the two men were within sight of each other. And the scent swelled in Quintin's presence.

Another also noticeably scarce belowstairs these past days was Quintin's maid, Nanne, and it was well she was, for one had only to look upon her in Verdun's presence to know her feelings for him—and pain over what he felt for Thomasin. As for her son, Eamon, that affection Verdun did return. But whatever the tale there, Griffin was fairly convinced his daughter's husband had not sired the boy.

"Show me," Griffin said and held out a hand, into which Serle placed an intentionally small and dirty scrap of parchment.

On the morrow, it read, *pheasant hunting past the village of Lorria. Departing two hours ere noon.*

It was written as instructed, as were all of Serle's messages to the brigands, none of which had received an answer—and still no instruction to let the enemy into Mathe.

Previous messages sent by Serle had included assurances the families believed that if the Foucault threat had not died with Sir Otto, it was greatly weakened and would soon gasp its last; tidings Ulric was near enough death that the king's decree was to be fulfilled without further delay so the old baron might know peace upon the land ere passing; and word the wedding celebration that had delivered the Boursiers and Verduns to Blackwood would culminate in Father Crispin wedding De Arell to Boursier. To lessen the possibility of an assault en route, that last had not been revealed until the day the two barons set out for the barony of Blackwood.

"'Twill do?" Serle asked.

Griffin looked up from the parchment that would provide the brigands with another opportunity to attack the hunting party on the morrow if they did not take the bait offered this day—boar hunting far enough beyond the village of Cross to ensure the inhabitants were not at risk, but not so far it made the trap difficult to spring. A trap which Serle, at best, suspected.

"Aye," Griffin said, "'twill suffice." He jutted his chin for his brother to depart the solar, then motioned for Sir Mathieu to ensure the message was affixed to the farmer's cart and to bear witness had a message been left there for Serle.

When both men exited, Griffin crossed to the window and, as he waited for Serle and Sir Mathieu to appear in the bailey below, looked beyond the castle walls to the peaks of dozens of tents erected on the land before Mathe to lodge the sizable entourage that had accompanied Boursier and Verdun.

Mostly, the knights and men-at-arms were trusted by their lords, but lest another Sir Otto prowled amongst them, their great number had provided a reasonable excuse to keep them from entering Mathe—and a deterrent to the brigands who stood little chance of getting past warriors even were Serle able to open a portal to them.

Griffin moved his gaze farther out across the land. Men, who were not of the brigands, were hidden in the wood beyond the village of Cross where the hunt would take place this day. Under cover of dark on the night past, the wood watch—a half dozen warriors each from the three barons—had departed Mathe and now lay in wait should the brigands take the bait. If Griffin, Bayard, and Magnus remained on the hook, those of the wood watch would return this eve to be replaced by others who would set a new trap for the morrow's hunt.

"Take the bait," Griffin muttered, tensing in anticipation of the battle cry that would roar from his chest, the swing of his sword, and the shouts of pain amidst bloodletting that, God willing, would leave all three barons living and at peace.

He lowered his gaze and saw Serle depart the keep and move toward the kitchen's side entrance where the farmer's cart was being unloaded. At a discreet distance, Sir Mathieu followed. Then came Rhys and Eamon. The two were hardly friends, but there was grudging interest on Rhys's part toward the younger boy who, despite his mother's corrections, was disinclined to consider himself inferior to a nobleman's son.

Though Griffin's father strongly disapproved of what he witnessed of their relationship from his window, Quintin encouraged the boys to spend time together and Griffin, having satisfied himself the two argued and wrestled well together, let it be. Not only did he like Nanne's boy, but he hoped his wife's interest in Eamon and developing relationship with Rhys would ease her longing for children of her own body.

Remembering their nights together before the arrival of her brother at Mathe, Griffin was stirred at the prospect he would soon have her in his bed again, and they would resume the joy of teaching each other love but for love's sake.

Feeling a smile, he awaited the appearance of the one who, like Sir Mathieu, was instructed to keep a discreet watch over another, in this instance, Rhys. And there the man was, trailing the boys.

Griffin grunted. He hated that he could not allow his son to move freely about his own home, but soon the threat would be past.

"Take the bait," he growled.

"You," a soft voice said.

He turned and found Quintin in the space between door and frame. Silently cursing himself for lowered defenses that prevented him from hearing the door open, feeling the change in the air, and catching her scent as a warrior must to remain worthy of being that, he stared at her. And recalled the one word she had spoken that fit the fear in her eyes.

Though he had felt the disquiet of Thomasin and Lady Elianor since their arrival at Castle Mathe, both aware their husbands' plan to end the brigands could spill over into the wedding celebration, he felt Quintin's more deeply. Amidst others, she smiled and laughed and seemed to enjoy their company, but she was more watchful of the three barons, and often Griffin suspected she listened more to their conversation than that of her stepdaughter and sister-in-law.

"I know you are the bait," she said. "What I do not know is how you shall escape Simon Foucault ere he swallows you whole. Tell me you can." Her eyes brightened. "Promise you will."

Griffin strode forward and drew her into his arms. "I know 'tis futile to ask you not to worry," he spoke into the hair atop her head. "Thus, the only assurance I can offer is that never have I had as great a cause to be victorious than now you are with me."

She lifted her face. "I am glad, but 'tis not enough."

"It is all I have to give. As the brigands must be destroyed, I will do what is necessary to protect those I love and those whose well-being I am responsible for—as will your brother and my daughter's husband."

"This day?"

"Whenever they come for us. But be it this day or another, we are prepared."

"How?"

"Trust me." He touched his mouth to hers. When she did not respond, he said, "You are angry with me?"

"Nay—frustrated. And frightened you will risk more than is necessary."

"Trust me, Quintin."

She jerked her chin, but he was not certain it was in agreement. After some moments, she said, "I wanted to be with you last eve. Had you been alone, I would have come."

Griffin would not have turned her away, even at the risk of once more rousing her brother's displeasure. But like Sir Mathieu, Rhys had been displaced to accommodate the barons of Godsmere and Emberly— thus, consigned to a pallet beside his father's bed until the night of the day Griffin publicly wed Quintin.

"Four days," he said, "and ever your place shall be here with me." He loosened his hold and stepped back. "Your brother and Verdun will soon be ready to depart."

"This day boar?"

He inclined his head.

"I shall pray for good hunting." She drew a deep breath. "And more."

He brushed his fingers down her cheek. "I love you, Quintin," he spoke the three small words that, as told, served well when there was little time to linger over feelings.

"I still search for the right words that will be as memorable for you as yours are for me," she said low. "But know my heart is yours."

"I know, and I carry it with me this day as I have every day since you entrusted it to me." He sighed. "And now I am nearly late." He stepped around her and into the corridor, assured himself Arturo was where he ought to be, and strode to the stairs.

It was time to try again to sink a hook in Simon Foucault's mouth.

32

———

Diot was displeased, the expression of which Quintin had grown fairly accustomed to, the resulting din an indication the little beast was agitated by a visitor abovestairs. At times, the dog issued deep-throated growls, other times yips, sometimes both. But Quintin had only before heard such vicious barks when she had tried to breach Ulric de Arell's sanctuary.

And Diot was not the only one unsettled. Shortly after the little dog had begun its protestations, Arturo's growls had sounded, evidencing he had moved from the base of the stairs to the chapel door behind which his charge prayed.

Knees aching from the hour spent on them since the hunting party's departure, Quintin rose from the altar where Father Crispin had lit several candles for her beseechings for the safety of Griffin, Bayard, and Magnus. She glanced at the door of the small chamber to the right of the altar where, doubtless, the priest once more rested. He was in better health, the sickness that had feasted on him having lost much of its appetite, though it yet demanded daily feedings. Thus, Quintin continued to pray for Crispin's full recovery.

Upon reaching the chapel door, the sound of another opening made her look around.

"You do not intend to go abovestairs, do you, my lady?" Father Crispin said in a voice that cracked with the effort to be heard above the dogs' commotion.

"Verily, I did not think that far ahead, but something is amiss. The little one sounds as if he could murder, and Arturo is roused."

"Thus"—the priest moved forward at a speed that evidenced he should have remained abed—"your brother and Baron de Arell would wish you to remain here whilst I summon men-at-arms to investigate."

"Aye," she begrudged and nearly turned back, but it struck her the little dog's distress might be in response to the old baron turning ill or taking a fall.

"I will go for them," she said and, before he could protest, opened the door and slipped into the corridor alongside Arturo, whose fur bristled where he stood facing the stairs.

Quintin had not lied. She had meant to summon Rollo and others from the hall, but a shout sounded from the apartment, the little dog's bark grew more savage, and the wolfhound lurched forward a step before peering across his shoulder at her.

Rather than go right, Quintin went left, and though she sensed Arturo's uncertainty in permitting her that path, he advanced just ahead of her.

When she was on the steps, skirts high, she recalled when last she had ascended them in the hope of reaching the apartment before being intercepted by the one she had believed was her enemy.

Dear Lord, she sent up another prayer as the little dog continued its rant, *keep the man I love safe.*

As she followed Arturo onto the landing, she heard another shout that caused the wolfhound to bound forward and scrabble at the door. His din nearly drowning out the other dog's, Quintin reached around him and tried the handle. It was not locked, and a moment later Arturo leapt ahead of her into the chamber.

Quintin caught her breath at the enormity of the dim room, startled over the blur of fur that shot from the far end toward her. Fortunately for the little dog, he made it beneath the bed before Arturo reached him.

While he barked and the big dog growled and paced the bed's perimeter, Quintin looked to the far wall forsaken by the old baron's dog. Amid the shadows stood a figure clothed in a long, pale tunic.

"Get out!" a muffled voice called.

Certain this was Griffin's father, she said, "Are you well? I heard——"

"Out! And take that filthy beast with you!"

She glanced at Arturo. Assured he could not reach the little dog, she strode forward. As she moved past the bed, she took in the chamber's opulence. Ceiling-to-floor hangings partitioned the room, patterned rugs covered much of the floor, and the furniture—bed, chairs, chests, tables—was massive and intricately carved.

Despite the divide between father and son, Griffin honored the one who had sired him by ensuring his shrunken world was beyond comfortable.

When Quintin reached the center of the chamber, her eyes parted the shadows where Ulric de Arell held his back to her. Arms splayed, his gloved hands gripped between them what appeared to be a stick.

"Pray, what do you?" Quintin said loud to be heard above Arturo and his prey.

The old baron's head snapped around, and she halted at the sight of his eerie, expressionless face—a mask, worn to hide the ravages of leprosy. "Accursed Boursier!"

She was not surprised he knew who she was, having often sensed him watching her from his window.

"Leave!" he commanded.

Fairly certain he was well in spite of the clamor, wondering if he might be mad, she started to turn away, but another entreated, "Nay, Lady. Stay!"

Though she could not see who spoke, Ulric de Arell's voluminous tunic spread like a curtain and arms raised to the sides, Serle was on the other side of his father.

Almost wishing she could be as unmoved by the plight of a De Arell as before she had known Griffin, Thomasin, and Rhys, Quintin continued forward. And alongside her came Arturo.

"You trespass, Boursier!"

She did not break stride until she stood ten feet to the left of the old baron and saw Serle was pinned to the wall by a stick pressed to his chest, his one hand gripping its center as if for fear it would gain his throat.

"Stupid girl," Ulric de Arell snarled. "Know you not I am leprous?"

She stared into the mask's eye holes that did not let in enough light to show the glitter of life behind it. "Aye. What I do not know is for what you attack your son."

He grunted, and she noted Griffin had likely learned from him that means of expressing himself. "What I do not know," he said, "is why you concern yourself over this one after what he did to your brother— deserved though 'twas."

Ignoring that last, she looked to Serle and saw pleading in his face. "For the sake of the De Arells, Boursiers, and Verduns I care," she said. "You must know Serle aids in misleading the brigands." At least, she prayed he did.

Ulric turned his immovable face to his son. "'Tis as he would have us believe. But this milksop stole abovestairs though I told I would not receive him. And for what? Not to be reunited with his sire, but to pry from one he believed vulnerable to death the plan to put the brigands in their graves. A betrayer!"

"Nay!" Serle shook his head. "I would know the plan, but not that I might do my family harm. I but seek reassurance Griffin moves against the brigands this day."

"What concerns you about *this* day that did not concern you about the day past?"

Serle's eyes darted to Quintin, then back to his father. "Providing the brigands are brought to ground this day, Constance will be safe."

"Ever Constance!"

"Aye, and ever it shall be. And that is why I came to you." Serle momentarily closed his eyes. "I have received instructions to let the brigands into Castle Mathe this eve."

"You lie! 'Twas reported this day is no different from the others— again no missive left for you."

"The message was there, not upon parchment but written in charcoal on the beam to which I affix the missives Griffin instructs me to write."

Ulric shoved the stick harder against Serle's chest. "If 'tis so, why did you not reveal it to your brother?"

"As he is ever telling me to do, I had to think—"

"What was there to think about?"

"How to ensure Constance's safety without letting in the brigands. And my word I give that never would I open Mathe to them!"

Ulric burned as he peered past the mask at the one he almost wished were not of his loins. Certes, what he did wish was that he had kept his word to his dying wife that their second son would be given to the Church so ever there would be one praying for the De Arells. But Ulric had believed two warrior sons were more impressive and valuable should one not reach adulthood. And both had proved worthy of being trained into the class of men that fights. Until Serle sacrificed all for a woman.

"Had Griffin done as I asked," that one continued, "had he delivered Constance here to keep her out of the hands of the brigands, she would not be of concern, but he refused."

"As well he should!" Despite the ache in his crippled hands, Ulric pushed harder against Serle's chest and was surprised when his son pushed back—so forcefully Ulric stumbled sideways. If not for the stick, whose end he slammed against the floor, he would have collapsed.

Desperately gripping the newest walking stick Thomasin had fashioned and herself delivered after her return to Mathe, he watched his son hasten toward the Boursier woman—only to jump aside when the wolfhound bared its teeth.

Raising his gaze, Ulric had his first near look at the woman Griffin wished to wed. Appearance suffering little from hair that was far from coursing her slender figure, her eyes shone with intelligence and her carriage was self-possessed.

A far different woman this was from Griffin's first wife. And yet she appealed, even though she had drawn a dagger on his son—or perhaps because she had, demonstrating she, a mere woman, would chance her life for those who belonged to her. Though Ulric's eldest son had said he would not risk his family for her, he might, indeed, risk himself.

Movement beyond Quintin Boursier drawing Ulric's regard to the doorway, he cursed. Though it was more than twenty-five years since he had looked upon the man there, he would have known it was Crispin even had he been unaware the stableboy who had become a priest was within his walls.

Loathing how weak he appeared, he walked his hands up the stick until he stood as straight as possible. And ached for the *quietus* ever denied him. "Enter, Crispin!"

"Lady Quintin"—the priest held to the door frame as if he were as deeply fatigued as Ulric—"you ought not be here. Pray, come away."

Followed by the wolfhound, she hurried to him.

The moment the big dog was past the bed, Diot raced to the far end of the room and once more took refuge beneath his master's tunic. Though the brush of fur against Ulric's ankles was mostly imagined, much of the feeling there lost to him, he found comfort in it.

Quintin Boursier touched the priest's arm. "Come, sit."

"My lady, best we—"

"I am not leaving." She drew him to a bench against the wall.

Ulric further considered the woman, wanting to find flaws in the daughter of Archard Boursier, the ally-turned-enemy who had wheedled Castle Adderstone out of the hands of one more deserving. However, a voice he hardly recognized for how often he closed his mind to it told him he was too many years past that offense and his end too near to waste the weeks, days, perhaps hours left to him. Thus, he tried not to hate this woman who would soon be a De Arell. And was amazed at how near he was to accepting her. Near, but never there.

"Tell me the brigands' plan, Serle," he commanded.

"They will come some time in the dark hours after middle night."

"How know you this?"

"Ere I was freed, I was told that upon receiving word to open Castle Mathe, I am to put powders in the wine served at supper to allow the brigands to more easily enter."

As had been done at Castle Adderstone last Christmas, Ulric reflected on that which had seen the wife of the Baron of Godsmere abducted.

"Whence did you obtain the powders?" Griffin's betrothed asked, resentment over her interference causing Ulric's hands to spasm on the walking stick.

Serle looked across his shoulder. "Packets were sewn into the hem of my mantle. But I vow, never did I intend to use them."

"You are to let them in by way of the postern gate?" Ulric asked.

"Nay. They are not so foolish to believe even a prodigal truly welcomed home would be given the opportunity to open an outer portal."

"Then how?" Ulric's saliva sprinkled the inside of his mask.

"I am to let rope ladders down the outer bailey's southern wall and the inner bailey's western wall. Upon reaching the keep, the brigands will enter by way of the garden portal that gives unto the hidden passage leading to your apartment."

Ulric felt as if struck across the face. "You told them of it?"

"Nay, Sir Otto learned of it whilst he served Griffin."

But had not breached it. The passage Griffin had ordered built into the inner wall when the diagnosis of leprosy had confined his father to the third floor had not only allowed Ulric to venture out of doors those first years before traversing the steps became too painful, but had provided access to the chapel for prayer and the kitchen cellar for viands during long nights when sleep eluded him. Doubtless, it was by way of the latter's concealed door Serle had this day stolen abovestairs.

"So you are to unlock the passage to better their chance of taking the keep," Ulric said.

Serle's jaw shifted. "That and, as told Griffin, ensure the deaths of those they seek first—Father Crispin and you."

Ulric glanced at the priest whose face reflected no surprise that he was so marked. "Ere they murder the rest of your family," Ulric said.

"And the Boursiers and Verduns."

Ulric jerked his head toward Griffin's betrothed. "What of her?"

"I heard talk she was to have been Sir Otto's, that his Foucault blood and Lady Quintin's would revive their line, but since he was revealed at Castle Kelling and is believed to have died, it seems she is destined for death like the rest of us."

Recalling the exchange with his eldest son following the unmasking of Sir Otto, Ulric knew it was not as simple as that. But then, Griffin was mostly convinced Serle was unaware Simon Foucault led the brigands. As earlier concluded, providing Denis Foucault's son could destroy the De Arells, Boursiers, and Verduns, he would seek to wed his niece in the hope of restoring the barony of Kilbourne.

"Thus," Serle said, "these things I must do to keep ill from Constance."

Just as Griffin had told that Serle was certain no matter how well he served those who had tortured him he would not be exempt from retribution, Ulric was certain Constance would find the same end as the three barons should the Foucaults prevail.

Would they prevail? If so, not by way of the garden door. To protect those inside the keep, Griffin had ensured that, in the absence of a key and inner access to raise the iron bar, it was impossible to breach without great time and effort that would alert the garrison.

Returning Serle to focus, Ulric said, "The plan to bring down the brigands is of less import than the key. That is what you came for."

Serle's gaze wavered. "Aye, but not to let the brigands in. To let myself out." He took a step forward, only to take it back as if for fear he would once more be pinned. "If Griffin does not work his plan this day, I would leave the keep by way of the passage ere the brigands discover I have failed them. Under cover of cloak, I should be able to gain the outer bailey and slip free of Mathe."

"And turn your back on your family."

Serle shrugged a shoulder into which Ulric longed to slam a fist. "This one-armed warrior will not be missed. And now that you know what the brigands intend, it can be turned to your advantage. That is of greater use than my intolerable presence here."

"It would have been of *far* greater use had you sooner revealed it!"

"I did what I had to, Father."

Ulric felt the ache he did on the rare occasion Griffin afforded him the title he believed his sire unworthy of. And his eldest son was not entirely wrong in that. Simon Foucault was not the only one who had made a tool of his son. Ulric had considered his own sons more a reflection of his prowess than theirs. Had his youngest become vulnerable to the foolishness of love because he too much lacked a good self regard beyond how it affected his father?

Ulric shoved the thought aside. Even were he responsible for who Serle had become—whose behavior had humiliated the De Arells—he was no longer accountable. A man could burden others with his shortcomings and failures only so long ere the excuse of youth was lost to him.

"Father, at least tell me I have hope Griffin will end the brigands this day."

A huff pulled Ulric's gaze to the wolfhound, who remained at Quintin Boursier's side though the mangy beast surely wished to pursue Diot. Having all but forgotten his son and he had an audience, Ulric cursed himself.

"Have I hope, Father?" Serle pressed.

If he spoke true of Simon Foucault's belief he had a means of entering Mathe this eve, it was unlikely the brigands would attack the hunting party unless they could be certain of victory. In the absence of that certainty, they had but to wait for night to fall to end the twenty-five-year feud in the blood of those who had gained from Denis Foucault's fall. Or so they thought.

"Nay," Ulric said, "I do not believe the brigands will find their end this day. But this night..."

"Then allow me to use the garden door so when the ladders do not appear this eve, I can assure Constance's safety."

Refusal sped toward Ulric's lips, but as he stared at his ruined son, he remembered his joy on the day the midwife had placed the squalling infant in his arms—another boy, unlike Archard Boursier who had but one son and Rand Verdun who had none at that time.

Realizing he was about to acquiesce, Ulric braced his legs apart. "I cannot."

Serle took a step forward. "Why?"

"I believe what you tell, but that does not mean I believe right. And for naught will I risk endangering those within our walls, especially my grandson who will be the next Baron of Blackwood." That last was for Quintin Boursier should she think to displace Rhys with a son made of her union with Griffin. "Now leave. All of you."

"Father—"

"Leave!"

The brightening of his son's eyes should have disgusted Ulric, but it was the jerk of his own heart that made him long to spray vicious words.

When the door closed behind them, he made good use of the walking stick to reach the nearest chair and eased onto the stuffed cushions. Once Diot was settled in his lap, he propped Thomasin's gift against his shoulder, removed the glove from his right hand, and watched more than felt his ugly fingers caress the beautiful wood as he entreated, "Quietus, Lord. Pray, soon. Quietus."

33

Hours. And despite the shadows with which the wood was intimate, the hotter the day grew. Only for that was Griffin grateful his shoulders were not weighted by chain mail. Were the bait taken, that protection would be missed—by Boursier and Verdun as well, where they rode on either side of him, faces and throats glistening with the sweat of vigorous pursuit.

The boar had eluded them, though only because those leading the hunt were loath to bring down their prey lest the brigands required more time to attack. Of equal import, the hunt had progressed too far beyond the wood watch—those men who had lain in wait since the night past to spring this day's trap.

The brigands were surely tempted, but something held back those who watched from the shadows cast by towering, heavily leaved trees and thick ground foliage for which Blackwood was named. Though Foucault and his men sought an end to De Arell, Boursier, and Verdun, they remained unwilling to bite, and the longer they circled the hook, the more likely harm would befall those Griffin loved. So perhaps the bait needed to be more appealing—to tempt men who were fighting temptation to bring that fight to their enemies.

When next the hunting party paused to refresh themselves and their mounts, Boursier and Verdun agreed to Griffin's proposal. A quarter hour later, they set out again, and when their game was sighted, strayed farther from the dozen who accompanied them.

The brigands were tempted often over the next hour, movement among the trees and the distant scattering of birds and rodents marking their places, but it was not enough.

As the false prey was allowed to escape, the boar's pounding hooves causing the dirt to spray, its grunts and squeals growing distant, Griffin cursed beneath his breath. And let in a thought he should not.

Three on the hook was too many to turn the brigands reckless, but one…

Surely among Foucault's men were a few foolishly eager enough to embrace the opportunity to gain their leader's favor—and riches—to go against orders.

Think much. Regret little, Griffin tried to subdue the impatience to which he was rarely susceptible. *There is yet the morrow and the morrow after.*

Having slowed his mount alongside Boursier and Verdun, he peered up and, reading the slant of light forcing its way through the canopy, knew it was mid-afternoon. After a look behind at the knights and men-at-arms who made up the remainder of the hunting party, he said, "When next we flush out the boar, we bring it to ground."

Boursier's lids narrowed. Then, spear in one hand, he raised the other that held the reins and thrust auburn hair off his brow. "Aye, if that does not draw them out, we will try again on the morrow."

Black hair clinging to his skull like a cap, Verdun nodded. "The morrow."

It was another hour before they once more set a boar to flight, this one larger in height but also girth, which slowed it. Still, it escaped when they attempted to shepherd it back toward the wood watch.

It was then Griffin caught movement in the direction the boar fled. But it was not of that creature, who lacked the speed to have so quickly distanced himself. As he looked nearer upon the figure before it melted back into Blackwood's shadows, he saw it was a man astride, and was fair certain it was the knight who had tried to kill Thomasin and her husband, and who had thought to make Quintin his prize.

Griffin spurred forward though Boursier and Verdun shouted for him to halt. Leaving behind the protection afforded by the wood watch, he tried to think, but his blood was shot through with anger, impatience, and that which drove Simon Foucault—revenge.

Griffin knew this dark wood, and that such intimate knowledge would make it difficult for the hunting party to stay near, but there was Otto again, wildly guiding his horse between the trees.

Hearing more shouts and the ring of steel, Griffin jerked his head around and saw temptation had won out, that the two barons absent the third and distant from the rest of the hunting party were being set upon by a half dozen brigands.

Griffin slammed his teeth together and turned his destrier. For that, the arrow that punched through skin and muscle before being stopped by bone embedded in his shoulder, rather than his heart.

With a shout less pain than anger, he saw it was too late to escape those closing around him. But there were only four, including Otto, who had turned back.

Griffin halted his horse and snapped the arrow shaft near its entrance. "Four," he growled, three of whom were on foot, one brandishing a bow whose string was being fit with another arrow, two advancing with drawn swords.

Even with his injury, blessedly to the left shoulder, Griffin was certain he could put down the two with blades. Thus, the sound of battle at his back, he leveled the spear that was to have pushed through the thick skin of a boar and commanded his horse toward the bow-wielding brigand.

The man loosed another arrow, but a yank of the reins caused the shaft to soar past its target. And then the spear hit its mark, and the man howled out of a toothless mouth as he slammed to the floor of the wood to become fodder for scavengers.

Griffin looked around and saw reluctance in the speed with which Otto advanced. Fear over engaging with one whose sword skill surpassed his own? Or did Otto see no need to bloody his hands when there remained two willing to wet their own?

Fear. Otto knew what the one who had been his lord was capable of. And so Griffin gave further proof, riding on the nearest brigand, swerving to avoid the man's blade, and slicing his own sword just above the neck of the shabby mail tunic. As the brigand dropped, the great vein pulsed its last, turning the rusted links of armor red.

Two remained, and still Otto was in no hurry to take the fight from the brigand who beckoned with his sword.

"Eager to die, are you?" Griffin shouted, grateful for the bloodlust distracting him from the scream of torn flesh.

"Betrayer!" the brigand spat.

Griffin glanced behind at the hunting party. They appeared to be having the same success as he, the wood watch having come out of hiding to quench their blades' thirst.

Kicking his mount forward, Griffin swung his sword high and leaned hard right to extend his reach and keep his opponent's blade from his horse. Steel clashed, the force of the blow spinning the brigand and dropping him to his knees.

Griffin reined around, and before the brigand could heft his sword high enough to defend his life, ended that life.

"Otto!" Griffin bellowed, and seeing that one fled again, urged his horse after him.

"De Arell!" The Boursier called.

Griffin knew he should look around lest it was a warning—that he should *think*—but as single-minded as a starving dog a nose away from a meal, he pushed his mount hard to keep Otto in sight.

"Accursed, puking Foucault!" he roared Ulric's insult, the force of which momentarily distorted his vision and reminded him of his blood loss. But he did not turn aside. He was too near his daughter's would-be ravisher and murderer...would soon have Otto begging for mercy.

A moment before the blow to the back of his head knocked him over his mount's neck, past the sound of blood pounding in his ears, he heard hooves approach from behind. Then the ground below sped past, and against that blur he saw his son's face, next Quintin's. And as darkness pushed him to the back of its throat, he felt that which so burdened a soul.

Regret.

Terrible regret.

I live. Or do I?

Over and again he questioned how deeply he must regret the pain throbbing through the back of his head, shooting down his spine, and feeding the fires in hips that vied for notice over the burn in the shoulder that had taken an arrow.

If he lived, he was grievously injured. Had he died, God's displeasure was surely upon him. No heaven, this dark place.

Or was it dark? He lifted his lids and, wincing as light rushed into his eyes, focused on the rough-hewn floor.

Not dead. Merely dying?

Merely, he turned over the word used to describe a death that would leave his son fatherless and his wife a widow, and gave a grunt of wry laughter.

"De Arell."

He jerked at the voice so near his ear he felt its gust, grimaced as he drew breath amid the odor curling into his nostrils. Desperate to place himself, he sought saliva and found a small pool beneath his tongue. Scooping it onto his palate, he held it there.

"He is conscious," the voice once more assailed Griffin.

"Now." The answer was distant and gruff, and as Griffin's consciousness further roused, fingers scraped the back of his injured scalp and the hairs protested as they were gathered tight and his head yanked up.

Even before the face of the one before his own shed its blurred planes, before he noted the fairly recent cut that ran jaw to cheek, which Thomasin had dealt to avoid ravishment, he knew it. Otto.

Aye, Griffin de Arell lived, though it was intended he would not much longer.

He did not know what made him smile, but he felt how uneven that unfitting expression was and thought of Quintin, who had hated it ere she loved it.

"This will make you scream," Otto said, though what shone from the eyes above that mouth belied satisfaction. Weariness there. Fear. Regret.

As Griffin swallowed the precious saliva, he mused it was good he was not alone in feeling regret. And if there was any way to cast off the fetters he was only now becoming aware of, he would make certain the last thing this one felt on earth was regret so keen all of him would be flayed ere hell embraced him.

"Now!" That other voice again.

Griffin slid his gaze to the right. By the light of a dozen candles and slices of day shining through the seams of shuttered windows, he saw the figure before a set of doors, a black cloth wrapped around his head and lower face.

Realization struck, but not as to the identity of the one giving the orders. That Griffin knew and was certain was the same who had landed the flat of a sword to the back of his head. It was the place to which he had been brought that surprised—the small church outside the village of Cross where he and Quintin had wed.

If he looked left, he would see the altar before which the nuptial mass had been intoned, if he looked down, he would see the kneeler upon which he had perched beside his wife to pray for their marriage. And to which he was now bound, the padded bench beneath his knees, the raised wood shelf beneath his upper chest and shoulders. It was the latter that caused him the greatest pain, his weight on the shelf pressing the arrow deeper. But though tempted to raise that shoulder to relieve the pressure, it likely kept him from bleeding out.

Strain and numbness in arms stretched taut over the front of the kneeler, wrists secured by a rope whose tension he felt in his ankles, he guessed the rope was threaded beneath the kneeler to ensure he remained hunched over with his back exposed—his flesh bared.

Whatever awaited him, and he could imagine it, having seen what had been done to Serle, he *would* want to scream, and who would hear him but—?

He yanked his thoughts around and was ashamed to only now question the fate of the priest who had wed Quintin and him. Had they killed him?

Returning his gaze to the one who was to do the other's bidding, he snarled, "Where is the man of God?"

"Absent."

Did Otto speak true? Was the priest ministering to the villagers? Before Griffin could enquire further, the one at the church doors shouted, "Do it now! They draw nearer."

Once Griffin made sense of that last, he was suffused with the satisfaction of knowing the Foucaults were as trapped as he—that Boursier, Verdun, and De Arell men were outside the doors.

No longer feeling the strain at the roots of his hair, realizing he held up his head though fingernails dug into his scalp, he determinedly raised both sides of his smile. "Aye, boy, do as told."

The younger man drew breath through quivering nostrils, exhaled against Griffin's brow. "'Twill be over all the sooner do you scream," he said so low it seemed his words were meant only for Griffin.

Griffin stared at him, then said loud, "Now, knave, ere Simon Foucault once more turns his knife on his beloved son."

Otto's eyes sprang so wide his lashes bent beneath his eyebrows.

"Aye, I know you lied when you told Verdun your father died in France," Griffin pushed his voice to a strength that made his throat feel bloodied. "We all know, just as King Edward shall soon learn the truth of the mercenary who serves him for his own ends."

Footsteps sounded—boot soles scraping, leather uppers creaking. As they advanced, Griffin chuckled at the color draining from Otto's face. But then his throat closed, and he coughed to open it. The jerk of his bent body thrusting his shoulder against the wood shelf and driving the arrowhead deeper, he suppressed a groan and called, "You would have a boy work a man's ill? Of course, mayhap this mistake of your loins is more man than you."

The boots halted to his right, and he peered sidelong into eyes the same color as Quintin's. "Whether you call yourself Sir Francis Cartier, mercenary of King Edward, or Simon Foucault, baron of naught, you lose."

Seeing Foucault draw an arm back, he was prepared for the blow and the cut of the ring from cheek to nose that was little compared to the injury dealt his shoulder and the back of his head. Next a blow that would bruise his jaw, and another that would swell his eye closed.

You are not thinking much, he told himself. *You are not thinking at all. Think, Griffin, else regret will be the death of you.*

"How long have you known?" the mercenary demanded.

Discovering Otto had released his hair, Griffin turned his face back and saw Simon Foucault had dropped his head covering down around his shoulders.

"Long enough to lay the trap into which you blundered." Griffin deliberately moved his gaze over the puckered skin of the man's lower face. "Hurts, does it not, those steel teeth tearing through the flesh of your deceit? Cracking the bone of your plan to put Kilbourne back together?" He sighed. "I had nearly given up hope of bringing you down this day—thought 'twould be the morrow ere we could try again—but of a sudden there was Otto." He flicked his gaze to the son. "And now I am fair certain you are quite short on brigands. Thus, you are finished."

He had not thought Simon Foucault could be more unsightly, but when his ruined mouth expelled a curse past bared teeth and gums, he was monstrous.

Griffin steeled himself, but when he jerked, it was from surprise that it was Otto who was knocked back by Simon's fist.

"You showed yourself!"

Otto raised an arm before his bloodied face, splayed his hand as if that would prevent him from being struck a second time. "I vow, 'twas not my intention."

"This night! You had but to remain out of sight, and this night we would have been inside Mathe, our blades dripping with the blood of our enemies!"

"You do not know Serle would have let down the ladders—that he would be able to access the garden passage!"

As Otto once more suffered a fist that collapsed him against the altar, Griffin quaked with the effort to contain the fiery pain of injuries stirred by anger. Telling himself strength would be wasted on raging against bonds he could not break, he forced himself to delve the reason Serle had not revealed he was to admit the brigands to Mathe this eve.

Because he had no intention of doing Simon Foucault's bidding? Because he feared his family would further distrust him? Or had he held that knowledge close in the hope that if the three barons failed to end the Foucault threat, he might still save Constance—that, pressed, he would have let in the brigands?

Griffin quaked again. If Serle had revealed the attempt to breach Mathe this eve, the trap in the wood would not have been necessary. Instead, the trap would have been set atop the walls, and those who climbed the ladders slain. Rhys's father and Quintin's husband would not be here now.

"Serle!" The name ripped from Griffin's throat like a blade scoring the inside of its scabbard as it was wrenched free.

And Simon Foucault laughed as he straightened from Otto whose gushing nose painted his teeth red. "Not surprisingly, betrayal runs deep in your family." He peered into Griffin's upturned face. "A brother's betrayal—more difficult to stomach, I wager, than that of men who vow to put their liege first. I almost feel for you, De Arell." He looked back at Otto. "Get up. There are deeds to be done and messages to be sent."

As his son gained his feet, Simon nodded at Griffin. "Do it."

Otto unsheathed his dagger and moved behind and to the side of their captive. Then a hand was on Griffin's back as if Otto sought to brace himself for what was required of him.

When Griffin felt the horizontal line cut into his flesh—the top of a T—he did not cry out as he had been warned he should.

"Deeper," Simon commanded.

Otto did as told. But when only a groan escaped Griffin, Simon shoved a hand between the kneeler's wood shelf and his captive's shoulder and dug his fingers into the torn flesh around the arrow wound.

"Almighty!" Griffin roared.

"Ah, the price of dirt," Simon bemoaned. "Never did your father believe 'twould be this high, hmm? And what pleases me most is the debt is far from paid."

The next dig of his fingers shifted the arrowhead, and Griffin's bellow nearly covered the pounding on the door.

"Simon Foucault," Boursier called, "release the Baron of Blackwood and your deaths will be mercifully swift."

"We should have left De Arell to die—should have ridden on!" Otto cried.

Folded over the kneeler, narrowly peering at beads of perspiration sliding down the hair before his eyes, Griffin anticipated the blow it seemed Otto did not—that which caused the dagger to slip and open their captive's flesh where a cut was not intended.

As before, he withheld his shout, but Simon once more commanded it by jamming his fingers into the wound.

"God's eyes!"

"Better," Simon drawled, then called, "Move away from the door, else I gut him."

Between deep breaths and the gnashing of teeth, Griffin listened.

"You know what he is thinking, De Arell?" Simon said. "That here is an opportunity to rid himself of an alliance he never wanted—to keep his sister out of your bed."

Griffin considered the possibility, but the Bayard Boursier and Griffin de Arell of years past were no more. All Simon Foucault had spent his life upon had crumbled.

There—a murmur of voices and retreating footsteps.

Simon clicked his tongue. "Alas, your men and Verdun's are with him." He lowered his hand to his side and wiped bloody fingers on his tunic. "You secured the rear door, Otto?"

"Aye," his son choked, then said with accusation, "We shall die here."

"Quite possible."

"I am not ready to die!"

"Pity. 'Tis easier done when one is ready." Simon returned to Griffin. "You are not ready, are you, De Arell?"

Quietus, Griffin reflected on that which his father had only once spoken of, though Griffin suspected it was often on the old baron's mind.

"You still have hope you may yet bed Quintin Boursier, hmm?"

Quintin *de Arell,* Griffin silently corrected. A good reminder of those for whom he had reason to live. Rhys. Thomasin. Quintin. He lowered his lids, imagined awakening with his wife curled against him. Watching her. Awaiting the opening of her eyes upon him—eyes not at all like Simon Foucault's though the color was the same.

"If we take him with us under threat of death should they follow," Otto said, "we might escape."

Simon sighed. "They will follow, De Arell will die, and then we shall die."

"We must try!"

With effort, Griffin lifted his head and peered across his shoulder at where Otto grasped his crimson-edged blade.

"We make our stand here," Simon said.

"But—"

"'Tis decided, though if you are eager to say your last prayer, I can do this alone."

"D-do what?"

"Take our revenge on those even more deserving than Ulric de Arell's whelp. Now if you are with me, cut him."

Otto's throat bobbed, but he drew near again and once more set a hand on Griffin's back. Then he made the cuts while Griffin pressed his tongue hard to his palate and turned his mind to what was being carved into his back. Two letters now. And when the word *traitor* wept crimson down his back, what then? Would they cut his chest as had been done Serle?

If so, it would require untying the rope binding him to the kneeler to turn him. And therein lay opportunity.

"And now we ask for terms," Simon said. As the bracing hand on Griffin's back tensed further, Simon said, "You will like these terms, De Arell."

When he revealed them, Griffin shouted again, demanding in a voice he feared would not carry to those outside that the terms not be honored. But another blow to the back of the head returned him to the dark of what could as easily be death as life.

34

Lady Elianor did not suspect, worry and pregnancy-induced fatigue having taken her abovestairs minutes past.

Lady Thomasin did not suspect, worry and her offer to escort the other lady to her chamber having removed her from the hall as well.

Thus, it was all for Quintin to question the urgency surrounding Sir Mathieu when he entered the hall. With an obvious effort to appear as if naught were amiss, he ascended the stairs and went from sight.

Quintin glanced at the servant she had instructed to tell Cook to proceed with the stew of mixed meats for supper now it was too late to bring boar to table even if the hunting party returned to Mathe this moment.

Why have they not? she questioned what normally would not concern her. Often a hunt required substantial daylight hours to deliver enough meat to feed those who took their meals in the hall, especially when hosting a great number of guests.

"My lady?"

She looked to where Rhys sat at a small table across from Eamon, who had surprised the nobleman's son with his knowledge of the game of chess that had occupied them these two hours.

"Aye, Rhys?"

"No boar for supper?"

"I fear not. And 'tis likely the meal will be served later than usual."

"I grow hungry."

"As do I," Eamon said and received the usual—though increasingly less severe—reproachful look from his companion.

"Take yourselves to the kitchen. Cook will prepare something to keep you until supper."

The boys murmured agreement but returned to their game.

As expected, Arturo came out from beneath a table to follow Quintin across the hall to the stairs, which would prevent Rollo from following.

Upon reaching the second floor, she heard Elianor's and Thomasin's voices behind the door of the chamber the Lord and Lady of Godsmere had been given and determined it was best neither was disturbed by what might prove unfounded suspicion.

"But you…" Quintin glanced at the wolfhound keeping pace with her. "…I do not suppose you will allow me to proceed alone?" When he began the ascent of the stairs beside her, she muttered, "Of course not."

Not that it mattered. With or without Arturo, Diot would alert the old baron of a visitor, as evidenced by the little dog's bark long before they reached the door.

As Quintin raised a hand to knock, the door opened.

"What do you here, my lady?"

"Discovering what *you* do here, Sir Mathieu," she said loud to be heard above Diot.

He glanced at the growling Arturo. "I intend no disrespect, but I consult with the old baron on a matter I am certain your"—he cleared his throat, likely to mask having nearly named Griffin her husband—"betrothed would not wish you bothered over."

She did not like the guardedness in his eyes, to which she had not been subject since before the day he had witnessed her marriage. "Your lord has sent word?"

His jaw shifted. "My lady—"

"Is it the brigands? Did they take the bait?"

"Lady Quintin, I—"

Ulric de Arell called something she could make no sense of above the little dog's din, then she was yanked inside in an attempt to keep out Arturo. But the wolfhound lunged past the door whose closing struck him in the haunches.

While Griffin's senior knight cursed, the big dog raced forward and Diot sprang from the foot of the bed to the head where his master sat propped against pillows.

"Down!" the old baron shouted and swung the walking stick up off his lap and cracked the wolfhound across the muzzle.

"Arturo!" Quintin cried, hastening to where the dog backed against a wall and shook his head and rubbed it on a foreleg.

When she bent to him, he bared his teeth, and she drew back in remembrance of the day Griffin had prevented him from ripping out her throat. But then he lowered his lip and lifted his head toward her.

Relieved there was no blood on him, though that side of his muzzle would surely swell, she cautiously set a hand on his head and turned toward the bed.

Diot was tucked beneath an arm on the old baron's far side, only his head visible. Blessedly, he had exchanged barks for growls.

Though tempted to berate Ulric for striking Arturo, Quintin knew it had been necessary to subdue the wolfhound. Looking from the masked man to the knight who had positioned himself between Quintin and the bed, she said, "Tell, Sir Mathieu."

He glanced at the old baron and received a nod. "I have word of Baron de Arell's capture by Simon and Otto Foucault."

She sucked a breath, groped a hand down Arturo's neck, and gripped his shoulder. "Is he…?"

"He lives and is held at the church outside the village of Cross."

Where they had wed. "My brother? And Baron Verdun?" Had they been lost on some meadow defiled by slaughter?

"Minor injuries only," the knight said, and as she thanked the Lord, continued, "It appears the brigands are defeated. Only a handful escaped."

She swallowed. "How many brigands are in the church?"

"'Tis believed only Simon and Otto Foucault."

"What of the barons' men?"

"Few fatalities, though a good number were injured and have been taken to the village to be tended by its healer."

She nodded. "Was it my brother who sent word?"

"Aye, he and Baron Verdun have surrounded the church, but..."

"What?"

"They dare not try to take it lest the Foucaults further harm or kill Baron de Arell."

"How do they know he lives?"

Another glance at Ulric, who himself answered, "They torture my son."

That nearly sending her to her knees, she dropped onto a bench to hear the rest.

"Each time an attempt is made to breach the church," Ulric said, "Griffin is subjected to pain so great his shouts reveal he yet lives. Though in what state..." On a breath that echoed inside the mask, he murmured something that sounded like *quiet,* then directed Sir Mathieu to finish the tale. A tale erected on the lie that were the two remaining betrayers of Denis Foucault delivered to Simon Foucault, the Baron of Blackwood would be released.

"I do not believe it," Quintin said. "Still your son will die, the only difference being you shall die alongside him."

Ulric inclined his head. "And the priest, if he can be convinced to meet Foucault's terms."

"Father Crispin will not require convincing. Do you go—"

"Of course I go! And if the Lord goes with me, I shall find a way to ensure Foucault keeps his end of the bargain. If not..." He drew his gloved hand from his little dog's chest to its head. "...Rhys will be fatherless and motherless and you, Lady Quintin, will be less one betrothed."

Quintin tried to imagine the leprous old baron and ailing priest prevailing over Simon and Otto Foucault and thought it only possible providing the Lord did, indeed, go with them. Thus, she grasped for a means of increasing the chance of bettering the Foucaults. And found one. "Mayhap they would trade Griffin for me."

Sir Mathieu made a sharp sound of dissent and Ulric said, "You?"

"Simon Foucault wished me for his son's wife."

The old baron snorted. "'Tis what Otto was led to believe, but methinks you were ever destined for the father. Regardless, 'tis too late. Now Simon is known to be Sir Francis Cartier, his plan to regain Kilbourne through marriage to you is trampled, all hope lost save that of taking his greatest enemies with him into death. Thus, even if 'tis true you would sacrifice yourself for my son—"

"I would."

"—you are no longer of use to him."

Thoughts whirling, she plucked at pieces, forced them together, and stood. "I am of great use to one who, for a quarter of a century, has lived for revenge and must now settle for far less than he believes his due."

"Nay, my lady!" Sir Mathieu protested.

She ignored him. "Does Griffin die, I lose more than a betrothed. I lose my husband."

The headboard creaked with the lurch of Ulric's body. "What say you?"

"We wed in secret after Christmas. Were that revealed to Simon Foucault, he might grasp the opportunity to take from your son what he loves." She pressed a hand to her abdomen. "And what he would love."

"You are with child?" Ulric demanded.

Wishing she could see his face to know if there was something beyond disapproval there, she said, "I am not so blessed, and never shall I be, but Foucault does not know that."

"You make no sense."

"I cannot give your son more heirs, so you may rest well knowing never will one of my body threaten Rhys's succession."

The silence stretched so long she felt it in the roots of her hair. "How can you be certain you will bear no children?" Griffin's father finally spoke.

She could reveal the injury done her by his youngest son, but there was no gain. "It matters not. What matters is I am precious to my husband. Thus, Simon Foucault will want me all the more if he believes that in stealing me away he also gains his enemy's unborn child."

"There is no good in this," Sir Mathieu growled.

"Mayhap there is," Ulric said.

"My lord, even if you cannot acknowledge it, you love your son, and the greatest love you could show him amidst the evil beneath which he suffers is to keep those dear to him safe. And that includes his wife."

"Who will not be a wife if Griffin is taken from us," she pressed. "More importantly, Rhys will no longer be a son."

"I will not allow it!" Sir Mathieu said.

"If I allow it, so shall you," the old baron snarled.

The knight looked between them. "My lord, your son is no longer a youth whose life must be directed. He is well-proved a man, one who would forbid his wife to be exchanged for him."

Quintin stepped nearer. "Baron de Arell, you know what I propose is for the best. For Rhys. For Blackwood. For your people."

"Quiet!" He backhanded the air, and the little dog barked as if in agreement.

He would relent. Had to. For all that was dear to him—and that she was not. "Do you meet Simon Foucault's terms," she ignored his command, "you and the priest will die with your son. Three deaths when only one life need be risked—that of one who has a greater chance of surviving Simon Foucault."

Ulric considered her, then shifted Diot onto his lap and said, "You truly believe you can better him and his son, Quintin Boursier?"

"I am Quintin de Arell," she reminded him, "and, certes, they will be less prepared for a woman to thwart them."

"My lord," Sir Mathieu returned to the conversation, "whether in life or death, never will your son forgive you should harm befall his lady."

The old baron stroked the little dog's back, with regret said, "You are right, Mathieu, and so we give Simon what he demands and see if we can free Griffin."

"Nay!" Quintin cried.

"Sir Mathieu, go to Father Crispin and tell him I have a boon to ask of him."

"You would sentence a Holy man to death?" she demanded.

"I but strive to meet Foucault's terms. 'Tis for Father Crispin to decide if he joins me. And since he has been having long conversations with death the same as I, methinks he will decide well." He returned his gaze to the knight. "Also summon the physician. My son will have need of him."

Sir Mathieu strode to the door and paused to peer at Quintin.

But she was not leaving, and he loudly closed the door behind him.

The silence that followed was heavy, but finally Ulric said, "I am not altogether bothered you continue to trespass upon my hospitality, but if you think to turn my decision, you spill my time with yours."

"Not if you would better your grandson's chance of having his father's guidance as he grows into a man."

He sighed, patted the little dog who lifted its head and looked from her to the door and back. "Sir Mathieu gives good counsel, Lady Quintin. Ever I have aspired to order my son's life, and too often I have done harm. Thus, I will not risk taking from him again one for whom he has more a care than he ought to."

"Not even for Rhys?"

"Though I am not in the habit of trusting God to right the ills in my life, in this I give over to Him. As must you."

Grudgingly acknowledging he left no window open for argument, she said, "Since the brigands have been mostly defeated and your escort to the church will be sufficient to keep any who escaped from setting upon you, I would accompany you."

He gave a sharp laugh. "I am familiar enough with you treacherous Boursiers to know that, given a chance, you will do as you wish. Thus, as

I would bear the blame should ill befall you, you will remain here with Rhys. And if this day he loses his father alongside his grandfather, you will ensure he receives proper training to become a man worthy of lording Blackwood—preferably at Wulfen Castle."

That place where her father had trained and been awarded the coveted Wulfrith dagger she had brought with her to Mathe, the keen edge of which Simon and Otto Foucault were worthy as Griffin had never been.

"Promise me, Quintin de Arell," he said, and her heart leapt to hear him give his name to her, "you will do whatever is necessary to see the son of the man for whom you say you would sacrifice yourself become a warrior worthy of lording Blackwood."

Whether she succeeded or failed at accompanying him, the promise would be fulfilled. "My word I give."

"And Diot. Do I not return to Mathe, he is to be given to my granddaughter."

"My word I give," she repeated.

"Then my blessing I give your marriage."

Emotion gripped her. "I thank you."

"And I you—that you loved my son."

She barely caught those last, whispered words, but she knew she had not misheard, that he spoke as if Griffin were already lost. "Baron de Arell—"

"Go!" He flicked a hand toward the door.

"'Tis possible—"

"Leave me!"

Arturo at her side, she crossed to the door and looked back. "I agree 'tis best Rhys knows naught of this, but should not Thomasin be told her father's life is in danger?"

"Nay. Like you, she would risk herself to save him. And me."

He was right. Aching for how slight the one who had been a formidable warrior appeared on his bed, she opened the door and stepped into the corridor. And swallowed surprise at finding someone awaited her there.

35

⸺❈⸺

"Ask me anything, De Arell. You have questions, and I am bored enough to while away the time until next you or your would-be saviors give me the pleasure of making you scream."

T and R, Griffin silently named the letters cut into his back. Only two. Unless Simon could be incited to finish the word and start on his captive's chest, the rope would not be loosened to turn Griffin.

Seeking to end this before the terms of his release were met, Griffin had taunted Simon for what seemed hours as the light of day gave unto the light of dusk seeping through the shutter's seams.

First, he had disparaged the Foucaults' traitorous bent, wondering aloud if it was passed from Denis to Simon to Otto by way of blood or merely example. Next, he had mused over further evidence of their traitorous ways, citing the two brigands who had served their leader well only to be gutted and their corpses presented as gruesome wedding gifts to Thomasin and Magnus.

He had congratulated Simon on the traitorous son he had produced, one worthy of the family name, as evidenced by Otto putting an attempt to ravish Thomasin ahead of his father's plan to restore Kilbourne.

He had mocked Otto's failure to enact Simon's plan for Thomasin and Magnus to be burned alive in retaliation for Thomasin's sympathetic response to the agony Sir Francis Cartier had suffered in the fire that ruined his countenance—the attempt to give her personal experience with that agony having aided in revealing his identity.

But for all of Griffin's taunting, Simon found too much satisfaction in digging into the shoulder wound that had first yielded the pained shout he required.

If only I had done as Otto advised, Griffin wished. *Had I screamed when he cut me.*

The back of a hand against Griffin's mouth returned him to the present. "Ask me, De Arell!"

Mouth moistened by the blood of a split lip, Griffin narrowly opened his eyes—the left by choice, the right by the constraint of swelling. So pained. So weary. But not as much as he would have Simon believe in the event the miscreant could be incited to finish branding his captive a traitor.

With a good effort made to appear a great effort, he raised his gaze up the man who stood before him with legs wide. "My father told you were as much a lover of gentility as beauty." Though his throat ached for moisture, he allowed bloody spittle to stretch from his lower lip toward the floor. "Though I know the years can be cruel to those who work the land, for what did you choose one such as Agatha of Mawbry to make a child upon?"

The hands at Simon's sides moved toward fists, but he eased them into deceptively benign hooks. "Aude was her given name."

As only Thomasin had known her, it seemed.

"One of several children made on common women by the lord I served in France." He laughed. "Such high regard she had of herself, believing she was equal to her legitimate sister, whom she served as a maid until that one..." He clicked his tongue. "...died."

"Aude killed her?"

"That does occur. Aude was of a jealous nature and her sister had an eye for a particular knight with whom she, herself, was besotted." He shrugged. "Very possible."

"Then seeing a kindred spirit in the vile person of Aude, you took her as your lover."

Not insult enough, he lamented when Simon dropped to his haunches to peer past the hair fallen over Griffin's brow. "Though she had a lovely figure that made her desirable from the backside, Simon Foucault was never more than tempted."

Griffin knew he was being led deeper into the story to alleviate the miscreant's wait to see if Ulric and Father Crispin would be delivered, but he continued to play the game in the morbid hope of pushing Simon to order Otto to resume cutting on their captive. "You speak of yourself as if you were not present, implying you did not father so unworthy a son."

Simon sighed. "Certes, he is of these loins."

"Then?" Griffin croaked, and when he coughed hard, found some satisfaction in flecking his captor's boots with bloody spit.

"As told, Simon Foucault was never more than tempted. Thus, Aude was the seducer when he was…well, no longer himself."

Griffin considered the pastorela Thomasin had learned from that woman, the song of a nobleman's pursuit of a half-caste shepherdess who spurned his advances. If Simon spoke true, in his case it was the nobleman who had done the spurning. For a time.

Griffin shifted on the kneeler and did not hold back the groan roused by his fiery shoulder, throbbing back, and aching knees. "'Twas not until you became Sir Francis Cartier you let her into your bed."

"Once I looked like this and had not a full purse to pay for better than Aude, there were few women willing to comfort me upon the sheets. Too, since Aude saved my life, it seemed only right I repay her." He jerked his head at where Otto sat on a front pew—elbows on knees and dagger loosely grasped between them. "And *that* happened."

There was such disgust in Simon's voice Griffin wondered if Otto was thinking not of the next cut to Griffin, but of the one to whom he wished he were man enough to retaliate.

"Aye," Simon breathed past his burned smile, "he hates me, even more than I loathed my father, but he fears me more. And rightfully so." Meaning if Griffin harbored hope of Otto's aid, he should abandon it.

"Then you are a worse father than Denis Foucault. That is much to be proud of, Simon."

Muscles at the man's mouth and eyes spasmed, but he was not moved to further torture. "Ask me another question. You know the one."

Sweat rolled down Griffin's nose, curved beneath it, and slid its saltiness over his lips. Too little to swallow, he said, "How did Aude save your life?"

"There is the tale!" Simon looked to his son. "He wishes to know of your mother's great love for your father."

Otto lifted his head only enough to meet Simon's gaze, then shifted his regard to Griffin.

"He pouts," Simon grumbled, then continued, "You heard I died in France days ere I was to depart for England to take back the lands awarded to your three families?"

"That was the tidings delivered us—that you were lost in a skirmish defending your lord."

"Nearly true. The attack moved from the wood to the town outside the walls of my lord's castle. I was ordered to gather the straggling townsfolk and get them inside the walls ere the drawbridge rose, only to find myself shut out with them. I hid us in a stable, but the fools could not keep quiet, and we were discovered and the building set afire."

He swallowed noisily, and though Griffin did not wish to feel the other man's pain, he did.

Simon coughed as if to clear the memory of smoke from his lungs. "It was Aude who pulled me from the fire and stole me away. She tended me for months, and each time I tried to be done with this foul life, she dragged me back with acrid draughts that made me heave and stinking salves that barely quieted my screams. But you know what kept me alive? That which Aude overheard my lord tell his captain of the guard that delivered her to the town in time to pull me from the burning stables.

That which made me dream of vengeance upon those who had stolen all from me. "

"Tell," Griffin said.

He shoved his face nearer his captive's. "Either you do not know what my lord ordered, or you hide that knowledge well."

"I know not."

Simon tilted his head. "You know the Bible story of David and Bathsheba?"

Griffin raised his eyebrows.

"Recall that after David impregnated Bathsheba, he attempted to conceal his sin by ordering his general to place her husband in the front lines of the battle where he would more likely die, and so he did die." Simon's smile turned more hideous. "What Aude overheard condemned me to play Bathsheba's husband to your father's David."

Inwardly, Griffin recoiled, but he kept denial from his tongue.

"I sense genuine surprise," Simon drawled, "and yet you do not gainsay me. Because you know 'tis possible, aye?"

Had Ulric persuaded Simon's lord to place his household knight in danger in the hope Denis Foucault's heir would not return to England to attempt to regain Kilbourne?

Griffin tried to find a fit for his father and concluded it was possible Ulric had been capable of such. But what made it unbelievable was that the newly titled Baron of Blackwood had not possessed sufficient influence or funds to cause another lord to condemn a loyal vassal to death.

"Nay," he said, "'tis a lie to which you have clung—one spun of Aude's imagination."

Simon's eyes widened, and his hand shot up, but he stopped it and bit, "Why would she lie?"

"*Think*, Simon. She was besotted with one she could not have. The only way to keep you in her power after pulling you from the fire was to sever your connection to your French lord, allowing all to believe your corpse was one of those pulled from the ashes. And you, poor Simon, were not only indebted to her, but you depended on her to aid in your revenge. You needed her—and the son she gave you. *That* is far more possible than my father possessing the means to convince a lord across the narrow sea to send one of his men to his death."

Simon slowly straightened, and as he began to pace the dais upon which the altar was raised, Griffin looked between him and his son who warily watched.

Shortly, Simon returned to Griffin. "And so I took the name Francis Cartier," he said as if naught had disturbed his reality. "As my reputation grew in France, I became known as the Merciless Mercenary." He gave a satisfied sigh. "When one has only revenge to live for, a formidable foe they make, and that inspires others to follow. Thus, when I returned to England, I was accompanied by a score of mercenaries, the ever-loyal Aude, and a son."

Neck strained, pain, fatigue, and blood loss vying to render him senseless, Griffin once more let his head hang between his bound arms that had lost much of the feeling fingertips to armpits.

Opening and closing his hands to restore circulation, he searched for words to move Simon Foucault to resume his torture.

"I made myself and my men indispensable to King Edward II ere his son took the throne from him," Simon continued, "and in between the tasks set me, I became a scourge to those who called themselves the barons of Godsmere, Emberly, and Blackwood, working ill on these lands to further the feud each time it waned. Much easier that became when Otto was of an age to be fostered and Aude began to move about Kilbourne, calling herself Agatha of Mawbry and securing the position of maid to Constance Verdun." A chuckle. "And we know how that ended, aye?"

The cuckolding of Bayard Boursier—and worse.

Another back of the hand. "You are not asking questions, De Arell. 'Tis ill of you to make me carry the conversation."

Conversation, Griffin mused as he raised his chin. "Forgive me." He winced at the gravel in his voice. "I thought you but wished me to listen to you listen to yourself talk."

More anger, but Simon laughed it away. "Very well, *I* will ask a question. For what did the king place Otto in your service? Recall, 'twas not only my father who was betrayed. Your fathers betrayed Edward II by bringing the baronage down upon the Foucaults for remaining loyal to the king. Thus, though that Edward bowed to the baronage's demands, the longing for revenge against your three families burned. When I revealed myself to him and promised satisfaction, he accepted wardship of my son and saw Otto trained up into a warrior."

Of course that was how it came to be. And ere the old king lost his crown, he had sent Otto to serve at Castle Mathe.

"Does our young king know you are Simon Foucault?" Griffin asked.

"Good question, De Arell!" Simon patted Griffin's cheek. "Since Edward III lacks the desire to avenge those who betrayed his father—embraces them, even—I thought it best he remain unaware. You see, our relationship is different from the one his father and I enjoyed. 'Twas not mutual need for revenge that gained me Edward III's favor, but the aid I gave in securing his throne when Mortimer and his mother sought to keep him their puppet."

This Griffin knew—that Sir Francis Cartier had earned his place near the third Edward by helping end Mortimer's power at the end of a rope.

"Next question, De Arell."

Shamed by limbs that had begun to tremble as if he were chilled, he said, "Was it you who murdered your own sister, Lady Maeve? Who drugged the household of Baron Boursier? Who stole away Lady Elianor and delivered her to Aude for execution?"

"Aye, aye, and aye. Of course, all did not come about as planned, but such one must expect in relying on others. What else would you know?"

More than anything, how to rile him sufficiently to make him finish branding his captive. "Is your son aware it was ever intended Lady Quintin—your niece—would be your bride?"

Simon's nostrils flared. "He thinks to turn you against me, Otto, in the hope you will put your blade through me."

"I know what he does," Otto said dully.

His apathy sickened, especially as it further tempted Griffin to that same place of powerlessness. "Regardless, I speak true." He peered sidelong at the young man. "Just as I do in telling what a disappointment you are, Otto, and how shamed I was to learn the truth of one I esteemed as being among my most capable and worthy knights—so much I trusted you to keep my daughter safe in her wanderings."

"Hence, the fool you are," Simon said.

One too many regrets, Griffin silently conceded. "I did feel the fool, but less now that I understand how I fell prey—how I did not see the coward behind the face of Sir Otto of Castle Mathe." Gathering breath, he momentarily closed his eyes.

"Enlighten us!" Simon hissed.

Griffin lifted his lids, and as his vision slowly returned to focus, longed for a spoonful of even the most brackish water. "It has all to do with the one who leads," he rasped. "Whilst Otto followed my direction, he rose to what was expected of him, exhibiting courage and good sense that masked who you made him to be—a frightened, deceitful little boy who went against his conscience and God to keep his father from hurting him."

Simon snatched Griffin's hair and wrenched his face up. But whatever punishment he meant to deliver was stayed by a shout outside the church doors.

"Foucault!"

Simon thrust Griffin's head down with such force, his captive's chin struck the kneeler's upper shelf. "Boursier!"

"I have word Ulric de Arell and Father Crispin ride from Mathe."

Distantly grateful for the moisture provided by his bitten tongue, Griffin bellowed, "Nay!" and wrenched at his bindings. "Do not—"

A fist slammed into the back of his injured shoulder, impaling him on pain so sharp darkness opened its great maw.

As he struggled to remain conscious, Simon called back, "Then De Arell's suffering ends soon."

"Yours will not," Boursier answered. "Many a blade out here is parched for want of your flesh and that of your son."

"All the better," Simon answered. "More of you to kill."

Silence. But what more was to be told? Griffin mused. If whatever The Boursier and Verdun planned to thwart the Foucaults failed, his father and the man of God would die alongside him.

Nay! he rejected the comfort of apathy. *Think much. Regret little.*

But he could hardly think anymore.

Then pray, another voice entreated. *Pray much, Griffin.*

Body quaking, he silently called on the Lord, *Keep me right of mind that I might smite those evil of mind.*

The black before his eyes graying, he drew forth a psalm. *Let the wicked fall into their own nets, whilst that I withal escape.*

"Otto," Simon said, "look again."

Griffin lifted his head and watched the knight heave his body off the pew with the effort of one twice his weight and cross to the nearest shutters. He put his face to the center seam, then moved to the other shutters before returning to his father. "They keep their distance. Their numbers appear the same."

Griffin dropped his chin, and as he stared at the floor spattered with blood, felt consciousness slacken. But he could not afford to go into the dark. Did he, when next he came around, Ulric and Father Crispin might be here. Then it would be too late.

Opening his eyes wide, he once more set his mind to gaining Otto's blade to the back.

"Twenty-five years," he rasped, "and this is how it ends for you, Foucault. Failure. The death of a warrior you can best only by taking him from behind and binding him. The death of an old man who is already far along the path leading out of this life. The death of a sickly priest." Forcing laughter, the pressure of which nearly made him shout, he looked up. "You are less worthy of Kilbourne than your traitorous father."

Candlelight revealed the flush rising up Simon's neck.

Lest the anger once more slipped away, Griffin continued, "On and on you drone as if your tale will end in some great victory of which you are deserving. But we all know it ends here in disgrace. And that is justice. Not only for our families but your father."

Simon blinked rapidly, doubtless trying to make sense of what was said.

Griffin smiled and tasted blood as his split lip protested its stretching. "You were, after all, the first to betray him, Simon. I was young, but I remember a visit to Castle Adderstone with my father on the day his liege received your answer to his summons to return home and begin learning the responsibilities of lording the barony."

Simon took a step backward.

"Your father raged over your refusal and suggestion Archard Boursier continue to serve Kilbourne in your absence as would also be expected of him once you assumed the title. And then Denis Foucault wept to have sired so traitorous a son. More, I wager, than you have wept to have made Otto on Aude."

"Cease, else I will cut out your tongue!"

"And his prized ring he sent as surety he was ready to pass Kilbourne to you…How he lamented bestowing it on one so lacking honor."

Was Simon panting? Aye, and there could be little feeling in hands clenched so tight they were white.

"And further you betrayed by not returning the ring with your refusal to leave France." Griffin channeled his pain into a heavy frown. "The same ring you years later sent to your sister to prove you lived to force her to aid Aude and you under threat of harm to her daughter."

"Be silent!"

Fighting the longing to comply, he said, "And so the greatest traitor of all broke faith with himself, the discovery of that ring by Bayard Boursier and his wife revealing the part you forced Lady Maeve to play to keep her daughter safe."

Simon lunged, and the fingers that tore into Griffin's bleeding flesh made the chapel reverberate with his shout and once more moved the gray of lowering day into the black of night. As he was dragged into it, he almost hoped this was death lest he awaken to find his father and the priest dead alongside him.

36

"I AM ONE promise you will not have to keep," Thomasin said low, chin trembling with emotion that evidenced she understood enough of the conversation she had overheard to know her father's life could be forfeit. "And Lady Elianor"—she glanced at the one who stood at the stairs—"is a promise you will not have to make."

Hand on the door she had quickly closed upon identifying who stood outside the old baron's apartment, Quintin whispered, "I shall go to my husband."

"And we shall accompany you." Thomasin nodded toward the stairs, and Quintin and Arturo followed her and Lady Elianor to the second floor corridor.

Thomasin turned to Quintin. "We came to the chapel to pray, and finding the door ajar, heard Sir Mathieu tell the priest of the brigands' defeat and that our husbands' men have surrounded the church where the Foucaults hold my father."

"You know the boon your grandfather asked of Father Crispin?"

"Aye, thus we came abovestairs to learn more."

"And discovered I was in your grandfather's apartment."

The young woman raised her eyebrows. "Most unexpected."

"I was not there by invitation," Quintin said lest Thomasin was hurt that Ulric had confided in a Boursier over his granddaughter.

"When Sir Mathieu entered the hall, I sensed something amiss and followed."

"'Tis true my sire lives? That my grandfather and Father Crispin must trade their lives for his?"

"Those are Simon Foucault's terms."

"And Sir Otto's."

"He *is* the side of his father."

"If we are to join those departing Mathe," Lady Elianor said, "we must act now."

Quintin glanced at her sister-in-law's belly. "Certes, my brother would have you remain at Mathe."

"Aye, just as your husband and Lady Thomasin's would have you remain. But as the brigands are defeated, my babe and I are less at risk than when we journeyed from Godsmere to Blackwood."

Quintin could not argue that, though still Bayard would disapprove.

"We do this together, Lady Quintin," she said. "And we begin with Rollo."

The big man's eyes found them the moment they came off the stairs, and as he strode forward, Quintin was relieved to see Rhys and Eamon disappear down the kitchen corridor. She told Rollo what needed to be done, the tasks set him possible only because Sir Mathieu would be occupied with removing the old baron from the keep without alerting his grandson to the situation.

Rollo was disturbed by the request, but his cooperation was gained by her assurance and Lady Elianor's that he would be at their side to protect them.

Their departure came together so efficiently Quintin marveled as she often did over the man-at-arms' wit in matters relating to his duty to protect those in his charge. Thus, Elianor, Thomasin, and she—less Arturo, whom she managed to lock in the solar—appeared in the outer bailey with half a dozen each of Godsmere and Emberly knights.

As a murmur moved among those amassed to ride from Mathe, Sir Mathieu turned from having aided the cloaked and hooded Ulric de Arell onto a horse between those of Father Crispin and, surprisingly, Serle.

"My lady, none of you should be here." Sir Mathieu looked to his lord's daughter. "You know your father would not like it, Lady Thomasin."

"Still, we ride with you," Quintin said and was pleased to see Rollo exit the stables, followed by grooms who led the horses required to enlarge the entourage.

Sir Mathieu's brow lowered. "Your betrothed would have you remain at Mathe."

"I know he would be pleased by your determination to keep safe those dear to him, but until your lord weds me before all, I am my brother's charge. And since The Boursier is not here, with the aid of his men I assume responsibility for my well-being."

Something gathered in the silence that drew Quintin's gaze to Ulric de Arell, and as she stared at him, it struck her this must be the first time in years he had been outside the keep.

"You lied, Quintin Boursier!" his voice shot from his masked and hooded countenance. "You gave your word you would not tell Thomasin."

His granddaughter stepped forward. In her hand was the walking stick she had retrieved from his apartment, and over which she had cried upon discovering the dozens she had fashioned for him over the years, having believed he had tossed them on the fire. Now she smiled up at him. "I am at fault," she said. "Your *Sin* was up to no good as usual, listening in on others. I vow, Lady Quintin did not reveal your plans."

He pondered that, then said, "You shall not ride with us."

Her smile lowered. "I am sorry, but this I shall do." She glanced at those of Emberly whom Rollo had called to her side. "And of course, so shall Lady Elianor. Now let us delay no longer. My father—your son—awaits us."

His hesitation made Sir Mathieu say, "My lord, do not allow this."

The old baron grunted. "What of Rhys, Thomasin?"

"He knows not—is in the kitchen answering his hunger."

"My lord!" Sir Mathieu protested again.

Ulric raised a crooked hand. "If the husbands of these ladies wished them confined, they should have seen them locked in their chambers. 'Tis not for me to do."

Quintin laid a hand on Sir Mathieu's arm. "You have done all that can be expected. Now you must ensure the Baron of Blackwood's heir remains safe."

His nostrils flared, but he said, "Pray, my lady, be of good care that you not further injure my lord by sentencing him to longing without end."

"I shall and, God willing, your lord and I will return to Mathe together."

He looked to Thomasin. "And you as well, my lady." He pivoted.

As he strode opposite, Quintin crossed to the priest. "I wish you would not do this," she said.

"And I wish you would remain at Mathe. Thus, we are both—all of us—in God's hands."

She inclined her head, and when he jutted his chin toward the old baron, she saw Thomasin raise the walking stick to Ulric. "I know my gifts offend, Grandfather, but this once would you not make use of one—if not to lean upon, to slam upside Simon Foucault's head?"

Though Ulric's expression was unseen, it was in his voice that sounded as if squeezed through a reed. "I shall." He accepted the stick. "Now mount up, Granddaughter."

Night had begun to extend its dark fingers across Blackwood when the Baron of Godsmere and a handful of his men rode from the torchlit church to meet the approaching party.

Despite the lighter shadows that was all that remained of day, Quintin knew the moment her brother sighted the women who rode at the center of the escort. Shouting something, he urged his destrier to greater speed.

The Blackwood knight given charge of the escort signaled a halt and, moments later, Bayard drew rein. "The reason these ladies accompany you must needs wait," he said as he moved his gaze from his wife and sister to his men, "but when this ill business is done, I shall have an answer."

He urged his horse near Ulric, whose hood had fallen to his shoulders during the ride.

"Baron de Arell," Bayard acknowledged the masked older man.

"How fares my son?"

"It has been quiet this past half hour, but I will not insult your good sense with the lie 'tis no cause for worry." He glanced at the physician. "God willing, 'tis but a sign your son has found temporary relief."

Senselessness only, Quintin determinedly named her husband's silence.

"How are we to do this?" Father Crispin asked where he sat his horse alongside Ulric's.

Bayard's scope of vision limited by the loss of an eye, he turned his head slightly to answer. "With every appearance of compliance, my friend."

"Appearance?" Ulric said sharply.

"Aye, my lord. Though I know you answered the summons thinking to sacrifice yourself, no other will lose his life to Simon Foucault."

"What of my son? You would allow him to die?"

"I have not long been acquainted with Griffin de Arell beyond that of the enemy the Foucaults made of us, but I am certain that just as the deaths of others for whom I have a care would be worse than my own death, so 'twould be for him. Thus, the only assurance I can offer is that the end is nigh, and once 'tis upon us, I shall do all in my power to bring him out of this alive." He moved his gaze to Serle, and despite the dim, his disapproval shone.

Ulric also noticed. "Aye, you must suffer his presence. Regardless of my fate, I would have him witness the demise of the one who branded him a traitor. Now tell me your plan."

"'Twill unfold better do you concern yourself only with the appearance of being a sacrifice, Baron."

Dear Lord, grant him success, Quintin sent heavenward and glanced at Thomasin. Her head was lowered, and Quintin imagined their prayers meeting in the air and rising together to fill God's ears.

"Now come," Bayard said, "the sooner the Foucaults know you are here, the sooner we can end this."

They are here. It was Griffin's first thought when he heard the sounds of gathering horses and voices amid the ache of returning consciousness.

Though he longed to rage at being unable to prevent others from dying for him, he was in no state to do so.

Slowly moving his mind up his body, he discovered the pressure on his knees was light, his weight spread from feet to hands stretched overhead. Prostrate, then. And the pain...

The back of his head ached, his carved flesh burned, and his shoulder throbbed—that last offering some relief though he did not doubt it would be short-lived. Of further relief was the cool breath whispering across the top of his head—as if through a seam.

Guessing he was laid out before the church doors, he tested his wrists. They remained bound, the rope's fibers pricking his raw flesh. The same could not be said of his ankles, and he understood the reason. When he was displayed to those who sought his release, he would do so upright, appearing able to go forth to make the trade that was all pretense.

"Is it Ulric de Arell?" Simon's voice came from behind.

"'Twould appear. He wears a leper's mask, and now they have him out of the saddle, a walking stick bears much of his weight."

"And Crispin?"

"Certes, that is the priest. He looks tired but no worse than he appeared at Lady Thomasin's wedding."

"What else do you see?"

"What I did not expect—the ladies Elianor, Thomasin, and Quintin."

Be still! Griffin silently commanded. If he died here, his daughter and wife would bear witness. However, as his anger moved toward Boursier for summoning them, he snatched it back. The Baron of Godsmere knew that if his sister's husband could not be saved, she would be forever haunted by what happened here. Thus, the ladies' presence had to be of their own doing.

And therein lay the folly of wedding strong women who refused to be moved about like chattel. But more, the blessing, he conceded, remembering Quintin at his side—sitting at table, walking the bailey, riding the land, lying in bed.

"That *is* unexpected," Simon drawled, "and welcome. For the death of your mother, Lady Elianor will witness our revenge. For the ill worked upon you, Lady Thomasin will watch die those she loves. And Lady Quintin shall lose her betrothed of whom she is much too fond."

"Then you will kill Baron de Arell regardless if his father and the priest trade themselves."

"Not I. You, Otto. And soon." When that was met with silence, Simon's creaking boots carried him forward and one delivered a blow to Griffin's ribs that sent the air out of him on a loud groan. "Awaken, De Arell. The sacrificial lambs have arrived."

Griffin raised his gaze up over Foucault to the man's dark eyes.

"'Tis a marvel you live considering how much blood you have lost." Simon shifted his regard to the floor, moved it toward the altar. "A pity we had to drag you so far. The village priest will not like his floor being marked where a De Arell paid the price of dirt and betrayal." He sighed. "And now 'tis time to make a trade—of sorts."

The thought of his father's and the priest's deaths tearing at him, Griffin assured himself Boursier and Verdun were not so fool to believe a trade would be honored. They but did what he would do—sought opportunity in the appearance of answering Simon's demands. He had to believe that, else whatever sense was left to him would be given to raging.

Another kick to the ribs, this time a crack of bone that made Griffin call upon the Lord.

"On your feet, De Arell!"

He pulled a long breath, then slowly heaved onto his knuckles and knees. Feeling the pain of his every injury, he straightened and braced his legs to counter the shifting floor and walls and take another accounting of his body. With only the binding about his wrists, he was no longer without recourse.

"Come, Otto," Simon said, "prove yourself worthy of the Foucault name and—"

"Fear not," Griffin said. The words sounding as if dragged across rocks, he tried to stir moisture from his mouth. Finding little, he continued, "'Tis no feat to prove worthy of that name. You have but to look upon the letters cut into the back of a man strapped to a prayer kneeler to know you have many times over proven yourself."

Simon once more thrust fingers into the arrow wound, making Griffin arch his back and nearly dropping him as he withheld the bellow of pain he would not have his daughter and wife hear.

"Foucault!" Magnus Verdun shouted as Griffin willed away the lights shattering before his eyes.

Simon pulled his fingers from the wound. "Otto!"

As the candlelit room returned to focus, Simon's son stepped to Griffin's back. Then it was that one's blade at his throat.

Griffin watched Simon position himself before the doors and press hands to them as if to throw them open. Though to do so would expose him to an arrow or spear, he need fear neither with his captive visible behind him, a blade at his neck.

"Your terms are met!" Verdun called.

Simon lowered his head as if in prayer.

Griffin did not want to believe one as godless as he would dare entreat the Lord to bless his murderous endeavors, but just as Griffin had asked the Lord's blessings upon his acts against Boursier and Verdun whilst they feuded, justifying what he did as retaliation meant to keep the wolves from his lands and his people, Simon surely believed himself in the right—and that if he could convince the Lord of it, he would bathe the ground in blood.

"I want to live," Otto whispered.

Though that did not surprise, Griffin's failing body jerked. Keeping his gaze on Simon, he said low, "Then cut my bonds, yield the dagger… and we shall let the king decide what to do with you."

A huff of disbelief. "I will hang or worse."

"Certes, if you do your father's bidding, here you die. Cut my bonds."

"After what happened with your daughter, you will kill me."

It *would* be a great temptation. "My word I give," Griffin whispered. "Do you get out of my way, you will not die at my hands. Now do the only honorable thing left to you."

The blade against his neck momentarily eased, then Otto said, "I cannot. Either way, all is lost, revenge the only purpose I shall serve in this life."

So be it, Griffin silently agreed.

"Make ready," Simon barked, then tossed open the doors to torch-light that momentarily blinded Griffin and sharpened the pain slicing through the back of his head. Determinedly resisting the weight in every muscle and bone, he moved his gaze over those outside.

Boursier and Verdun were mounted side by side, their men and Griffin's forming a wall left and right that surely encircled the church. Just in front of them stood Ulric and Father Crispin. And in back of Boursier and Verdun were the wives King Edward had forced on the three barons—solution and punishment to their feuding. Now blessings.

Quintin's gaze awaited Griffin's, but he held it only a moment. There was too much fear and longing there, distracting him from what was more important at this moment—finding the narrow opportunity when the weapon the Foucaults made of him could be turned against them.

Think much, he reminded himself. *Pray much. Regret little.*

37

⁓∞⁓

THE PAIN OF looking upon Griffin's suffering nearly bent Quintin over her horse. Were he not a powerfully-built man, he would be on his knees, perhaps even dead.

The light of torches spilling into the church's dim interior revealed one side of his face was darkened with bruises, a wound to the shoulder glistened with blood trailing down his bare chest to his chausses, and the skin over his ribs on the other side was flushed and swollen as if having sustained a terrible blow.

"Preserve him, Lord," she whispered. And was grateful when her hands were gripped by Griffin's daughter on the left and Bayard's wife on the right.

Seeing Thomasin spilled her own sorrow down her cheeks, Quintin squeezed the young woman's trembling fingers and looked to the church where knights on either side hunkered in the shadows awaiting an opportunity to enter through the shuttered windows. And the mounted men surrounding the church were weapon ready—arrows trained on Simon Foucault, hands on sword hilts.

"Oh, have mercy!" Thomasin gasped and began to whisper the paternoster.

"He is not alone," Elianor said softly.

Quintin looked around and nearly sobbed at the compassion on the lady's face.

Now it was Bayard's wife squeezing Quintin's trembling fingers. "We are here with him the same as the Lord," she said and bowed her head.

Quintin knew she should resume her own prayers, but movement at the church doors drew her gaze.

Her mother's brother stepped outside. Torchlight cruel to the lower half of his face, he raised his arms high and dropped his head back. "Thou prepares a table before me in the presence of mine enemies. Thou anoints my head with oil. My cup…" He splayed his hands. "Lord, how it runneth over!" He dropped his arms and slapped a hand to his sword hilt. "What think you, Crispin? Is God not on my side this day?"

The priest was long in answering, and when he did, there was strength in his voice Quintin had not heard in a long time. "Certes, son of Denis Foucault, you are in the presence of enemies, but those of your own making, those who seek an end to the suffering to which you have sentenced the people who are no longer of Kilbourne but of Godsmere, Emberly, and Blackwood."

Foucault snorted. "With your aid, they first made enemies of me. And when this is done, I will not go into that hell of their making alone. You shall be on my left, and the most unworthy of my father's liegemen will be on my right." He looked to the old baron. "Remove the mask that I might be certain 'tis truly the feeble, worm-eaten Ulric de Arell."

When Ulric did not comply, Simon said, "Having found a more satisfying means of making your heir scream like a woman, I have not finished branding him a traitor as I did your youngest son. Hence, remove the mask, else I shall see him cut again."

With a shaking hand, Ulric slid the mask up off his face. Whatever he revealed that Quintin could only guess at from the little she knew of leprosy, it made Simon Foucault crow.

"Justice! A long, painful, grotesque death. Why, had the devil to choose between you and me, I would be bound for heaven even had all of me been burned alongside my soul."

"Craven, half-faced, flap-mouthed canker!" Thomasin cried.

Simon Foucault moved his gaze to her. "Ah, *Lady* Thomasin, the foul fruit of her father's loins. I was disappointed when Magnus Verdun rescued you from my men ere they could work their perversions on you for my enjoyment."

"Men you murdered!"

He shrugged. "They proved useless—should easily have felled the tic-ridden Baron of Emberly. But I righted their wrongs, honoring you and your husband by making wedding presents of their corpses."

"Verdun!" Bayard said sharply, and Quintin knew Thomasin's husband had made as if to move against Foucault.

"Aye, Verdun," Simon drawled, "control thyself—always, lest the truth of you be known." He glanced behind. "I quite like this, Otto. Keep up your guard lest these traitors attempt to take this from me as well."

Attempting a broad smile, he moved his gaze to the woman beside Quintin. "Elianor of Emberly, you proved a good diversion for Aude when your uncle sent her to serve you after Constance was ordered to the convent and Serle sent on pilgrimage." He shifted his gaze to the latter. "I wonder, if not for this day, would you have let me into Mathe this eve? Or would you have betrayed me?"

Though Serle seemed to sink into himself, he said in a voice that belied his shame, "Never would I have let you into Mathe."

Simon played the silence well, letting it cast doubt on the verity of that claim.

And making Serle shift nervously. "This chance to wreak revenge on my family was your only chance," he said more loudly.

"Ah, but what *was* has become, and I intend to wreak much." He returned to Elianor. "As told, you were a good diversion. How Aude laughed at your gratitude as she stingily doled out powders to keep your first husband from your bed—almost as much as she laughed over the coin he paid her to keep watch over you lest your eyes and thoughts strayed to other men—"

"Enough!" Bayard shouted, and now it was Verdun holding him back.

Though Elianor appeared to have gone completely still, Quintin felt the quake of her hand.

"You are right. I go too far." Simon raised a gloved finger. "One thing more, then I shall address my brother."

Quintin glanced at Rollo who sat his horse alongside Elianor and noted the big man's narrowed lids.

"Most unfortunate for you, Lady Elianor, the tales Aude carried to your husband pushed him to his worst, causing you to huddle beneath the covers, claw at the sheets, and pray—oh, how you surely prayed!—for his death."

A sword exiting its scabbard sang a song of steel, but whatever harsh words Verdun spoke to Bayard stayed the Baron of Godsmere from spurring his destrier forward.

"Quite the friend you have there, Boursier," Simon exclaimed. "And I am sure the Baron of Blackwood is grateful to Verdun as well. But worry not, I am done with your lady wife. Rollo!"

"Simon!" the man-at-arms shouted with what sounded like challenge.

"You are among my greatest regrets. Had I known the half-wit I made of you would grow into an enormous man whom Archard Boursier would put to good use, I would have held you under the water longer to ensure you were not just dead, but very dead."

"'Twas the Lord what saved me that I could keep Lady Quintin and Lady Elianor from yer clutches. Ye is not a God man."

Foucault's eyebrows rose. "Ah, but I *am* a God man. Like Him, I have held the lives of many in my hands, and now the life of Ulric de Arell's son is mine to do with as I please. To trade or slay."

"For which we are here," Bayard barked. "As we weary of your boasting—your pathetic attempt to hold captive the last audience that shall ever suffer your presence—let us be done with it."

Simon laughed. "We are done with it when I say. Now let me think on what boasts would flay you, Boursier." He gestured at his eye. "That is already known—the cuckolding Aude and I planned and which you, Constance, and De Arell's pup so eagerly accommodated. Ah, your father!"

"I am aware your lover poisoned him, that when Lady Maeve discovered it, your threats against her daughter's life made her your pawn."

Simon groaned. "You spoil my surprises."

"It sits well with me."

"What of you, Lady Quintin? Will you also disappoint me?"

She blinked at finding Foucault's eyes upon her. "Already I have. Never will I be your prize, and after this day, the Foucault name will be no more. A good thing." She glanced at Rollo. "Nay, a God thing."

As she waited out the silence, she looked to Griffin whose chest glistened with what she feared was fever. How much longer could he stand? How much more blood could he shed ere he was lost to them?

She released Elianor's and Thomasin's hand and urged her horse forward.

"What do you?" Bayard demanded as she came alongside.

She leaned near. "My husband dies. This must end."

"Not with you. Never again will you place yourself between warring men." Then he called, "Your terms are met, Foucault. Send forth Baron de Arell, and his father and the priest will come to you."

"Ha! I am to trust a Boursier? Nay, when I am ready to trade, 'tis me you will have to trust. And I am not ready. My niece and I have much to discuss."

Quintin sat straighter in the saddle. "I have naught else to say to you."

"Truly? No questions needing answers? No accusations?"

"'Tis enough to know you are my uncle in name only, that when the devil moves among God's people he does so in the person of Simon Foucault."

His upper face flushed. "Clearly, you need convincing. Otto, make Griffin de Arell scream."

"Nay!" Quintin cried.

Another horrid smile, then he crooked a finger. "Come closer."

"Do not!" This from Griffin, loosed at the same moment Bayard snatched hold of her reins.

"Not again," her brother said.

"But Griffin is—"

"Not again!"

Her tears were not meant to move him to a place he had vowed he would not allow her to go again, but when she glimpsed softening in his singular gaze, she said low, "There is not yet a means of freeing Griffin, so allow me to venture a bit closer. My word I give I will not move beyond Ulric and Father Crispin until you tell me 'tis safe."

His nostrils flared.

"Bayard, I love as you love, and since I cannot swing a sword to protect one dear to me, allow me to be the distraction your men need to free Griffin ere 'tis too late."

He turned his face toward the church, and she found hope in that.

Griffin must have as well, for he called, "Do not, Boursier!"

"If I lose him, Bayard, I lose myself."

He looked back at her, jerked his chin. "Go only as far as a pace back from the old baron and Father Crispin. And if you are tempted to break your word to me, consider that if your husband survives and you do not, he will go to his grave trying to kill me—all the good come of our marriages undone."

He could not have said anything else that would have better enticed her to keep her vow. "Save the man I love," she said and began to dismount.

How Griffin bellowed! But there was unexpected good in his protest she saw as she stepped from the stirrup to the ground. Under cover of his din, one of the knights on the right side of the church opened a shutter and disappeared inside.

Lest her notice captured Simon or Otto's attention, she did not attempt to delve the church's dim interior to ascertain how far the man advanced on Otto. Her task was to allow him and others to draw near enough to bring Griffin out alive.

"That is far enough, Quintin," Bayard called.

She halted behind Ulric and Father Crispin, one to her right, the other to her left.

"Closer!" Simon Foucault commanded when Griffin quieted.

"So you can murder me as well as my betrothed?" she scoffed. "Nay, I shall not further dishonor the Foucault name by being so fool to believe our kinship means anything to you."

Though she feared he would order Otto to make Griffin scream, he said, "You are close enough. 'Twill suffice."

Ignoring the threat in his words, she said, "Now a question to which I am fair certain I know the answer. Was it you who murdered my mother?"

"'Twas. And it was easily done since that Christmas Day at Adderstone was the first I had looked near upon her since she was a girl I called my little Maeve."

Quintin had expected as much, that all communication between brother and sister had gone through Agatha.

"But old Maeve forced me to it. When she recognized Sir Francis Cartier as her brother, I knew that if not that day, another she would betray her family again, revealing all she had held close to keep you safe. A pity she proved so resistant to the plan to restore Kilbourne."

A plan Quintin was tempted to reveal had been doomed from the moment the cuckolding of Bayard Boursier was conceived.

"Had your mother stayed the course, I would have spared her though she happily wed one who betrayed our father. And so she died, though I vow it was a kind death."

"Kind!" Quintin exclaimed louder than intended when she glimpsed not one but two shadowed figures beyond Griffin and Otto.

"Aye, I let her go quickly and quietly, rather than slowly and screaming as she deserved. Only the softest, feather-filled pillow for my old Maeve."

Conjuring a vision of her mother's struggle beneath that pillow, Quintin choked, "You sicken me."

He fanned a hand before his face. "Alas, it cannot be helped."

"Nay, I am sickened by what is inside you. Rather, what is *not* inside you."

"Ah well, the De Arells, Boursiers, and Verduns must answer for that, not the heir to the great barony of Kilbourne who waited more than twenty-five years to reclaim what was stolen from him."

"And who failed. Utterly."

"Not utterly. Though I did not foresee this day when all I would have to show for my efforts was..." He lifted a finger. "The death of Archard Boursier." Another finger. "Bayard Boursier's eye. Serle de Arell's sword arm. Verdun's whore of a sister sentenced to the convent. My sister's death." He looked to his five raised fingers, folded them, and lifted two. "And soon the lives of Ulric de Arell and the traitorous priest." He chuckled. "Now I count them, it occurs Aude and I did quite well."

"But not Otto?" Quintin said, then exaggerated a gasp she prayed would cover the creak of a shutter. "Of course not. He shall number among those you count on your fingers like a child citing the reasons he deserves another pastry." She moved her gaze to his son's face visible over Griffin's shoulder. "I am sorry for you, Otto. Sorry you are but a finger on your father's hand when you could have been a knight of great standing and honor. I know it. I saw it in you the same as did your lord, who would not otherwise have entrusted you with his daughter."

A shiver went down her spine when she caught the glitter of tears and movement of the dagger that opened a gap between the blade and Griffin's throat. Then fear raced back up it when her husband's head lowered to hang upon his chest. If the knights drawing near did not act quickly, Griffin would collapse.

"The siren tries to lure you, Otto," Simon called.

"Sadly, she does not speak false," his son said. "And long I have known it, that you—"

Griffin's head snapped up and back, and a crack like lightning sounded, followed by Otto's cry as the blow to his face knocked him back and splayed his arms.

Then everywhere, motion and clamor.

Griffin swung his bound arms around and followed Otto to the floor.

The men who had stolen into the church transformed from shadows into warriors.

Horses hooves, barked orders, and the ring of bridles and rattling of spurs.

The flash of steel as Simon Foucault lunged toward the defenseless Ulric de Arell, Quintin, and the priest.

Her name shouted, the sweep of an arm from the left and right, one striking her in the chest, the other across her middle.

The breath of arrows set to flight, a glimpse of their penetration of the arm, belly, and thigh of Simon Foucault whose sword swung from on high, Bayard spurring past her.

Then she hit the ground, and a shout in her ear that sounded of Father Crispin and moisture slashing across her neck and chest.

"Bayard!" Quintin tried to send her brother's name past her lips, but the weight on her chest denied her air. She pushed it off, and as it rolled to the side, she saw it was the priest, his face clenched with pain. And pinning her shoulder on the other side was the unmasked, heavily panting Ulric de Arell.

Realizing the two had borne her to the ground and the moisture on her was blood, she cried, "Nay!" and sat up. As she dragged Crispin into her arms, she saw the hopelessness of Simon Foucault.

Though put through with arrows, chest torn open by what had to have been Bayard's blade, he struggled up from his knees and, retaining hold of his sword, stumbled back from the two barons who had come down from their horses.

"Dear Lord, dear Lord," she chanted as she searched beyond them.

Griffin was on the church floor, but that was all she could see past the knights bent over him. She had to reach him, but Crispin bled—

And forget not the promise you made, she reminded herself, and only for that was she grateful for the need to hold the priest. Otherwise, she might find herself at the mercy of a dying Foucault.

Lowering her head toward Crispin's, she prayed for him, Griffin, and Ulric, and all those who risked their lives to end the Foucault threat. As she did so, she fumbled a hand to the old baron and set it on his shoulder.

"My son?" he croaked.

"I know not," she whispered, "but no further harm can be done him." Then she returned to her pleading with the Lord that when Ulric passed from this world he would do so knowing he left his son behind, and that she would grow old at the side of the man she loved.

Simon Foucault was dying. Not on the edge of Boursier's or Verdun's sword, but on the arrow shafts leaking the life from him. And he was not going quickly or quietly. But his son...

Griffin raised heavy lids and focused as best he could on the one lowering beside him. Not Quintin. The physician. As the man set to tending the arrow wound, Griffin turned his head to the side.

Neither was Otto going quickly, but he was going quietly, the light in Foucault brown eyes dimming as he cupped a hand over his neck as if it were possible to keep the blood in. That injury he had dealt himself.

Amidst Simon's boasting, Griffin had awaited a moment worthy of risking all to free himself—and thought it lost when Otto tensed with the creaking of the shutter. But rather than warn his father, he had hesitated, and that hesitation had stretched when Quintin challenged Simon over his son's worth.

Though the young knight had seemed close to abandoning the Foucault cause, when a space opened between flesh and blade, Griffin had seized that opportunity.

The blow to his injured head had been blinding, the backward thrust of Otto's body causing the dagger's point to rise and catch Griffin's jaw before—ironically—slicing his captor's throat. Thus, Otto would pay the highest price, one Griffin might also pay, but not until Quintin was at his side. He must remain conscious.

"Griffin." Her voice was taut with the pleading of one who feared an answer would not be forthcoming, and he realized he had closed his eyes.

As he struggled to open them, she said, "Can you save him?"

"He has lost much blood, my lady, and I know not the extent of the injuries to his head and innards, but I shall do all I can."

"Quintin, come away." This from The Boursier. "Allow the physician—"

"I will not." She caught up Griffin's hands. "Pray, cut his bonds, Bayard."

Griffin felt the flat of a blade between his wrists, then the rope fell away and one of his hands was fit into his wife's and raised to soft lips.

"Griffin"—her breath fanned his skin—"this morn…" She swallowed. "This morn you said never had you as great a cause to be victorious than now I am with you. Pray, continue to be victorious—for your family and your people. For me."

He narrowly opened his lids and saw a smile of encouragement move onto her lips. "There you are, my love. Do not go into the dark. Draw near me."

The dark was tempting, so weary and hurting was he that he had not enough strength to do more than groan as the physician probed his gored flesh. But he lifted his lids higher and rasped, "I am with you. My father?"

She muffled a sob, said, "He fell hard when he and the priest protected me from Simon, but methinks he will be fine."

"Father Crispin?"

She hesitated. "He took Foucault's blade to the back, but he lives."

"How long?" he croaked.

"I know not." She looked up. "Bayard, your wine skin."

As liquid sweeter than any Griffin had tasted trickled across his tongue, he saw Thomasin lower alongside Quintin, her husband over her shoulder.

"I must extract the arrowhead ere we move him to Mathe," the physician said. "Give him as much wine as he can take."

As more was eased past Griffin's lips, Simon Foucault shrieked a curse at his son, causing Quintin to peer over her shoulder.

Following her gaze, Griffin saw Otto draw a rattling breath and shift near lifeless eyes to the one who was to have been his prize. "Lady, I thank you…for seeing in me…what could have been. Had I known sooner…"

She inclined her head. "I spoke true, Sir Otto, and also wish you had known sooner. I shall pray that what you had not on earth you find when you leave us."

He looked past her. "Lady Thomasin, I hope one day you will…think upon forgiving me."

"Aye," she said small.

Eyes closing, body easing, he went into the dark where Griffin commanded himself not to go. But as Quintin once more slid wine onto his tongue, consciousness receded and he silently pleaded with the Lord that he not wander too far from her.

38

⸻

"The physician does all he can, but he has not much hope. He says 'tis for God to decide."

Emotions clamoring for expression since the day past when word had come of Griffin's capture, Quintin lowered her chin and let her tears fall to her clasped hands. "If only he had not made himself my savior."

Bayard touched her shoulder. "'Twas instinct to protect one he loves—the same as once you sought to protect me."

She looked up. "But 'twas not necessary!"

"He and the old baron could not have known there was space enough for me to ride on Simon Foucault ere he reached you."

"And so we shall lose Crispin."

"If the Lord does not answer our prayers as we wish."

"Then we must needs pray harder."

"So we shall." He jutted his chin toward the bed. "Your husband?"

Grateful for the constant Arturo stretched on the floor alongside his master, eyes on his mistress, she looked to Griffin. Though the sheet drawn up his chest concealed the worst of his injuries, his face was a mess and looked all the worse for the bandage wound around his brow that secured a poultice to the wound at the back of his head. Of less concern were the cuts to his back—providing they did not become infected.

"Several times throughout the night he briefly awakened, and always he knew me and asked after Crispin and his father. But only once this day, when Rhys was within, did he return to consciousness. Though he assured his son he will soon be out of bed, he struggled to hide his pain."

"The physician remains confident he will recover?"

"Aye, but I fear for him."

"You have not slept, Quintin. You must rest."

"My place is here."

"So 'tis. Thus, you ought to lie down with your husband."

That surprised. As it was not yet known she was Griffin's wife, it would appear unseemly, whether it was the physician, a servant, or Rhys who next entered.

"Until you awaken," Bayard said, "I will keep watch over you both."

She was so weary she felt nauseated, but before she could speak one way or the other, her brother swung her into his arms and carried her across the solar. Lowering her to the right of her husband, he left a space between them she longed to cross. But it was best she not disturb Griffin.

As Bayard ignored Arturo's growl and settled into the chair on the opposite side, Quintin turned toward Griffin, slid a hand across the mattress, and curled her fingers over his. And slept.

The scent of torches.

The rumble of lowered voices.

Quintin opened her eyes to find night had once more drawn its curtains closed. Beside her, torchlight kind to his beaten face, Griffin conversed with Bayard who sat forward in the chair he had surely occupied for hours.

"So now the missive is sent, we wait on the king's response," her brother said. "As there are witnesses aplenty to attest to the truth of his prized mercenary, I anticipate no retaliation. Indeed, we may even be shown favor for the wrong done us—hopefully, beginning with your brother."

"For Constance," Griffin said, "I fear Serle would have let them into Mathe."

Quintin basked in the sound of his voice. It was not its strong, gruff self, but neither was it weak and disjointed as it had been during his earlier awakenings. It sounded unhurried and even—much like after they made love.

"Thus, Serle cannot long remain upon our lands," Bayard said. "For that, I once more asked the king to use his influence to release Constance from the convent. With her at his side and a purse full of coins, they can make a life far from here."

"Aye, for the best." Griffin sighed. "Now, ere I once more sleep"—he looked around—"I would speak with my wife."

He had known of her awakening, and neither did her brother's face reflect surprise.

Bayard rose stiffly from the chair, flashed her a smile as he pressed his shoulders forward and backward, then strode across the solar. "The physician has come and gone, Sister," he said as he opened the door. "The night is yours."

She sat up. "Father Crispin?"

"He remains with us."

"What does the physician say?"

He hesitated. "There is hope, but Crispin was not well ere he was injured."

She nodded, and as the door closed, sent up another prayer. When she looked around, her gaze was momentarily captured by Arturo, who had risen to his haunches to rest his chin on the mattress alongside his master.

Quintin studied Griffin, noted the fresh bandage on his shoulder, and set her eyes to blue. "Good eve, Husband."

"Good eve, Wife."

"I am ashamed to have slept through the physician's visit. Certes, he was scandalized to find me abed and that my brother allowed it."

He slid his hand out from under hers and touched the ring that had slipped from beneath her bodice. "He knows. I showed him this. And soon all will know how long we have loved."

She raised her eyebrows. "Then no wedding before all?"

"Aye, still we shall publicly speak vows so others may celebrate our blessing, but until then, you shall be at my side whenever and wherever you wish."

"That is ever and ever."

A twitch at his mouth promised a smile. "I am tempted to forget to be angry with you, Quintin."

"Angry? With me?"

He closed his eyes, and when he opened them, he did so narrowly. But not out of censure, she was certain. Sleep called to him. "Aye, angry with you. And your brother for placing you in danger."

She scooted nearer, put an elbow to the pillow alongside his, and propped her head on a hand. "In defense of Bayard, I gave him little choice. In defense of me, 'twould seem the only way to keep me out of harm's way is to stop me from loving. And surely you do not wish that."

Another promise of a smile. "Better that than lose you."

"Of which there is much less chance now Simon and Otto Foucault are dead."

He squeezed his eyes closed, opened them wide. "Though I do not approve, I am grateful you helped make possible an end to the Foucaults—that my son is not fatherless, my wife is not husbandless." He shifted on the mattress, groaned. "My back aches. Would that I could turn onto my side."

Unfortunately, the opposing injuries to shoulder and rib made that impossible.

"But far worse it would be had Otto cut all of the word into my flesh," he conceded.

She shivered in remembrance of what she had seen in aiding the physician. "Only T and R," she said.

"And the cut where the blade slipped."

"Aye, curved—makes the T look nearly a P."

"Does it?" At her nod, he said, "I had thought the T would serve as a reminder to *think* much, the R to *regret* little, but when I could think no more, I told myself to *pray* much. Thus, mayhap a P it will be."

"Pray much. Regret little."

"A good thing." He lowered his lids. "The physician's draught presses upon me."

She lightly touched his bruised cheek. "I will be here when you awaken, and then I will tell you what I have wanted to give back."

"Hmm. Words of love?"

"Aye, I found—Nay, not found. I drew them from the well of my heart."

He was silent so long she thought he slept, but he murmured, "Though acts of love, with which you have gifted me, are of greater import, still I would hear the words now."

"But what if you do not remember?"

He chuckled. "They can be spoken only once?"

"Of course not."

"Then tell me so my sleep will be sweeter. Do I not remember, you have but to tell me again, as I pray you will do often throughout our long lives."

She brushed her mouth across his. "You, Griffin de Arell, are the beginning and end of me. The now and then of me. The keeper of my joy and my heart. The future I did not know I could possess, and the only one I would have. That is how I love you. How I shall ever love you."

There. A small, uneven smile that returned her to the day she had first laid eyes on him when, unmoved by the great number of enemies before his walls, he had looked down upon her with that infuriating, crooked smile. And in the midst of their contentious exchange, he had bitten into an apple.

"Certes, those words I shall not forget," he said. "And when I awaken, we shall speak of them."

"Will we?" she teased.

"Aye, they bear closer discussion."

It was nearly what he had said the day he had come down from the gatehouse. And when she had entered his walls, his hand had closed over hers and they had both felt something that made him suggest there could be good between them.

"Aye, Husband, it does bear closer discussion."

He gave a barely perceptible nod. "I love you, Quintin de Arell."

Epilogue

—∞∞∞—

Wulfen Castle
England, 1350

"Do you think women will ever be admitted?"

The words seeped into Quintin as she considered the great edifice that was Wulfen Castle, for centuries renowned for training boys into men and where her son, Rhys, had earned his spurs and a Wulfrith dagger four years past—as had Eamon a year later.

"Admitted, Lianor?" Elianor laughed. "Of course you do not speak merely of a woman being permitted to observe warriors in training."

"I do not," agreed the eldest Boursier child, all sixteen years of her.

"What think you, Thomasin?" Elianor asked. "Will there be lady knights in England?"

Quintin glanced at her daughter and saw she would not be distracted by such talk, no matter how well-intentioned, while her twin boys remained in sight. But they would not much longer. In the company of their male kin, they neared Wulfen Castle where they were to begin their knight's training.

Touching the weapon she wore on her girdle despite the protests of men who called it sacrilege for a woman to don a Wulfrith dagger, Quintin shifted around on the stallion Griffin had gifted her years ago despite the disapproval of those same men who believed only a mare was tame enough for a lady.

"Methinks one day, dear niece, women will openly train to become warriors and fight alongside men to protect their loved ones and country."

A snort sounded, and she picked out the perpetrator—one of a dozen soldiers left behind to watch over the women.

Rollo muttered it was a man's duty to bear arms, glanced at her father's dagger, and grinned.

How she loved this big man who, in wedding Elianor's maid, had fathered half a dozen children. She returned his grin, then continued, "However, 'twill be many years beyond your own, Lianor."

"Unless she dares what Lady Annyn Bretanne dared two hundred years past," Thomasin said, though still her eyes were on her youngest sons.

"Annyn Bretanne?" Lianor said. "What did she do?"

"What she wished to do." Thomasin nodded at the fortress. "She cut her hair and, disguised as a squire, trained whilst awaiting an opportunity to work revenge on Baron Wulfrith for what she believed was the murder of her brother."

"Tell!" Lianor exclaimed.

"Do not encourage her, Thomasin," Elianor teased.

Magnus's wife glanced at those who awaited the return of their men. "I do not suggest she do the same. I but make the wait for the return of a certain De Arell more tolerable."

Lianor gasped. "What do I care when, where, and with whom goes Rhys de Arell?"

Quintin exchanged a look with Elianor. Until a year past, Lianor and Rhys had carried on well. But shortly after celebrating ten and five years, Lianor had become easily offended by her cousin who, eight years her senior, continued to regard her as a child while flirting with other women not much older than she.

Her behavior annoyed Rhys. Were he not like his father in temperament, he might have been harsh with her. Instead, he mostly ignored her, but the tension was growing so thick it seemed one of them would say something unforgivable.

Last eve, Quintin had pressed Griffin to intervene, but he had said that though his experience was limited to his Boursier bride, such dissension could prove the way to great love—so many obstacles that one could not long hide one's true self, and in overcoming them together, a man and woman would be more strongly joined.

Though she had liked that, she had said she but wished her niece and son to return to friendly terms. He had laughed, swept her into his arms, and made love to her. Before falling asleep, he had whispered, "They are cousins by marriage only. Though Rhys fights it, he is ever more aware they are far more man and woman."

"Well?" Lianor returned Quintin to the present. "What do I care?"

"It seems much," her mother said.

Before the young woman could object, Thomasin sighed loud. "Now they go."

So her sons did, having been greeted on the drawbridge by one who came on foot—the lord of Wulfen Castle.

"Pray, look back," Thomasin beseeched.

And one, then the other of her sons turned in the saddle and raised an arm.

"Oh, have mercy!" Thomasin gasped.

Quintin urged her horse near and laid a hand on her daughter's back. "They will visit at Christmas."

It was the same reassurance Griffin had given her when Rhys, then Eamon, had begun their knight's training. Her boys. Her sons. And years from now, when Justina wed, he would reassure her again.

She considered the top of her nine-year-old daughter's head. Hair confined to a braid that held tight to its crossings, its strands thick and golden, it was much like Griffin's. Her disposition, however, was more like Quintin's. One would never know their blood did not flow through the girl.

Eight years past, the club-footed babe had been abandoned at the church outside the village of Cross. During a visit with the frantic priest, Quintin had assured him she would find a home for the child. And so she had.

Griffin had been doubtful, more so than when she had wished to bring Eamon into their family following his mother's death from fever, but Justina quickly became as beloved to him as she did to Quintin—Quintin who was now the mother of three children, grandmother to Thomasin and Magnus's children, and quite the aunt. And that was not all.

Arturo was now gone, but his sons and daughters roamed and protected Castle Mathe. Too, she had one of Diot's daughters, given her by Thomasin who had accepted her grandfather's gift when he had attained his quietus a year after the deaths of Simon and Otto Foucault.

"Look, Mother!" Justina exclaimed. "'Tis Eamon."

Quintin squinted at the one who guided his mount beneath the portcullis. Though she saw her youngest son twice a year when he left his position as Wulfen Castle's armorer to visit Mathe, he would not miss an opportunity to greet his mother and sister.

As she watched, he embraced Griffin, Magnus, Bayard, then Rhys.

"The Lord is good," Quintin said.

"Always," spoke the one behind.

She peered over her shoulder at the priest who had insisted on making the journey to Wulfen though the injury sustained to protect her years ago made it difficult for him to sit astride longer than two hours at a time, and for which their party had departed a day early—as the three families did each time they delivered a son to Wulfen, now seven in all.

She inclined her head. "Father Crispin."

He smiled. "As ever, I am blessed to be here with you."

"As ever, we are blessed to have you with us." Though it had taken months for him to recover from Simon Foucault's blade, he had finally wed Griffin and her. And as on that day as this, she had worn the beautiful dark blue gown Elianor and Hulda had made for her during her grieving all those years ago.

"There are your brothers, Lianor," Elianor said.

The fourteen-year-old had his father's hair, the eleven-year-old his mother's, and both were of a size that belied their ages.

"And my eldest," Thomasin said, her sorrow at seeing her twins away eased by the joy of her impending reunion with Rand. And when they departed Wulfen Castle, she would find further ease in the child pressing its way into the world. Perhaps when the babe was delivered four months hence, it would be a much-longed-for daughter.

A thrill flew through Quintin when she saw her men and those of Elianor and Thomasin put heels to their mounts. And then Eamon was at her side and out of the saddle. He lifted Justina down, whirled her around, and returned for his mother.

"I miss you always," he said as they hugged.

She drew back and cupped his face between her hands. He was not handsome—too rugged for that—but he drew the attention of many a woman. "And I you, dear Eamon." She had known she could not replace Nanne, but the boy had allowed her to become the mother he needed and returned her love.

"Father says the king has granted a license to build another castle on Blackwood," he said as they stepped apart.

Which would make three, the second recently completed to be administered by Rhys until he came into his father's title. God willing, a score or more years from now.

"So Edward has. Did your father tell he would have you be its keeper when it is completed"—she gave a short laugh—"ten years hence?"

"Aye. By then I ought to be ready to leave Wulfen and take a wife."

"'Tis as your brother and I would have it," Griffin said, striding toward them.

Seeing Justina had captured her father's left hand—out of affection, rather than the need to counter the hitch in her step—Quintin took her husband's right and turned with them to watch the reunions of the other families.

"Rand Verdun shall have his pick of the ladies," Quintin said. "He is more handsome each time I see him."

Griffin chuckled. "The Verdun Curse."

In looks only, it seemed, none of Magnus and Thomasin's boys presenting their father's nervous tics and intense need for control.

"A fortnight past," Eamon said, "Baron Boursier's eldest son and Rand stole out of Wulfen and took to drinking at a nearby inn. Likely, they would have avoided discovery had not Lord Wulfrith stopped there upon his return following a sennight at court." He lowered his voice. "Rumor is the king honors him with membership in his Order of the Garter."

"Impressive," Griffin said.

Quintin silently agreed, the recently formed order exclusive to the worthiest of King Edward's nobles—a total of twenty four. "Was young Verdun and Boursier's punishment fair, Eamon?" she asked.

"Aye, lessons well-learned."

Griffin considered Boursier's youngest son, a quiet, serious youth. "He fares well?"

"Mostly. Though warring does not come naturally, he is determined to be among the class that fights. And that counts for much."

Though initially denied entrance to Wulfen, it believed the Church a better fit, Bayard's son had pleaded to train with Rollo. Quintin knew it had bothered her brother that he could not himself bring forth the warrior in his son, but as Elianor had assured him, it was not for lack of trying. Blessedly, what the boy could not excel at beneath his father's guidance he had learned well enough from Rollo to gain admittance to Wulfen. All he had required, it seemed, was distance from comparisons between himself and his father and brother.

"Poor Lianor," Justina said, and Quintin followed her gaze to the young woman.

Past her embrace of the oldest of her brothers, Lianor's eyes were all for Rhys—whose eyes were all for Wulfen Castle where he stood alongside his horse idly running a hand over its neck. Though his training there was long past, he surely missed the years that had ended with him as first squire to Lord Wulfrith.

"I shall distract her," Justina said and hastened forward, unconcerned her step was less than graceful. As it should be. Years ago, when Griffin's brother and wife had journeyed from Spain to visit, Constance had despaired in Justina's hearing over the girl's clumsy gait. In Constance's hearing, Griffin had told his daughter a graceful heart was far more important and *that* Justina had in full—unlike others.

When Eamon strode from their side to join Rhys, Griffin said, "Well, Wife?"

She slid her arms around his neck. "Husband?"

"I do not need reminding, but..."

"You would have me speak it again."

"You were warned."

She repeated the words of love she had given him sixteen years ago, ending on, "That is how I love you. How I shall ever love you."

He kissed her and repeated his own. "What I did not know was missing from me, I would never cease to miss were it lost. Thus, I will do whatever is required to keep you safe."

"A promise kept," she said and claimed his kiss.

For new releases and special promotions, subscribe to
Tamara Leigh's mailing list: www.tamaraleigh.com

Excerpt

LADY EVER AFTER

———⚬⚬⚬———

A clean-read rewrite of *Unforgotten,*
published by HarperCollins, 1997
Releasing Fall 2016

From Tamara Leigh, USA Today best-selling author of the acclaimed *Dreamspell,* comes another medieval time travel romance set during the 15th century Wars of the Roses conflict.

Lady Catherine Algernon, dreaming of her death at the hands of traitors, is stunned when a handsome stranger from the twenty-first century saves her life just as her nightmare is about to come true. Look for *Lady After* in Fall 2016.

PROLOGUE

———❀———

Northern England, May 1464

SHE HAD SEEN her death. Though the dream had come to her every eve for a sennight, that from which she now awakened had been this-worldly—so real she momentarily considered this was the dream.

Chemise damp with the sweat of fear, Catherine turned onto her stomach, reached beneath the bed, and patted a hand over the floorboards until her fingers found the hilt.

"There you are," she whispered. "There." She started to draw her hand back but could not.

Every night before attempting a few hours of sleep, and each time she came up out of the dream to find the dark still upon her, she felt for the dagger to reassure herself it could be brought to hand. This night was different, the living, breathing memory of her death demanding more than reassurance.

She curled her fingers around the hilt and dropped onto her back. Clasping the sheathed blade to her breast, she stared at the ceiling. But try though she did to resist the dream, fatigue once more thrust her into that world.

Her enemies were upon her. Before, behind, and beside her. Every one of them faceless, though she need not see their coarse jaws, gleaming eyes, and grinning mouths to know them for traitors.

The stench of their bodies making her swallow hard, crude taunts stirring the fine hairs across her body, she held. Though her defense of the gatehouse would be for naught, never would she surrender. Thus, she must be felled, and the warrior who broke from the others believed he was the one to do it.

Straining beneath the weight of a sword whose point sought to be more intimate with the floor than the air, Catherine added her left hand to the hilt and hefted the weapon as the man drew near enough that he appeared faceless no more—whiskered jaw, leering eyes, moldering teeth.

Moved by fear of a strength that allowed her to sweep the blade high, she sliced through his sword arm.

The long silence of disbelief. The roar of pain and anger. The sword clattering to the floor. The savage warrior coming for her.

Catherine stumbled back against the portcullis winch and tried to raise her sword again, but too late. Ever too late.

The devil wrenched the weapon from her, and without a pittance of hesitation, turned it on her.

She could never remember his face upon awakening. But now she saw clearly his contorted features as he drove the blade through her, barked triumphantly, and lurched back, brandishing steel whose silver was terrifyingly more beautiful varnished in crimson.

Catherine dropped her chin. Blood spread across the bodice of her cream-colored gown, but where was the pain?

She almost laughed when it answered like a child eager to assure its mother it was here.

Oh, how it was here! As torturous as the sear of a hot iron one should not trip fingers across and yet foolishly and fiercely gripped.

She opened her mouth to drag in air needed to lend voice to her agony, but there was no breath to be had.

'Tis good, she told herself, embracing what was to be her last pleasure—denying these traitors the satisfaction of hearing her scream like

a lamb put to slaughter by one incapable of delivering a mercifully swift death.

Accepting her battle was terribly lost, grateful it was finally done, she slid down the winch to the floor.

Lord, Lord, she called ahead of what she prayed was her ascension, *if only I had my life to live over...*

1

England, Present Day

COLLIER MORROW ENDED the call, dropped the cell phone on his desk, and dug his fingers into his neck muscles.

"Bloody rotter," he growled, envisioning his older brother smiling his maddening smile, feet up on the desk, unlit cigar jutting from his mouth.

And James had every reason to wallow. His latest acquisition was no minor conquest. Indeed, there was none beyond it.

Collier dug deeper, pushed and pulled at the muscles.

There had always been rivalry between the brothers, encouraged by their father who had seen it as a means of ensuring it could never be said he had produced weak sons. But the lessons Winton Morrow had taught them had not died with him six years ago. If it wasn't James scrambling to snatch a property out from under Collier, it was Collier returning the favor the next go-around. Always a higher stake. Always a way to better the other. Until now.

It had been their father's greatest aspiration to recover Strivling, the castle that had been held by the Morrows from the fifteenth century until the nineteenth when it was sold to raise the family out of debt. Having failed in that endeavor, his sons regarded it as the ultimate prize, the victor never to be outdone.

And Collier's defeat was all the harder for the company it kept with reminders of the injuries he had sustained a year ago. His neck, arm, and ribs aching—he choked down air and slowly exhaled. But there was no lessening of the pain. No relief.

Knowing where he was heading, he struggled against the need and told himself it would pass, that he had only to wait it out.

But for how long? An hour? A day? Longer?

He released his neck, thrust a hand into his pocket, and clamped his fingers around the vial.

Two, he promised. *No more than three. And if it gets bad—*

"Your home is beautiful."

He snapped his head up and stared at the woman who stood in the doorway of his office. Auburn hair framing a lovely face, sky-blue eyes steady, Aryn Viscott gave a half-hearted laugh and stepped into the room. "Not the reception I was hoping for."

Telling himself he felt neither pain nor anger, Collier drew his hand from his pocket and strode from behind his desk. "I'm glad you're here."

"Are you?"

"You know I am, darling."

She raised her eyebrows. "You were going to meet me at the airport."

And would have had he not been derailed by one call after another. Although pricked by guilt over sending a driver for her, he'd had no choice, not with Strivling at stake. "I apologize. An important business matter required my attention."

"Problems?"

Ignoring the invitation to elaborate, he said, "Nothing I can't handle," and drew her to him.

She tensed, but when her chest brushed his, she dropped her purse and leaned up and into him.

He closed his mouth over hers, felt his aches ease as his body was wonderfully and uncomfortably stirred by being so near her.

Thinking that if he could lose himself in her arms, then that part urging him to lose himself in the vial would be quieted, he was tempted to lure her beyond this place he had moved her past only once—much to her whiter-than-white regret. However, he had agreed to her terms, and for it would not have all of her again until the ring in his desk was on her finger. Soon though, and for that he had moved their eighteen-month courtship to England where they would make a life together.

The phone rang.

Grateful for the interruption that made it easier to pull back from the line they were not to cross, he lifted his head. "I'd better take that."

Face flushed, breath quick and shallow, Aryn said, "Under the circumstances, I suppose you ought to."

He retrieved his cell phone. "Morrow here."

"Hello, little brother."

Relieved his back was turned to Aryn, Collier fixed his gaze on the clouds gathering outside the many-paned window behind his desk. "James."

"Have you heard?"

"I have."

"Then I won't keep you."

Were he alone, Collier would have slammed the phone down, but he would not have Aryn see what teemed beneath his skin in such abundance his longing for her shifted to the vial in his pocket.

He placed his phone on his desk and turned.

"Why did James call?" she asked.

Her knowledge of the discord between the brothers was limited to the little she had pried out of him. And that was enough. "Nothing you need worry about." He took her arm. "How about I show you around the manor?"

She pulled free. "You have to end it, Collier. Whatever this thing is between your brother and you, it has to stop. Look what happened with—"

"It's under control," he said and felt the urgent press of the vial against his thigh.

She narrowed her lids. "Are you sure?"

Until three weeks ago, his dependence on painkillers *had been* under control. However, when the bid for Strivling started going James's way, the pain had climbed up out of him. For days he had struggled to reject the promise of relief, then that long, excruciating night...

But he could quit. He had done it before.

"Quite sure. Now would you like a tour, or should we continue where we left off?" He moved his gaze to her lips.

Though her suspicion continued to fill the space between them, she said, "A tour would be safer."

The strain about his mouth gave way to a smile that felt almost genuine. "In some things, Aryn, you are too proper—like the English of old."

She bounced her eyebrows. "Who knows? Maybe this American's roots were pulled from your English soil."

He impressed her face on his memory, though it was hardly necessary since he would soon awaken to it every morning, happen upon it every day, and kiss it every night. But always this feeling it might be the last time he looked upon her...

"What is it, Collier?"

He blinked. "You're right. Who knows?" He offered his arm. "Shall we?"

The final stop on the tour. Probably one they should have skipped, Collier reflected as Aryn stepped ahead of him into his bedroom.

She halted before the fireplace and tilted her head back to study the portrait to which he awakened when he resided at the manor. "How unusual. It's a woman, isn't it?"

He came alongside her. "It is." At first glance, the mash of colors were without sense, making it appear more a piece of modern art than a portrait commissioned in the fifteenth century. But it did belong to that distant past, as did the lady revealed here and there through the landscape painted over her during the sixteenth century.

"Who is she?"

"It's believed to be Catherine Algernon. The picture was removed from Strivling Castle in—"

"Strivling?" She looked around. "Didn't it once belong to your ancestors?"

Once, and now again, but not to Collier. Forcing the darkness down, he said, "It did," and returned to the safer topic. "The picture was believed to be merely a landscape."

"No one knew what lay beneath?"

"Not until it had hung in the library of this manor twenty-five years with the morning sun on it. Then the top layer of paint began to peel away."

"Why would someone paint over her?"

"She was never completed." He pointed to a gap in the scenery which revealed the outline of hands, the only color that of the red rose clasped between them.

"I see."

"Since the portrait would have been deemed useless in its unfinished state, it was overpainted with the landscape, a not uncommon practice with canvases never completed or deemed inadequate."

"Aren't you curious to know what, exactly, she looks like?"

"Always."

"Then why not have the portrait restored?"

"It's been attempted, but the landscape gives up only what it wishes, when it wishes."

"As if it guards a secret, hmm?" She reached up and touched the frame. "I wonder why it was never finished."

He considered the still blue eyes staring out from the canvas. "If it is Catherine Algernon, her sudden death would account for that."

Aryn looked across her shoulder. "How did she die?"

He smiled. "You would know if you were English," he said, though the truth of it was that the legend of Catherine Algernon had died long ago. Only the generations of Morrows kept it alive.

"Well, since I'm thoroughly and pitifully American"—she returned his smile—"you'll have to enlighten me."

He loved the sparkle of her eyes, one of the many things that had first attracted him to her.

"Was she a significant figure?"

He braced an arm on the mantel. "No. It was her death that put her name on men's lips."

"Which brings us back to how she died."

"Have you heard of the Wars of the Roses—the House of Lancaster against the House of York?"

She wrinkled her nose. "Sounds familiar, but history and I aren't on the best of terms."

"It was a civil war waged for the throne of England. Catherine Algernon supported the Lancasters"—he indicated the red rose—"whereas the Morrows supported the Yorks whose badge was the white rose."

"Hence, the Wars of the Roses."

"As it was later called. In 1461, the Yorkists overthrew King Henry the sixth and installed Edward the fourth on the throne. In an attempt to subdue the northern barons who continued to support Henry, Edward sent a man named Montagu to besiege their castles. There was resistance, but eventually surrender. Edward's policy being one of conciliation, he restored the castles to their Lancastrian lords. But in 1464, they revolted again, and with the same result. Among the last to fall was Strivling Castle. Catherine died in the final engagement."

"Go on."

"Legend has it that, following the death of Lord Somerton and his son—Catherine's betrothed—the lady took control of the castle's defenses."

Aryn's smile widened.

"Let me guess. This bit of history you do like."

"Of course. It's nice to know not all damsels were in distress. Continue."

"Montagu announced that the man who succeeded in opening Strivling would be awarded the castle. Being a landless knight, my ancestor—Edmund Morrow—accepted the challenge. Unfortunately, he and the others who offered their services were defeated, and those not killed were captured and imprisoned, Edmund among them. On the day following his capture, he led an escape from the dungeon. He and his followers had just taken the winch room when Catherine—"

"Winch room?"

"It's where the winches that control the portcullis and drawbridge are located." At Aryn's nod, he said, "Catherine defended it with this sword." He touched the blue-black hilt of the weapon on the mantel.

Aryn gasped, evidencing she had been too engrossed in the portrait to notice the sword. "She actually used that?"

"She did, but though she had the passion for fighting, she had none of the skill or strength. The sword was turned on her and she was slain."

"Edmund killed her?"

Collier shook his head. "The man's name was Walther, a mercenary knight the same as my ancestor. Catherine cut his sword arm and, in his fury, he killed her."

Indignation rolled into Aryn's eyes. "Chivalrous! Her life for a few drops of blood."

He chuckled. "I'm sorry to be the bearer of bad news, but regardless of how your Hollywood portrays knights, chivalry was often forgotten when there was blood to be shed and plunder to be had—especially when a man's pride was trounced as Catherine trounced Walther's."

Aryn grunted softly, slid a finger down the blade.

"Careful. The edges are as sharp as the day they last drew blood."

She turned her blue eyes on him. "So with Catherine dead, her enemy was let in and your ancestor awarded Strivling Castle."

"Actually, Edmund's reward was even greater. He was granted the entirety of the barony of Highchester, Strivling being one of its three castles."

"Impressive. What of that pig, Walther?"

"Edmund awarded him charge of one of the lesser castles. Thereafter, the mercenary fell into obscurity."

"Not soon enough for my liking."

He grinned. "It's over five hundred years in the past. Nothing to be done about it now." He pulled Aryn toward him.

Shedding her indignation, she wound her arms around him, and Collier kissed her long.

"How I like what you do to me," she whispered against his lips. "Too much."

He groaned, raised his head. "Meaning *stop*."

She lifted a hand and tripped fingertips over his stubbled jaw. "Afraid so." She nodded at the bed. "Dangerous."

Beautifully dangerous. He sighed and pulled back.

"I want it too, Collier, but…"

"I know." That faith of hers he wanted to hate but could not, it being so much a part of her—though he had proven it could be scaled the night he had seduced her.

She caught up his hand and pushed her fingers through his. "I love you."

He wasn't as uncomfortable with her declaration as he had been the first time he had sensed she risked much to speak it. However, he wasn't ready to return the sentiment. But soon, there being no way around it if he was to secure her *yes*—the prerequisite for sliding his ring on her finger.

He bent again, kissed her quick and chaste. "Let's get you settled in, then we'll go downstairs and have a nice, candlelit supper."

Her smile wavered, but she firmed it up. "I'd like that."

"Your mind's elsewhere," Aryn said where she sat with his arm around her in the library.

She had been silent so long Collier had begun to think she slept—had prayed she did. But having little practice at prayer since his father had deemed his sons' church attendance a waste of time, he supposed he couldn't fault God for not doing him a favor. Of course, the motive for wanting her to drift off might be more the cause of an unanswered prayer than his lack of practice.

She shifted on the sofa to face him and laid a hand on his chest. "Collier?"

Lest she feel the erratic beat of his heart, he clasped her fingers and set them on his thigh. "Elsewhere? What makes you think my mind isn't on you?"

Firelight on her upturned face reflected a wry smile. "It's pretty obvious when your mind is on me, and it wasn't. So if I had to guess, I would say James is your *elsewhere*."

Diverting the tension from his hand on hers to his jaw, he clenched his teeth. The strain of keeping his emotions and pain in check was exhausting. Aryn had asked him to stay while she unpacked, next they had prepared supper and lingered over their meal, then tea in the library and talk. Hours of talk. Now, nearing midnight, still he was denied the relief he had vowed he would not seek until she slept.

Almost feeling as if he went through withdrawal again—yawning and perspiring, flesh peaking in goose bumps, muscles beginning to twitch—he wondered how much longer he could endure.

"I guessed right, didn't I?" she pressed.

James. "Forgive me for being so preoccupied. I had a poor start to my day."

"But it got better, didn't it?" She grinned.

The pain in his ribs joining that of his neck and lower back, he said, "It did."

"Whew!" She blew a breath up her face.

"Since we have an early start tomorrow to show you the sights of London, we ought to get to bed." He drew his arm from around her.

"It doesn't have to be an early start, and since I'm not tired and you seem fairly awake"—she shrugged—"you could tell me why I have yet to be alone with you."

James, the bloody rotter!

Get it over with, he told himself and sat back against the cushions. "I lost a property to my brother, and not just any property. Strivling Castle."

She drew a sharp breath. "You didn't tell me you had a chance to purchase it."

He felt her hurt. But it was business, nothing to do with their relationship. "A chance, and that's all it was." He flexed his shoulder.

After a long moment, during which he sensed she gathered up her hurt and put it behind her, she said, "I'm sorry, Collier. I know it must have meant a lot to you. What do you think James will do with it?"

Trying to move his mind from the pain shooting shoulder to hip, he said, "He plans to take up residence there."

Aryn made a sound of approval. "It could be worse. He might have wanted to transform it into one of those castle hotels."

Her words rattled him, especially since his brother's decision to maintain it as a private residence was a strong factor in his acquisition. So had Collier been wrong in thinking to carry out their father's plans for Strivling?

No. The maintenance of something that immense and old was exorbitant. If James didn't wish to bankrupt himself, eventually he would have to sell it or develop it.

"It's midnight," he said.

"All right, all right." She unfolded and pushed up off the sofa.

He rose beside her, took her elbow, and led her from the library and up the stairs.

At the door to her bedroom, she turned to him. "I love you, Collier." She levered onto her toes and kissed him. When she drew back, she was frowning. "You feel warm. Might you be coming down with something?"

Warm, and yet so cold. Forcing a tone of amusement, he said, "A combination of sitting before a fire for hours and being in the company of a desirable woman."

She rolled her eyes, shook her head, and opened the door. "Good night."

Now, his pain said as she closed the door. *Two. No more than three.*

He pressed a hand to his pocket. Empty. But he knew where it was. Time and again distracted by the vial while he and Aryn prepared supper, he had slipped it in a drawer.

He started back toward the stairs. And halted. He was in pain, but less so than earlier. If he could sleep through it, he would be that much closer to beating this thing.

One, then, pain bargained. *No more than two.*

One was reasonable. And didn't slowly weaning one's self offer a better chance of success than going cold turkey?

He growled low, turned on his heel, and strode to his bedroom where he removed only his shoes before stretching out atop the covers.

Staring at the ceiling, he forced his thoughts to the phone calls that needed to be made before dawn, to the day he would spend with Aryn, to anything other than that which called more loudly to him with each passing minute. But sixty of those minutes later, he was no nearer sleep.

He cursed, sat up, and dropped his feet to the floor.

2

—∞∞∞—

SOMETHING SKIDDED ACROSS his desk and fell to the floor.

His solicitor's voice on the other end of the line becoming white noise, Collier stared at the vial whose contents had spilled across the carpet, then swiveled his chair opposite the window.

Aryn stood in the doorway, eyes wide, chest quickly rising and falling.

"I'll call you back, Heath." He ended the call.

Aryn swallowed loudly enough to be heard across the room. "I forgot my shampoo…thought I would borrow yours." She pointed to the pills. "Surprise."

After downing one last night and two this morning, he had left the vial on his bathroom counter. *Fool!*

"You lied to me, Collier. You told me you were off them."

He could lie to her again, but he wouldn't. She would just have to understand.

He pushed his chair back and stood. "I *was* off them."

"But?"

"I needed them again."

"Strivling?"

Though he knew she sought more than confirmation, that was all he could give. "Yes."

She swung away.

"Aryn!"

She halted. "I'm leaving."

Not just leaving. Walking out of his life. "Stay." His voice was so choked he wasn't sure it was his.

He heard her swallow again, and when she turned back, her eyes brimmed. "I can't."

He jerked his head at the pills. "They have nothing to do with you."

Her huff of disgust caused the tears to spill over. "That's the problem. Those things shut me out. Not that I wasn't out before, but I was finding you under all those layers. But you don't want to be found, do you, Collier? You don't want anyone that near you."

Pride kicking and screaming all the way, he said, "I want you, Aryn."

"Want me, but don't trust me."

"Of course I do." A pitifully automatic response. He didn't trust women—not since his mother had walked out on her tyrannical husband without looking back at the sons she left behind.

"No, you don't. If you did, you would have told me about Strivling."

"We've discussed this before, Aryn. It's never a good idea to mix business with personal."

Bitter laughter. "Do you love me? And if you do, can you say it?"

Did he love her? Was that what moved through him even in her absence—when he had only the memory of her beside him? "I want to marry you, Aryn. I'm ready." There. That ought to be enough.

She quickly shuttered her surprise. "What about love?"

Silently, he cursed her for pushing him, demanding of him what he couldn't give. But he could lie...

Once more rejecting that option, he opened the center desk drawer. "I want to marry you," he repeated and reached for the elegant little box. And drew his hand back. This was not how he had envisioned proposing to her. Far from romantic—worse, desperate.

"You do love me," Aryn said and briefly closed her eyes. "You just can't see it past those pills and the drive to outdo your brother."

He eased the drawer closed. "If you believe I love you, why are you leaving?"

"Because I'm not supposed to have to tell you what you feel." She drew a shaky breath and crossed the room.

He turned to her, but though he longed to take her in his arms, she would not welcome his embrace.

Leaning up, she kissed his cheek. "Goodbye, Collier." Then she was gone.

He wanted to go after her and tell her he loved her if that was what it took to hold on to her, but he turned to the window. A quarter hour later, he watched her duck into a cab.

As the car wound down the driveway, he assured himself he would get her back. All Aryn needed was time. All he needed was a way out from under the pills beneath his feet.

Staring into clouds as the plane rose through them, Aryn tried to swallow the lump in her throat, but it was stuck and would only be dislodged by the muffled sob she finally let past her lips.

Turning to the window, she let the tears make a mess of her. She cried for the day she had met Collier, the one night they had made love, his continued pursuit of her though she refused to repeat the mistake of falling into bed with him, and a hundred other remembrances of the man she loved. Then she cried for the climbing accident that had been the beginning of the end of them.

The large dosages of painkillers prescribed to ease Collier's suffering had caused changes in his personality—so marked that, six months following his accident, she had issued the ultimatum that if he didn't break his dependence on the pills, their relationship was over. Where he had gone wrong was in believing he could handle the withdrawal without professional help.

A sudden tightness in her chest, she snatched her purse from the floor and rummaged through it. Where was it? In a zippered pocket? Her cosmetics bag? What if she had packed it in her suitcase? Beginning to cough, she dug deeper and—blessedly—closed her fingers around the cylinder.

Relieved she hadn't misplaced the inhaler as she sometimes did, she put her mouth around it and dispensed the metered dose. Shortly, it was as if the asthma attack had never been. But Collier had been.

Hurting so much she wanted to cry aloud, she closed her eyes.

A hand touched her shoulder, and the elderly woman who had earlier taken the seat beside her said, "It will all work out, dear."

It wouldn't. Her battle for Collier was lost as surely as Catherine Algernon's battle against the Yorkists. Perhaps in another time and another place, but not now, not here.

"Another time, another place," the woman said.

Drawing a sharp breath, Aryn peered into the matron's softly wrinkled face. Her eyes glittered like moonlight on snow, mouth curved sweetly, and over her brow fell a lock of dark hair that contrasted with the silver crowning her head.

"You will see." She settled back and closed her eyes.

Aryn stared at her until the woman began to softly snore, then she turned her face to the window and tried to see beyond the impenetrable clouds.

Lord, she silently appealed, *if only Collier hadn't fallen. If only he had that day to live over...*

ABOUT THE AUTHOR

Tamara Leigh holds a Master's Degree in Speech and Language Pathology. In 1993, she signed a 4-book contract with Bantam Books. Her first medieval romance, *Warrior Bride*, was released in 1994. Continuing to write for the general market, three more novels were published with HarperCollins and Dorchester and earned awards and spots on national bestseller lists.

In 2006, Tamara's first inspirational contemporary romance, *Stealing Adda*, was released. In 2008, *Perfecting Kate* was optioned for a movie and *Splitting Harriet* won an ACFW "Book of the Year" award. The following year, *Faking Grace* was nominated for a RITA award. In 2011, Tamara wrapped up her "Southern Discomfort" series with the release of *Restless in Carolina*.

When not in the middle of being a wife, mother, and cookbook fiend, Tamara buries her nose in a good book—and her writer's pen in ink. In 2012, she returned to the historical romance genre with *Dreamspell*, a medieval time travel romance. Shortly thereafter, she once more invited readers to join her in the middle ages with the *Age of Faith* series: *The Unveiling, The Yielding, The Redeeming, The Kindling,* and *The Longing*. Tamara's #1 Bestsellers—*Lady at Arms, Lady Of Eve, Lady Of Fire,* and *Lady Of Conquest*—are the first of her medieval romances to be rewritten as clean reads. Look for *Lady Ever After,* a medieval time travel romance, in Fall 2016.

Tamara lives near Nashville with her husband, sons, a Doberman who bares his teeth not only to threaten the UPS man but to smile, and a feisty Morkie who keeps her company during long writing stints.

Connect with Tamara at her website www.tamaraleigh.com, her blog The Kitchen Novelist, her email tamaraleightenn@gmail.com, Facebook, and Twitter.

For new releases and special promotions, subscribe to Tamara Leigh's mailing list: www.tamaraleigh.com

Made in the USA
Columbia, SC
12 January 2018